The Artisan

A Novel

by

Gene Luke

This book is dedicated to the forgotten Serbian Warriors of World War II

 Originally published by Prosveta Publishing House of Belgrade, Yugoslavia, under the title *Tima Tišler* and subsequently translated by the author into English. The revised edition was submitted to the Florida Writers Association Royal Palm Literary Award contest for unpublished books, where it received second prize for the best historical novel of 2016.

ISBN: 978-1-941254-03-5

Printed in the United States of America

X IX VIII VII VI V IV III II I

Worldwide Distribution by

Amazon.com and IngramSpark.com

For my sister Dusica,
a kind soul of unwavering character

As I look back on the long and difficult process of translating and editing this novel for the US/English-speaking world, one person shines out with her dogged belief in this tale about the extraordinary goodness of people and their perseverance under threat of global annihilation. My true friend, my editor, and my patient guru, Bonnie Cassis Helmer.

Contents

Contents

Contents

Contents

Editor's Introductory Preface

The title above suggests the multiple nature of this introduction and thereby echoes the multiple nature of *The Artisan* itself. It is at once a fictionalized record of situations Serbs found themselves in during World War II, an homage to their bravery and sacrifice, and an ode to the power of love. It also expresses both the author's and the editor's hope that the novel will make the Balkans seem a little less foreign to us all in the United States.

The atrocities we witnessed on the news in the 1990s were the culmination of a long history of oppression and conflict. The Balkans (the former Yugoslavia, as well as the new states arising from and neighboring it) embody a crossroads between Europe and the Middle East. Under the Ottoman and Hapsburg Empires, they became a melting pot where ethnic identities mattered less than one's relationship to the ruling state, and individuals moved throughout the region without significant concern for maintaining a "homeland." The Empires, however, often played these ethnic groups off against each other—as the Ottoman Empire similarly did in the Middle East—in an effort to make these regions easier to rule and to oppress.

After the dissolution of those Empires, beginning with the two Balkan wars in 1912 and 1913, and on into this century, nationality, language, and religion have become critical issues. Mortal conflict has continued to arise over attempts to create sufficiently large territories with a majority of people who identify themselves in the same way: Serbia and Serbs, Croatia and Croats, etc. We see these same difficulties continue also in the Middle East, today reaching a scope that threatens the peace and prosperity of all Europe, and perhaps even of the US.

The Artisan

Born and raised in Serbia, Gene Luke interviewed twelve Serbian compatriots who served in WWII, and he came to admire deeply their commitment and compassion. Though many of the events chronicled in the novel are based on their reports, this work is entirely fiction, the tale of an Everyman caught in the darkness between Dueling Powers. It outlines some of the consequences the name "Serb" foists upon him and how he meets that fate and rises above it. It reminds us also of most people's genuine kindness and of the horrors of war and its aftermath—softened only by seeing them through the eyes of a generous and forgiving man.

The English text has been greatly expanded over the popular Serbian edition and contains ethnic references not in the original, since readers of the original would recognize ethnicities by a person's name as easily as we in the US would know the background of a Smith or a Lopez.

Serbs use the Cyrillic alphabet, more familiar to the West as "Russian." Transposing it into Latin letters often results in confusion over pronunciation. I requested that we include guides at the first occurrence of Serbian names to help increase the reader's comfort with the sounds of the Serbian language. For a full explanation of the alphabet, please see the guide on pages 344 and 345.

Also, since much of Balkan geography is unfamiliar to us in the US, we included at the end the map of Yugoslavia, delineating Timo's travels throughout the area.

Bonnie Cassis Helmer
Las Vegas, Nevada

Long Beach, New York 11561
October 30, 1991

Dear Andrew,

Your decision to join Doctors Without Borders in Yugoslavia distresses me deeply. The reports I read in *The New York Times* *are very discouraging. You write that you have joined a dedicated group of medical professionals from all corners of the world who are helping to save wounded Serbs, Croats, and Bosnians. But you do not tell me how you plan to handle your confrontations with the brutal realities in the Balkans.* *The Times* *states that "medical vehicles and personnel have been fired upon. Serbian insurgents have held medical personnel hostage and mistreated them during detention. Serbian rebels, Croatian security forces, and the neutral Yugoslav Federal Army have all beaten their prisoners." No side in this fight is blameless.*

I cannot sleep at night knowing the conditions you will face. I often see you in those horrific situations and I pray for your safety.

You have your mother's soul. You are wise and strong, just as she was, but you are also young, and, like every young person on this planet, you hope to save the world. I praise and respect your love for humanity. You and Sophie have accomplished more than I could ever dream, and that gives me great pride. You both give me so much joy.

I cannot explain the lure of the Old Country for the two of you, and I do not understand how it came about. I avoided talking about my homeland to both of you. Neither did I glorify Serbia to kindle fire in your hearts. Perhaps your exposure to the festivities of the Serbian communities here in New York may have created a glorious picture of Serbian history, tradition, and culture. Or maybe reading those heroic songs and tales—mostly myth—so richly decorated with sacrifices, martyrs, and national tragedies, may have sparked your desire to counter the efforts of yet another bloodthirsty conqueror in a long line of vicious conquerors.

With both of you risking your precious lives trying to save others—Sophie at the Embassy in Belgrade and you somewhere in Croatia—even now in my old age, I want to rush to your sides to care for you, to make sure you dress warmly and eat all your favorite foods from my hot stove.

But I can hear you saying, "No, Dad, I am grown up now."

The running news line tonight says, "Civilians and persons placed hors de combat have been summarily executed by both Serbian insurgents and Croatian security forces."

What if they catch you? What if they don't realize you're a doctor? What if you cross a line of fire? What if . . . ? A thousand questions rage in my mind day and night. Should I cry for your return, or should I resign myself to the role of my forefathers and celebrate your decision to join the army, in this case the army of physicians?

Perhaps I am too sentimental or over-protective, but your beloved mother would want me to express our feelings. Someday you also will have children and you will forgive me for allowing emotion to overcome me. I still carry your late mother's love—as well as my own— for you and for Sophie, and as long as I live, you will hear your mother's voice through me.

I was slightly younger than you are now when they drafted me. I have not shared my story with you before. I would like to do that now.

Chapter 1

Recruitment

Teardrops of moisture trickled down the small window through which my father and I watched for signs of dawn. Slowly a sliver of light eased above the horizon, and, for an instant, the field of wheat across the road came alive, its leaves tipped in gold. Then, just as suddenly, grey clouds again engulfed the sky.

My father—the lines in his face seeming even deeper than usual—could not look me straight in the eye. He squeezed my shoulder.

His voice faltered. "God be with you, Timo."

I was then a twenty-year-old married man, and the Yugoslav Royal Army had summoned me to serve, as it had all Serbian men of recruiting age. My mother had stuffed a woven satchel for me with smoked meat, ham, cheese, and bread, and filled my father's old water flask from the First War with our best vintage brandy.

Though this happened over fifty years ago, in May of 1940, I remember with vivid clarity that cold and rainy day when she, my father, and my pregnant Roda escorted me to the gate in our yard in the small village of Krušar [***Kroo**-shahr*] near the Velika Morava [***Vey**-lee-kah **Moh**-rah-vah*] River. With orders in my hand, I took a deep breath, threw the satchel over my shoulder, gave my tearful, worried Roda a quick hug—under my parents' watchful eyes—and started my ten-mile walk to receive further assignment from the regional headquarters in Jagodina [***Yah**-goh-dee-nah*].

As I reached the city, I saw recruits waiting for trains going north and south jamming the streets of our district's military administrative center. Some of the men I knew from nearby villages. Some came from the western banks of the Morava. All were young peasants whose fates now lay in the hands of the big powers.

War loomed on the horizon for our virtually leaderless country, as it did for all Europe. The air buzzed with the possibility that we might enter it voluntarily. Despite the heat of the passionate analyses I heard everywhere, lingering uncertainty sent a chill through my heart. *How can a seventeen-year-old king make such a decision?* I listened to learned men tell us that we Serbs should align with our old allies, the French and the English. A Croat in the group zealously believed our best move lay in siding with Hitler. Others tried to convince us that no stronger and mightier army existed than that of the Yugoslav King's Army, and so we had nothing to fear come what may. Such discussions raged among the conscripts and among all the relatives there to give their sons a customary send-off.

An old Serbian tradition dictated that we celebrate lavishly this most revered male rite of passage. Proud fathers joined former generations by gladly shouldering the honor of handing their sons over to the military and loudly trumpeting the news to all their friends and relatives. At the homes of most recruits, the festivities began with toasting, singing, dancing, and roasting a pig or calf for a crowd of guests. The parties went on for days.

Happily for me, we had wrapped up our party several days before, so I could spend those last few precious moments alone with Roda, Father, and Mother. But many of the parties even continued at the railway stations, as they did here in Jagodina. Several Kolo[1] circles had formed

[1] The Kolo is danced by virtually all Slavic peoples. It is performed with groups of people (from three to several dozen) wrapping their arms around each other's waists (ideally in a circle, hence the name, which means "circle"). There is almost no movement above the waist. The basic steps are

by the tracks, each with an accordion player in the center or a gypsy brass band loudly playing ballads, dances, and Kolos. The cacophony perfectly suited the raucous exuberance of the occasion, with most of the gala participants either too drunk or too tired to notice the dissonance. Mothers hugged their sons and cried. Fathers hid their tears by singing songs of parting, toasting from a big jug of plum brandy passed from mouth to mouth, and hugging their friends and relatives to assuage their secret pain.

Assigned to my regiment all the way from the town of Apatin in Vojvodina [***Voy**-voh-dee-na*], a nearby fellow recruit had gathered a small group around him, all firmly embroiled in fervent argument. Of Hungarian origin, the draftee had a pale face, with black hair and eyebrows that moved to the center of his forehead every time he blinked. Although named Ištvan Sebenyi [***Isht**-vahn **Se**-ben-yee*], at home they called him Pišta [***Peesh**-toh*]. I could hear his voice above the rest insisting that he should join the Hungarian Army, not the Yugoslav.

"But you live in Yugoslavia, and you are a Yugoslavian citizen, aren't you?" asked an older gentleman also standing near us.

"I am, but I'm a Hungarian citizen too through my parents. Hungary recognizes dual citizenship for all Hungarians born in the territories of the former Austro-Hungarian Empire. A year ago your Regent Prince Paul

---

easy to learn, but experienced dancers perform with great virtuosity due to the different ornamental elements they add, such as syncopated steps.

Each region has at least one unique Kolo; it is difficult to master the dance and even the most experienced dancers cannot master all the regional variations. The dance is accompanied by instrumental two-beat music (bearing the same name), performed most often with an accordion, but also with other instruments, frula (a traditional kind of recorder), tamburica, or šargija.

approved this stipulation in the nonaggression agreement between Hungary and Yugoslavia."

"It didn't specify that Yugoslav citizens serve in the Hungarian Army," the older gentleman retorted. "Besides, the Yugoslav Government does not summon our Serbs in Hungary to serve here." He turned away, shaking his head. "We never had these kinds of arguments when I served in the Big War."

"But you had only Serbs in your army," interrupted Pišta, stepping around to face the man once more.

Shaking visibly, the old man looked into his eyes. "Very true. And we were the victors. Do you know why? Because we united in support of our cause, and our military did not tolerate saboteurs like you."

"I am not a saboteur, and you have no right to call me that. I only mean to say that I should not serve two armies."

The son of the older gentleman pulled his father aside and reprimanded his intolerance.

Pišta looked discouraged and walked away from the group.

Another recruit placed his arm around Pišta's shoulder. "Why do we discuss such matters? It's not up to us where and who we serve."

"You're right, Simo. Let's join Kolo," said a third.

The three young men stepped off the platform and walked over to the first Kolo circle, cut in, and became a blur among the fast-flying dancers.

As we received our assignment papers, a military commander ordered me to join the 46th Infantry Regiment in Knjaževac [***Knyah**-zheh-vats*], where a transport waited to take us to the city of Bitola in Macedonia. They loaded us on a train already filled with soldiers from the 29th Artillery Regiment, also assigned to Bitola. We edged our way into the old passenger cars and stopped wherever we could find space.

Once underway, I pushed to get closer to a window, but the car was so packed I could make no progress. Travelers seeking fresh air had left the windows open. When I finally reached one of them, the sooty smoke pouring from the engine choked me in every tunnel.

When we disembarked for a break at Vranje [***Vrahn**-yeh*] Station, I took a deep breath of fresh mountain air and let it linger in my lungs. During the hour that we waited there, an express train from the south thundered through on its way to Belgrade. The first-class car passed quietly, but the second-class passengers crowded the windows, waving and hollering, "Long Live the King! Long Live the Army!"

Serbs. Army. Always the same. We love our military more than bread. We defeated the Ottoman Empire, then the Habsburg, for God was always with us.

I crossed myself and took another long breath of fresh air.

Back aboard the train, we continued south. After almost twelve mind-numbing hours, the train finally arrived at our destination.

Before us lay Bitola,[2] picturesque with its white painted houses, its Turkish verandas, red tile roofs, and small clear glass windows dressed with handmade draperies. In the bright gray and light blue rays of the morning sun, this Macedonian town of mythical beauty and holy silence quickened our heartbeats and left us breathless. A deep joy and a strange, unexplained lightness glinted in our eyes. Just as water from a mountain spring refreshes even the smallest muscle of the body, the

[2] The name Bitola is derived from the Old Church Slavonic word meaning "monastery, cloister," as the city was formerly noted for its monastery.

dancing beauty of this panorama awakened our finest sensibilities.

Too early for visiting, for sitting on front porches, or hosting guests in the shadow of thickly twined grape vines, the city lay quiet. We shuffled through silent streets.

Solomon

In the Main Garrison outside the city, junior officers assigned us to our units and marched us to our barracks. Before entering, we received our uniforms, boots, caps, guns, blankets, and food rations.

About thirty of us entered the large barracks building and rushed to pick the choicest beds of the twenty double-bunks lined up against the walls. I quickly seized the first bottom bed near the entrance, and everyone else scrambled for the other lower bunks. When only uppers remained, some skinny, wiry boys scaled theirs in one jump, while the short, chubby ones tried repeatedly to get to the top.

The fellow who claimed my upper bunk caught all our attention. From his traditional costume, I recognized the colors of the Southeast Rumanis, the gypsy tribe renowned as entertainers and musicians. A red bandana wrapped over his tar black hair held tight a black silk cone cap. His vest had gold and red tassels on the epaulets. When he bounced, trying to hoist himself up, his long-sleeved white shirt, with traditional blue and red stripes embroidered around the collar and cuffs, twirled in the air. He had tied his striped black and brown pants neatly below the knees. Nevertheless, the yellow chevrons on each side of his legs moved in and out like an accordion with his every attempt to mount the bunk. A long yellow sash around his waist held his shirt in over his balloon pants, and, if he hadn't had pigskin moccasins with a white wrap going up to his knees, from behind I would have thought him a girl in a skirt.

Almost a midget, he tried with all his strength and climbing skills to get to the top. He fell down several times and rolled like a beach ball between the bunks, bringing forth gales of laughter from his now spellbound audience. He lunged toward the bunk and caught it below his armpits, his short legs dangling high above the ground. Then he tried several times to wrap a leg around a bedpost, but his grip gave out, and he tumbled down every time.

We howled and roared with laughter, calling for another performance, to which he willingly obliged, clowning all the way to the top. When he finally made it, he stood upright and extended his arms proudly, like a circus performer.

"Solomon at your service, my brothers."

I tossed him his bag, and he pulled out a small violin, brought it quickly to his left arm, and started fiddling some spritely, though unfamiliar, melody. We applauded and cheered, loving every moment.

Thwap! The door of the barracks flew open, cutting short the gypsy's performance. A stocky sergeant in his late thirties stepped inside, followed by a tall, slim corporal. Everyone jumped to attention.

"I am Sergeant Gubar," he thundered. "You will be under my command. This is Corporal Ravasi. He will make it his life's work to get you in shape for this army. Do you hear me?"

"Yes, sir! Sergeant, sir!" we responded in unison.

"I didn't hear you, you miserable worms," he barked.

"Yes, sir! Sergeant, sir!" we shouted again more loudly.

"I give you two minutes to get out of your stinking rags and into your uniforms, ready for inspection. You got that, you prissy girls?"

"Yes, sir! Sergeant, sir!"

Two minutes to put on our uniforms? Impossible. These uniforms require time and experience to get into. But we followed orders, many of us struggling miserably to meet Gubar's demands.

Meanwhile the Sergeant paced angrily on short legs, as he eyed each of us. He had the face of a Krajišnik[3] [***Krah**-yeesh-neek*], angry eyes, high cheek bones, thin lips and a wide nose on a large round head with very light hair and a short neck. In addition to the handgun that constituted part of the standard uniform, he carried in his left hand a finely honed, handmade willow switch that struck fear in all our hearts.

Cpl. Ravasi followed him intently, hands clasped behind his back, carefully mirroring his sergeant's every move, then stepping aside promptly at each turn. The Corporal's narrow face displayed a carefully trimmed mustache beneath a long, curved nose, and his eyes, when not glued to his sergeant, exuded the kindness of the typical mild-mannered Dalmatian who always aims for peaceful solutions.

As we all raced to meet the Sergeant's demands, Solomon struggled most. He removed his hat and bandana, unwrapped his sash, and tried to take off his shirt, vest, and pants, but he got tangled in the process and fell down. He wiggled around in an effort to remove his shoes and pants, thereby catching Sgt. Gubar's eye.

"What's wrong with you, you lousy gypsy?"

---

[3] A Serb from Bosanka Krajina [***Krah**-yee-nah*] on the Bosnian frontier.

Gubar strode over to him, a fierce frown on his face. "Why are you down on the floor, you baby-stealing lout?"

Horrified that such a specious accusation could still be voiced in our day and age, I watched the Sergeant raise his switch. "Get your lazy gypsy ass up, you filthy son of a bitch."

He paused momentarily, then roared again. "Get up!"

The switch went even higher in the air and came down swiftly, striking Solomon across the back. Then, right there in front of us all, Gubar whacked him again and again, on his arms, legs, feet, behind, and even several times across the face.

We stood frozen at attention, totally bewildered and helpless.

The little musician, scared and subservient, covered his head with his hands and cried with such pain that the rest of us fought to keep back our own tears.

Why do people in power like to abuse the weak, and why do the weak put up with it? I could feel my jaw tighten and my face redden.

My heart went out to Solomon. I watched that beast continue to batter his small body over and over, until I couldn't bear it anymore.

Involuntarily my arm went out, grabbed Sgt. Gubar's arm, and held it firmly. We glared at each other. His hate and anger cut into my glower, but I stood determined and strong, my grip tight.

His shoulders relaxed. His eyes stared in disbelief. Defeat and frustration rolled over his face.

He turned and stormed out of the barracks with a thunderous slam.

Everyone was quiet. Dumbfounded. Something extraordinary had just happened. Something unthinkable. I strove to grasp the weight of my action. I tried not to think about it.

The little musician trembled and said, "I'm sorry. Oh, I'm scared. For both of us."

I put my left hand on his shoulder and offered my right. "Call me Timo."

Soon the door opened and our Serbian Sgt. Simić [***See-**mitch*] stepped in.

"What happened here?"

The room burst wild with noise as my barracks-mates surrounded the Sergeant, all talking at once. Sgt. Simić extended his hand and lowered it slowly, signaling for us to quiet down.

"Hold on. Stop." He pointed to the tallest man. "You there. Tell me what happened."

"Well, Sergeant Gubar was beating up little Solomon really bad. And well--"

He hesitated. "Timo grabbed his arm and stopped him. Then Sergeant Gubar tore out of here in a rage."

"Yes, Sergeant Gubar went directly to the Garrison Commander. He was fuming."

He turned to me. "Timo . . . You did this?" Sgt. Simić looked puzzled, but a corner of his mouth showed a touch of pleasure.

"I'm sorry, Sergeant." I shook my head. "I just couldn't watch it anymore. It was brutal, inhuman, and I reacted . . . I don't know." I lowered my eyes and shrugged.

When I looked up again, I saw Simić surveying me compassionately, but he didn't say a thing. He just turned and walked out.

An hour later a couple of regulars came and took me to the Commanding Officer on Duty. When informed of my action, he didn't even look at me. Through his thick mustache, I thought I saw a smile. He ordered seven days of incarceration for me in the guardhouse jail at the front entrance to the compound.

The cell had a small window on the door, a bed, and a bucket. Although I felt slightly depressed for the reprimand, I welcomed the punishment. I needed some rest.

While the others marched under the hot May sun, choking in clouds of dust, I slept contentedly without a shred of guilt to trouble my conscience.

Military Training and Trade

At the end of my week in prison, I resumed standard military training. March left! March right! Count off! Step up! About face! Rifle at ready! Rifle at attention! To the ground! Get up! Attack! Stop! Attention! At ease! One, two! One, two . . . and so on, all day, every day. We wore out our boots in a couple of months. Peter, the military shoemaker, then skillfully glued and nailed onto the soles the leather and rubber pads they gave us to extend the boots' lives for another few months.

Before long I got sick and tired of marching. *If God himself hadn't chosen us, we would march even on holy days.*

Our Sunday break from marching consisted of religious services that lasted from eight in the morning till noon. In the middle of our marching field, Father Tomo would chant the liturgy, say prayers, sing psalms, give blessings, and celebrate Holy Communion. One old soldier, his cantor, chanted, "Bless us, oh, Lord," and rang the hand bell whenever Father Tomo looked at him, but, for the most part, the priest conducted the entire service himself, from the first liturgy to the last sermon.

Exhausted from rapid-marching in full gear for ten-, fifteen-, and sometimes twenty-kilometers on Saturday, we recruits stood at the back, bolt upright, behind rows of officers and non-commissioned officers, thinking, *Lord, when will this service end?*

Many of us envied the minorities who were not required to attend our long Orthodox services. Croats (deeply Catholic), Slovenians (either Catholic or Lutheran), and Muslims all relaxed by the barracks or played soccer while we stood in the hot sun. They had different services at different times, Catholics and Lutherans in the early morning and Muslims in the evening. Serving their mandatory army terms as regular army chaplains, their priests, ministers, and imams dressed in soldiers' uniforms without guns. These chaplains neither battle-trained nor participated in basic training, though some received officer status and had many perks, including separate accommodations, separate dining facilities, and free passes out of the garrison.

Our disparate group of Yugoslavs all marched together, slept one right next to the other in group tents, fought for and against each other in mock battles, and ate together in small groups, exchanging silly jokes and farts from the bean soup. Nevertheless we felt something in the air, something different and solid, like a wall between us that separated us.

Croats had proudly and faithfully served the Hungarian Empire, while Serbs died valiantly to wrest their freedom from it. The Albanians of Kosovo fought for total independence and separation, while Turks continued to dream about the return of the Ottoman Empire. Macedonians, long victimized by Italy and Bulgaria, felt betrayed by the Yugoslav government when it made pacts with both those countries for economic reasons. The list goes on and on, like the proverbial catalogue of grievances among step-children. It kept us from developing into true comrades in arms, from opening up to each other as good soldiers do. It kept us from becoming brothers.

For some of the games we played, teams formed based on nationality, and then the competitiveness rose to outright hatred between opposing sides. Croats eagerly hurt their opponents physically, while Slovenians joyously shouted oaths in their own language at every successful score. Benevolent, peace-loving Bosnians always took a beating in those ugly skirmishes. Serbs and Croats typically managed to avoid direct confrontations between each other, while gentle Bosnians and Macedonians received the brunt of brutality from both sides. Although "Bosnian" defines a people who constitute a distinct collective cultural identity with three different religions, regardless of the religion they practice, they never initiate a fight unless seriously provoked. When occasional fistfights did, however, break out, the officers in charge never called the military police. They resolved the issues on the spot and refused to let the men carry grudges into the barracks.

I thought this a wise and practical policy.

Somber centuries, however, had nursed these ethnic antipathies. Neither the officers' principles nor the Corfu Declaration—though it guaranteed religious freedom and universal suffrage, with equality before the law for all ethnic sects, as well as equal status for both Latin and Cyrillic alphabets—could adequately neutralize what so much table talk had so diligently fostered.

Three months of military training finally came to an end. Those in authority singled out the tradesmen and assigned them to a special regiment. As a carpenter, I was promptly promoted to lead the carpentry shop for the entire division. They put me in charge of all tools and told me to guard them with my life.

They assigned another Serb, Kosta Popović [***Poh**-poh-vitch*], to work with me full time. A city boy, Kosta had grown up as a poor helper in a woodworking shop, but once I trained him, he quickly became a great asset on all our projects. We also had several men who helped on an as-needed basis: Marko Čanić [***Chah***-*nitch*], a tall fellow Serb with a dark complexion; Bruno Kremović [***Krey***-*moh-vitch*], a friendly Croat from Slavonia who talked a lot, and Sulejman Agić [***Su***-*leh-man* ***A***-*jitch*], a Muslim of Bosnian origin we called Sule, who claimed he was a Turk and used every opportunity to promote Islam.

We made new doors and windows for all the barracks, repaired chairs, benches, and tables for the dining rooms, and constructed bookcases for the General and the Colonel. We skillfully and efficiently completed all our assignments.

Sometimes I went to Bitola to buy materials. On Saturdays, market day, this bustling small town became crowded with people from the surrounding areas. Villagers came to trade, to buy, or to enjoy a little entertainment in the town's festive atmosphere.

Everyone and everything that moved enchanted me. And when the young maidens promenaded down main street, oh, what a sight. The old town folk sighed, while young men lined up close to Mustafa's Gate for a better look. There, maidens passed proudly, displayed their innocence and beauty, then wove in and out through the stalls of the colorful marketplace.

Looking like a dandy with my soldier's cap tipped to one side and my clean, pressed uniform—pants and shirt shining of starch—I too found time to steal a moment of pleasure by trying to catch the eye of a young girl. A geyser of passion would begin to boil in me, and I would think lustily about my own vibrant brunette, Roda. *Oh, how I miss her!* Time seemed so long until my first furlough. I daydreamed about her, pregnant, with her little round belly. *How we caressed each other. How I loved to cup her sweet, round face in my hands as she ran her fingers through my chestnut curls.* An enormous storm of lust brewed within me.

I often lost myself, gazing at this circle of young maidens.

Then Uncle Vane [***Vah**-neh*] broke the spell. "Don't bother looking at them, son. It will come for you also. She will be as pretty as a dove."

I did not reply, nor did I tell him about Roda.

Mid-afternoon I would return from Bitola on a horse-drawn wagon loaded with lumber and carpentry supplies from the Macedonian Vane's store. Kosta and I would unload the wagon, then go to the kitchen, where Joseph the Czech saved lunch for us, along with wine left over from the officers' dining room. After lunch and a short nap, we would attack our latest project.

In those days the craft of carpentry was a true art. We did everything by hand—cut our own lumber, shaped the boards and planed them. Kosta and I worked contentedly for hours on end, chatting and sharing gossip as we chiseled and planed. I also owned a special set of tools for woodcarving newly constructed items. The basic set consisted of sharpening stones, carving knives, gouges, a v-tool, and a veiner—a deep gouge tool with a U-shaped cutting edge. I delighted in these instruments the way a painter dotes on his brushes and palette knives.

When the opportunity arose to embellish a piece, my hands—possessed by some inner spell—spewed forth gardens of flowers. Roses blossomed at my fingertips. Leaves unfurled when chisels danced over wood grain. My mind dissolved into a world unknown to me. It stood outside any motor connection, watching as a bare oak plank sprang to life with each skew and gouge to become a beautifully ornamented door. Egg and dart, bead and barrel, acanthus, palmetto, Greek key. The rosettes and other flowers I carved on the doors compared well to pictures in a museum.

At times while I worked, Kosta just stared, mesmerized by the devilish dance of these tools in my hands. He watched silently, barely breathing, then his eyes would widen as a simple cut burgeoned and spread, like the real branches of an enchanted tree. When I stepped back to survey, he would sigh, surface, and return to his task. Or, if he had finished and was ready for a little break, he often murmured, "What an artist."

Adem Aziz

Kosta always seemed to be in on the latest news.

One day he told me that they had arrested the Albanian Adem Aziz for subversive actions against the Yugoslav Royal Army.

"How can that be, Kosta? He's the best marksman in the whole Rifle Company?"

"You see that? The whole camp is talking. And we all thought he was just a joker who likes to chase Albanian girls and sing songs to put us to sleep." The deep scar on the left side of his forehead twisted with his concern.

Just then, Marko, Bruno, and Sule all appeared to join us for lunch before their shift. A large pile of doors and windows with missing and cracked panes crowded our work area, so we needed to finish the job quickly just to have space to work.

"Bruno, have you heard about Adem Aziz? What do you think will happen to him?" I asked.

"What will happen to him? They'll shoot him." His brows furrowed, making his narrow eyes even narrower. "There's no democracy in the army. What do you think? That the Army will forgive him? Ha! They caught him at the gate smuggling out a big bag of ammunition."

He smoothed an invisible wrinkle from his carefully pressed pants, then shook his head from side to side. "And he brags about all of his romantic adventures. Conqueror of girls' hearts. Ha! He committed treason! He was supplying those Albanian fascists with *our* ammunition. Who knows how many times and how much smuggling he did? And now maybe our own bullets will be waiting for us around some corner."

"I don't know what to say," Kosta responded, his blond hair falling across his wide face as he shook his head and shrugged his shoulders. "I don't understand many things. When we're together with other Yugoslavs, we sing and dance and celebrate holidays in the same spirit. Our Serbian music and dances are so popular. Even the Croats cheer up and get into Kolo. Just the other day we all danced together and competed to see who would lead Kolo. We sang and said heroic poems of the past. We circled and danced, smiles on every soldier's face, whether Albanian, Macedonian, Bosnian, Croatian, Slovenian or Serbian."

He spread his hands out before him, palms up. "But when we're alone with just our fellow countrymen, it seems we despise each other, and the happiness when we danced wasn't real." Kosta let his hands drop and shook his head again, eyes downcast. "The longer I'm in this army, the more I feel we're all strangers in some foreign militia."

He turned back to his work. "I'm not wise enough to dwell on this subject."

Marko scoffed. "One of the sergeants said he expects the country to collapse, since we have no strong government and we show signs of breakdown."

With a heavy accent, but with a good dose of confidence, Sule started laughing like crazy and spoke half in Serbian and half in Turkish. "Aferim,[4] Brothers. It will be

[4] Have courage! (literally, Bravo!) in Turkish.

what is not supposed to be. Allah protects us all. Come. Convert to Islam before it's too late, and all will be well."

Sule looked down at the ground, musing, "Ah, good old Turkish times. It will never be the same."

"Go to Hell, you son of a Turkish bitch," Marko thundered, as waves of anger rolled over his king-sized belly. "They should have dealt with you long ago for subversion."

His heavy hand dropped down on a workbench with a loud thud.

"Let him be, Marko. He is a simpleton. Don't you see?" I said, calming Marko down.

"Fool or not, he spreads this religious crap around all the time. They should have discharged him months ago. That Bosnian Colonel Mehmedović [***Meh**-meh-doh-vitch*] at Headquarters protects him. I know it."

He jutted his head so far forward you could almost see a neck. "Those Muslims protect their own."

"What did I tell you?" said Kosta, still shaking his head. "There is no hope for us."

He gently set his tools on the workbench. "Let's go eat. I'm hungry."

Gen. Stošić's Order

Not long after starting my position in the carpentry shop, an order came to make all new doors for Gen. Stošić's [***Stoh**-shitch*] house. A fellow Serbian, Gen. Stošić summoned Kosta and me to his office and showed us the plans for two double doors and five single doors for his two-story residence. This cigar-smoking, puffy-faced general did not exhibit the typical arrogance of higher ranked officers. Instead, with his bright, encouraging eyes and constant smile beneath a thick mustache, he prodded us to express our honest opinions and accepted all our suggestions.

He wanted the best materials, so we sent for mahogany from Greece. We ironed the boards for a whole week before we started to plane them. This involved clamping the boards together and pouring very hot water over them to soften the surface. It took Kosta and me two weeks to make all seven doors. We decorated the insides with flowers and the outsides with coats of arms, wheat, eagles and hawks.

By some Divine Grace, when we finished and installed them, we received a week's furlough from the General.

"Ah, Mila," Kosta sighed. *Ah, Roda!* My thoughts echoed his words.

How happily we scampered to the barracks. Once there, we hurried the officer on duty to issue our passes as quickly as possible. Joseph immediately filled our bags with food, and off we ran.

We arrived at the railroad station three hours ahead of our night train and bought our tickets to Skopje [***Skohp**-yeh*].

As we settled into our seats, I could hardly calm the fire blazing within me.

Home.

Roda.

Leave

The warmth of late September helped me sleep all the way to Ćuprija [***Tchu**-pree-yeh*]. Kosta had gotten off at Aleksinac, some sixty miles earlier. I did not notice his absence until some rowdy recruits from Niš [*Neesh*], who were reporting to the local cavalry battalion at Ćuprija, awakened me just in time for me to disembark.

I stepped down at the station. Everything was silent. Only the dogs barked to welcome me. The road to Krušar led across the Morava. I flew over the bridge as if on wings.

Fresh air, the smell of mown hay, September grapes and corn made my heart cry with joy.

I arrived home as the villagers of Krušar began their daily tasks—men with their cattle in the barn or field, women with their pots and pans, roosters trumpeting their morning calls, and cows mooing thanks for their morning milking.

Father will have driven the herd to the lower meadow by now, and there's smoke from the summer kitchen. Mother has already started the fire.

My eyes strained to catch sight of Roda. *She will be pretty heavy now and of little help around the house.*

As I entered slowly through the gate, I heard a child's cry.

I stopped on my heels. *Has she already given birth?*

At that moment Mother ran from the kitchen and reached up to embrace me. "My son, you have a daughter. A month old already. May God bring you happiness."

"Thank you, Mother." I returned her embrace. "Daughter, eh?"

I slowly entered the house and dropped my sack. Roda was resting and feeding the baby.

"Timo, a daughter. She's so pretty, and she looks so much like you. Look at those dreamy brown eyes!"

Roda's proud smile swelled my heart.

"Roda, thank you," I stuttered and somehow moved closer to them.

We kissed each other quickly, shy at Mother's presence. I stared at the baby, who pulled on Roda's breast with her tiny mouth as if there would be no milk tomorrow.

So small, with a little lock of hair on her head.

She seemed like the little angel painted on the wall of Jagodina Church. "How beautiful she is," I mumbled.

Roda held my hand while I beamed in silence.

Called up by Mother from the lower meadow, Father arrived a few minutes later. We embraced and sat down. Mother brought a flask of brandy, removed the rag-covered hemp plug, and poured us each a glass. We toasted the birth of my daughter, then another for my return, one for my health, and again for the rich harvest. The crop that summer had come in greater than ever before.

We polished off the flask.

Neighbors brought more, and the drinking went on into the evening. Shortly before dawn, dead drunk, I fell asleep on the summer sofa in front of the kitchen.

Father woke me at dawn and sent me to the well to refresh myself with Krušar's cold water. After a rough body rubbing with a linen towel, I sobered up and got my strength back.

I returned to find Roda alone in the house. Mother had taken the baby and the crib outside. Roda had unbraided her dark brown hair and put on a white sleeping gown with a red shawl around her waist. She placed a red rose between her breasts. I was like a wolf. We must have awakened the entire neighborhood.

When we stopped for a short pause, we heard voices on the front patio. Village women had gathered there to gossip. With the men in the fields, the women cackled playfully about us young lovers. Mother served coffee and tried to calm them down, but they persisted. They could not neglect such an opportunity to joke and tease.

I did not leave our room for dinner. Roda brought some pork roast, cream cheese, and bread, but I wasn't hungry.

I wanted only her. So we played out our passions on into the night, and when everyone else went to bed and fell asleep, I walked out to the front yard and spun round in circles. Everything smelled of Krušar, of the whole Morava region, of meadows and forests, of creeks and ditches, of all the places where I had run with my childhood friends.

Roda came out of the house and joined me. We sat on a bench in front of the fence and gazed at the clear, star-studded skies.

Our parents had arranged our marriage when I was eighteen, and it had taken us a while to like each other and become husband and wife. Here together under the stars, my soul melted and oozed out of me. I felt as though I should inhale as much of this beauty as I could. Passion mixed with happiness, while my heart danced, leapt, sang with joy.

The bounty of it all quenched my thirst. The family had reaped huge crops of wheat and corn. The cattle were healthy. The sows were big and had birthed many piglets. Our sheep bore many lambs. And the yard was full of poultry. Barefoot children ran vigorously across the meadows, while my wife sang under the eaves.

My soul and heart filled with joy. We lingered there until midnight.

Before returning to bed, I watched my daughter in her crib for a long time and wondered when I would be home again to see her. *God willing, next spring.*

The week went by like a day, a little with Father, some with neighbors, and mostly with Roda. Then the time arrived when I had to go back. I put on the uniform. Mother packed my bag full of food.

I kissed my daughter and said goodbye to my mother and father. Roda did not want to come out of the house. She cried and sobbed. I started for the gate, and she ran out to me weeping softly. I embraced her, and we stayed like that awhile, holding each other tenderly.

I remember Mother wiping a tear with her apron, while Father himself seemed ready to cry.

"Roda, I must go."

I left through the gate, through Krušar, and over the Morava to Jagodina, where I caught the train south for Bitola.

As we pulled into Bitola Station, I imagined the walk to the garrison that lay ahead of me. I thought of Roda, and somehow it seemed that my life would never be the same again.

Return to the Garrison

On the first market day after my return, as usual I visited Old Man Vane's store and purchased all the supplies for the garrison carpentry shop: boards, veneer, glass, locks, hinges, and other materials. After packing and loading everything, I paused in front of the store for a little chat with Uncle Vane.

It was a warm afternoon, and the cold soft drink he offered refreshed me. I told him about Serbia and the Morava valleys and hills. He stroked his beard absentmindedly, yet followed every word.

In his younger days he had traveled through Serbia to trade with sawmills, foundries, and rope factories. He loved our peasants very much. "With them," he said, "I could make the best deals and the best trades."

At dusk, after our friendly talk, I drove my wagon out of town toward the Garrison.

Behind me cannon shells fell on Bitola.

Explosions erupted around the valley.

I stopped abruptly and looked toward the barracks where panic and commotion had broken out. Trumpets sounded formation and movement of troops. Lit lamps clicked off.

I hurried my horse through the abandoned gate and rode to the workshop where Kosta hastily filled the cart with tools.

No one knew who bombarded us.

Frightened, Kosta ran around collecting everything we needed to take with us. I dismounted to help him. Soon ready to go, he looked at me, ran his hands through his blond hair, and bit his lip.

"Slavko ordered us to leave with the 46th Regiment for Resen. Sleeping in tents."

"Why do we have to take the tools along?" I asked.

"Because it's our duty. We're responsible for the tools. Where we go, the tools go."

"Then we won't return?"

"It's what Sergeant Slavko ordered, so that's how it must be." Red-faced, Kosta cut me off and walked away to harness the horse.

Among the last to leave the barracks, we could not hear the trumpets anymore. Shells whizzed over us constantly. All night long we hauled overloaded wagons. Then, sometime before dawn, we caught up with our regiment near Resen.

At daylight we were ordered to settle in the nearby forest. We set up tents. The food wagons prepared breakfast. We ate, and then, exhausted from the previous night's ordeal, we rested until noon, lingering in the shadows until dinner.

Then the order to move came—direction: Ohrid.

Sometime around midnight we arrived at Ohrid Garrison, where we met with the Second Battalion of the 46th Regiment. The Garrison's barracks and military structures were primitive. The whole thing looked like a big barn. They stationed my company in an abandoned building, occupied earlier by monks who had apparently pulled out in a hurry, leaving behind all their valuables.

The next day we learned from the Garrison Commander that the Italians had accidentally bombed Bitola. In response to this "mistake," our government submitted a stern warning. They quickly covered up the whole thing, and no one talked about the attack after that.

A week passed, during which I did not open my toolbox. I read books from the diocese library, played cards with Kosta, and waited for further orders, as time slipped slowly away.

At the end of the week, the Company Commander received orders from Regiment Headquarters to transfer me to the battalion workshop on the other side of the camp. They wanted it done quickly. This distressed us all.

Kosta nearly buckled over when he heard the news. I reminded him that I would not be far away, and we would see each other, but both of us had a feeling in our stomachs that contradicted my words. As I saw sadness and worry darken Kosta's face, I could feel a black cloud enter both our souls.

That's when I parted from Kosta, never to see him again.

Later I learned that Albanians had killed him during our retreat through Macedonia.

The news stabbed my heart.

Chapter 2

Quiet Before the Storm

The battalion workshop was located near the garrison entrance. Even though Mr. Boro and I were the only carpenters in the entire Ohrid Garrison, we did not have much work. Additionally, we knew how to arrange it to make plenty of time for other activities. So the next few weeks proved to be the most peaceful and beautiful part of my army life.

Mr. Boro loved to gamble. He spent much of his time playing cards with lower ranking officers, who often owed him their entire monthly salary. For him, card playing became a ritual. He would put on a clean undershirt, clean dress shirt, and freshly pressed trousers, comb his wavy dark hair, part it down the middle, trim the edges of his mustache, check it all in his pocket mirror, smack his lips, well-pleased, and walk out confidently swaying his tall frame.

I, however, had such a great desire to expand my knowledge that, ever since childhood, I had used my free time to read. My elementary and middle-school teacher, Joseph, had encouraged me to read and learn as much as possible, and often lent me books to take home. My father grumbled and did not like to see me waste my time reading. He wanted me to become a carpenter.

Knowing my love for books, my tiny, good-natured mother would, however, secretly sneak into my room and prepare the gas lamp for me every night, enabling me to devour the pages of our classics, and the histories of the Greeks, Romans, old Slavs and Serbs. I read the Old and New Testaments, learned by heart passages from Njegoš's [*Nyey-gohsh*] *Mountain Wreath*, memorized numerous heroic poems, and became totally obsessed with the adventures, discoveries, and travels of the maritime explorers.

By age fifteen, I was so far ahead of my classmates that Jagodina Real Gymnasium wanted to make me a sophomore. But my father would not allow me to continue my education. He considered mastering a trade more important than all the schools in the world. Teacher Joseph arranged to have me transferred to Jagodina, but my father would not let me go. For him, a trade provided bread, while books and education afforded a pastime for gentlemen—not peasants.

Nevertheless I continued to read. Teacher Joseph persisted in encouraging me and in supplying me with the most appropriate books for a boy my age. Thus I became a good storyteller. Later master carpenters, journeymen, helpers, and my army pals all listened eagerly to my tales of Magellan, Marco Polo, Amerigo Vespucci, and Cortez.

Here at Ohrid, through books, I led another life, in another world—a world untouched by war.

Thus arrived the frigid winter of 1940, and I did not even feel it. No matter how cold it became outside, our workshop remained warm with the heat of burning sawdust and wood chips. Upon finishing my work, I read volumes that I borrowed from the Serbian battalion doctor Cvetić [***Tsveh**-titch*], who also enjoyed good stories and novels. At first, my choice of subjects puzzled him, but since we often talked about these books, he came to understand my hunger and began to support my further education. He directed me to read about medicine, science, dead and living languages; and he taught me some words of German and some expressions in Latin.

Through him, I learned the phrase that has become my lifetime favorite: *Omnia mea mecum porto.* "All of mine I carry with me."

Such truth in this little sentence. Wherever I went, I carried those words.

All Is Lost

By the end of January 1941, the Greeks had pushed the Italians off the northwest mountain region of Greece. The Italians, exhausted and frightened, had retreated across the Yugoslav border to surrender to our army. We sheltered them temporarily in the Garrison, then transferred them to the Kičevo [***Kee**-chey-voh*] camp. From there, many returned to Italy.

A people of music and poetry, Italians made truly miserable soldiers. God only knows what made them go to war. Mussolini did them an obvious injustice. He forced these peace-loving, ordinary men to join the Fascist Italian Army and face zealous and rabid Greek freedom fighters. They looked so pitiful that we felt sorry for them.

Winter here turned mild. Already in February buds sprouted in the forests and meadows near our barracks. Looking for nesting spots, birds landed on trees in bloom. Rising streams rushed to the Drim River, rippling loudly through the mountains' bare canyons. Mud became the heaviest burden for our already overloaded infantry. It stuck to their boots, making every step heavier and more tormenting. Even the horses carrying raging officers got stuck. They neighed shrilly at the spurs that mercilessly jabbed and bloodied their flanks.

Foreboding lurked in our souls. Regional Command appeared confused, disoriented, lost. Officers became nervous and inscrutable. They hid themselves in cocoons, awaiting direction from upper command while our generals remained silent.

When, on 25 March, our government and the King's Regent, Prince Paul, signed the Tripartite Pact to join forces with Germany, they informed our regional commander about it in strict secrecy. But somehow everyone in the Army knew.

Two days later, a pro-Western military coup took down the King's government and installed the Serbian Gen. Dušan Simović [***Du**-shahn **Si**-moh-vitch*] at its head. Simović dissolved the newly formed alliance with Germany, bringing pure joy to Serbs. But our delight was short-lived.

On 6 April, Croats, Slovenians, Montenegrins, and Bosnian Muslims–who had observed the coup indifferently–reveled at Hitler's crushing air attack on Belgrade, and a country, that for so long stood on only the weakest foundation, disintegrated.

It collapsed on the rotten pilings of profound hatred among ethnic groups.

On 7 April our artillery opened fire on the Italian troops that reached Struga. The Italians returned the shelling from across the Albanian border. This battle lasted until 12 April with no casualties. Neither the Italians nor we advanced or retreated.

On 13 April, our regiment commander ordered the Army to pull back. We left a few machine guns behind, however, to protect the retreat of the 46th Infantry Division, which had already started to withdraw in chaos and panic.

Regional Command then vanished with the entire headquarters. The remaining officers and non-coms struggled to organize the cavalry, infantry, and artillery behind the Black Drim in some sort of assembly that would calm the men's spirits and bring order back to the army. But their calls, threats, and pleas fell on deaf ears.

Soldiers fled in terror to the northeast.

I crossed the Drim with my sergeant, and we headed through a clearing in the forest toward Skopje and the

Tetovo Garrison just west of there. We lost contact with the other groups, but we managed to follow the route based on the topography map that Sgt. Simić carried with him.

Around midnight we arrived in a village, fortunately inhabited by Macedonians. They received us heartily, gave us food to eat and put us up near the fireplace. At dawn, our host woke us and advised us as to which road was safest to travel. He told us we would get to Skopje in about three days if we took care to avoid the Arnauts.[5]

This group of Albanians would intercept Serbian soldiers, offer money and jewelry for their guns, and, when the famished and bewildered soldiers agreed to a deal, the Arnauts would kill them with bayonets and knives to save their ammunition. Then they robbed the dead soldiers, stripped them naked, and left them to rot in the ravines and rocky canyons of the Šar [*Shahr*] Mountains. Thankfully, Macedonian shepherds and peasants happened onto at least some of the victims and gave them a Christian burial.

Sgt. Simić and I walked mainly at night, rested in the daytime, and kept careful lookout for Arnauts and their villages. Sometimes they followed us and watched from a distance, waiting for the right moment to attack. But they could see we remained prepared to confront them.

Exhausted, we finally joined the rest of the army at Tetovo, where our men had gathered from all directions awaiting their next orders.

The entire city swarmed with Yugoslav soldiers. Without our knowledge, Hitler had already conquered Serbia, shattering what little resistance it made to the roaring German war machine. Downed communications

---

[5] Albanians—who formerly constituted the Sultan's Guard under the Ottoman Empire—ruled Kosovo and other areas with an iron hand. Their vicious oppression continued after the ousting of the Empire, when they became known by this derogatory epithet.

and railroad lines, however, had interrupted all correspondence with Supreme Command in Belgrade. So the officers' echelons that made it to Tetovo by horse or on foot still expected to receive direction from above. We all milled about in the huge open field near the garrison, trying to get information and remaining at ready for the moment it would come.

That afternoon the Germans entered the city. One lieutenant and ten soldiers on motorcycles. The soldiers had sidecars with machine guns pointed at hundreds of us spread out in the field. The lieutenant stepped off his motorcycle, strode out into the road overlooking our army, and addressed us in German.

Soon one Croatian soldier came forward to translate his words: "Your government has fallen. You are now war prisoners of the German Army. I order you to fall under my command. Lay down your arms."

Those words hit my ears like a blow to my face.

They echoed across Serbia.

We stood there dumbfounded and hesitant. *But we'll eat them up.* I then spoke the same out loud with like-minded hundreds of others. Nevertheless, when the German lieutenant ordered our officers to dismount and join the soldiers, our would-be resistance collapsed.

I watched as our officers—yesterday's wolves—dismounted. To my great consternation, a Croatian colonel came forward immediately, smiling broadly. Shoulders squared and head held high, he saluted the German officer, removed his sword, ripped off his epaulets, took off his cap, and threw them all to the ground, spitting on the pile with disgust.

The gasp from the men would have broken a pig's heart.

He then removed his pistol from its holster and—turning the handle toward the German and looking him gleefully in the eye—placed it directly in his hand.

Without breaking eye contact with the Croat, the German tossed the pistol onto a blanket that lay to his side. With a big, happy grin, the Croatian saluted again, turned on his heel and returned to our ranks.

A low grumble rolled through our group, and everyone glared at him as he took his place off to the side.

Next, a colonel I didn't know walked slowly forward, looking down at the ground—paused briefly, then looked up at the German lieutenant, saluted, unbuckled his sword, and gently dropped it and his pistol. As he returned to the ranks, one of the German soldiers went over, picked up the sword and gun, and placed them on the blanket with those of the Croatian.

All of the majors and captains under the command of these two colonels lined up to follow suit, and one by one they unbuckled their swords and dropped their pistols on the blankets spread out in front of their enemy to receive them.

The lieutenants under these men made a move to step forward, when the one bright moment in all that shame lit our hearts. Col. Radić [***Rah**-ditch*], a Serb who already stood front and center, refused to unbuckle his sword. He stood there, firmly determined not to surrender, eyes locked with those of the German officer.

When the latter stepped forward to within a meter of the Colonel and drew his pistol, Col. Radić continued to glare at him, jaw clearly set.

The German moved closer.

Radić held firm.

The shot stunned us. The Colonel went limp and collapsed to the ground. None of us had the presence of mind even to gather up the body.

The German lieutenant stormed back to his elevated position on the road and shouted in German again.

From my place just a few rows back, I spat to the side and threw my rifle on the ground. Twenty other soldiers behind me did the same. At the crash of all the dropped rifles, the men in front of us turned around and threw their rifles to the ground also.

This act of revolt riled the German officer, who shouted out his next command.

The Croat translated his sharp words: "If anyone disobeys, he will be shot on the spot."

One of the German soldiers pointed a machine gun at us and fingered the trigger.

We were petrified. It was over.

Our Army had surrendered.

Journey into the Unknown

After the surrender, the eleven Germans then drove an entire division of the Yugoslav Royal Army like a flock of sheep into the closed circle of Tetovo Garrison. We stayed there for a day.

Then they loaded hundreds of us into cattle cars bound for Skopje. What a nightmare, full of confusing phantasms that hardly seemed real but were. My mind grasped for meaning, but so many bleak scenes piled one on top of another made everything hazy, like some foreign film I couldn't understand.

We arrived in Skopje at dusk. They unloaded us in front of the main train station, where another German patrol waited to escort us to Skopje's garrison. Exhausted, thirsty, and starving, we slept on our blankets in the garrison yard. For breakfast the next day, they gave us hot tea and a piece of bread.

At about ten o'clock, they separated us by nationalities. They gave the first group of about a hundred Croats travel passes and some sort of ID cards, then did the same for the several Slovenians, Muslims, and, finally, for the Montenegrins, the largest group. Perhaps three hundred or more proudly waved their passes as they exited through the main gate, shouting, "Long live Freedom! Long live our Duke!"

Totally worn out, I did not notice the goings-on around me. Soon I understood that they had only taken us Serbs as prisoners. No other Yugoslav regional governments had supported us. In the now smaller circle of captives, I searched for my corner of shame. I attempted to hide my misery and disgrace by covering my face.

I felt worthless and nameless for the first time since I had become a soldier.

From Skopje, our next train arrived at the Pirot Railroad Station, and they finally gave us something to eat. The meal, served by Bulgarian soldiers from a wheeled kettle, consisted of a dry biscuit and a cup of potato soup. One of the Serbian soldiers addressed the Bulgarians:

"What's going on? Where are they taking us?"

A Bulgarian soldier giggled. "Well, brother, that's the way it goes. If the Germans win, you are ours, and if the English win, we are yours."

In WWII Bulgarians aligned with the Axis powers, so Germany took command of their army. The Germans, however, treated the Bulgarians with suspicion, as in this case, when they shouted at them and chased them away from the train cars to prevent them from talking to us.

In Sofia they moved our transport to an auxiliary track, and we stayed there overnight waiting. Apparently no one felt the need to hurry. From the soldiers' conversations with Bulgarian friendlies, I gathered that Hitler planned to attack Russia, but Yugoslavia had already delayed him six weeks. He had to secure passage through Greece and did not want the Balkans to become a southern front. Thus the prisoner-of-war transports moved slower because the rail cars for transporting the German Army to the Eastern Front claimed higher priority.

The following day our transport cars returned to the main tracks, and we continued to the northeast, burrowing deep into the heart of Bulgaria. From the day of our surrender and imprisonment, beginning at Skopje Garrison, and during the long journey through Yugoslavia and Bulgaria, we would have suffered a great deal more if it weren't for little Solomon, our gypsy comrade. He became our cheerleader, the bright star in our otherwise cloudy sky. He played his violin and danced for us, then told jokes till we laughed so hard a passer-by might have thought we were all on our way to someone's wedding.

Solomon never complained. Whatever little food we got, he often shared his measly portion with the hungriest eyes. He always seemed happy, no matter what, and consistently entertained us with cheerful melodies. He refused to play ballads that would have racked us with nostalgia and driven us further into despair. He knew the Serbian soul, for he had spent many long nights playing for us sentimental fools, and he appreciated our great love for homeland, monarchy, and family. As a Muslim, he never drank, but he told us he had three children, with a mother for each kid. He claimed his religion allowed him to have more wives, and we teased him about it to no end. He just smiled and called us unfortunate.

When we left Sofia on the way north, he played some softer melodies with a touch of sadness. I asked him why.

He looked at me mysteriously and said quietly that he had heard the owl, which meant that he would lose his best friend that day. I didn't insist on an explanation, assuming it an old gypsy superstition, and walked away. He kept on playing and entertaining our carload of soldiers, but every so often he would stop and listen. We didn't understand his intuitions, so we brushed it off as "Solomon."

In the small town of Ginci [***Gint**-see*], the train stopped to replenish the water supply. We walked out into the sunny bright day and enjoyed spreading out along the tracks.

Whenever our train stopped at some remote station like this, either to let another train pass or, as here, for supplies, the German soldiers traveling in passenger cars with our train would line up in front of each car and wait at attention. With their dogs at the ready, the German guards kept their eyes on us. The officer in charge had a chair set in the shade of the passenger car, where he drank his lemonade and smoked a cigarette.

As usual, Solomon pulled out his fiddle and began some gypsy melody. Refreshed by his eternal good humor, we enjoyed his soothing strains, as we watched him sway with the magical moves of a female dancer. Then he changed the tune to a more vivacious melody and started dancing on the tracks. He looked like one of those trained monkeys in the circus, walking a tight rope, playing a fiddle tied to his left sleeve, with a bow tied to his right hand. He would walk along one of the rails, then hop to another, dancing faster and faster and jumping higher and higher till he worked himself into a trance.

All at once the heavy arm of the commander grabbed his neck from behind, ripped his fiddle out of his hands, and with a big swing, clobbered him over the head with it.

Bang! Twang! The instrument broke into several pieces, as the strings attached to the broken fingerboard wound themselves around Solomon's neck. This small and gentle cream puff of a man screamed with pain, bent to his knees, then started collecting the broken pieces of his best friend. He cried like a little boy.

It took only a few seconds. We watched bewildered.

Why? Solomon played at many stops before? Perhaps the owl had indeed foretold his future.

The German officer walked back to his chair, wiped his hands with a towel, poured some more lemonade, and smiled sadistically. He raised his glass to Solomon, and in response, Solomon lifted his arms, the pieces of the violin held high, and replied:

"Allahu akbar!"[6]

Loaded back in the stock car and on our way again, the heat and stuffiness overcame us. There was a Schwaben[7] among us, born in Paraćin [***Pah**-rah-tcheen*]. His parents had moved there as engineering experts in a glass manufacturing plant. He accepted Serbian ways and was assimilated into Serbian culture. We pleaded with him to ask one of the German soldiers to save us from our misery. Someone mentioned the Geneva Convention. Others simply begged.

He refused to listen. He did not want to reveal his German origin and risk release on that account. He told us that he was Serbian and that wherever Serbians go, he goes too.

On some other occasion this would have tightened our throats and brought tears to our eyes, but then it only

[6] "God is great!"

[7] In the late 1920s and early 1930s, Yugoslav industry invited various German expert engineers to establish their careers and become secondary citizens of Royal Yugoslavia. Their children, referred to as "Schwaben," grew up among Serbians, acquiring Serbian customs, language, folklore, and culture. Many never returned to Germany.

angered us. We grumbled and swore, but he would not bend.

We journeyed through northern Bulgaria for most of the day, passing valleys and canyons, until we stopped at another remote station. The train to take us in another direction was late, so we waited, packed like sardines, the heat of the sun wringing every last drop of sweat from our bodies.

After several hours of this agony, I heard a sharp commanding voice from our wagon speaking in German. The guard on the station platform turned in the direction of our car: "And you? What are you doing there? You're German, aren't you?"

"I'm a Serb, but I learned to speak German in school," said our Paraćin Schwaben. "Please ask your commanding officer to divide our overcrowded car. We're suffocating and cannot continue this way anymore. It's inhuman, and you're violating the Geneva Convention."

"One moment, please," said the guard and ran to the passenger car.

A few minutes later a German officer arrived, ordered all of us out, then split us in two equal groups, and sent half, escorted by guards, to the last empty stock car. I went with the second group to that car. Everyone was relieved. Our Paraćin countryman hurried to fill our empty flasks with water, and so we all drank thirstily as we ran to the new car. When I stepped in, I felt as if I were entering the hall of our headquarters back in Ohrid with all its empty space. We rested on clean hay and continued to wait.

We did not travel long to the River Danube, not more than an hour. At the last station, we disembarked and walked for two or three kilometers along the riverbank. Night began to claim the surface of the river, and we could hardly distinguish the pontoon bridge stretched between the banks. A line of exhausted prisoners dragged itself across to the other side. We sprawled on unpitched tent canvases and fell asleep immediately.

At dawn we learned that we had reached Romania on St. George's Day, 6 May 1941—patron saint of soldiers or no, we had nothing to celebrate. We stayed there a week, waiting for transport and catching up on our rest.

During our week there, a Romanian delegation appeared with a permit from the German Authority to liberate all those prisoners of the Yugoslav Royal Army who were Romanians, or who declared themselves Romanian. The Kingdom of Romania, under orders from the Nazi occupying forces, had annexed the Serbian counties of Požarevac [***Poh**-zhah-reh-vahts*], Negotin, and Resava, as punishment for their disregard for the Regent's pact with Germany on 25 March. Romanians, however, never officially occupied those territories and left the local Serbian authorities to govern during the war; but technically—and as far as the Germans were concerned—the three counties had become part of Romania.

The delegation began to select their countrymen, and soon a small line had formed in front of their field desk. A distant relative of mine, Velibor, whom I had stumbled onto when we crossed into Romania, confronted me now.

"Come on, Timo, let's register. We're also from Negotin County."

"You are, but I'm not."

"Who cares? Stay close to me. I know a little Romanian and we'll make it through."

"I can't. You go though."

I walked away from him so that the other Serbs would not hear. I was ashamed of such an act. *Is there no one who will not desert us?*

With silent cursing and hatred, the eyes of my countrymen watched vigilantly every Serb in line. Velibor joined the queue. I thought for a moment, and then approached him again.

"Listen, Velibor. Could you do me a great favor?"

"Sure, anything, Cousin."

"You see that little fellow over there?

"Yes, I see him. The little gypsy."

"Right. Him. Could you squeeze him in line with you and help him pass as a Romanian from Negotin Krajina [***Krah***-*yee-nah*]?"

"Well, I don't know, Timo. He's a gypsy . . ."

"C'mon. You have to. He's so helpless. He won't last a day as a prisoner of war. Please, Velibor. Do it for our sake. I'll be indebted to you forever."

"OK, brother. I'll take him," he said, as he shrugged. "Call him."

I waved to Solomon and he approached sheepishly.

"This is my cousin Velibor. I want you to go with him. He is going to declare you a Romanian from Negotin Krajina. Just follow him and don't say anything. He will talk for you. Do you understand?"

Solomon looked confused. Knitting his eyebrows, he looked up at me, then hugged me.

"Thank you, Timo. May Allah bless you. I will pray for you."

I shook his little hand and waved him off. The two of them got in line in front of the Romanian Delegation table. When his turn came, the Romanian delegate asked Velibor whether he spoke Romanian.

"I do, a little, but not very good."

The Romanian smiled through his mustache, wrote Velibor's name on the pass and, looking well satisfied, handed it to him.

When Solomon's turn came, I heard my cousin tell the Romanian, "He's also from Negotin Krajina but he doesn't speak Romanian." Then he added, "He'll learn quickly."

The Delegate handed a pass to Solomon.

Thus my relative, along with twenty others, including smiling Solomon, went back to Serbia. I secretly waved to him, but he did not see me.

I remained with my own kind, again alone.

Escape

On the seventh day, the Germans moved us to the railroad station at Turnu Măgurele [***Tur**-noo Meh-**goo**-rey-ley*], Romania, and we again boarded a transport. I counted twenty-four stock cars, one passenger car, and one steam locomotive. I was again in the last car but with a different group.

We traveled west all night and all the next day. Sometimes we followed the Danube, but sometimes the tracks ran between the hills not far from that mighty river, and we wondered about our distance from the riverbank.

I had lain down to sleep toward the front of the car when I overheard a conversation among three soldiers.

"Mr. Božo [***Boh**-zhoh*]," said one, "we can pass through that small window at the top."

"There are iron stairs leading from the roof so that we can descend to the platform," said the second Serbian soldier.

"Boys, I know," the older fellow replied. "But how can we jump from it?"

"Not to worry. I will go first, and you watch how I jump," said the first soldier.

I recognized the voice of the older man, whom we called Mr. Božo. He had spent a considerable amount of time with me making brushes in the workshop of our specialty battalion at Ohrid. Much older than regular recruits, Božo Lukić [***Lu**-kitch*] had mastered the art of drawing horsehair through a wooden base with soft wire. That's how we fashioned the best handmade brushes for the entire division. He did not talk much, but he loved listening to my polemics in a warm workshop. I often recited passages from the books I had read, and he would say he had learned something.

I opened my eyes slowly and whispered. "Mr. Božo. It's me, Timo!"

Surprised, he looked at me and smiled. "Timo, how are you? These are my fellow villagers from the Šabac [***Sha**-bahts*] region. Allow me to introduce you: Lazar and Gavro from Koceljevo [*Koht-**sehl**-yey-voh*]."

I shook hands with the two young men and moved to join their circle. Božo turned carefully so the larger group could not hear him. He bent his head toward me, almost touching my ear.

"Timo, we have decided to escape. Would you like to join us?"

"I would," I replied without hesitation. "When?"

Lazar, the first young man, with a tiny moustache and long neck, leaned forward.

"Tonight, we'll arrive at Đerdap [***Dgehr**-dahp*]. The tracks there climb the Canyon, and the train will slow down greatly. The passage through Đerdap lasts almost an hour, and that will give us enough time to climb out and jump off."

Excited and ready for the next challenge to this useless fate, I listened to the escape plan. First, we would all help Lazar reach the top front window and squeeze through. Then he would descend the stairs to the bottom platform step, where he would wait for Gavro. After him, Božo would get out and stand at the top of the stairs, where he would help me through. Lazar would jump first. Gavro would follow, then Božo, then me. The entire process should not take more than thirty minutes, and the escape would start the moment we slowed down through Đerdap Canyon.

The train meandered west into the night, as though entering ever deeper into a dark cave. It tore the stillness of the northern riverbank with the balanced rhythm of its pistons. Everyone in our car slept, and only the four of us peered determinedly through the slats, waiting for the right moment.

I had drifted into dreams when Božo pulled my sleeve.

"Timo, we've arrived. It's slowing down. Prepare to go."

I looked around in search of the other two, but they were no longer inside. The train had slowed, and we moved as agreed. I helped Božo get up to the window, through which he quickly disappeared.

Then I raised myself and squeezed my head and upper torso through. I saw Gavro's shadow separating from the car and falling into darkness along the railroad tracks. I descended the iron stairs, clinging tightly, when I felt Božo help me step down to a flange with hardly enough space for my toes.

The old man shivered as he clung to a metal bar, preparing himself for the jump. It would not be easy, though the train moved much more slowly. At last he leapt from the moving car. I thought for a second that I heard a painful scream, but the loud squealing of the train wheels on the curving tracks masked any other sounds.

I crossed myself, said a short prayer, and dove into the darkness, my hands straight out in front of me. I felt the sharp pain of thorns in my palms, but my inertia continued to roll me through the briery bushes. Finally, I came to a stop in front of a tree and lay spread out on wet ground.

I looked and listened. Nothing but black and silence.

I slowly got up, as fear slithered down my spine. Exhausted, I wondered what to do next. I straightened up and quietly called out to my companions.

Nobody answered.

I called a little louder, and my voice echoed through the valley.

I groped my way up the hill and began to recognize solid forms. Dawn was slowly dispersing the circle of darkness, and I recognized the bulwark of tracks three or four meters in front of me.

The noise of the train gradually disappeared beyond the high cliffs of the canyon, and I heard only the awakening of the forest and the murmur of a creek in the distance. I called again to my cohorts and started moving along the railway.

Soon I heard a subdued moan, and I rushed, calling louder. I got there just as the other two descended from the tracks down the slope to where Božo's body lay curled up on the edge of a ravine. He moaned and whimpered so dreadfully that it made me shudder.

We tried to turn him, but when he screamed in response, we let him alone for a moment. When we finally got him on his back, his head was all covered with blood, and his right hand hung bent in the direction opposite his elbow.

Horror-struck, I froze.

Then, pulling myself together, I ordered the other two to start a fire and bring water in their hats from the creek. I pulled a handkerchief from my pocket and got closer to Božo, who quivered in pain. In the firelight, Božo's exhausted and pale face told us that his wound was indeed very serious. I began to console him. I tried to straighten his arm, but he let out such a terrible shriek that I stepped back.

"Timo, don't," moaned Božo. "It's broken."

I hesitated. "We must straighten and set it, Mr. Božo."

Without much knowledge, I took on a task I had never done before. While my hands maneuvered blindly, I silently prayed to God to help me. I steeled myself against Božo's screams, and instead, told Lazar to hold him tightly while I set his arm.

Božo cried out again, but not like the first time. I lifted his arm and pulled slowly. His eyes reflected the fire, and the light from the flames flickered across his ashen face as it contorted in pain. Holding him with my left hand under his elbow, I pulled a little harder and felt the bones set in place.

Božo calmed down a bit.

I sent Lazar to find a piece of wood to use as a splint. We bandaged the arm with our kerchiefs, and then we washed Božo's bloody face, dislodging all the dirt that had caked on his scratches and skull.

Poor old Mr. Božo was totally crushed, but when we gave him fresh water from the creek, he gathered his strength and got up on his feet.

Then we all set out along the tracks, heading west.

Romania

The slowly rising sun warmed our backs. Weary, we eagerly inhaled the fresh morning air. A soft breeze brought the smell of surrounding forests, blooming trees and meadow flowers. It gave us new energy that revived our confidence.

After a few hours of moving slowly, we saw around the second bend—about five hundred meters ahead—beautiful hillsides with pastures, where smoke spiraled into the sky from a small village. Our faces lit up, and we started down the slope, then uphill toward the first cottage.

In front of the cottage, an older woman wrapped in a wool scarf sat near an older man with a large mustache and a lambskin jacket. A young boy drove sheep from a barn.

With some knowledge of Romanian—but also pointing to my mouth and stomach—I asked for some food for the four of us.

The old woman did not need much explanation. She went into the cottage and brought back a large piece of bread and a loaf of cheese. She cut the bread and cheese, placed it on a shallow wooden dish and signaled to us to help ourselves.

We, the young ones, attacked the food like hungry wolves, while Božo finished his cigarette, then, with his left hand, calmly put it out, broke the bread and cheese in small pieces and appeared to enjoy every mouthful. The boy also brought out a hunk of ham that the old woman offered to us after carefully cutting it in four equal pieces.

Our strength returned at every savory bite, and slowly we began to relax.

As daylight filled the forest clearing nearby, we watched the dance of the remaining shadows with dreamy eyes. The splendor of colors dotting the meadows and the movement of stems at the smallest breeze in the woods trapped bits of fog on the hillside. A flock of birds sang, flying in and out of the trees, while in front of the cottage, sheep grazed on young grass and bleated.

Behind the cottage, we fell asleep on the rugs that our hosts laid out for us.

I don't know how long I slept, but late afternoon had already arrived when voices in front of the cottage woke me. I saw three Romanian soldiers calmly smoking their rolled tobacco and occasionally looking in our direction. Božo was awake, while the other two still slept soundly.

Puzzled, I looked at the old man, but he only nodded his head and said something unintelligible.

I tapped Lazar and Gavro and alerted them to our capture. They had not yet awakened completely, but after hearing my words, they suddenly shuddered and turned pale.

Božo, seeing their fear, tried to cheer them. "Boys, don't be afraid. What God has meant for us will happen. God is great, and He will protect us from every evil that looms over us."

When the Romanian soldiers led us over the hill, the sun was already setting. I turned around and saw the old woman nodding her head sorrowfully, and the boy waved until we vanished into the woods.

After a half hour of walking, we arrived at a hilltop where, down in the valley below us, we could see the reflection of sunset from the mighty Danube. At the foot of the hill, we saw the building where the border guards then led us.

They placed us in a large barracks. We sat down on wooden benches next to the window. Depressed and helpless, we lost hope. We had endured terrible suffering, and now the pain grew greater.

Gavro sobbed.

Lazar tried to calm and console him, as we trudged toward our next prison cell.

That same evening they took us to the garrison's commanding officer on duty. He was a tall young man, with black hair, olive colored dark eyes, and a finely cut mustache. He reminded me of that movie star perpetually cast as the romantic lead. The neatly ironed uniform, shiny boots, and cigarette holder in his mouth emphasized his noble class even more. *We could have a famous actor standing in front of us, or an officer on parade, as easily as a border garrison officer.*

He received us with kindness. An interpreter asked questions with sympathy and understanding. He wanted to know whether they had fed us, whether Mr. Božo had received medical help, how he currently felt, and whether his soldiers had treated us with respect.

We acknowledged his concern and expressed our gratitude. A feeling of hope seeped back into our dejected hearts.

"Serbia is our closest neighbor. The affinity between us is both profound and longstanding. Our royal families have intermarried."

He took a drag on his cigarette and continued, "However, as you yourselves know, Romania is in chains."

Visibly upset, his voice became elevated. His eyes shot bolts of lightning, and strong emotions colored his words of anger and agony. "The Germans have occupied us, as they have you, with one exception. They have not taken us prisoner—yet. Instead they have enslaved us in our own country."

He shook our hands. "Had you been civilians when we captured you, I would have had you transported across the Danube to your homeland and set free tonight. That, however, is not in my power. German Command Headquarters already knows that we have apprehended you."

Božo thanked him for his kind words, and, before parting, the old man embraced him with his healthy, left arm. As a memento from us all, I handed the officer an icon of the Holy Mother of God that I had carved when I was in Bitola.

Touched by this act, he stood there for a moment, crossed himself, then kissed the icon and placed it on his chest. Large tears, as clear as water from a mountain creek, illuminated his dark eyes. He wiped them shyly and waved to a guard to take us out.

We returned to the barracks, ourselves deeply moved.

They kept us there for three days. We bathed. Their barber cut our hair. They gave us shaving cream and razors, washed our laundry, and mended our uniforms. We felt as if we had returned to our own army. They offered us plenty of food, and we, fearing where our path would lead next, ate as if these meals were our last.

On the fourth day, they told us to prepare, as they had been ordered to release us to German Command. Before dusk, a German truck with two soldiers appeared, took charge of us, and drove us back to their command post. Our recently acquired hope disappeared when we found ourselves behind the walls of the old city of Drobeta-Turnu Severin.

At dawn they brought us in front of the German commanding officer, who proceeded to interrogate us: "Where did you come from? What prison camp did you escape from? Did you kill any German soldiers?"

He pounded on the table and glowered at us unconvinced as we gave answers about how, during a short break, we had fallen behind at a station near Đerdap Canyon, how the train had left without us, and how we had followed the tracks until we got to the Romanian border garrison, where they took us in.

Our story sounded persuasive, but the facts contradicted us. Wounded Božo provided sufficient reason for the interrogator and the commanding officer not to believe us, so they transferred us back across the Danube to a collective prison camp near Kladovo, Serbia.

Return to Serbia

I don't know whether the suspense of not knowing our fate or the return to Serbia in chains demoralized us more. Dirt roads along the Danube raised turbulent clouds of dust behind the Krupp-Protze Kfz.70, where the four of us and one German guard sat on the wool rug covering the open truck bed. A second guard, in the cabin with the chauffeur, started a conversation, but his companion would not respond.

After about a half hour, we arrived in Kladovo. When we stopped at the main square, the guard ordered us out of the truck. He left on foot with the chauffeur. We sat on the ground alongside the truck, awaiting his return.

The young guard tried awkwardly to roll a cigarette.

Mr. Božo, seeing his difficulty with the tobacco, handed him one of his.

A few minutes later, our fellow countrymen from the surrounding area gathered around the truck. "Where were you captured?" "Where are you from?" "Have you seen my son?" "Have you seen my cousins?"

We remained quiet, waiting for permission from the guard. We looked at him timidly.

One nicely clothed lady addressed him in German: "May we talk to our countrymen? Perhaps they know something about our own. Please, sir, in the name of the Lord, let us talk to them."

She startled the young soldier, who appeared more surprised than frightened. He nodded his head.

The questions continued from all sides. It stung to tell the unfortunate parents that their sons had been taken to Germany. Women cried. Men held their heads, trying to hide their helplessness and pain.

As the group dispersed, one of the men turned back. "Are you hungry?"

Before we could answer, a lady asked the guard if they could prepare some food for us. He again agreed. Old and young ran in all directions. They brought bread, cheese, smoked meat, sausages, fruit, and fresh red peppers and tomatoes.

We began stuffing our shirts, when our guard emptied a laundry basket and offered it to us to put the food in. The nicely dressed lady thanked him profusely. He loaded it onto the truck and ushered us in. As we climbed aboard, our people surrounded the truck, folded their hands in prayer and bowed with gratitude to this young fellow.

The warmth of our people overwhelmed him. A faraway look appeared in his eyes, as though fond memories of his youth were rekindled. A tremor crossed his face. He looked confused, nagged by some inner guilt, derailed from his mandatory coldness, foreign even to himself.

A young child ran to us and handed a small Serbian flag to Gavra. "Give it to my daddy. Tell him Momma and I are waiting for his return. He must come. Tell him Zoran . . ."

The truck pulled away, and we waived solemnly while the small boy yelled the imperceptible words of his message. We tried to keep our tears back, as our people stood waving and sobbing. They cried for us, for all the sons of Serbia, and for the Fatherland. We endeavored to remain strong, but our hearts trembled with pain, and our blurry eyes unwillingly drowned in a contagion of sorrow.

The young guard sat silently and watched us curiously. When we had gone some distance, he handed us the basket. During the trip, we stopped three times and shared the blessings of our Serbian people with the chauffeur and the two guards.

At one point, I saw the young guard wipe away his tears, and I heard the older guard ask with surprise, "Hans, what is it?"

"Nothing. I don't know. What did these people do to us?"

"Hans, be careful what you say. You're a soldier."

They stopped talking.

Astonished and confused, I understood the young man's anguish.

I felt sorry for him—and for us.

Meeting with Father

We arrived in Negotin before nightfall. They kept us in a German army barracks for three days, then transported us in another truck to Zaječar [***Zah**-yey-chahr*]. The city jailhouse there served as a prison camp. They locked us in with fifty other Serbian soldiers.

At dawn they took us all to do forced labor repairing our homeland's roads. All day long we worked on city streets, repairing old Turkish cobblestone, filling potholes with crushed rock, and packing the fill with heavy sledgehammers. At main intersections, we laid stone sidewalks and street pavers, as well as stone fences. From the compassionate passers-by, we begged cigarettes and packs of tobacco. They threw them to us secretly when the guards weren't looking. Late in the day, the guards escorted us back to camp, totally exhausted.

Nevertheless, in those warm May afternoons, we young people had enough energy to spread stories full of hope and high expectations. Many claimed the Germans would let us go when we finished the road repairs. They believed the war would soon end because—they thought—Germany had already defeated France and England, and Hitler now held most of Europe. They even talked about additional agreements between our King and Hitler. The starry-eyed storytelling started at our return to camp and continued into the following day, becoming ever more and more imaginative.

One day, while we worked near a small park, I got the courage to ask an older gentleman to get me a stamped postcard so I could inform my family of my whereabouts. The next day I saw him walk by, cough casually, and drop the postcard on the cobblestones.

The following week my father arrived. Others also received visits from their parents and close family members. They let us out in the jailhouse front yard for a moment of privacy.

My father brought a bag of food and greetings from my mother and Roda.

We sat silently for about ten minutes.

Then I told him about the escape. His old face twitched and became anxious.

We were silent again.

"My daughter? Did you christen her?" I asked suddenly.

"We waited for you to return, but when you were taken prisoner, we called the family together and christened her. We named her in honor of your grandmother. Her name is Vasilija [*Vah-**see**-lee-yah*]."

I could feel my eyes twinkle. "After Grandma Vaska. That makes me happy."

And then, we fell silent again. Our conversation was no more than a sigh.

"How is Roda? Is she helping you? Is she a good daughter-in-law?"

"Yes, son, Roda is a very good woman. She watches over us and takes care of us as if she were our own."

"And, my daughter? Is she getting big? She must be ten months old by now. Is she walking yet?"

He nodded. "Yes, ten months, son, ten, and she grows more every day. Soon she will walk. She crawls all day long, and your mother is with her all the time. Roda is in the fields, and I am in the shop."

He paused and looked away, then hugged his left shoulder with his good arm and took a deep breath. "And so the days go by. Days without you."

He paused again before turning back to me.

"Oh, my son, we hope you stay alive and healthy. Take care of yourself wherever you go."

"Don't worry, Father. Soon, they will let us go home. That's what we hear."

"May God help you."

We crossed ourselves and finished our hushed conversation. When the bell announced the end of our visit, my father embraced me, his mouth close to my ear:

"Timo, my son, promise me something. Don't ever try to escape anymore. This time you were lucky. They could have shot you."

Tears filled his eyes. Then his face tightened again. A burst of emotion broke free from behind valiant stoicism.

We cried quietly, in the last embrace.

I stammered the promise.

He turned to go, then stopped, pulled a small note from his pocket, and placed it in my hand.

We parted with heavy hearts.

As I watched him disappear down the road, I opened the note. It was from Roda. *But, how? Who could have written it for her?* On the back, scribbled in tiny letters:

> May God save you, my favorite student.
> Teacher Josef

Dear Josef. How much I owe him.

I pictured Roda asking his help, then turned to her letter:

> Dear Timo,
>
> When I heard the Germans took you prisoner, my heart sank very low. May God protect you!
>
> I am good, and little Vaska is an angel. She smiles a lot. When we take her with us to the fields, she just sings all day. I help Father Milovan in the fields and with the cattle, and most of the time Mama Bosiljka [*Boh-**seel**-kah*] takes care of little Vaska in the house. I learn from your mother about cooking, knitting and cheese making. We have lots of lambs this year, and Father Milovan also bought a mule for pulling the straw wagon for harvest and fertilizing.
>
> The village has not changed much, but only the old men are left. When Father goes to market in Ćuprija, he takes me with him and we trade for goods, since no one has money anymore. We got a little, though, and I bought cloth to make a sun bonnet for Vaska to match the scarf you used to wear in the fields.

The letter started to blur. I had to blink several times to be able to read the rest.

> I hope they will let you come home—very soon.
>
> I miss you, and your mother and father miss you. We all need you here.
>
> With all my love,
> Your Roda

I thanked God for all our hard labor. It eased our pain and made our time in Zaječar go by quickly.

Departure for Germany

When we finished the road repairs, they again loaded us into cattle cars. I was separated from my escape crew, Bozo, Lazar, and Gavro. Whether cousins or neighbors, I never knew, but Gavro and Lazar stayed together always. At the end of the war, I met them at a Hamburg railroad station on their way home to Serbia. Later, it saddened me to learn that the communists had captured and killed them somewhere *en route* in Slovenia.

Without them, I felt very much alone again. Soon though, we were joined by a group of young civilians from the concentration camp in Niš. They had failed to avoid capture in the villages and cities of eastern Serbia. Within a few days the count reached two thousand Serbian POWs and civilians loaded onto long trains going north to serve as forced laborers for the Germans in their underground factories.

For the first time in my life, in the very blood of my veins, I felt defeat. That vital fluid rushed excitedly forward from my heart, but returned to it dejected, doomed. The top of my skull strained like an anchored balloon trying to ascend to unknown heights, while the unbearable drums beating in my head choked my tired soul.

Clouds of fear and panic howled through the gorges of Morava, spreading the bleak cries of us conquered warriors across the mountains and valleys of our beloved homeland. The wind moaned in mourning for her sons of Serbia. She attempted to revive our spirits with the warm touch of early summer and the smell of ardently blooming meadows, of nectar and sweet pollen.

And indeed the fragrances on the wind did ease the souls of us poor peasants, who looked dully out into the unknown. Hillsides painted with the perfect colors of nature changed spontaneously with the rhythm of the iron wheels. Pictures of the countryside turned like the pages of a photo album. We Serbian soldiers stared longingly through small holes in the train cars. In our minds we opened the doors of distant homes, silently called our beloveds, and unconsciously let out sounds that echoed and vanished with the loud whistle of the locomotive.

But soon we lost souls began dreading our future once more, and an already high tide of terror rose anew, mounting ever higher and higher.

Wooo-wooo! The train whistle jolted me out of my stupor.

The sweet smell of the meadows, the fragrance of my birthplace, entered my lungs from afar, and I recognized the valleys, blooming orchards, plum trees, and gardens along the rising Morava. The aroma reminded me of the times before the war when I would return home with my father from Jagodina or Paraćin, and the bouquet of our meadows enchanted me. I inhaled it, as if with my last breath. My eyes and skin bathed in its waves, skimming lightly across the surface of a secret sea, and my entire body became a sail in fond anticipation of another energizing gust.

I peeped through a hole in the door and recognized the town of Ćuprija.

The train slowed. I hurried to find a piece of paper and scribbled the following message:

To Milovan S. Tomić, village of Krusar
by Ćuprija.

We left for Germany. Take care of
yourselves! Your son, Timo

I beg anyone who finds this message
to take it to Milovan S. Tomić.
Much obliged,
Serbian war prisoner,
Jeftimije [***Yef**-ti-mee-yeh*] Timo Tomić
[***Toh**-mitch*]

Once we had crossed the bridge over the Morava, I pushed my note through the hole, and it landed in a mound of wildflowers along the railroad tracks.

A soldier behind me scoffed, "That's useless."

"It's OK. It doesn't matter. Maybe someone will find it," I replied confidently, although in fact, I doubted that anyone would.

Serbia gradually vanished behind us. I felt her with all my soul but I could not touch her. I raised my eyes to soak in as much of the scenery as I could, while it shifted before them as if in a magic kaleidoscope. Those pictures imprinted vividly on the pages of my memory. I returned to them over and over for a long time afterward, whenever I searched for solace.

Leaving the last hills of our homeland, I felt as if I had entered a tunnel of darkness with no daylight at the end. I tried to erase myself from this speeding train of the damned. Deep anxiety clawed its way into my soul. I closed my eyes to resist it, dreaming of happy moments, of dancing in the circles of my youth.

I thought of Solomon.

Among all these silent, unfortunate prisoners, I started moving, two steps to the left, two to the right, attempting to perform my own little Kolo in this tightly crowded space. I held my head high and accompanied myself with the imaginary twittering of metal flutes and the wheezing of weary accordions.

Soon the two men on either side of me also started to dance. They each wrapped an arm around my waist and we began to move as one. We gathered strength from each other and our stomps became bolder.

One by one, my circle dance expanded, swaying from side to side, jumping, kicking as best we could, gathering men and speed and determination, until the entire wagon of warriors' boots pounded in rhythm, stomp, step, step, stomp, stomp, our bodies bound together in a tight core of defiance.

The two Slovenians, Janko and Lubo, and a blond Slavonian from Osijek [***Oh**-see-yehk*] watched intently, then one by one they too joined in, moving awkwardly in the beginning, until the mystical rhythm entered their souls. Their eyes filled with tears of joy and sadness. They pounded their boots in concert with the rest of us. Pride shone from their pale faces. Soft humming spilled from their throats. They were Serbians, even if only for the moment. We became one.

We danced our last dance—resolutely—a shimmer of the sublime in the gloom of a bitter reality.

We are all of us one.

Chapter 3

POW Camp

The hearty determination of our communal dance dwindled bit by bit as the train wended its way out of Serbia. The long trip through the somber valleys of Slavonia, the seductive hilly regions of Austria and Czechoslovakia, and on into the green hills and valleys of Germany drained from us the last drops of our youth and filled us instead with a darkness that we allowed ourselves to wallow in.

When Germany fired the first shell on Belgrade, it nearly overwhelmed our resistant clamor with one mighty blow. Our famous Serbian fighting spirit had died. From that point on, the silence of defeat conquered the souls of hundreds of thousands of Serbian soldiers and followed them through all their years of captivity.

What I lived to see could not be tied with any threads of reason. Instead some secret fingers of malevolence pulled our strings to drag us across the stage of our existence. Life and Death strode as gladiators into the arena of human evil, while the merchants of hatred cheered from the stands of crazed nations.

I recall the details of our arrival at the prison camp in a jumble of numb impressions. Somewhere in the north of Germany, between Hanover and Hamburg, they unloaded our train cars in early July 1941 and drove us like herded cattle into Stalag 311. The prisoners there were mostly French, Belgian and English, along with a few Serbians, Ukrainians and Greeks.

I later learned that French, Belgian, and English prisoners had arrived a year ahead of us and had worked on constructing the concentration camp that formed the newest part of the entire prison complex. They had already cleared several acres of forested valley, fenced in the camp, and linked tall concrete columns with thickly intertwined barbed wire. They sawed lumber from tree trunks, and now they were clearing the surrounding forest for the so-called "no-man's-land" that lay between our prison camp and the camp under construction. Different nationalities bunked in different buildings, so our arrival provided us with a rare opportunity to meet men of other nations as we helped cut timber for construction.

A few days after our arrival, I got assigned to the work brigade, which needed three hundred rough-wood cutters, sawmill workers, carpenters, builders, and other skilled laborers who would build the camp.

Patriotism did not mean much when my stomach cried all night from hunger. In Zaječar, we were, at least, fixing streets in our own country. Now we labored to help the Germans in their war effort against us. But I could hardly wait for the canteen kettle with slimy cabbage soup and a small loaf of bread to share among five prisoners. Surfeit lasted an hour at most, and then the insatiable dragon in me would begin to howl. It felt like my pupils would stretch to bursting in search of anything edible. I chewed on an old leather wallet until it disappeared, and then I gawked at my comrades and begged for an extra bite of bread. For those of us who burned our meager provisions faster than others, work duty provided salvation. Double meal portions satisfied the call of our hungry stomachs for the greater part of the day, allowing a few tranquil moments to filter into our famished warriors' souls.

The concentration camp lay near Bergen-Belsen, about thirty kilometers from our main prison camp. I started working there around the middle of July, assembling barracks prefabricated in Holland. After putting the units together, we installed them on the east side of the camp toward the front. Those barracks furnished accommodations for the prisoners on the work brigade, for the camp guards, and for the officers of the company, and one of them provided space for the canteen where only Germans ate. Additionally, we assembled a storage barracks for food and tools.

The concentration campground spread over the size of two soccer fields. It had two barracks, one on each side of the entrance gate. Densely intertwined barbed wire encircled the camp, while tall guard towers stood about fifty meters apart. At night high-power searchlights illuminated the entire area. On the north side, the new gas chambers[8] of brick and concrete had begun to take shape, and on the south side lay the storage buildings and railroad tracks for loading and unloading of materials, people, and cattle. On the west side, a forested mountain slope supplied the logs for the French and Belgians to cut and transport to the sawmill. On the east, a barbed wire fence about three meters tall and ten meters wide separated the concentration camp from our prison barracks. We called it "The Forbidden Wall," because they prohibited us from crossing it. A dense forest, hung with yellow and black warning signs, lay beyond the outside fence with a ten-meter wide clearing between them.

That vortex of human horror opened right in front of our tired eyes one sunny day. Our hunger had become its

---

[8] [Author's note] Although the gentleman I interviewed, who lived through the events referred to in many of these episodes, claimed that Bergen-Belsen had gas chambers, the evidence denies it. One can only assume that, after the war was long over, my source's memory projected the existence of gas chambers there on the basis of the reports of so many others across the country. I choose to respect the story he told and his sense of shame in sharing responsibility for their existence.

hunger. Over the next several years, its amazingly straight geometric forms would devour thousands of innocent souls. The whiteness of its perfectly square concrete columns, with the silvery reflection of barbed wire, its guard towers and new barracks, and, at a distance, the gas chambers and smoke stacks, all hid evil behind a mask of pristine construction.

We stared in wonder, unconscious of our contribution to this crime against humanity. We had built Death, and Death tilled our lives.

Ice Hell

Militaristic pomp created an imaginary fortress of invincibility for Hitler's disciples, transforming customary German obedience into blind conformity to Third Reich ideology. With lightning speed, 208 divisions of the insatiable German war machine stormed into Russia on 20 June 1941. By the end of July, twenty thousand Russian prisoners found themselves in concentration camps in Germany. Hitler did not consider them war prisoners because Russia had not signed the Geneva Convention. Instead, the Reich considered them no different from Bolsheviks or Jews, and therefore treated them as lacking human rights, as non-Aryan people born for extinction. They provided Russians no quarters in the barracks, and only the sick were housed in the tiny infirmary—constructed merely to appease the Red Cross. So Russians slept on bare earth, packed like sardines. When the heat of summer scorched these godforsaken grounds, Russian soldiers stoically endured sharp straw, mud, the slops the Germans served once a day, and the stench of open latrines.

But summer was ending, and a north wind carried the dank hint of a long winter. Darkness had begun to fall over Germany. The sun disappeared behind thick black clouds, and only a reflection of the far polar light would sporadically brighten the eternal dusk of this hollow land.

Glancing occasionally beyond the forbidden wall of barbed wire that divided us from the concentration camp, I saw the empty eyes of desperate Russian prisoners, staring at a far-away, invisible horizon with the look of abandoned souls. Mute cries echoed, visibly tearing the silence, although bodies continued upright. I walked catatonically through streets of hell, witnessing lost specters with deeply sunken and dazed eyes watch jocular devils in *Feldblusen* play at target practice.

The fiery colors of autumn withered into leafless limbs wrapped in coats of ice, and the frigid whistle of winter silenced the last call of migrating birds. At times, I couldn't hear myself over the moans that yowled from across the yard, and shadowy captives followed me with every step I took to get away. Other times, I watched, transfixed, as worn-out bodies wrapped themselves in stacks of intertwined arms and legs, searching for a single remaining particle of heat. Occasionally, with its last drop of energy, a shadow struggled to carry its skeleton to the gate. Gazing far to the east, eyes glowed—for a moment or two—their last farewell to Mother Russia. Then the body crumpled into the abyss, finally finding peace.

In September, ten Russian bodies fell daily, without pain, without a scream. We made coffins for them and buried them near the compound. Then, as the number of coffins grew, they were removed from camp to some unknown grave.

When October came, and ice covered the earth, the Germans did not bury them in coffins anymore. Dredging machines with long forks loaded corpses in trucks, and newly arrived Jews became gravediggers. The forbidden wall between our barracks and the camp became the stage upon which the dance of Death played interminably.

Striving to escape, shattered nails scraped holes in the frozen earth. Hollow moans mutated into death screams or gasps of "Oh, Mother," as semi-dead extremities twitched with life's last spasm.

Insane hunger degenerated into cannibalism. Prisoners' eyes burned with fever. Bodies shivered in cold panic. The muffled cries of the dying and the hysterical howling of flesh-eaters pierced our souls. This choir from hell broke the silence of the night, while stone-faced German guards watched the Russian contest with Death—then counted corpses.

November and December brought the last waves of agony to those remaining on that icy altar of Death. Each night my fellow Serbian co-sufferers and I also sank into that frigid hell with our very first dreams. All of us felt thousands of feet and legs walking over our beds. Arms grasped at us from under our blankets, dragging us down in desperate attempts to raise themselves. The spirits of the dead hugged us with frozen hands. Screams of horror blended with sobs of dying. Delirium mixed with dejection, as all of us shriveled into putrid shadows.

In our warm barracks, with blankets over our heads, we tried to hide from the brutal reality, but the wind of truth woke us each dawn with the howling of despair.

Then the epidemic came.

With the last Russian prisoners gone, it struck the Jewish gravediggers and a few German guards. Next it spread through the rest of the Jews and Germans. They quarantined the camp, so those in charge transferred us to another camp nearby. They locked us in a new quarantine and forbade us from having any contact with German staff. They starved us for almost a month.

Then a group of doctors arrived from Hamburg to test our blood. As a result of the analysis, they lifted the quarantine, and in January 1942, they transferred all three hundred of us Serbian prisoners to Staub, where daily meals at last returned a little peace to our souls.

The scenes of horror from that distant concentration camp slowly faded from our memories, and our dreams began to lead us back to the sweet past before the war, among all our families and all our own people, in the hills and valleys of our homeland.

But the winter that year proved interminable. Daylight lasted only a few hours—and even then, the sky was deep gray, congealing into thick, impenetrable darkness with approaching night. Icy rain mixed with snow kept falling, while freezing winds from the north chilled our bones.

We had watched the Russians die from starvation and ice. Now the turn fell to the Germans. Columns of German vehicles, bearing their own troops returning from the Russian front, passed our camp almost daily. We gaped at trucks loaded down with men devastated by frost, heads without noses or ears, hands without fingers.

Fear set in for ordinary Germans not caught up in the Hitler euphoria. The cold spell bewildered local peasants. No one had previously experienced such bitterness. They became frightened and no longer totally confident in their Reich. A secret doubt regarding Hitler's invincibility began to sprout under the roofs of families whose sons had left their bones in the frozen suburbs of Moscow.

The arrow of time had become a pendulum that swung not only between day and night, but also between the terror that ruled in the souls of conquered and conquerors.

Painter's Workers

In our new quarters after the epidemic, we ate better and moved about more freely. But in reality, the entire region formed a huge camp. All along the hundred kilometers between Hanover and Hamburg, barriers of intertwined barbed wire lined the roads between POW and army barracks, concentration camps and military factories. If some poor bastard tried to escape, the Germans would catch him immediately and punish him severely. Thus few attempted to break free.

On Sundays we did not work. I passed my time with the other prisoners playing Spanish Monte with a pack of old, worn-out cards. I learned the secrets and finesses of this simple game, and I routinely beat every soldier in our barracks. After the war, the game would serve me as a supplemental source of income.

Encouraged by imaginings and rumors of faraway Allied victories, a trace of hope sparked in us. Dreams once again became our impermeable shield from the brutal storms swirling about us. We heard that the Red Cross would deliver packages to all POW camps starting in March, and we reveled in the thought that soon we would enjoy the goodies. Everyone longed for the day when we would receive them, and delays in delivery brought great gloom upon us all. Some prisoners talked so much about the contents of the packages—exaggerating their size and quantity—that they sickened with overwhelming desire and rolled on the floor with cramps born of the clash between Hunger and Reason.

Peter, a neighbor of mine from Ćuprija, knew how to cut glass. So a local craftsman, painter, and glass cutter, Mr. Frederick Holz, took the two of us, Peter and me, to work for him. That's how we came to labor for the camps and local villages in February 1942.

One day, they took us to a big military bakery to paint. The bakery was only about three kilometers from our prison camp, so we could walk there every morning and return each evening without escort. The bakery had two doors, the front entrance door and the rear door next to the railroad tracks, where they loaded train cars with shelves of bread for the military.

In March the Red Cross packages, containing canned food, cigarettes, chocolates, and coffee, began to arrive. We supplied cigarettes to German soldiers, and they supplied us with old socks, old boots, and padlocks, as well as the boards from which Peter and I made soldiers' trunks for our fellow prisoners. Almost everyone had a wooden footlocker with a padlock that secured the valuables they traded on the flourishing black market.

Work in the bakery was not hard, but the smell of freshly baked bread drove us crazy, so our empty stomachs howled even louder at the end of the workday. The hot steam from the ovens glued a thick layer of flour and moisture to the walls and ceilings. It took three weeks with hammer and chisel to remove the accumulated stucco of grain dust.

Meanwhile, we learned how the bakery functioned. A big clock in the village church tower banged out the hours. The bakers fired up the ovens at two or three o'clock in the morning. They kneaded the dough, placed it in molds to rise, then put it in the oven to bake the first batch at four o'clock. Next they would start work on the second batch, and at six-thirty they loaded it in the oven. This process cycled throughout the day, except for when, at ten minutes to ten, they recharged the ovens with coal.

At ten o'clock, all first-shift bakery workers went for lunch in the factory cantina near the main entrance. When the last batch came out in the afternoon, the workers would end their shift and leave the bakery. At three o'clock, the second shift of Germans—the only nationality allowed to work in the bakeries and food factories—would arrive.

While we worked, a German civilian guarded us. They never left us alone. During our lunch hour at four in the afternoon, they let us rest outside, but they did not offer us any food. To calm our hunger we would collect crumbs from the layers we removed from the walls, but they were so bitter that we couldn't eat them. We continued to starve but kept a watchful eye out for the right moment.

After several weeks, with the cleaning complete, we began to paint. Although the pastel green paint created a strange effect in that atmosphere of moisture, heat, and clouds of white flour dust, we did not wonder about the choice. We started painting at the main entrance and continued to the back door. We painted the ceiling during the workers' breaks, and sometimes we would stay on our ladders during both their lunch hour and ours, and then take our rest after the second shift's break time. By the time we finished, everything looked like a meadow of green wheat.

Around the time we finished painting half the bakery, a bold thought overtook me. I noticed that during first and second shift lunches, our old German guard paid less attention to us, joining the others in the cantina for about ten minutes. Peter always brought a couple of cigarettes to smoke during our break time, and the old German would ask for a half, so that he could smoke it with his coffee in the cantina.

One day before second-shift lunch, I asked Peter to give our German guard a whole cigarette. Peter did not like my proposition, but I explained that I would work alone during lunch hour, while he went to the front of the bakery to guard the entrance.

Peter stared at me. "Guard the entrance? Why?"

"Yes, guard it," I said and outlined my plan.

Peter crossed himself. "Are you crazy? Have you forgotten that the punishment for stealing bread is death?"

Despite the fact that—from the moment I decided to do this—I could not calm myself, I somehow convinced him. I trembled and worked, waving my brush back and forth, back and forth over the ceiling, while seeing only bread loaves stuffed between my arms, German Shepherds, German soldiers with automatic rifles, and the firing squad that waited for me beyond the fence.

But the power of Hunger proved omnipotent and ripped the fear-mongering picture from my mind.

Lunch hour finally arrived. The gong banging in my skull echoed through the empty bakery. I rushed out the back door, hurried to the train car, and grabbed four loaves from the upper shelves. With a strong swing, I pitched them all over the fence through the open door on the other side, and then watched them disappear behind the dry bushes.

I returned to the bakery with a deep sigh of relief. My heart pounded so fast I felt faint. Sweat oozed from all my pores.

In delirium, I walked out to the main entrance and mumbled to Peter, "It's done."

"You're either crazy or stupid," he said.

"Probably both."

I had not thought about what might happen with our loaves in the meantime. Would we find them on the way back? Perhaps a stray dog or some animal might smell them and eat them. But these possibilities never occurred to me as I scrambled to secure the loaves. In my mind, I saw only fresh bread, and I basked in its intoxicating aroma.

When we walked out through the main factory gate that afternoon, our eyes, guided by our stomachs, pointed toward the section of road that hid the secret object of my insane courage. Those bakery rear doors adjacent to the railroad platform lay quite a distance from the main gate. The building blocked them from the view of the armed guards who walked the inner circle along the barbed wire fence. We sped up to get to the bread and hurriedly collected the loaves before the guards reached that spot on their rounds. We slipped them up our sleeves and rushed back to camp.

Just before dark we passed the camp guard in our usual manner, without salute.

With our last burst of energy, we ran into our barracks.

We had tested our courage to the limit, but that night we beat our hunger. It did not visit us as it had every other night, and we didn't wake to empty stomachs in the morning. We slept contented and happy.

After that, Peter and I brought loaves almost every day, and our hungry brothers enjoyed every bite, as though it were covered in honey and the supply would go on forever.

Hungry and Crazy usually walk the same path. We walked in their footsteps.

When we finished painting the bakery, our boss took us to a military garrison where we had to replace all the windowpanes. We parted with heavy hearts from our source of fresh bread. Our whole barracks mourned on that sad, sad day.

Bread for Russians

Frederick, our boss was a good man. He respected us as skilled workers and let us do our job without much instruction or supervision. He took us to the work place, and then left to shop for supplies or other things. We mainly replaced broken glass on military barracks' windows. Sometimes we repaired and painted doors and windows on nearby residential housing. We used a dull gray and an ugly green color. They seemed to be the only choices in the region—maybe in all Germany. In this grayness, everything became invisible, unreal, thoroughly blended into a somber landscape. From the day we arrived to the day we left, I remember only dark clouds, and I often ask myself whether the sun ever shone there.

In the military camp where we replaced window glass, they offered no supplemental ration. Our Hunger returned, as did we to that miserable slice of bread and that pathetic bowl of soup from cabbage or potato peelings. The repulsive liquid would warm my stomach, awakening the dragons that then tortured me all day long. At times my sharp sense of smell would catch the aroma of food from the nearby kitchen that served German officers, and I would double over from the sudden, gut-wrenching pain. While in my semiconscious state, my vision would blur from my enormous desire for just one bite of their rich feast.

After the first week, I was so hungry that I dared to address a German officer in front of the kitchen.

"Captain, Sir, we're hungry. Please, give us a piece of bread."

His left eyebrow shot up. He measured us from head to toe with a certain scorn, and then waved to a waiter to give us a piece of bread. The waiter saluted, looked at us with suspicion, and signaled for us to follow him. He left us in front of the door and returned carrying a box with three or four pieces of dark bread that looked more like burnt logs.

We took the bread from the box and hurried back to our bench to enjoy it. Between my teeth I felt the cracking of bitter flour, sand, and coal. Astonished, we looked at each other and spat out that disgusting mouthful as though it were poison. We cleared our mouths and throats, while the waiter and the cook laughed loudly from the kitchen door.

"It looks like the Serbian pigs do not like the bread we make for their Russian brothers," the cook said.

Peter stormed away, spitting out the last grains of sand and burnt crumbs. "For Russians? Fuck their German mother. They're human filth. May God let the Russians roast them on a spit."

I will never forget the taste of that bread. And today, when I see dark, over-baked bread, I wretch as I recall that disgusting mouthful.

We continued to work for Frederick Holz, sometimes traveling to Soltau, where he would purchase supplies and treat us to fresh rolls and coffee. We labored in the surrounding villages, at the workshops and farms, painting walls and furniture, lacquering tables and chairs.

We were eternally grateful to Frederick, because he always demanded that the owners serve an afternoon meal to us and thus extended the good part of our prison lives. German peasants treated us with constrained hospitality. And though they did not degrade us nor hate us openly, they were cold to us and kept their distance. They never invited us to come to their table. They brought the remaining meal portions and placed them near us without a word, as though serving their domestic animals.

Hunger did not care.

Walsrode

In the summer of 1942 they divided our camp of about three hundred prisoners into two work groups. They moved my group to an underground munitions factory near Walsrode and the other group to a metal working factory about seventy kilometers north of Bergen. About a hundred and fifty of us worked in the munitions shipping department, loading tank and cannon shells onto freight cars. They had us dip our hands into buckets of resin to improve our grip and to protect us from ripping away our skin on the icy cylinders.

Lifting big cannon shells from the factory floor with semi-frozen hands, then carrying them along a slippery path required steadiness and mental concentration. Many weaker men failed and ended up back in the main POW camp. I stayed vigilant, measuring every step cautiously.

In the underground factory, they rewarded us with an abundant meal. The Germans gave us plenty of bread, potatoes, beans, slices of cooked ham, and sometimes thin slices of yellow cheese as a treat. Usually we ate around three o'clock, and then they would let us rest for about half an hour.

They allowed us to walk around the huge factory hall, where they served smaller meals to the female laborers brought in from several countries. These women—Poles, Russians, Belgians, several Germans, and a few Serbians—sat at the other end of the hall, about twenty meters from us. Our guards prohibited us from socializing with the women during lunch breaks. The sentries, however, ate their meals in another hall, so after a week, we conquered our fear and made contact. We spoke to them in rapid, short exchanges. We asked for their names and places of origin, and they quickly told their stories.

On the seventh day I met two Serbian sisters who described their experiences as follows:

"Ustaše [*U-stah-shey*][9] took us from Kostojnica [***Koh**-stay-neet-sah*] first to Jasenovac [***Yah**-seh-noh-vahts*].[10] But luck was on our side and we are still alive, thanks to the Germans who wanted forced laborers. They brought us to this underground factory in May 1941. We have not seen the sun for over a year. Only darkness and tears."

The sight of their fair complexions, their shapely figures, and the soft tones of my beloved language brought me back to a life that—in my Hunger—I'd almost forgotten. I felt helpless and lonely. *I haven't heard from my family since I last saw Father in Zaječar. I have no way of communicating with them.*

The women told us about one of Tito's followers, a Yugoslav Partisan[11] guerrilla the Germans brought to the factory. They said she tried to kill herself but the bomb did not detonate. She told them she died long ago, and they

---

[9] (also Ustashe, Ustashas, or Ustashi) The movement emphasized the need for a racially "pure" Croatia and promoted persecution and genocide of Serbs, Jews, and Gypsies. The Ustaše were responsible for the murder of around 300,000 "undesirables" during WWII.

[10] During World War II, Jasenovac was an extermination camp established by the Ustaše regime in the NDH (Independent State of Croatia). Although not operated by Nazi Germany, it was one of the largest concentration camps in Europe.

[11] The Yugoslav Partisans, or the National Liberation Army, was Europe's most effective anti-Nazi resistance movement, and was led by the Communist Party of Yugoslavia during World War II. Its commander was Marshal Josip Broz Tito.

The Četniks, also a WWII anti-Axis movement, opposed the Partisans' long-range goals for Yugoslavia, favoring the retention of the Yugoslav monarchy. They engaged in resistance activities for limited periods. The Četniks played a role in the pattern of terror and counterterror that developed in Yugoslavia during World War II, particularly against the Yugoslav Partisans and their supporters.

saw only her dead spirit walking through the hallways of hell.

I also met two Russian women who begged me to help them escape from that dungeon. They wanted to walk out with us on our return to camp. They had even secured some uniforms. Unfortunately, they never had the chance to wear them. I would have helped them, but my comrades refused—afraid that all of us would get caught.

After eleven weeks of hauling bombshells that carved depressions in my shoulders, the steady rhythm of hell's circle totally consumed me. But the Germans knew exactly how our stomachs worked. We all lost our sense of time and gnawing Hunger alone reanimated us just before lunch. Yet even with rest, I felt my knees give out and my body sway. Only the harsh winter kept us alert, with surges of brutal winds that pierced our cold bones, stabbing us to attention in our semiconscious confusion.

Sometimes someone behind me would cry out and fall; another would moan and sob softly. To make that cruel and icy trek to the loading ramp, each of the rest of us, one by one, and step by step, would silently follow forward the footfalls of the forlorn foot soldier in front of him.

German Christmas[12]

Christmas had arrived for the Germans, but we Serbs did not even realize it. Thanks to Lubo, our Slovenian friend, who served as an interpreter, we learned that the very next day was 25 December—even though we considered it still two weeks away by our Julian calendar.

[12] Since the Serbian Orthodox Church still used the Julian calendar at this time, 25 December for them fell on what was 7 January in countries using the Gregorian calendar (most Western countries, as in this case, Germany).

Christmas or not, we were hungry and worn out. Our beloved Ivo Andrić[13] wrote about poverty during the Holidays when he knew it in Vienna:

> December afternoons provide bitter satisfaction for beggars. On Christmas Eve we walk the wet pavement with a sad happiness, as Christmas trees glimmer in windows, rain beats on us and fog chokes us. A holy night rests upon the entire city, where citizens eat, drink, celebrate God, and ride their fat wives. And on Christmas Day, they share a festive lunch in a restaurant, with white coffee, four buns, and 101 dirty jokes.[14]

Walking along the nicely decorated main street of Walsrode on Christmas Eve, I felt the wisdom of his words. As I passed yards with Nativity scenes and doors ornamented with winged angels, every vapor wafting from the warm kitchens smelled of one big, long cake. As the irresistible scents got stronger, our pace slowed and my stomach howled its crazy sounds, followed by echoes of emptiness.

I would stop for a moment, take a deep breath, fondling the luxurious fragrance, and then continue to walk without exhaling until I began to lose consciousness.

My next breath would suffocate me with the stench of all the living and dead beings that had wandered these streets since ancient times.

---

[13] (born: 9 October 1892; died: 13 March 1975) A Yugoslav novelist, short story writer, and the 1961 winner of the Nobel Prize in Literature. His writings dealt mainly with life in his native Bosnia under the Ottoman Empire.

[14] From Andrić's *Memoirs*.

It seemed ironic to me to imagine a German celebrating Christmas, obeying the Gospels, kissing the Cradle, praying for mercy and forgiveness of sins, and departing from church sprinkled with holy water—only to destroy, kill, and strangle his own kind—all the while praying and expressing joy for the birth of Christ. For on Christmas Day 1942, Germans celebrated that unfortunate Jew Jesus by sending thousands of similarly innocent Jews, Russians, Poles, and Serbs to join the heavenly choir, thereby multiplying its prayers for all sinners with the anthems of thousands of arriving souls.

But Hunger does not obey boundaries or fear. Hunger indisputably challenges man's fortitude. She drives the mind to invent. She forces him to look into the eyes of Death and to confront Her. A man leaves fear behind and seizes from a dining table the fruits that momentarily quench this primal instinct.

Christmas? On Christmas, even we *are not forced to work. German Christmas is* our *salvation.*

I addressed my comrades in our barracks:

"Men, tomorrow is German Christmas, and we would do well to offer best wishes to local households. I suggest that two of us take a bag and set out at dawn in the residential part of camp and go from house to house, wishing everyone a Merry Christmas. I believe the Germans will offer us something."

Befuddled, Mito Bogdanović [***Mee**-toh* ***Bohg**-dah-noh-vitch*] held his hand in front of his chest, palm up and fingers splayed. "Timo, you are crazy! Where did you get that idiotic idea?"

He curled up his nose and shook his head. "The Germans will kick us out like dogs before they give us anything."

A burly man with eagle eyes and a big crooked nose, Mito was an economist before the war, and at Staub he took it upon himself to manage all our incoming packages from home, Red Cross packages, and trades with German guards. He was honest and fair, never taking advantage or cheating.

"Will we greet them in Serbian?" asked Paul.

"We'll ask Lubo. He knows German. He'll teach us," I replied.

"I'll go," said Bogdan Pantić [***Bohg**-dahn **Pahn**-titch*], a dumpy man, with a short mustache and a big nose.

"Me too," said Čedo Janjić [***Chey**-dah **Yahn**-yitch*], getting up. "Paul, go find Lubo, and bring him here."

Lubo, the Slovenian, a trim, fit man who looked like an upper-class Austrian, was a POW like all the rest of us. He married a Serbian woman before the war and lived in Kragujevac [***Krah**-gu-yeh-vahts*] before he was mobilized. When the Yugoslav Army surrendered, he did not admit he was Slovenian and joined us Serbians on the same train to the same camp. He knew German perfectly, so they transferred him to the command barracks, where he became their main interpreter and provided a link between Serbian soldiers and Germans. He spent his free time on Sundays with us, and so, from time to time, he would let us in on local and world events. He was Our Lubo.

When he arrived and heard our plan, he laughed like a joker. "Timo, you are the biggest fuckoff. But, ya' know, this time, ya' done good, kiddo."

Then he turned to Čedo and Bogdan: "OK, look guys, this is what you need to do. Go up to the door, bow to the host, and together say, '*fröhliche Weihnachten*.'[15] Then, you open your bag."

---

[15] "Merry Christmas"

Everyone stared at him wide-eyed.

"Look, no one will turn you away, because it wouldn't be Christian. Wait until they give you some stuff, and then go to the next house."

He started back, and then turned around with a laugh. "And hey, when you bring the goods, don't forget to call me. I want my cut."

Čedo and Bogdan spent almost all night practicing *"fröhliche Weihnachten."*

That morning we felt no hunger. Worry over how this unusual mission would end bloated our stomachs. At dawn Čedo and Bogdan had each taken a large bag and set out to visit all the German residences in the compound. Meanwhile, we roamed through the barracks yard, trying to get a breath of fresh, crystal-clear morning air, but cold gusts pushed us back inside. There, we coughed and cleared our throats in a vain effort to breathe, as tobacco smoke mixed with our own stench to irritate our sensitive lungs.

At last Čedo and Bogdan returned. They stood there, bags in hand, grinning like children visited by the tooth fairy.

We cheered.

They emptied their bags of goodies onto a bed covered with a white sheet.

The sight was splendid.

Bread, cakes, and loaves with curled braids and various designs on the white surface of their baked crusts, rolls of liverwurst, salami, headcheese, ham, cookies, and sweet rolls filled with jam. The spread of sundries looked like a heavenly banquet prepared for us desolate beggars, whose bewitched eyes already ravaged the profuse blessings.

If no one had thought to set the table and divide the food, we would have remained staring all afternoon at this bountiful sight, the last drop of saliva perishing in our dry throats.

But Mito quickly took charge and ordered two men to divide the food. He arranged the barracks in three groups of eight and started handing out portions. Mito packed an equal share for Lubo and placed it in his chest. Each of us received a sizable quantity from the rich table, and we still had some left for the next day—Saturday—as well.

And thus we surrendered ourselves to the pleasures of German Christmas 1942. All bitterness vanished from our tormented faces, as glimmers of satisfaction shone forth from our hollow eyes, and our lips smacked pleasantly with every sweet bite. For many of us, it was the most beautiful Christmas ever.

Later, as we wandered through life, we often reminded ourselves of this cherished event. We treasured our memories of that brotherly feast in our POW camp when every bite we took seemed sweeter than any before.

On 29 December we had only worked three days of the previous five, but sometimes rest and good food just gives Fatigue a chance to catch up with you. Not long before the end of my shift that day, it overwhelmed me. Feeling as though wrapped in a poultice of broken glass, I managed to lift a shell to my left shoulder and stabilize it there, but when I tried to pick up the second, I had to see-saw it into my arm while I leaned my left shoulder against a post and shimmied up, heels digging into the floor to try to keep my balance as I levered the weight.

When I finally got both shells on my shoulders, I started to sway.

My eyes blurred. My ears buzzed.

I could barely feel my legs move as I stared at the path of footsteps in front of me. I lurched toward my target.

The distance seemed like the trip from home to Jagodina. I tried to think of those comforting hills to muster my strength and keep me moving forward, but my swaying led me further and further from the path.

Nevertheless, I managed to get to within a couple yards of the train-car door when I realized that my next step would take me onto a piece of ice.

I swung left.

My right foot went out from under me, and I jostled and twisted and hurled my body in an effort to keep myself and the shells from falling.

Aiyeeeeeee!

Everything pierced me.

Cold.

Wet.

Black.

Chapter 4

Hospital

I woke up in a hospital. After three days of delirium, I began to distinguish forms and shadows of people moving around my bed. Muffled conversations, instruments clattering, chairs moving, iron beds squeaking, and someone's painful cry, all failed to make this suffocating space more real. A montage of my past reeled through my mind in a turbulent nightmare, while angry faces from a dark history burst out at me.

Faraway screams echoed occasionally through this bottomless space, but they quickly died down, affording me momentary tranquility in sharp contrast to the agony they expressed. For a long time I followed moving faces on a blurry screen, looking for smiles and words of comfort, but those appeared only in the twilight of my dreams.

Immersed in this hazy sea, my eyes finally locked onto two unfamiliar spheres bent over my bed, speaking fluent Serbian:

"He's awake," said the first one.

"Yes, I see that he's waking up. How are you, Timo?" asked the second fellow.

The pain from my right arm pounded like a big hammer on an iron gong, while the curious eyes in my heavy head strove to converge on these two faces.

"I'm Doctor Stojan Pavićević [***Stoh**-yahn **Pah**-vee-tcheh-vitch*], and this is my colleague, Doctor Svetomir Pajić [***Sveh**-toh-meer **Pah**-yitch*]. You had a bone fracture that we barely succeeded in setting. We placed it in a cast. Your pain will last a while longer, but you must endure it because the hospital doesn't have painkillers."

He looked up at his colleague, then back down at me. "Ask for us if you need anything."

The two heads disappeared from my view.

Pain returned, and I could hear only my own desperate voice screaming across the hospital hall. I became conscious of my surroundings, and I screamed even louder. As I surfaced more fully, I could see patients lying in beds arranged along the walls under large windows. My bed stood next to the hall entrance. As if in sympathy, some patients howled along with me, others swore, and some growled hoarsely. Then the noise of the wounded quieted down. The hall transformed into a beehive of activity, accompanied by the hoarse resonance of scurrying footfalls and hushed voices.

I closed my eyes, allowing myself to drown again in darkness.

A week later they lifted me out of bed and took me for a walk in the hallway. My arm still hurt very much, but the entire muscle system had adjusted to therapy, and I could then endure the attacks of knife-like stabbing without further howls.

In my thoughts, I often returned home. With no mail delivery, I felt completely isolated from the world. I worried about my father, my mother, Roda and Vasiliya. Two years old by now, my daughter probably ran around all day talking. I imagined her chirping around my mother, chasing the little chickens, hens and roosters through the yard, amusing her grandfather and being caressed by her mother when she returned from the fields. I would take a deep breath and continue longing for them.

I dreamt of Roda coming to me at night, but my passionate expectations would greet the morning disappointed by reality. I yearned for her very much, and my desire for her became even greater as time in the hospital dragged on. I wondered how she dealt with her need for me.

Rehabilitation lasted five weeks. Then they took off the strap that kept my arm bent. A swelling above the fracture had appeared, however, and my fellow-countrymen doctors decided to request help from a specialist.

A German doctor arrived from Hanover and, after a brief exam, ordered my cast removed. Under the cast, the dark blue color of my arm did not indicate a good recovery. The doctor examined the healed fracture, felt the muscles under the swelling, consulted with our doctors, and ordered six more weeks of rehabilitation with special massages, salt baths, and heating pads.

Although hospital life bored me, and my restless spirit suffocated in that atmosphere, I rejoiced at the additional recovery time granted me, and I expressed my gratitude to the German doctor.

Finally I received a letter from my father! He told me that a peasant passing by our POW train on the way to Germany happened to see the note flying out of our car. He retrieved it and took it to my father. Roda and my parents cried for three days, and later the whole village buzzed with news of the unlikely incident.

When I left the hospital my arm had recovered considerably, and, thanks to the rehabilitation, I could lift up to twenty kilograms easily and without pain. Good hospital food had fully restored my body, and soon I felt the old peasant spirit working again in my muscles.

Lomnitz

Back at the main POW camp, Hunger again drove me to despair. At noon I received the day's rations of a small slice of bread and a cup of tasteless potato soup. *Why can I not endure Hunger like all the others? What kind of insatiable dragon do I carry in my body that will not leave me at peace?* The old depression returned, the feeling of helplessness in the face of constant stomach howling.

I went to find Lubo the Slovenian to beg him to get me a job with a work brigade. It didn't matter where, because I thought I would go mad thinking about food.

He tried to dissuade me, knowing that hard labor would exhaust me. Rarely would anyone volunteer, but I wanted to get away from this mortuary, no matter the price.

A few days passed and Lubo came to our barracks. He sat me down and calmly described the choices.

They needed some men in a local malleable iron foundry.

"It's tough, man, and noisy as hell," he said, shaking his head. "They make you sleep at the factory, so they can drag your ass to work any time, day or night, and you only get two meals a day."

He looked down at the papers he held in his hand. "Or you can dig canals and trenches somewhere near Bremen."

He shuffled the papers, then looked straight at me. An extra glimmer appeared in his always happy eyes.

"But, hey, look at this. You're gonna' love this. You grew up on a farm, right?"

I nodded.

"So you know a lot about farming. Well, man, this is the job you want!" He pointed to the forms in his other hand. "I can manage to squeeze you in as a replacement with the Prezelle/Lomnitz group."

"Oh, Lubo, you saved my life. I'll never forget this. I swear."

I jumped up and hugged him.

"Hey, hold on," he said, breaking our hold. "Let me see what I've got for ya'."

He pulled a little package from his pocket and handed it to me. "Look bro. Here, this oughta cheer ya' up. A nice chunk o' hard cheese. Oughta keep ya' for a couple o' days—if you nibble at it nice and slow."

He gave me a sly grin. "I swiped it off a lieutenant in the officers' lounge."

I didn't say a word. I just kept holding his hand as if I would never see him again.

That good man was the best friend we had. God bless him.

A week later an older German with red hair and a red face escorted me to my new quarters about thirty kilometers from Staub. Along the road that ran from our prison camp to Lomnitz stood a dormitory where young German maidens had once learned home economics. There I would join the work brigade assigned to the farms in the villages of Lomnitz and Prezelle. Facing the main road and not considered an actual prison camp, the dormitory was surrounded by barbed wire to remind local residents that prisoners of war lived there. Beyond it and Lomnitz, the road led to Prezelle, and then continued on through a number of other German villages and farms.

I joined the other six men already working in Lomnitz, so our group consisted of seven Serbian war prisoners. Twenty-eight of us resided in the dormitory, including the team that worked in Prezelle. The German who had escorted me there, Stefan, a portly middle-aged, short-legged man with a happy attitude, guarded "our village camp." He had a small room behind the main door, while we POWs shared the four large rooms, with seven people per room. Our entire Lomnitz team thus shared one room, with all of the Prezelle workers in the other three rooms.

We each had a mattress made of thick linen, filled with dry straw and moss. The space proved ample, and we could move about without difficulty.

The German Work Authority supplied us with gray jackets and trousers that hung on our skinny bodies like burlap bags, while our boots could have told stories of many other feet. They paid us in bonds, and naturally, we had to reimburse them for the clothes, boots, luxury accommodations, and food from our measly—and rarely received—wages (equal to about twelve German marks a month).

No matter the wages. We could not have conceived of a way to spend them anyway.

The village of Lomnitz lay only about half a kilometer from our dormitory. In the beginning, the heavy-set German soldier would take us all every morning to each farm, and in the evening, he would escort us back to our quarters. Stefan tried to carry out his duties eagerly, even though time had passed him by and no one expected much of him due to his age.

Lomnitz had a population of about a hundred residents. A grocery, tavern, village hall, Lutheran church, and elementary school formed the center of the town. Village houses lined both sides of the main street. Farms, fields, yards, gardens, and barns lay on both sides behind the rows of houses. The townsfolk gaily decorated the fronts of their houses to look like an eternal celebration. We admired their neatness and cleanliness but never fully understood it. In Lomnitz, as in other towns, only old fathers and grandfathers had remained behind when their sons shipped out to the Eastern front in 1941. Their wives and mothers now carried the biggest workloads on the farms.

Although about twenty families comprised the village, not all were farmers. Our little group of seven worked for both rich and poor alike. Rista, a fairly dark-skinned man with a big nose, worked for Bauer, the tavern owner. He constantly carried things in and out of the cellar, a process that required him to haul bottles, jugs, kegs and other paraphernalia out the back door, around to the side of the building, through the cellar doors, then down a long flight of stairs. At six foot six, Mile Stojković [***Mee**-ley **Stoy**-koh-vitch*] returned on his long legs every evening, exhausted from working for Farmer Hoffmann, who swamped him with a multitude of tasks. Spasoje Užičanin [***Spah**-soh-yeh **U**-zhi-chah-neen*], with a receding hairline and big feet, worked for another farmer. Radenko Skerlić [***Rah**-den-koh **Skehr**-leetch*], the youngest of the group, with bushy brown hair and green eyes, worked at the other end of the village for a young widow with three children. Nedeljko Polovina [***Neh**-dehl-koh Poh-**loh**-vee-nah*], who was built like a boxer, worked for the old peasant Slinger and his wife, and Aleksa Pitić [***Pee**-teetch*], the handsomest of the group, with light hair topping his six-foot frame, served the village mayor. These six had much more work than I.

Every day we would rise at five in the morning. At six we would go to work in the villages, the seven of us for Lomnitz, and the other twenty-one for Prezelle.

It didn't take long for red-faced Stefan's attention to slacken. He began to neglect his daily duties as he spent more and more time with the village widows whose husbands had vanished on the Russian front. After unlocking the gate in the morning, Stefan went back to sleep until noon, and then he would go to Lomnitz or Prezelle for a big lunch as the guest of some farmer.

No matter where he started, he usually ended up in a tavern or at some peasant's house, where they served him homemade schnapps and beer. Homemade beer was ubiquitous, to the point that in May the entire village smelled of overripe yeast bubbling away with molasses in the pigs' troughs. But any time of year, Stefan would often get drunk with his countrymen of Prezelle and leave us on our own to take care of ourselves. Nobody escorted us to work or brought us back anymore.

Thus I undertook my assignment on the farm of Berthold Fiske, who, at that time, served in Greece with the German army. His seven children, old father, mother, and wife, all lived in the same house. They had a few acres of land where they grew potatoes, corn and wheat. They had only two cows, some pigs, chickens, geese, and ducks. They usually kept one of the pigs for themselves and sold the rest along with the chickens that crowded the front and back yards. I wondered how such meager holdings could support so many people and what work they would give me when they already had so many hands.

Sober-faced and narrow shouldered, Old Man Fiske got me started planting potatoes right away. Afterward we cleaned the barn, repaired the roof and did some small things that did not take much time.

Elsa Fiske's youngest, two-year-old Anna Marie, often played around my legs, reminding me of little Vasilija. She got used to me quickly and began to call me "Daddy." Elsa did not care, but the old man, Günther Fiske, got angry and moved Anna away from me.

I yearned for my little girl and fell in love with this button-nosed, blond-haired child to fill the void. Children can feel this, and, since they have no bias, Anna Marie expressed her happiness whenever she saw me. I enjoyed her innocent attention more and more.

Even though I had many small errands, my work was not hard, and thanks to the ample homemade food on the farm, I again felt peace in my stomach and strength in my muscles.

When Old Man Fiske discovered I did carpentry, he found numerous things for me to fix, and I no longer had to do any farming. In the beginning I repaired all his farm tools, then all the windows in the house, the dining room furniture, and all the barrels in the cellar.

Word about my woodworking skills soon spread through the village. Lomnitz residents began to drop by and admire my workmanship. They gathered together newer tools for me. Old Fiske cleared a small space under the covered patio attached to the barn and set up a flimsy old woodworking bench for me. I began to plane, iron, and restore all the furniture and tools in Lomnitz.

I enjoyed it all, the work and the complete freedom of movement it gave me. I plied my trade without pressure or supervision and improved my knowledge of German by talking with the local people.

All this thanks to the vocation I loved so much.

Return of the Birds

Spring flourished in the nearby meadows and woods. Flowers bloomed in rainbow colors. Blossoms covered the trees. Green forests drowned in the deep shadows of old pines, while bees and other insects carried pollen from one flower to the next.

My colleagues and I had already adjusted well to our duties, and we knew almost everyone in Lomnitz by name. We shared our impressions, experiences, and everyday events. Rista had the most tales to tell, because Bauer's tavern filled daily with locals and travelers who brought stories about everything and anything, but mostly about the war and the conditions they lived under. Staunch champions of Hitler's ideology, most Germans supported the Third Reich and its plan to conquer the world. In their eyes, everything the Reich decided made sense for Germany. And everything that made sense for Germany must be good for Germans.

But the peasants wondered, "Why now, after four years of war, do we have to give more than ever? Didn't we already conquer Europe? Have the French and Flemish gone on strike? And should we not talk about the people of the Ukraine, Hungary, and Romania, who have never made good allies? Send them all to Asia or Africa. Only the German people should live on these fertile lands." The chatter reinforced everyone's belief that the rest of the world opposed them and that only cleansing Europe and populating it entirely with Germans would solve the problem.

Rista listened to and remembered almost all of these discussions. He spoke excellent German, but he never revealed it to his master or to the local people. Everyone knew dinky-looking Rista as Bauer's servant. He would occasionally disappear to the tavern cellar to arrange wine jugs, to pour wine from barrels into bottles, to record inventory and then submit daily reports to his master before leaving. The few words he used sufficed for basic communication, and it delighted Bauer no end that he could consider Rista a hard-working, honest man.

After the first several weeks, Bauer left all the work to Rista and dedicated his time to his clients, with whom he often shared both his wine and his opinions. Little Rista, with his olive skin, kept his head down and hid his eyes from his master, as he looked a lot like those of the "undesirable race," and even more like those in the nearby towns who wore yellow ribbons and Stars of David before the war. Serbians were Slavic, considered undesirable, but tolerated as workforce, servants, slaves. And so Rista moved among the local people, and no one paid attention.

Others among our group also retold their daily events. Stories about the young widow, Irma Steiner, particularly interested us, and every evening we badgered our young, bushy-haired Radenko to tell us in detail about the events surrounding her. Radenko looked at us, and, checking his confidence, put his right thumbnail between his front teeth, then sighed and threw his hands in the air.

"What do you want me to tell you, fellows? She's young, she's beautiful, she's a widow, and she keeps her distance," he said, shrugging his shoulders. "I like working on her farm. She treats me well. The children love me. They even gave me a pet name, 'Raden,' and they're constantly finding something for me to help them with. Mrs. Steiner—"

He looked down. "I call her that, although to me she's always 'Irma.'" He smiled, his green eyes glowing.

"—anyway, she doesn't mind having me around her children, but she runs a very tight ship. I work there from morning to evening almost non-stop. We take a break for lunch and dinner—" He laughed. "—and she cooks some mighty tasty meals."

He shrugged again. "What can I say? I wish she would be more . . . ?"

"Like a woman, you mean?" said Nedeljko, fluttering his thick eyelashes in jest. "Don't you get any signs? Some hot looks? Some occasional touch?"

"I don't know. Sometimes I feel something, but a minute later she's as cold as ice."

"She needs a man," Aleksa forcefully asserted, as he leaned back to relax his six-foot frame. "She's probably yearning for you, and you don't even see it." He sidled up to Radenko and whispered, "Look into her eyes. If she blushes, she is ripe. If she stays pale, stay away from her."

Radenko winced. "Look folks, I don't know about these things. I'm not married. I never had a woman before."

"You never wrapped your legs around a woman's ass?" Spasoje jumped up from his chair, landing flatly on his big feet.

"Let him be, Spasoje." Mile called from his bunk, nodding and grinning. "He's still a virgin, but I'm sure it won't be too long before he enjoys a woman's warm embrace."

He looked at Radenko. "Tell us a little about her farm. We pass by, but we don't know how big it is or what she raises."

Radenko's face lit with pleasure. He smiled at his long-legged pal Mile, then turned to the rest of us.

"She has about fifty acres where they used to grow wheat and corn. They had a herd of cows and lots of poultry. But that was all before Mr. Steiner was killed. Now she plants only corn. They have six cows, some pigs, poultry, and two old mules she uses for plowing and pulling the wagons. She also grows lots of vegetables. She sells her corn, vegetables, poultry, and pigs, and with that money, she buys household supplies, clothes for the children, and other basic needs. She's very frugal, doesn't spend money foolishly, and doesn't show off with fancy dresses, hats, and all that woman's stuff."

He paused and his voice became quiet. "Sometimes I feel like she has a hard time dealing with everything, especially the things she doesn't really know how to tackle." He pursed his lips and turned away. "I want so much to help her, but I can't talk to her. That darn German is so hard to learn."

"I'll teach you some. It's not so hard. A few words here and there—"

"Yeah, Timo, teach him," Spasoje interrupted to taunt Radenko. "Show him how to wrap his legs around her sweet butt. He won't need any words after that."

"You old goat. Stop teasing him." I scolded, then turned back to Radenko. "Don't pay any attention to him." I laid a hand on his shoulder. "Really, I'll spend some time teaching you a few basic words."

"Would you, Timo?" Radenko asked eagerly. "That would mean so much to me."

"Of course. And if I don't know something, Rista will help us. Won't you?" I said looking at Rista. He nodded and smiled.

"How many children does she have?" asked Mile.

"Three. Max, Peter, and Zella. They're wonderful. Very kind and courteous. I like them very much."

"How old?"

"Max is five, Peter, three, and Zella is two," he replied, then became more animated. "But I'll tell you. They sure seem a lot older. They know their chores. They do everything Irma tells them to do and without complaining. I do some heavy lifting for them, but their mother won't let me help them too much. She points her finger at me and tells me no, no," he said, shaking his own finger and head, then shrugging.

"So I watch them with a heavy heart. It's so hard to see them struggling to drag a loaded basket of chicken feed across the yard, or buckets of cow dung from the animal stalls to the compost pile, or huge water pails to water the animals—all the heavy farm stuff that only men should do."

He looked down and murmured, "They're so young."

"How does she communicate with you then?" asked Aleksa, his handsome face curling into a question mark.

"She doesn't. She just points and I do."

His voice grew earnest. "If I could only talk to her, she wouldn't have to push so hard."

He sighed.

"Sometimes I feel like she's standing behind me, looking at me, but when I turn my head, she quickly looks the other way."

He became more animated, his face beaming, "When we get our daily chores done early, she takes the children to the water hole and waves to me to join them. I love it. We splash water on each other. The children run around and sing their kiddy songs, and Irma seems different."

"Different how?" I asked.

"Warmer. More human. Less tense and less rigid. Like this is our five minutes of playtime, and we can all just be children. It's wonderful!"

He leaned forward and placed his hands over his heart, then punctuated his phrases by moving them outward.

"It makes me feel so happy because she smiles, she laughs, she plays. Sometimes I wish we could spend the whole day at the water hole."

He sighed. "But the next day she's back to her strict routine. I hate it."

He shook his head. "I just don't know how to read her."

Spasoje and Nedeljko snored loudly, while Aleksa and Mile played cards. Only Rista and I continued to listen to Radenko's outpouring of feelings.

"You love her, don't you?" said Rista, breaking the pensive silence.

Radenko blushed and nodded.

"Well, be very careful. If she doesn't condone your signs of affection, she can report you to the authorities and you'll be severely punished. Be prudent. Watch your step. Don't let your emotions control you. Remember that," Rista said, patting him on the back.

"OK," Radenko timidly agreed.

"Don't take it so hard," I said. "You didn't do anything to offend her. Just be patient. She'll give you a sign if she wants you. But be careful. Rista is right; the risk is much too great for you both."

I hugged him. *Poor kid, he is so much in love with her already. We trounced his soul ruthlessly. Time will tell.*

In an effort to help him keep his sanity, we stopped teasing him. But the bees had already spilled their pollen in his love garden, and the flowers of delight and happiness shone on his face, until obstacles to his beloved Irma flared rays of distress from his dark eyes.

I asked myself how soon Irma might discover these subtle flames and begin to tremble once more with yearning, yearning that she'd skillfully denied herself since her husband had left for the front.

Our Serbian brother was a sincere and patient young man.

Wait, Radenko, wait.

As spring overtook Germany, the war vanished from view. I continued with my job, but Old Günther Fiske got sick and died. The whole village gathered to send him off. The Mayor gave an appropriate speech. The Lutheran minister said a prayer. Oma Fiske, with her stone face, said goodbye by throwing dirt on the coffin, and only Little Anna Marie and the rest of the grandchildren cried for their opa.

Berthold

A week after the funeral, Berthold arrived from being stationed in Greece. He had a leave of absence thanks to his father's death but spent most of the week just getting home. When I reached the Fiske's that morning to report to Elsa, he came out yelling at me. Elsa, a shapely blonde with pouty lips and high cheekbones, appeared a moment later, a look of concern on her face.

"Berthold, don't abuse Timo, please! Opa liked him and treated him very decently. There's no reason to be mean to him. He has helped us a lot and kept things running smoothly, especially since Opa took sick."

"Why are you standing up for him?" Berthold's nostrils flared above his small, round mouth. "He's nothing but a Serbian *Schweinhund.* None of them deserves to be treated kindly. Those Serbian guerrilla bastards blew up the bridge over the South Morava River, and we had to circle all the way around through Bulgaria and Romania just to avoid them."

"But it's not *his* fault. Why take it out on him?"

She opened the door for him to pass through in front of her. "Please, come into the house and I'll make you breakfast. The children will be up soon."

"*You* mind the house, woman."

He snatched the door from her hand and slammed it against the jam.

"Go get me that bottle of schnapps first, and then you can make breakfast."

He gave her a shove toward the door. "I'll take care of him later."

She opened the door again, and he followed her into the house.

Feeling distressed and uneasy, I turned to my workbench. I had a couple of chairs from Bauer's Tavern that needed repair, so I got to work on those to take my mind off the confrontation.

After a while Berthold approached my workbench and stood there smoking and glaring at me as I sanded and glued. Half-finished with his cigarette, he flicked the butt at me, but it missed and fell to the floor.

"Please, Sir. I have highly flammable chemicals here. I would respectfully advise you to dispose of your cigarette butts elsewhere."

"Who do you think you are, talking to me like that? You're nothing but a *Schweinhund*."

He spat on me.

It hit me right on my cheek, but I gritted my teeth and ignored it.

Then he barked, "You pick that cigarette up right now."

I bent down and picked up the sizable butt, still lit.

"Now, put it in your mouth and smoke it."

I looked at him dumbfounded. *What a monster!* I thought to myself. *I have never smoked in my life.*

"Go ahead," he shouted. "Inhale. Deeply."

I tried to inhale, but I just coughed and gagged. My eyes popped, I turned all red, and my body twisted from the sudden pain of this ghastly tobacco encounter.

He laughed and pointed at me, doubling over in hysterics. The howls from his small, round mouth brought Elsa and the older boys out, curious about what had happened.

Elsa ran to the pump to fill my cup with water and made me drink it.

I slowly got my breath back and leaned on the wall.

He continued to laugh as he walked away. "Boys, get your butts at that table. It's time to eat. You, Elsa, come with us."

The day passed without any more incidents. But fear of his return made me ill.

The next morning Elsa told me that he had drunk a lot the previous night and that he was sleeping late.

I hope he stays in bed until he returns to his post. But my hope vanished that afternoon with the sight of his drunken shadow swaying on the wall.

"You bewitched my family, you *Schweinhund.* I'm going to kill you," and he spat on me again.

With an unsteady hand, he pointed his handgun at me as he circled and searched, his eyes closing and opening between states of consciousness and unconsciousness.

He leaned his narrow shoulders on the outside wall and yelled, waving his gun to direct my movements, "Down, you Serbian pig. Get down!"

I sprawled on the floor, terrified, counting the last seconds of my life.

Elsa ran out and screamed, "Bert, you fool, do you want to go to jail? If you shoot him, they'll either put you in prison or send you to the Eastern front."

She stepped toward him.

"Give me that gun," she said, taking the gun away. Berthold crumpled to the ground in a drunken stupor.

Elsa took a step toward me.

"Timo, you can get up now. He won't bother you anymore today."

"Thank you, Elsa." I whispered. "He would've killed me."

"No, he's just a drunken fool. He's hateful, but harmless."

She lifted Berthold's snoring body off the ground and stumbled with him into the house.

Luckily for me, he spent most of the rest of his three-week furlough at the tavern drinking and talking with the locals—other than a day or two working in the fields with Elsa. But somehow he always managed to find a moment here or there to indulge his sadistic pleasure in torturing me with demeaning orders, then threatening to kill me like a dog if I refused.

And then, one day, he took a big ham—telling Elsa that he wanted it as a gift for his captain—and he simply packed up and left.

I took a deep breath and thanked God for his departure.

Mrs. Gottfried

The days had become longer, and we seven passed our time before bed in the yard behind the dormitory. Since anyone could squeeze easily through the barbed wire, some brave ones began to disappear in the first hours of night. A few slipped away to deal on the black market. Inevitably someone would try to run away but would quickly get caught and returned to Staub where he would permanently lose his farm work status and privileges. Some went to female friends, since Radenko was not the only one of us to tremble at the coming of spring.

Cupid's arrows struck me then too.

At the end of May, the Lutheran Church asked me to repair the balcony casing of the old bell tower and return it to its original state. At first glance, I could see it was ready to crumble.

One afternoon there, as I replaced some rotting sections of the rafters, I heard a voice flowing in a wave of mystical melodies. It bounced off the inner walls of the bell tower like an intoxicating gust. In some unintended mid-space between life and death, it penetrated my soul to join my secrets in the fairy circle of my deepest desires.

I did not exist.

Time stopped, and all else became silent at the flurry of otherworldly sounds.

I had flown to paradise and angels sang to me.

I absorbed those beautiful tones with all of my being. I closed my eyes and soared on the silvery-voiced wave, then descended on the fluttering ripple of the piano. I hovered over unknown spaces and I faded away, as that enchanting voice, with its thrilling rhapsodies broke the barriers of sleeplessness, awakened dull visions, and tore realities apart.

This mysterious heavenly concert lasted for about twenty minutes, and then stopped just as suddenly as it had started. I sat with closed eyes recalling the music I had heard and trying to imagine the angel who had anonymously shared such a feast with random passersby.

Still in a dream state, I finished my work and returned to the village camp astounded. I sat silent, remembering, turning those sounds round and round, reliving every soul-stirring moment.

That evening my companions sat lazily recounting their tales. As the storytelling languished, I dared to ask if anyone had heard a woman's voice singing near the church that day. Everyone looked at me curiously since no one had heard anything.

"You must have got sunstroke and heard the angels singing," said Nedeljko, his calm eyes clearly laughing behind those thick lashes.

I gestured scoffingly at him. Rista coughed lightly and gave me a signal to take a walk, so I got up and followed him, for I impatiently burned to hear what he would tell me.

I prayed he knew.

"The voice you heard belongs to Mrs. Hanna Gottfried. Although she currently teaches in Lomnitz, she's a superb mezzo-soprano, who sang with the Hanover Opera Company. When the war started, she gave up her highly successful career to come to Lomnitz and teach."

Rista stopped walking and looked pensively at his feet. "She undoubtedly sang something from Wagner, probably the *Wesendonk Lieder,* known for their lyrical and passionate yearning. They supplied many of the musical ideas that Wagner later used as the basis for preludes, arias, and even the love duet in *Tristan und Isolde.*"

He turned to look at me.

"Young, pretty woman. I find her enchanting. But don't be fooled. She's a Nazi sympathizer and a model German, extremely proud of her husband Colonel Gottfried. Although, God knows, poor man, he understood his fate completely when they packed him off to the Russian front in August of '41."

I had envisioned a young, proud blonde that did not fit my picture of arrogant German women. *Could someone with such an enchantingly angelic voice do evil, harm a soul, destroy a human being?*

I refused to believe what Rista told me—to accept such a cruel possibility.

"What's an aria?" I asked.

"An aria is a musical piece in an opera for solo voice with orchestral accompaniment."

"Doctor Cvetić told me about opera, but I could not understand it. It seemed silly to watch people singing stories to each other. But when I heard her voice, I found myself in the middle of some tragedy that I understood in my own way. I felt a heavy pain and tears rolled down my face."

"Yes, she does have a dulcet voice." He shifted his weight to the other leg.

"Unfortunately, it's not for us. Don't let her captivate you."

He shook his finger at me. "You'll be risking your life."

"How did you get to know so much about music?" I took a seat on a log in the yard.

"I studied music in Zagreb before the war." He sat down next to me. "I attended the opera regularly and heard many world-renowned soloists and orchestras from Italy and Austria. Fabulous times."

"You lucky man." I laid my hand over my heart. "I would like to hear even one opera."

"If we survive, I will take you to the first opera available to us," he promised, as he got up and went off to bed.

That night, in confused dreams, my inflamed imagination shaped the image of this German goddess with beautiful melodies that wandered above unknown horizons and opened new sights filled with grace and noble pleasures. The continued rapture of those days working on the church bell tower and listening to divinity sing transformed my soul into a lake where melodies flowed in mighty waves and echoed all night with magnificent choirs of perfect voices and the sounds and harmonies of bewitchingly uncommon compositions.

When I finished the bell-tower job, I returned to the Fiske family, who heartily welcomed me back. Many small tasks had piled up and sorely needed doing since Old Fiske had died, and I had been busy with the Church. As I tinkered with them, I thought about Mrs. Gottfried, whom I still had not met.

On the way to and from the Fiske's, I would pass by the school and Mrs. Gottfried's two-story house. I always searched for her shadow, but I could not catch sight of her. Alluring dreams of a blond angel disintegrated by daylight to torments that filled my daydreams with pain.

Rista recognized my anguish and warned me very sternly about the dangers.

Each time I passed the house, my eyes searched, as my mind pondered the image of the stonehearted angel who had destroyed my peace.

With the passing of Grandpa Günther, little Anna Marie emboldened herself completely. She constantly played near me. I had come to enjoy her, and in my free time, I carved some wooden toys that made her extremely happy.

Elsa demonstrated her gratitude by doing everything she could for me. She made excellent snacks, sometimes cold cuts of smoked pork ribs, ham and bacon, and often some pies with strawberry jam for dinner. A pitcher of beer became a daily treat, and very often Elsa would join me in my afternoon meal, sharing a glass of beer accompanied by happy chattering and giggling. If not for the obligation to return to the dormitory every night, I would have felt like the head of the Fiske family.

At that time I did not know what thoughts spun round in Elsa's head. Often I was tempted to grab her—so full-bosomed and cheerful—and to lay her down on the straw rug. But I never did, probably from fear that she would refuse me and become my ruin, when in truth I loved another.

Fortunately, our relationship became like family. I took care of all of them, and she took care of me. She sewed my socks, made me a pair of shirts, altered Old Günter's jacket for me, and supplied me with all my basic necessities.

Elsa became my confidante and new friend, through whom I could trade. She sold our Red Cross cigarettes, coffee, chocolate, sugar, and other delicacies to the Germans and acquired boots, jackets, suits, padlocked wooden footlockers, tools, and other desirable goods that we resold to the prisoners of the main camp. Our black market trade flourished, and I established with Elsa an uninterrupted channel of exchange that fed us all and prepared us for life after the war.

Summer

That summer Old Mrs. Fiske went to bed one day, never to get up again. When she died a few weeks later, Elsa had no one but the children and me.

Summer came and brought with it a deep beauty. The sun conquered those icy regions and melted the last remnants of snow from far away mountaintops. Green spread through the fertile valleys and hills, with fruits ripening—as if overnight—from yesterday's flowering orchards. Ears of wheat, corncobs, vegetables, and wild forest berries all ripened. Farmers' faces reddened with sunshine. Children ran through the open meadows of summer vacation, and life in Lomnitz became a festival of gaiety encapsulated in space and time. The inhabitants of the village kept themselves isolated from the everyday events of warring Germany. Although horror and evil, sorrow and misery, despair and madness swirled everywhere around them, they shut all these out with their good peasant common sense and covered their heads, leaving such realities to others.

I continued to do carpentry work in Lomnitz and occasionally I would go to Prezelle, passing by Mrs. Gottfried's house on the way. I would slow down, hoping to hear her voice—that heavenly intoxicating concert—or at least to see her shadow—that vision of my dreams.

Summer brought the music of birds, insects, domestic animals, forest winds, and human voices, while those fragments of arias vanished from the daily repertoire of the mystical fairy of Lomnitz.

Is she hiding behind the summer curtains?

She sang only just before dusk, when the heat and humidity began to fade. Sometimes, enchanted by the rise and fall of her tremolos, I would slow my pace or hide in the bushes along the road and cherish every moment.

No one cared anymore whether or not we returned to the village camp, since portly Stefan was one of those goodhearted Germans whose main goals consisted of a heavily laden dinner table, fresh beer, and merry company. He liked (while he still could) a plump (like him), full-of-life, juicy maiden, divorcée, widow, or even married woman. Thus our drunken old guard often stayed overnight with some widow, and we no longer worried about a timely arrival.

Stefan had adjusted to us, and we had adjusted to him. He watched out for us, and we watched out for him. If someone from the SS Command suddenly announced a visit, we ran to find him and get him back to the dormitory to prepare the prisoners for inspection. We quickly cleaned up the rooms, hid all traces of black market deals, and then presented ourselves—suitably for war prisoners—as miserable and sorrowful. Stefan would receive a commendation when they passed through our little village camp, and he proved himself ever grateful to us and to the farmers for covering for him.

One day I learned from Rista that Adolph Eichmann[16] would pass by our barracks after visiting the Russian enclave at the concentration camp. We lined up along the fence when a column of automobiles and armored vehicles thundered by. I thought that in one of those vehicles I saw

[16] (born: 19 March 1906; died: 31 May 1962) A German Nazi SS lieutenant colonel and one of the major organizers of the Holocaust. Eichmann's duty was to facilitate and manage the logistics of deporting masses of Jews to ghettos and extermination camps in German-occupied Eastern Europe during WW II. In 1960 the Mossad, Israel's intelligence service, captured him in Argentina. Following trial in Israel, he was found guilty of war crimes and hanged in 1962.

a skinny, short fellow peering out at our group. Many years later, looking at photographs in history books, I realized that I had witnessed one of the infamous monsters who had ruled half of the civilized world.

Harvest

Summer began to fade behind the pale redness of the sun, and autumn slowly invaded the forests and meadows with occasional gusts of cold currents from the far mountaintops. Farmers rushed to harvest their crops and to gather their produce, filling their silos with corn and wheat and their cold storage cellars with fruits and vegetables.

This year had yielded an abundance of everything. The enormity of work needed in the fields far exceeded the number of available hands, so they brought an additional thirty prisoners from the main camp to supplement the work force. We felt sorry for these wretched men. Exhausted and hungry, they could barely move through the fields and orchards, so we worked harder on their behalf to protect them from being sent back to Staub. We fed them and nurtured their return to health, arousing their wholesome needs and desires.

With the harvest complete, they left full of physical strength but with empty hearts. Sorrowful and bitter at the prospect of returning to the main camp, they cursed their miserable lives. Nevertheless that month of recovery helped most of them survive to the end of the war.

On the last days of harvest, as we passed by the school, I strove with all my might to hear the voice of Mrs. Gottfried. Once I thought I saw the draperies quiver and imagined her peering out from behind them. I fell behind the group and with a sudden burst of courage I looked directly at her window.

I felt her.

Our looks met somewhere in the dusk, sensing each other and vanishing in the vanity of hope.

I walked away dejected, miserable—and entirely bewitched.

Fall

With fall, children returned to school. Birds migrated south. Insects became silent. Under the cold roofs of peasants' homes, the wind whispered the nearing of winter. Autumn dressed the trees in the villages and forests like the paradise landscapes of Grimm's fables, full of beauty, fairy-tale dragons, and the unimaginable secrets of the Germanic peoples.

Toward the end of September, I returned to my carpentry work. Elsa did everything to please me. She even had the shop enclosed with brick and a fireplace installed to keep me warm all winter. The glow in my heart for this family made me content to be part of a circle born of dark soil, raw but honest principles, linen towels and dark bread. My peasant roots had grabbed hold, and it did not matter what language I spoke—a help no doubt in assuaging my nostalgia and inner unrest over Roda, Vasilija, and my parents.

On a Saturday afternoon, with the sun slowly gliding to the west, I was outdoors, polishing a chair with California wax, when a bicycle stopped in front of me and Mrs. Gottfried slowly descended. Illuminated by the sun, her white gossamer dress glowed, veiling the delicate figure of a young woman.

Blinded more by her appearance than by the sun, I raised my arm to shade my view. I saw a long, rigid face with piercing blue eyes. I rose and bowed, with an awe that I have never felt for anyone, not even as a child.

I rushed to say something before she could stop me with her commanding voice.

"Good afternoon, Madame," I said.

"Why do you stare at my window?"

Remembering Rista's warning, I was petrified, and then, taking a deep breath, I answered thoughtfully.

"Your voice is beautiful, and I'm enchanted when I hear you sing. Please forgive me if I've disturbed you."

I quickly took another breath.

My soul trembled and my heart pounded, but I did not dare to look at her. I don't know whether my natural stubbornness overwhelmed me, or my curiosity about those piercing blue eyes got the best of me, but when I raised my eyes to look, I felt myself drowning in a cold and bottomless lake.

Her reply surprised me.

"This means that you love our music?"

Unexpectedly I felt that I now walked more steadily on shifting grounds. She had addressed me with respect, not as at the start.

I responded excitedly. "Yes, Madam, I love it very much!"

She looked at me curiously one more time, turned back to the west, and with a short goodbye departed from my shop.

Disturbed, scared, and overjoyed, I followed her every motion until she disappeared from my sight.

My courage amazed me, as did my confidence and my knowledge of the German language.

Elsa, who had witnessed the visit from a distance, came over to the shop and looked at me inquiringly. I flicked off her unstated question with a wave of my hand and said that Mrs. Gottfried had come out of curiosity, that she probably had a job for me, that she wanted assurance of my skills.

I lied.

Elsa looked at me. "Frau Gottfried does not like foreigners. And certainly not war prisoners. Be careful what you say to her."

"Thank you, Elsa. I will be careful."

I returned to my polishing, but my thoughts ran only toward her, her shapely body, her extraordinarily still beauty and absorbing blue eyes. I felt goose bumps rise on my arms and legs, and a hot flash zipped through my exhausted frame. I shuddered to shake off the thought that forced itself upon me. I drank a cold glass of water and poured the rest over my hot head.

My Lord, is it possible that behind such loveliness a demon lies? Perhaps Rista is right. And Elsa.

But my heart objected, *No! She is an angel in a human body. I cannot believe their warnings. I cannot believe in a reality more cruel than those I have already lived through.*

Shadow of Sorrow

I was already in love with my scintillating vision of Mrs. Gottfried. In my sleep she came to me on the steps of her melodies. I tried touching her in a moment of passion, and gusts of cold morning air would wake me from my burning. I arose sleepy and tired and would only open my eyes when we exited camp.

My dear Elsa would greet me with a hot cup of coffee—supplied by our black market trades—and a small meal that we all shared. The older children had already left for school, and we each went about our own duties. Elsa did not ask that I help her with farm work. She did most of it herself, except for seeding and harvesting, when neighboring farmers helped.

A strong woman, full of energy, Elsa looked young and desirable even after the birth of her seventh child. I told her stories about my village, about Roda and little Vasilija, about my father and mother. She would listen carefully and occasionally ask questions about tradition, religion, and work. Almost everything interested her, as though she searched through any information for an explanation of the situation we all found ourselves trapped in. Sometimes, in the corners of her eyes, I noticed a shadow of despair arise, and then spread slowly over her entire face. She felt a natural insecurity about the events surrounding her, and she appeared to search for emotional support from me, even though in reality she held the upper hand.

When alone I thought of the blue angel. Her eyes watched me from every corner as my captivating fantasies warmed the workshop. I heard her haunting melodies inside my head and saw her on sunrays floating through the eternity of the cosmos.

The soft flickering of the stars drew us upward and lifted us above the mountaintops. Enraptured, we saw the beauty of the world spread out before us.

I inhaled her sighs and absorbed the trembling of her lips.

I felt her in all of my pores.

I vanished from the chains of reality and disappeared in my yearnings for her.

Yet my Roda, little Vasilija, and my old parents forever remained in the back of my mind. Guilt encumbered my steps when my mind turned toward Mrs. Gottfried. Thus I found myself at odds between two poles—so far apart from each other—yet both inside of my conquered heart.

These new feelings of love differed from my love for Roda. Somehow they reflected a higher meaning, more subtle and innocent. Next to Mrs. Gottfried I felt like a boy with a red face, while with Roda I felt like a stallion.

I understood that neither Roda nor I knew much about love. Our parents made the arrangement, and we adjusted to the tradition, without dating, flirtations, or yearnings. Although both of us had liked someone else secretly, we submitted to our parents' wishes and soon we adapted to life together. We got along well both mentally and physically from the very first day, and thus we relaxed into the traditional mold of Serbian love that parents had arranged for centuries.

Several months passed and I had not received a single letter from home. I sent letters weekly to the family, yet nobody answered. Finally one arrived for me, forwarded to Staub through the efforts of my countryman, Milentije Nikolić [*Mee-**lehn**-tee-yeh **Nee**-koh-litch*], who hailed from a neighboring village back home. My father had sent it, and I was overjoyed. I grabbed it from the guard who distributed the mail and started reading voraciously:

> Dear Son,
>
> It has been a long time since we heard from you and I asked Ljubisav [***Lyu**-bee-sahv*] to attach this letter when he sends his to Milentije, since he told me that he receives mail from him regularly, while we did not get a word from you.
>
> We got scared that you might be ill, or, God forbid, disabled, as dark thoughts can think the worst, while my heart and your mother's heart were breaking apart. But tragedy struck us and I don't know how to begin this letter and not break your heart.

My hands trembled.

Two months ago God took our little Vasilija and took our souls with her. Little Vasilija died from some kind of cough. We took her to a doctor and to a local healer, but nothing helped. Little Vasilija just smiled, so sweet like honey, then her eyes withered and closed, and my heart broke in a thousand pieces. From that day, I cannot sleep anymore.

Tears rolled down my cheeks.

My Bosiljka [*Boh-**seel**-kah*] grieved for two weeks until her eyes dried up and her throat tightened like an old rag, while Roda sobbed long and sad. And then she locked herself in a room and did not come out for a week. When she came out, she had become a different woman. She was no longer good, obedient Roda. She went to her parents and stayed for a week, and when she returned, she did not say a word. She moved about the room, flipped some things around, stared at the dresser for hours, and then she packed up and went back to her mother. She does not see or hear us. We have not seen her in a month. I didn't say a word. Nor did your mother. It is a heavy load. But no one bothers to ask us.

While she was here that mailman Stanko followed her and constantly talked to her about something. He hates me and when he sees me he threatens often that he will eliminate all of us. It looks like he has become some sort of communist. They are all over this region, and there is a constant change of power between Četniks and Partisans. And they all take forcefully from us and threaten our lives if we don't give. But we do not care. We'll remain on this earth with whatever little we have. God watches over us and we pray to Him to watch over you, too.

My son, if you are alive, please send your letter through Milentije because I am certain that Stanko is stealing our mail, and I will send my letters from the post office in Ćuprija.

Please stay alive and healthy,
Your father Milovan and mother Bosiljka

I pounded the wall. I buried my head in my pillow. I mourned my little Vasilija all night long. I cursed God for taking her.

Why? So many sins are on almost every footstep of this damned land and You take her*!*

Dawn arrived with a cold wind filtering through the window cracks of the dormitory and bringing the sharp, icy breath of the coming winter. We put on overcoats and started down our usual path. My friends felt sorry for me, but they kept it to themselves, recognizing my need for solitude. We did not talk, and we parted in silence.

Elsa felt the change in me. She noticed a cloud in my eyes and left me alone in my shop.

Little Anna Marie hugged me with her small arms and started singing her favorite song. I cried softly and she too ran out and into the house. My sobbing had frightened her.

Elsa returned and embraced me. I cried while she held me in her gentle arms and comforted me. She sensed a tragedy but could not have imagined what had really happened. She continued to console me, but I could not calm down. Through my sobbing I whispered Vasilija's name, and she knew.

Her tears poured out joining mine. She cried softly with great emotion.

I choked and gasped for air.

She brought me some water that I drank thirstily then fell into her arms again. Her warmth and loving care calmed me and I began to gather my strength.

Before that moment I had never noticed the depth of Elsa's emotions. With her hands around my neck, she kissed my closed eyes and forehead.

I hugged her and held her in my arms for a long while.

In My Shop

Several sad weeks passed by in silence, while thoughts of my family's tragedy loaded a huge weight on my soul. While my hands obediently did my carpentry jobs, my mind muddled through the nihilistic thoughts of a crushed being.

Meanwhile, Elsa managed to arrange with Regional Headquarters for me to stay permanently in my shop, allowing me to work and sleep in the same place. I appreciated her making it possible for me to leave that freezing cold concrete building that never heated up, though I missed my companions.

Occasionally they came by to keep me informed of the latest events. In that way I learned that Radenko had moved to Irma's and that nobody from Staub had bothered to look for him. Indeed everyone knew he and the young widow slept together, since he didn't return to the village camp at night anymore. Our guard Stefan no longer cared who came or went, having drowned himself in a barrel of alcohol.

By now I knew all the residents of Lomnitz, and they accepted me as one of their own. I found time to chat with them about anything and everything, but mostly about farm work. At old farmer Slinger's, where Nedeljko worked, I often repaired wooden carts and trailers and spent hours with him discussing inventions in transportation, steel bridges and ships. It appeared that everything interested him, and he needed to exchange thoughts with someone about anything—anything other than the war.

The farmers of Prezelle, on the other hand, shied away from any conversations with me. They would wave me away when I tried to ask a question, making me feel unwanted. When I finished a job, I would start to leave right away, and often they would not offer me food. I did not care because Elsa always made me a big meal, but the arrogance and unfriendliness of this group of German farmers bothered me. I wondered why the residents of these two neighboring villages differed so greatly.

On my return from Prezelle I always passed by the school on purpose, hoping to meet Mrs. Gottfried, or at least to hear her angelic voice. This game of cat and mouse I imagined between us had become a daily temptation that I could not resist. I had lifted her to a towering pedestal, and I strove to see her in my thoughts, if not in reality.

Every time I found myself by the school fence, I felt my emotions rise to flooding. I looked at her closed window and imagined that she watched me carefully and curiously from behind the heavy draperies.

When I heard her voice through the closed classroom door, I would stop, thunderstruck, and stare at the dark windows, imagining her figure as she moved about the room.

My sense of her closeness turned me into a petrified beggar whose eyes dripped tears of happiness. My love flowed from one lake to another and into a pleasure of endless dreams. Her melodies opened doors to eternity, and my lonely soul soaked in every tone as it yearned so desperately for her.

My body would continue down the street, but my awareness stayed glued to the frosted glass of her window.

My companions now stopped by my shop regularly, and Elsa made them feel at home as best she could. Mile smiled with delight when Elsa asked him about his origin. He replied eagerly, "We have a nice orchard up on Rudnik Mountain. We make the best plum brandy in all of Šumadija [*Shu-mah-**dee**-yah*]."

He turned to the rest of us. "You know the brand 'Stari Svat' produced by Vinarevo Wine and Liquor Company? That's *our* brandy, bottled and labeled under 'Stari Svat.'"

Proud of his family's accomplishment, he beamed innocently. "We sell Vinarevo two hundred casks a year as the exclusive supplier for this brand."

"Really? That's your brandy?" exclaimed Spasoje, leaning forward and pounding the floor with his big foot. "That stuff's potent. On my wedding day, my best man and our godfather got me so drunk from toasting with Stari Svat, I couldn't recognize my bride, and I almost took her mother to bed with me."

He shivered. "I never touched that bastard stuff again."

When the laughing subsided, Elsa turned her attention to our handsome Aleksa, "What did you do before the war?"

He looked surprised. He hadn't expected anyone to ask him about his past. He scratched his head and mumbled something out of the corner of his mouth.

"Com'on man. Speak up. We want to hear your story," Mile said gently, stretching his long legs out so he could listen from a more relaxed position.

"Well, my little brother and I lived with our grandmother on a small farm near Rekovac [***Reh**-koh-vahts*]. Both of our parents died from influenza in the 1920s. Our grandparents took us in and raised us until I was twelve. Then our grandfather got killed in a rock slide, and I became head of the household, taking care of my nine-year-old brother and my deaf grandmother."

He looked down at his hands, and then cocked his head to one side. "Needless to say, life was hard. Grandfather didn't have any horses, so I used a couple of cows to plow the fields and to pull the cart to market. My little brother helped, but at seventeen, the combine caught his left arm and ripped it out of his shoulder."

Everyone gasped.

Aleksa continued, "He survived, but I lost my big helper. So I got married that year and brought home a healthy young bride from the nearby village."

His fine features lit up, and a modest smile erupted from beneath his thin mustache. "She's a good wife and very caring."

Then he hung his head and sighed. "I've just been here for so long. I worry all the time about what's happening to them. I haven't received a letter in two years."

Elsa got up and hugged him.

He stiffened up, looked around at the rest of us, and then relaxed, patting her lightly on the back.

I suddenly felt very homesick. I wanted to say something but Nedeljko jumped in to bolster us with his hearty strength. "Oh, hell, guys, let's not spoil this lively moment with sob stories. Let's remember our beautiful country's happy holidays, county fairs, and our music and dances."

He leaned toward us, a sly grin on his face. "You don't know, but I played button accordion and spent most of my youth entertaining and making people happy. They danced their hearts out. They drank virgin brandy and got smashed, then they made love in the bushes and went home satisfied."

He shook his head. "Boy, I never met a sad person until I joined this Army."

He brightened again, stretching his muscular torso forward and throwing his arms out. "When life is good, we Serbian people know how to be happy. We're the happiest people in the world."

Then he started singing an old love song:

When I think of you, my darling,
I remember red blushes on your face.
Then I only drink red wines
From my banged up old dingy case.

When dreams of your lovely eyes
Come to me with great delight,
Then the barman does nothing else
But pour the wine all night.

And I sing, drink, and cry
From the joy that is truly mine,
But when I leave, I stumble and trip
From my love for you and my wine.

Everyone laughed at Nedeljko's song and the tone of the evening changed once again from sorrow to lightheartedness, but the nostalgia remained.

On several occasions, I noticed Mile trying eagerly to get Elsa's attention.

As we ate, we discussed the latest news and drank hot brandy that I made in our traditional way with homemade hot caramel. Elsa served us, with Mile following her every move and smiling at her every look. She also seemed to like this long-legged fellow with light brown hair, who blushed when he made contact with her blue eyes.

I noticed a touch of secret happiness entering her lonely heart, and something about her seemed to dance for joy at his growing attraction to her.

Mile and Elsa had found the bridge that would tie their hearts.

I remained alone, wandering the riverbank in search of a bridge to *my* angel.

The Shadow Spreads

One day before sunrise, Elsa received a letter—hand delivered by a lieutenant—from the Regional Office of Army Affairs, expressing their condolences and forwarding her a package of the late Berthold Fiske's personal effects. The farmers of the village had just started their morning chores, and, still bathed in deep darkness, dogs slept in their yards.

The lieutenant courteously remained several more minutes, then said goodbye and departed.

I stayed behind with her and the children. It was Saturday and the children occupied themselves building snow towers and castles in front of the house.

I watched Elsa as she stared at the letter with a blank look.

The package lay on the kitchen floor, so I lifted it and put it on the chair in front of her.

She continued to stare and reread the sentence informing her that Berthold had been killed in Romania.

She suddenly became aware of my presence and started shaking and crying without a sound.

I hugged her and sat her down. Little Anna Marie, who played nearby, came over and also hugged her mother gently, caressing her thick, long blond hair that hung behind the chair. With her little hands she conveyed so much tenderness to Elsa.

She murmured a little poem to her mother.

I left them alone and returned to my shop.

In the afternoon Elsa came to the shop entrance, swaying unsteadily, as if looking for something to lean on. Her skirt and dress were covered with snow and mud, and I realized that she had fallen several times on the way from the house. I took her in my arms and, through her blubbering, noticed a strong scent of alcohol on her breath. Her drunken, unintelligible words—pouring out tenderness, agony, and immense anger all at once—made conversation impossible. She choked and sobbed inarticulate laments.

I laid her down on the bed and tried to calm her, but she fought and turned over, hugging me passionately and trying to kiss my lips.

I separated from her and called Horst—the oldest of the children—to go and fetch Mrs. Hoffmann or Irma for some help.

Horst returned shortly and hollered from the gate, "Herr Timo, I brought my teacher, Frau Gottfried. She will help you."

She stood at the door draped in a beautiful handmade scarf, wrapped over a short fur coat. Her long sky-blue dress covered her black leather boots. Locks of her hair peeked out from under a black hat that had colorful flowers planted in the brim and a long silver ribbon wrapped around it. In the door frame of my shop, she stood there, resplendent, divine, like a picture from one of my forgotten books.

"What's happening?" she asked worriedly.

"Elsa cannot calm down," I replied. "You have heard about her husband?"

"Yes, Horst told me," she said softly.

This gentleness in her startled me. *Those words came from the woman I dream about, from the goddess I love, from sublime lips not severe ones.*

I watched her comfort Elsa.

She asked me to prepare tea for Elsa, and I rushed to the kitchen to do it. I floated on a cloud. So happy to help her.

But what I found in the house stopped me. The children played in a room now strewn with Berthold's things. On the kitchen table, a letter he had written sat open. I read it as I waited for the water to boil.

> Dear Gisela,
>
> I am writing this letter from the Southeastern Front, somewhere near the Ukraine and Romania, where I ended up in June of this year, and I do not know how long all this will last. I am hoping for an early return, because they promised me they would let me go home when my request was approved.
>
> I am sending you five hundred marks now, and when I get my next paycheck, I will send it to you because I have no need for anything here.
>
> I miss you very much and I miss our lovemaking. Since we met, I only think of you. I have forgotten Elsa and the children because of you. I hope you will not forget me. Take care of yourself and be patient. All of this will be finished soon, and we will be together forever then.
>
> Your sweet Berty

I could not believe it. *Can this be Berthold? That brutal simpleton who spat on me and bullied me no end?* I could easily believe him so venal as to abandon a wife and seven children, but . . . *Does* he *know how to love?*

I stared at the letter and thought about the tangles of the human heart when the teapot whistle aroused me. I dropped in a metal ball with English tea and rushed back to the shop.

It surprised me to see Elsa whispering to Mrs. Gottfried.

I served them tea and sugar and left.

I was playing with the children in the yard when both Mrs. Gottfried and Elsa walked out. Elsa had sobered, though still a little pale and very grateful to Mrs. Gottfried. She bowed three times and thanked her. Mrs. Gottfried advised her to take time to rest.

Before leaving, she looked at me with her beautiful eyes, "Good night, Timo."

"G-good nnight, Mmadame," I managed to reply, stupefied, then let my eyes follow her until she disappeared from my view.

It seemed as though she had tied her ribbon to my waist and it unwound into infinity.

Prezelle

In late November I received a request from the town of Prezelle to repair the handrails and steps of the Town Hall. I set out on my usual route past Mrs. Gottfried's, as always slowing considerably in the hope of seeing her. But that bewitching sight eluded me once more that day, and instead when I got to Prezelle, I encountered a considerably more disturbing one.

Five of the Prezelle work crew from my village camp had been stripped to the waist and tied to trees in the village square. The village teacher Mr. Thielke stood in front of them with a whip in his hand that he had clearly used quite mercilessly. A group of men stood around behind him, cheering him on as he laid into the chests and faces of the five again and again, until it became difficult to know for sure whether they still lived.

Since the Prezelle people had never proved very accommodating to me, I was reluctant to approach anyone to ask what was going on. I decided to hang back from entering the square and simply watch.

Just then six young Prezelle women with shaved heads stumbled out of the Town Hall and started down the street toward the men tied to the trees. When they got close enough to be able to see the men's condition, several screamed. They all started to weep, and a couple of them crumpled to the ground.

Another bunch of women came out of the Town Hall, following behind the first group, and started throwing rocks and dirt at them and taunting them with "Whores!" "Sluts!" and numerous other degrading epithets. It appeared, from the tufts of hair still clinging to their skirts, that the second group of women had shaved the heads of the first group, but didn't consider that sufficient punishment for—apparently—sleeping with those of my fellow farm workers tied to the trees.

When the shamed women reached the trees to stand in tears next to their lovers, who drooped bleeding and quashed, Mr. Thielke turned to address all the many townspeople who had, by this time, interrupted their normally busy workday to glower at and impugn these unfortunate wretches.

"Heil Hitler."

"Heil Hitler," the townspeople returned, along with the customary salute.

"These six women, whom we used to consider sisters of the town of Prezelle, have defiled our good name and our standing in the eyes of our glorious Führer by committing adultery with these Slavic dogs! Slavs!" He waived his arms and spit in the dirt.

"Can any of us imagine an act quite so low, so horrible? Our good Aryan women mating with filth? Well, we will show them what it means to mate with filth. We will show them how *good* Germans regard such acts."

He pointed toward the lovers, his nose wrinkled and his lips curled downward. "They will pay for their irresponsible, ungodly behavior."

He turned back to the crowd. "I thank all the people of Prezelle for supporting me in my efforts to right this terrible wrong that they have inflicted upon us. We are here today to cast them out from our society, to purify our town, and to make them pay for what they have done to us."

He clenched both fists and thrust them forward. "They must know that we will not stand for behavior that is such an affront to German honor and German sensibilities. They must know that we will not stand for behavior expressly forbidden by our glorious Führer. They must know that such filth only begets filth. Heil Hitler!"

At this everyone responded, "Heil Hitler," then cheered.

Thielke motioned to one of the men to take what looked like a huge pail of manure ready for the compost heap over to the first woman. Then, whip in hand, he followed behind his lackey.

As the man approached her with the pail, she cowered in fear.

Thielke raised the whip and, leaning in almost nose-to-nose with her, commanded, "Take this manure and feed it to your swine of a lover."

He hook the hand with the whip. "You are nothing but a beast to mate with such rubbish."

My stomach started to heave as I watched the poor woman take a handful of manure and, trembling, raise it to her lover's mouth.

He gathered enough strength to turn away and refuse to accept it, only to see his woman whipped for his resistance.

At the sound of her scream, he nodded and told her, "It's all right, my love. Give it to me."

With tears streaming down her face, she lifted her hand to his mouth and fed him the manure.

Even at my distance I could see the glee sparkle in Thielke's eyes. "Now you too," he said to the woman.

She returned his look with crazed eyes, searching his face for some pity, some mercy.

She found none. She hung her head, then reached her hand back into the bucket. Her whole body convulsed as she raised it to her lips.

"Good, now kiss," demanded Thielke.

Quaking, she turned to her lover, her chin smudged with feces, her tears still streaming relentlessly.

"I love you," he said to her. "You are my life."

Thielke spit on them. "Kiss!" he insisted.

Still reluctant, she raised her lips to his and cradled his head in her hands.

Their bodies relaxed as they took what solace they could from even this forced embrace.

She let go and hung her head, still crying.

My stomach was in knots.

Thielke turned to go to the next woman.

I decided that this might not be the best day to start work on the Town Hall.

I returned to Elsa's, not even glancing toward Mrs. Gottfried's windows.

The next day the whole town of Lomnitz was abuzz with the news of the happenings in Prezelle. The five men had not returned to the dormitory the night of the beatings, and when they also failed to show up that night, as much as I hated the thought of having those words cross my lips, I considered telling everyone what I knew.

Luckily for me, our handsome Aleksa, who worked for the Mayor of Lomnitz and his wife, spoke up and reported the entire story.

Needless to say, the group met his report with both anger and terror, but his coda to the tale afforded at least some wisp of comfort. He had overheard the Mayor's conversation with his wife, and, to the best of Aleksa's understanding, she had told her husband, "I am ashamed to see our people take these measures in the name of Germany and German honor. How can such actions ever be considered honorable? Thank Heavens I know that you would never allow such a thing to take place in Lomnitz."

At this, the Mayor had heaved a very deep sigh and replied, "In these difficult times, we do the best we can."

The Request

With Nature's typical contrariety, December 1943 arrived as mildly, quietly, and idyllically as in a fairy tale. As the month dragged on under the dark skies of the Luftwaffe, white clouds of Christmas began to gather over Germany, bringing holiday spirit to the frozen hearts of warriors, slaves, and innocent victims alike. Jesus had returned to people who carried the heavy shackles of war. A few days before Christmas, a deep calm covered the land and filled the skies. For an instant the Holiday restored confidence to the locals. Decorations again brightened yards and houses, and holiday happiness filled the hearts of children.

Germans cut Christmas trees in the nearby forests, transported them on sleds, and trimmed them at home. At Elsa's house, the children twinkled with excitement about the sweets tied to the branches of the freshly cut pine, now festooned with wooden dolls and porcelain angels, bells and silk flowers. They all impatiently touched the trinkets, admiring the sparkly reflections, enticing sounds, as they watched the mysterious shadows cast on the white walls by the fireplace's flames.

Elsa prepared for Christmas with special pleasure. Her face glowed with contentment. She seemed to race with time, cooking, smoking the ham, baking cakes and tortes, washing and cleaning every room, and shepherding the children to get ready for the big holiday.

It was not Christmas, however, that had caused her happiness. In her soul flames of love burned for Mile, and her eyes saw only his gentle face bringing torches of hot pleasures for her lips. They understood each other with the mute tongue of a euphoria that spontaneously filled their hearts and transformed each emotion into a romantic secret. Longing boiled over and spilled into a bottomless gorge of love, then welled up into a tide of discoveries. The source of their happiness masked itself with the cloak of the coming holiday, burgeoning silently in the shadow of the birth of God's child.

As my mind lingered on these scenes, Elsa's son Horst called me from the gate. "Herr Timo, I have a message for you."

I walked out of the shop and saw him skiing the cleared path in front of the house.

"A message? From whom?" I asked loudly.

"Frau Gottfried wants you to see her this afternoon. She has a request for you."

"Thank you, Horst. Please tell Frau Gottfried that I'll drop by at about three o'clock."

Horst continued on his way, and I returned to the shop.

I couldn't imagine what she might want from me, but the invitation excited me. My turbulent thoughts began once again to unhinge my enamored soul. I felt my heart pounding faster, pushing heat through my cold body. I turned nervously in a confusion of apprehensions and movements, trying to stay calm, but everything around me whirled in my bewildered head.

We will meet soon. What will I tell her? This is our first meeting. Alone. How will I behave? She is a lady. And me? At best, an artisan, a carpenter. Realistically, a peasant, a slave.

I continued pacing the shop when Elsa and Wilhelmina, her oldest daughter, entered.

"I heard that Frau Gottfried has invited you. You must get dressed."

Before I could say anything, she pulled a dark blue shirt and dark blue jacket out of a bag and laid them on the bed.

"Come on. Take off those rags and put this on. Berthold's clothes won't fit anyone but you. You must look nice." She indulged me with her sweet voice, while helping me to remove my work jacket and shirt.

"You must shave." She turned to her daughter. "Wilhelmina, honey, bring the shaving kit from Mama's bedroom."

I tried to compose myself, but I could not even say thanks to this blue-eyed angel who cared so much about me. I again thought of Mrs. Gottfried's cold look and arrogance, and I froze with fear at the thought that I might do something unthinkable.

Can this high society German woman possibly look at me as an equal? Perhaps she will order me to chop some wood, prepare the furnace for Christmas, or shovel snow in the schoolyard. Yes, no doubt she wants my assistance with something like that.

But, somehow, I secretly believed differently. I had seen the smile on her face, the joy in her eyes. A sense of pride rushed through my heart and I felt my smile flash for a second—long enough for Elsa to notice.

Elsa continued to mother me, and while I lulled myself with delectable dreams, she shaved me, washed my face and sprayed it with some kind of cologne.

In the small mirror she handed me, I saw a strange face. It stared at me. I looked different, still young, though much older than on the day I left Krušar.

"You enjoy my pampering, don't you?"

I nodded.

She combed my hair with her fingers and continued, "You're a very handsome man, Timo. With your curly chestnut hair and dreamy brown eyes—"

"Really, Elsa, I never thought—"

"I have my Mile now—that sweet and loving man. But I mean Frau Gottfried. Your warmth and kindness, your unselfish love for children—not to mention your love for people in general—these are qualities that make you respected here, among us villagers."

I looked up at her as she unbuttoned my shirt. "I know you and the children care very much for me." I looked down at her hands as she finished the last button. "But I feel less certain about the others. The good people of Lomnitz remind me of my own people, yet I try to remember that a German will always consider me a prisoner of war first and foremost."

"Timo, please listen." Elsa's voice turned serious as she helped me out of my work shirt. "In wartime a young lonely woman like Frau Gottfried can easily lose her composure. Be extra careful. I don't want you to get hurt by misinterpreting her request for help. Take it just as it's conveyed to you, whatever service she may ask for. Just do it and don't let on how much you admire her."

"But if she only wants me to do something for her school, why are you dressing me up?"

"You'll be a guest in her house—alone. Please, think about what you'll say. An upper-class woman like her will have no tolerance for small talk. Speak only when spoken to."

She reached for the shirt lying on the bed. "Now, let's finish fixing you up. I'd like that."

She put the shirt and jacket on me. They fit me really well. She dressed me as she would her own son.

I melted. This five-foot-ten carpenter felt like a little boy delighting bashfully in his mother's touch.

When she finished, her eyes flashed with satisfaction, and she patted my butt, saying, "Now go."

She shook her finger at me. "But be wise."

The Task

In an overcoat and clean boots, I started for the school about ten minutes before three o'clock. The school was empty. I walked to Mrs. Gottfried's house and knocked on the main entrance door.

A minute later she appeared and looked at me puzzled.

I took off my cap. "Frau Gottfried, I've arrived. You called for me."

She tilted her head to the side and looked at me again with disbelief.

"Frau Gottfried, it's I, Timo," I said confidently, realizing that she did not recognize me.

"Ah, Timo. It's you. Please, come in."

She moved aside to let me by.

I walked into a hallway decorated with various pictures from all corners of the world. I took off my overcoat and hung it on a coat hook. She led me into a beautiful salon with a magnificent piano. The open instrument had sheet music standing on the music desk. The black polished surface, decorated with lines of gold, white and pastel green, glistened in the fading sunlight, forming an unframed picture before my eyes. It enchanted me so much my hands moved forward to touch it.

I jumped back at the sound of her voice. "Please sit down, Timo."

I turned around and saw two chairs with colorfully quilted pillows next to the fireplace. Involuntarily, I looked at my slacks and didn't move another step.

"How can I help you, Frau Gottfried?" I asked, continuing to stand.

"But please, sit down, for Heaven's sake."

She smiled and took the chair across from me, then gestured for me to sit.

I sat somehow, humbly, almost not touching the seat.

"Tomorrow, I would like to go to the forest to cut down a Christmas tree for the school. Would you be willing to help me?"

"Certainly, Madame. It would be my great pleasure."

"I have already arranged with Herr Bauer to have the sled ready for us at eight o'clock in the morning. Is this suitable to you?"

She looked at my nervous hands that wandered from my pockets to my knees, and then to the chair arms.

"Absolutely. I can arrive earlier, if you like," I assured her.

My eyes, as if bewitched, had not turned from her piano. She noticed my intense curiosity.

"Would you like to touch it? Or perhaps, would you like to hear it? I'd be happy to play for you."

She stood up and turned toward the piano. "Please, come."

"No, Madame. I was admiring the workmanship," I said confused. "Uh—yes, I'd like very much to hear it."

She walked over and sat down on the piano bench, then tossed her head backward, spreading her long golden hair over her silk blouse. She lifted her arms and fixed her eyes on that ineffable wreath of notes. Her lively fingers ran across the keys to create magnificent harmonies, dancing in a circle of majestically moving fairies. The sound bounced off the walls, ceiling, and polished wood floor in an emanation of melody that charmed, undulated, opened mountains and canyons and ascended into the unknown.

Everything chimerical that I have heard before from a distance has become real, tangible, and so close.*—And yet, still so distant. Imponderable. Immaterial. That is music. The heartbeat that nurtures us in our mothers' wombs. The illusive melody we carry throughout our lives, never knowing where it comes from. The sounds of birth and death.*

Watching the passionate movements of her body, I floated on the stormy waves of an air, tied to the mast of an abandoned ship, expecting to sink with every strike of her fingers.

But then she lifted me up and directed me to the calm open sea where our eyes met. I felt as though our souls traveled together, and I longed to moor in the bay of her secrets.

The music softened, slowed.

Her fingers paused, hanging briefly above the keys as the final notes hung with them.

This miracle worker had transformed stone and dust into a human heart and soul.

Her soft voice woke me. "Did you enjoy the Beethoven?"

I took a deep breath and let it glide gently out again. "Yes. Very much. It was truly magical," I replied, even though I did not understand the question. *What is Beethoven? Perhaps a chair I am sitting on or some other object in the room?*

As if in answer to my silent question, she continued, "Yes, Beethoven is our greatest composer, and I love him very much."

I felt enlightened.

She looked down at the keys. "I often return to him when I am lonely."

She rose from the piano.

I got up and walked to the hallway. I put on my overcoat and bowed to her, just as Rista had taught me.

She extended her hand, and I kissed it with my warm lips. *Did I feel—or just imagine?—a slight tremor from that cold, beautiful hand, its skin like fresh cream?*

I walked out with dignity on the legs of a peasant whose body shook from overwhelming anticipation.

The Christmas Tree

The next day I woke up at dawn to the familiar call of a rooster. Joyful, I refreshed myself with cold water and started a fire in the furnace.

The sudden blast of heat enfolded my bare upper body, and I stood for several moments, staring at the flames that rose like a whirlwind. I imagined her face on the leaves of fire flowers and tried to grab it with my hands, but it vanished in a puff of white smoke.

I dressed and walked out. Fresh snow had covered the front yard, and I felt as though I trampled new cotton.

I entered the kitchen and started a fire. Everyone still slept. I poured water into a teakettle and put it on the stove.

The children had left the kitchen table covered with books and notepads they forgot to put away before bed. As I waited for the water to boil, I flipped through the pages of a book of Andersen's fairy tales. Elsa walked in.

"Ah, Timo. Good old Timo."

A dreamy smile spread across her face as she tried to blink sleep away. "You already started the fire."

She yawned as she approached the stove. "I'll make something for breakfast. What would you like?"

"I'm not hungry, Elsa. I'd just like a cup of tea," I replied.

She looked at me curiously, still half asleep, and turned to the stove to make breakfast.

I moved the books and notepads from the table, wiped it with a rag, and covered it with a tablecloth. She mixed the eggs, with an occasional glance my way.

Her curiosity prevailed. "What did Frau Gottfried want?"

"She asked me to help her cut a Christmas tree for the school. We'll do it today. I'll go there at eight o'clock."

"Ahh . . . Take the ax with you."

"Herr Bauer will prepare the horse, sled, and tools. I won't need mine."

While I prepared the tea, she continued to beat the eggs, which she then abandoned to sit with me so that together we could enjoy our hot tea.

We drank slowly, sip by sip, and exchanged questioning looks.

What do her eyes see? How much does she know, and how much can she guess? Elsa has Mile now. Why would she care about me?

"Timo, be careful. She's the wife of a high-ranking SS officer. Local Nazi members watch and follow her every move."

Erupting through her haze of sleep, Elsa's words spilled out and cut like the sharp blade of a drawn sword.

"Be cautious with her. She's not an ordinary woman. Weigh every one of your words and watch how you handle yourself. Keep a tight hold on what you feel inside."

I looked at her, confused and puzzled. Her words wounded me and woke me from a sweet daydream.

I shook from some unknown chill. I nodded.

What did I just confirm? That I understood? That I'm scared?

My passionate challenge to taste the secrets of the unknown had eternally glowed in my adventurous soul, but Elsa had extinguished it with a wave of facts.

What am I plunging into?

The face of Mrs. Gottfried once again appeared threatening and chilly as a statue from which the sun's rays deflect to leave it mute and somber.

I arose from the table with a heavy heart.

I trudged out of the house to the morning's cold harshness.

Jürgen Bauer busied himself in the schoolyard with a horse hitched to his sled.

I greeted him from the gate. "Good morning, Herr Bauer. How's business down at the tavern?"

"Good morning," he mumbled, not bothering to look up from tending the horse. "The handsaw and the ax are in the toolbox under the seat."

He walked around to the side of the sled. "This blanket's for the horse. Cover him when you stop to cut the pine tree."

He pointed to some blankets. "The fur cover's for Frau Gottfried."

"Thank you, Herr Bauer."

He pressed his lips together in a grimace.

"Dortich Forest is about three kilometers from here. When you leave the village, turn right," he pointed.

"After about one kilometer, you'll come to a small creek with a bridge. Drive over the bridge and take the road uphill until you come to an intersection."

He held up his hand with his fingers spread and grabbed his fourth finger with his other hand. "Five roads cross at this junction. Take the one that goes by a small chapel with a Crucifix. Dortich Forest begins about half a kilometer from that point. You'll see cut pine trees along the road."

He adjusted the horse's reins. "Bigger and prettier trees grow in the upper end of the forest, about a hundred meters from the road. But let Frau Gottfried decide which one to cut."

He finished fiddling with the horse. "Well, here she is."

A smile lit his face. He looked past me over my shoulder. "Good morning, Frau Gottfried," he shouted with obviously deep respect.

"Good morning," I turned and joined in hastily.

"Good morning." She walked through fresh snow.

She wore a dark blue wool dress, with an overcoat made of silver fox fur, and a brown fur hat and muff, where she kept both hands.

She is truly the most ravishing woman I had ever seen. I feel like a slave. She is my master and all else is nothing but a dream.

Pulling the sled over the snow-packed trail, the horse trotted slowly out of Lomnitz. Occasional snowflakes hovered, taking forever on their slow descent, like dandelion cotton flowers in a light summer breeze. Wrapped in them, the tree trunks and bushes along the road looked unreal.

Will I awaken from this dream? I asked myself trying to pierce the unknown. *Here the Third Reich doesn't exist. Yet they caused everything. The roads that take us to this fairy forest were cleared by Hitler's lunatic ideology of world conquest and annihilation of "unsuitable" peoples. Can Mrs. Gottfried truly support the Nazis?*

I glanced at her secretly, trying to solve the riddle hidden behind her blue eyes. Occasionally they reflected a wondering warmth. I embraced those flickers and felt happy and calm.

She obviously enjoyed the cold weather, the white forms in the silence of a crystal clear day. The profile of her pale face merged beautifully with the picturesque sights of the region, whirling through myriad irresistible poses in frame after frame of my imaginary photo album.

In my happy trance on the road to Dortich Forest, I convinced myself that she simply could not be like all the others.

No! She cannot believe in Nazi ideology.

Suddenly a doe crossed our path, gamboling lightly. Although the road here was smooth, Mrs. Gottfried bounced in her seat, eyes wide and glowing. "How adorable she is. How graceful."

"Yes, Madame, she is really beautiful."

"All the wonders of nature meet in her. She flows like the lyrical movement of a sonata."

She turned to me. "I would like to be a doe, to wander endlessly and enjoy space without borders and without people, listening always to the music of the spheres."

Her pupils widened and her voice became soft. "Wouldn't it be wonderful?"

"I think you'd be the loveliest doe in the world." My thoughts spilled recklessly from my mouth, and I felt I had said too much.

She did not answer.

Nor did she look at me anymore.

She scared me once more with her coldness and silence.

We came upon the intersection Bauer had described, and I directed the horse toward the forest. Soon we found the cut stumps of young pine trees, and I decided to stop at a clearing on the right side of the road.

She looked away as I helped her down from the sled.

We walked the hilly path toward the top where Bauer had told us the better trees grew. We slogged through snow up to our knees. She often sank into deep snowdrifts, and I would pull her out joyfully. She laughed with delight, her bell-like voice echoing through the forest clearings, dancing somewhere above the treetops, then fading away in the great beyond.

When we reached the highest point, we looked out over the vast spread of pines below us. Muffled with snow, they sang with the same silent beauty as notes lined up on a sheet of music.

We stood there awestruck.

"Please, help me select a tree," she said after several minutes of silence.

"I leave this to you," I replied.

"No, no. You know wood better than I do."

I saw that deciding caused her as much trouble as it did me. "I'll get the hand saw, and you, please, stay here."

"Have you made a choice?" she wondered.

"Not yet. When I return."

"Please hurry."

She laughed. "Since I'm not a doe, I'm afraid to be alone."

I ran down the hill and tumbled over a few times, entertaining her with my clownish acrobatics. She laughed delicately at my falls, which made me try harder to please her. In reality, I had slammed my head into a big pine tree and did not want to admit that it hurt, but my head would ache until evening.

Carrying a big handsaw on my return, I again acted the clumsy clown whose legs toppled him into deep snowdrifts from which escape proved difficult. Falling further and further into the abyss of deception, I tried to enchant her with my playful movements, mimics, and smiles—one-sided, yet, oh, so sincere.

Adoration lay open and visible on the face of a slave in the shadow of an unreachable goddess. Her laughter and joy inspired me even more, crowned by her hearty applause when I reached her. Ah, how I yearned for her tender glances, for her happy smile and her touch. My heart burst with exuberance, but fear mingled too in this cocktail of forbidden love, and cooling reason dropped ice cubes of brutal reality into the steaming brew.

A trace of confusion dimmed her face, and the shadow of reality damped the flame of brief bliss. She showed me the pine tree she had selected. Almost five meters tall, the silver pine grew among others at the bottom of the clearing.

I knelt down at her feet to cut it at the bottom of its trunk. When it fell, I wrapped the branches at the top with twine, tied the rope around the stump and pulled it slowly toward the sled.

We no longer spoke. Silence separated us as firmly as though we stood on different slopes.

I did not fall anymore, nor did I roll like a silly clown. Dragging the wrapped tree, I gathered my strength, and descended toward the sled. I walked with the firm step of a prisoner. Following my footsteps and the path of the heavy tree crown, Mrs. Gottfried walked confidently behind, without a sound or a word.

I packed the tree and lashed it to the sled. We climbed up on the front seat and started for Lomnitz. The sled glided on well-worn tracks, rising and falling over rough spots, suddenly dropping into a deep channel, leaning to the left and then to the right.

Through all this, Mrs. Gottfried held on tightly to the metal barrier of the carriage, taking care not to touch me, not even with her fur coat. This sled game excited me, and I wished that the ice wall between us would melt and convert back into the warm slurry of emotions that we had shared earlier.

But I hoped in vain. The sun over Lomnitz had already passed its midpoint. Mrs. Gottfried had returned to reality, and we arrived at the school without a word or a smile passing between us.

After unloading the tree, I took the sled back to Mr. Bauer and returned to the schoolyard.

Mrs. Gottfried called me into the schoolhouse, and, with dry syllables ordered me to start the fire in the classroom. Her words were sharp, like the jagged edge of a broken sword bouncing off a stone heart. I did not dare to look at her, but I felt her penetrating eyes follow my confused movements.

"When you finish, unpack the tree and take it inside to thaw out. I'll show you where you can find the base and tools for mounting it," she said over her shoulder, as she walked away.

This change of behavior totally surprised me.

Cold, commanding words do not come from an angel. A Nazi woman spoke them.

The blazing fire in the furnace now warmed the classroom, and the frost needles on the windows melted away. Back outside, I untied the tree and shook off the snow, then took it in and carefully laid it in front of the first row of desks. The remaining icicles and clumps of snow sticking to the branches melted and changed into gleaming puddles on the floor. I turned the tree over and kept wiping the floor until the last drops of water had fallen.

I went to her house and knocked on the door. She opened and pointed to the storage shed where I could find the base and tools.

She closed the door behind her before I could say anything. I felt as though I were with the farmers of Prezelle. Unwanted. Miserable. Hurt and disrespected, odious even to myself.

I found the large base and the trunk locking bolts.

Once inside again and not giving the weight of the thing a thought, I lifted the huge tree and wrestled it into the base. It took an extreme effort to lock it safely with the bolts.

I stood up and looked at this superb tree. Its silver blue branches, thanks to the heat, had spread like the extended palms of supplicants, decorating this space with the glorious spirit of the holiday.

I walked out of the school and went to Mrs. Gottfried's house. She opened the door and looked at me questioningly.

"Frau Gottfried, I finished my job. Can I go now?" I asked with uncertainty.

"If you'd wait for me, I'll get Herr Bauer to help you mount the tree in the base, and then you may go."

"I've done it already," I said proudly.

"How? Alone? Is it possible?"

"You may want to look at it. It's very impressive."

She walked again behind me—without a coat—and at the entrance stopped abruptly, astounded by the tree's splendor. She stood there, immobile for several moments, and then turned to me.

"Thank you very much, Timo," she whispered.

It seemed to me that her face now displayed a veil of happiness. She extended her hand as an expression of gratitude.

"You may go now, Herr Timo. It is truly breathtaking."

I kissed her hand passionately, made a deep bow, and walked away with a feeling of joy bubbling up in me.

I returned to the shop exhausted and lay down in the warm room that the children had pre-heated for me. No, this was not physical exhaustion, but some psychological drain that tired all my muscles, all my strength.

I fell asleep in my overcoat and boots, in a deep, sweet dream that carried me on the wings of the past through the blooming fields of my Serbia. The valleys of Morava teemed with rich crops, swarmed with sheep, cattle, pigs, and poultry, in a montage where I walked with my father, sparkling in the golden colors of wheat, bathed in happiness and gratitude.

Fourteen again and carrying the first bag of new tools that my father had brought me from Hungary, I proudly began my apprenticeship in his carpentry shop.

My First Music Lesson

My prison buddies, Rista, Nedeljko, Mile, and Aleksa, dropped by for a visit and woke me with their noisy joviality.

"Get up, you lazy bum," hollered our handsome Aleksa from the door. "Didn't you have enough sleep last night?"

Laughing, he bounced me on the bed. "We received the Red Cross packages, and we brought yours." He motioned to Nedeljko to bring it in.

"Hey, our package is a little bigger than usual this time," added Nedeljko, as he set a sizable package on the bench next to the window. "So everybody's celebrating."

"I'm going to see Elsa and get some brandy," said Mile. "We'll celebrate when I return."

When Mile walked out of the shop, Rista glanced at me. "Timo, you look quite depleted. What on earth did you do today?"

"I took Mrs. Gottfried to the forest to cut a Christmas tree for the school. The fresh air of Dortich probably wore me out."

"That's quite a distance from Lomnitz. I hope it wasn't a big tree."

"Five meters tall and about three wide."

"Five meters?" they all shouted. "Why, you poor fellow."

"No, no," I interrupted them. "We had a horse and a sled from Bauer."

I swung my legs over the side of the bed and sat there, my head cradled in my hands.

"But even so, I had to cut it from the top of the hill. Deep snow, fresh air, long road, and then mounting it in the classroom exhausted me completely."

I shook my head.

"When I returned, I fell asleep like a log—but with sweet dreams."

"Aleksa, fire up the furnace, please. It's a bit cold in here," Rista said.

I got up from my bed, took off my overcoat and began to search for the bottle of brandy I kept in my toolbox.

"Let's refresh ourselves."

I pulled out the bottle and poured glasses for Rista and Nedeljko. I found an old cup, filled it, and handed it over to Aleksa.

Then, holding the bottle up, I toasted. "In the name of the Lord, to our health!"

"For the end of our suffering!" toasted Rista.

"For the King and our country!" shouted Nedeljko.

"And for the two of us!" said Mile entering with a bottle of brandy in one hand and Elsa in the other.

Elsa brought several glasses and now we all stood, festively toasting and clinking our glasses together, eager to warm our bodies with the ardent spirits.

After the fifth toast, we slowed down, and, with thick tongues, we recounted stories of unrelated events, but mainly reminisced about the past. Rista sat next to me on my bed, Mile and Elsa on the little bench by the furnace, while Nedeljko and Aleksa sat on the floor. In the beginning, we all talked at the same time, not completely understanding the overlay of conversations. Then, in an effort to be heard, we continued, shouting.

We always painted "yesterday" with fantastic words tasting of honey, floating on the intoxicating melodies of our homeland and decorated with the rainbow colors of nostalgia. "Today" became a nightmare leading to the gaping mouth of a long, endless tunnel, and "tomorrow" wore the costume of uncertainty, painted with the fading colors of hope and shaded with a film of oblivion, where suffering souls called to us from the abyss.

Thus we talked about the past and the good old times, true or not. Sweetness, peace, and happiness poured out of our conquered souls, and we shared our talents—unrelated to reality—drunk, and conscious only of today's existence.

Tomorrow? Who knows?

I turned to face Rista directly and asked him quietly, "Tell me something about Beethoven and Wagner and about their music. My heart swoons with those beautiful melodies, but my brain captures nothing. Mrs. Gottfried talks about them, plays and sings their compositions, and she thinks I understand, but I'm like that chair that I thought was named Beethoven."

He smiled, stroked his bony face with his hand and fixed his eyes in the distance. Through a curtain of tobacco smoke, he unveiled a new world to me.

"Beethoven's music replenishes the soul. It exhilarates us, as it rises above the clouds, topples and dives into the unknown, then brings us back to heights that can only be scaled in dreams. The length and complexity of his compositions and his constant search for new vistas in music imposed heavy demands on his listeners, and often his compositions sounded strange to contemporary ears, but his output was prodigious."

He looked at me to see whether I seemed interested, then continued. "Of his nine symphonies, you'll most likely recognize the Third, *Eroica*—originally dedicated to Napoleon—the Fifth, *Fate*—which the Allies use as a call to victory, because the first four notes sound like the letter "V" in Morse Code—the Sixth, *Pastoral*, and the Ninth, *Ode to Joy*. Along with these he composed ten concerti—most notably *Emperor* for piano, ten sonatas for violin, and thirty-two for piano, of which the *Kreutzer* violin sonata and the *Pathétique*, *Moonlight*, *Waldstein*, and *Appassionata* piano sonatas rank as the most popular with listeners. Most likely Mrs. Gottfried enchanted you with one of these last four."

I absorbed this vivid story about Beethoven, bewitched by so many new expressions and all the new knowledge entering that hole in my head and planting deep roots that would later burgeon into the fruits of my musical education.

"Wagner, however, represents Germany and Europe in the dramatic epoch of the fermenting ideologies of socialism, fascism, and Jung. Of all composers, he sparked some of the greatest changes in music, art, and thought. His music awakens true passion in us in a way no other composer can. His works are equally hated and loved, but no one can repudiate their greatness."

Rista looked down at the floor.

"His membership in a socialist German nationalist movement, however, ended his welcome in Dresden and necessitated his escape to Paris and then to Zürich in 1848—where he wrote the *Wesendonk Lieder* and *Tristan und Isolde* that I mentioned to you before. In Zürich he also wrote a passionate anti-Semitic attack, 'Judaism in Music,' and showed his true face as a nationalist and a racist."

Rista stopped and turned to me.

"You asked me about what Mrs. Gottfried sang, which bewildered you with its mysterious charm and afterward deprived you of sleep. As a mezzo soprano, she wouldn't have practiced Isolde's rôle, which, when well-sung has brought audiences to a pitch of silent hysteria."

He laid a hand on my shoulder. "But I believe you may have heard parts of the *Lieder* that went to make up *Tristan und Isolde*, where Wagner went further than any previous composer to evoke sexual passion. In *Tristan* he succeeded in creating a rich, chromatic style that used dissonance and its drive for resolution to create tension and deep yearning."

He looked me in the eyes and nodded. "Your response to the music, Timo, is completely understandable."

Christmas Celebration

December 24, 1943 (Gregorian calendar): German Christmas Eve brought large snowflakes to dust the already frozen layer of a previous snowfall. Like the soft fur of white rabbits, the snow provided a cushiony playground for the children of Lomnitz. They happily rolled in it, spreading the holiday spirit of Christ's birthday throughout the village.

In the afternoon the villagers made arrangements for the evening church service, and Mrs. Gottfried gathered her pupils to go caroling at dusk. Hymns, prayers, and communions would parlay the enveloping turbulence of war into a tranquility of present blessings.

A rhythmic tinkling of glass bells approached my shop as I slowly packed my bag in preparation to spend Christmas in the main camp with my buddies. The angelic soprano voices of the children rose above the roofs in a harmonic choir, floating on invisible wings straight to the hearts of the villagers, while Mrs. Gottfried's voice opened the doors of all fortresses, producing joy on even the most somber of faces.

The skillfully woven harmonies of the children's bell choir gave me pause, and the beat of a small drum approaching Elsa's house changed the direction of my thoughts. I decided instead to leave early the next morning—with hot biscuits and the pot of fresh coffee that Elsa would prepare for us.

I walked out into the yard.

There, as if in a heavenly amphitheater, surrounded by small, crystal-clear-throated angels, I watched Mrs. Gottfried, my chest filling with bubbles of happiness, lifting me to bond with the warmth and love of the atmosphere surrounding their group. Mrs. Gottfried's hands rose and fell in accord with the bells and voices. Encouraging her cherubs joyfully, she drew from them the most endearingly natural tones. She trembled and glowed, transforming the scene into the perfection of an idyll.

My throat became dry, and my eyes filled with tears.

Elsa and little Anna Marie came to join me, and alone together we formed a magic circle, enjoying a divine cocktail of anthems to gratify our hearts' thirsty reservoirs.

When the group concluded, we—overwhelmed and full of enthusiasm—applauded and bowed to Mrs. Gottfried, who gratefully acknowledged our rapture with a small nod.

At Staub the next day, we prisoners spent German Christmas in the best of moods. We enjoyed the good food that we had gathered once again from the farmers, the good drinks that Rista had skillfully accumulated from Bauer's tavern, and the carefree, merry company that we had not shared all together for a long time.

For that brief span, we forgot time, space, and the struggle for our lives. We colored our hours with good cheer and danced on a platform of diversions, holding tightly to each other with the elemental ties of a shared past. Tears of joy decorated our faces, expressions of tenderness welled up from our breasts, and oaths of loyalty to each other until death sealed the fraternity of our festivities. Our foamy voices awakened thundering triumphs. With drunken pride and threats to the sun, our silent prayers flooded the dried creeks of our beings to allow our souls to swim once more toward an ocean of happiness.

In truth, we flew toward the year 1944, encouraged by secret hopes, lightened spirits, and the anticipation of blessings for the coming Orthodox Christmas.

Hope?

With the Holidays behind us, our thoughts turned once again to the crazy game of war that strutted on the darkened stage of death. Time passed slowly. An ever-simmering anger called for revenge on the Third Reich.

Then the winds of victory swooped from East to West and brought whispers of German defeat that kindled courage and defiance in the semi-dead eyes of us conquered soldiers.

And so arrived 1944, the year in which hope brightened our expectations and adorned our infinite dreams of tomorrow. But we hoped a hope without adequate foundation, a hope that toppled at the first breeze of doubt, a hope that faded when a flash of ambiguity threw us into the abyss of despair.

Yet we dreamed of freedom and we hoped. *What more can a man in chains expect than a chest full of dreams that feed on the promise of hope?*

My hope lay in my Saturday evenings and Sunday afternoons with Rista. He taught me about music, Mozart, Bach, Beethoven, Wagner, Strauss, and Liszt. I learned about the boundless repertoires of these magnificent composers and recited them for hours and days before meeting with Rista again in our camp. I found great pleasure in this new field of interest. Even though I did not understand the notes, nor the concepts of composition—and least of all the untranslated words of arias—Rista's own substantial education, his colorful description of the characters, and the rise and fall of the powerful voices that he occasionally imitated with his deep baritone, all brought me to feel the thunder, lightning, storms and hurricane winds of these masters. They carried me to clearings on foggy mountaintops, then brought me back into deserted valleys and barren fields, where everything flickered in the last rays of the setting sun.

Then I would hear her voice echoing in the dark canyons of forbidden spaces, far away and unclear, like a night bird that a man can hear best in his dreams.

My fellow prisoners often asked me why I wasted so much time on German music, but only Rista knew the real truth. Some surmised it. Others wondered about my persistence.

Rista taught me zealously, with obvious gratification. In turn, I felt I touched the sublime. I became more impatient and eager, due to this extraordinary wealth that fed my lust for delight. I got to know the virtuoso skills of Mozart's extraordinary compositions that formed one great garden of melodies. In Rista's words, one magic concerto could change from full to empty and back to full, on and on to eternity.

Soon Rista became impatient, wanting to teach me as much as possible, and even insisting on meeting two or three times during the week, in addition to our weekend sessions. But I could not take it all in, so I often switched the subject and asked about the events swirling around us.

Rumors about the growing needs of the German military machine passed continuously through our camps, leaving in its wake a variety of interpretations. I, however, favored Rista's explanations, since he provided the most reliable information about the events around us. Bauer's tavern offered his sources of information: locals gathering to relax, occasional soldiers passing through, army suppliers, escorts, as well as wounded soldiers released from duty due to serious injuries. All these and more found Bauer's tavern a refuge from everyday life—and from the War.

The entire camp gathered when Rista talked, often keeping him going until midnight. He told us about the increasing number of German defeats, on both the Eastern and the Western fronts, about the escalating Allied bombardments, about the mounting breakthroughs of the Red Army, and about the planned American offensive. He informed us of the Allied victories in North Africa, their invasion of Sicily, and Mussolini's capitulation. The news excited and encouraged us.

In this limbo of human destinies, the progress of the war between Axis and Allied forces inexorably affected the spirits of the local citizens—most notably the children. They touted the Reich's successes with heart-stopping pride at the first signs of defeat for Hitler's glorious, unbeatable army. Boys like Elsa's son Horst—who had just turned fifteen—competed among themselves to show their elders that Germany would prove invincible and Hitler the most ingenious military leader of all time. They forcefully asserted that he would conquer his enemies and give birth to a world order most suitable for *all* Germans.

Mothers shook their heads in confusion, while elders encouraged their boys, and Mrs. Gottfried attempted to reduce the number of juvenile soldiers by retaining in her care any older students who otherwise would have advanced to *Die Hitlerjugend* instead of high school.

Some of the older Nazis went to the fields next to the school on Thursdays and gathered all boys over twelve to teach them war skills. They dressed the boys in re-tailored soldiers' uniforms and had them carry wooden rifles. The boys marched, pointed their "rifles" at straw targets, and called themselves "Hitler's Youth," in anticipation of the glorious day when they would officially fight for the Fatherland. Proud of their new duties and their Nazi ideology, these Youths burned with the mighty flame of patriotism, abundantly fueled by hard core Nazis, whose own flames continuously roared in their fanatic breasts. I had known these boys for several years now, and I felt a certain pity for their future.

One Thursday Mrs. Schwartz, who had the house next door to the schoolyard, asked me to help repair their fence. Her husband was on the Eastern Front, and she lived alone with their children, both their parents having already passed away. The chickens they depended on for food kept escaping from the yard, and she had her hands full with three little ones, ages three, five, and six. Happy to help, I kept an ear out as I worked, in an attempt to follow the goings-on with the "Hitler Youth" practice.

The men of the village took turns with the boys, and the Mayor's turn had arrived that day. He didn't indulge in a lot of rhetoric, but simply had the boys practice and learn survival skills—lighting fires without matches, finding food and water in different environments, creating shelters with whatever might be at hand. All excellent skills for any young scout.

The day seemed to go very smoothly. The boys clearly cared very much about gaining these abilities, and they seemed quite in awe of the Mayor.

When the time for "target practice" arrived, one of the boys piped up, "My uncle Kurt came to visit, and he told me that we are harboring a Jew here in Lomnitz. He thinks the man working for Herr Bauer is a Jew. Is that true, Mayor Riedl?"

I listened closely for his reply.

The Mayor took a deep breath.

"While we honor ourselves and our country by carefully obeying Our Führer, when it comes to questions about people, we need to take care not to allow ourselves to be fooled by appearances. Just because a person has dark hair and skin, doesn't mean he must be a Jew. Look at the Reverend Zeidler. His hair is dark and his skin is far from fair, but is he a Jew?"

The boys all shook their heads.

"Of course, he isn't a Jew. And look at Herr Thielke, the schoolteacher in Prezelle. You've all seen him. He has a huge nose. Do you think he's a Jew?"

Everyone laughed and shook their heads.

"So you see, we must be careful about the judgments we make. We do well to let a man's actions speak for him. Has anyone seen this man do anything bad or wrong?"

Once again all the boys shook their heads.

"My dad goes to Herr Bauer's tavern whenever he's on leave, and he always says that he doesn't know what Herr Bauer would do without the help. He's gotten so old and weak, and he has so many heavy things that need lifting," one of the boys offered.

"Indeed," the Mayor continued, looking each of the boys directly in the eye, one by one. "We should all thank God for helping us in our time of need by sending us such kind men as those war prisoners who toil with us on our farms and in our businesses."

Contented with the day's lesson, the boys returned to their "guns" and "target practice."

In the end, we POWs remained skeptical about Allied victories because we could not yet see any meaningful change within our somber circle. Everything continued its usual routine. The men at Staub still teetered on the verge of deadly starvation. Those in the dormitory still scrambled to play their charade for the SS Command. Radenko and Mile continued to wince at the mention of Prezelle. Long days rapidly replaced long nights. Years passed. And we Serbians remained conquered.

Spring Kites

In March southern winds animated the buds of the already blooming forest flowers, and the snow melted away practically overnight. Farmers rambled through the meadows, and cattle went into the fields. Peasant women began the long process of washing winter clothes, drying them on ropes, beating dust from rugs and runners, and preparing the house and front yards for the coming Easter holiday. This year, German Easter[17] came earlier, and everyone rushed around feverishly, as if surprised and unprepared. Even Gunther Zeidler, the Lutheran minister, sent his sexton to the post office in Prezelle daily to check for deliveries, as he fretted that his new robe would not arrive in time.

I had not seen Mrs. Gottfried for a long time, even though I often passed the school. I asked Rista and Elsa, but no one had seen her. Horst came to the shop occasionally, and I would carefully inquire about his subjects, homework, other students, and superficially about her.

Horst took after his mother Elsa. More physically developed than his peers, he had a mild nature and a great deal of curiosity. He did everything asked of him and never objected. His big eyes reflected Elsa's warmth through the innocence of a child's heart and soul. He always admired my carpentry skills and was thrilled when I taught him how to handle one of my tools. Gifted, he learned quickly, so I put extra effort into teaching him my trade. Elsa liked it because she reasoned that carpentry would provide him

[17] Orthodox Easter always falls after Passover. So if the first Sunday after the first full moon after the vernal equinox (Easter in Western churches) falls before Passover, Orthodox Easter will fall on the following Sunday, with Passover taking place between the two Easters.

a better future than farming, so she encouraged him to spend time with me when not in school.

One day he told me matter-of-factly that he didn't have school because Mrs. Gottfried had taken ill. Elsa and her neighbor, the old widow Berta Celler, stayed with her to help.

Although frightened and worried, I didn't dare ask further questions. The whole day I paced, torn by fear.

Horst sang as he planed a small tabletop that I had made for him.

I wandered out of my shop, trying to find something that would distract me from my terrible thoughts.

Elsa returned in the afternoon. From the moment she stepped through the door, I peppered her with inquiring looks of distress and impatience. Surprised by the obvious depth of my emotions, she took me into the kitchen and ordered me to sit down.

From a brandy bottle, she poured each of us half a glass, and we drank it together in one swallow.

Her whole body trembled. "Frau Gottfried is very ill. She has pneumonia, and she's simply fading away by the hour. Old Frau Celler's making some wet covers and massaging her with alcohol, but it doesn't help much."

She looked at me, her eyes clearly red and wet. "I prepared some chicken soup with vegetables. She didn't touch any of it."

Elsa rocked back and forth, her shoulders curled over her chest. "She needs help, but we don't have a doctor or medicine," she sobbed. "I'm afraid she won't last long this way."

I listened in disbelief and felt myself choke. I needed fresh air, space where I could scream out my agony.

With a pained and questioning stare, Elsa looked deep into my eyes.

I went blank.

Her loud voice roused me. "Timo, take another drink. It will be good for you."

Still shaking, she handed me a glass. I grabbed it and emptied the last drop.

I calmed down and looked at her pleadingly, as if asking her to save Mrs. Gottfried herself.

My mind scattered at the speed of light.

I stumbled out of the house and, having no clear sense of my actions, I started running toward Staub. I felt certain they would have the proper medicine. *They must have medicine for this type of illness. They treat so many soldiers for this and similar diseases. I will tell them it is for one of us. I must lie.*

I forgot about myself and my miserable status as I plunged into danger, not worrying about the consequences. I felt as if I flew on wings that belonged to some other being. I covered the distance without touching the ground.

At the camp's entrance, I showed the guard my pass and breathlessly explained that I must get medicine. He lifted the turnstile and let me through the main gate. My steps pointed me to the clinic, with its English and French doctors and nurses.

When I got to the hospital barracks, I found an English doctor to whom, mixing German with a few words of English, I explained why I had come.

He pulled out two small packets of powder. "Give him the medicine with a warm drink. If it doesn't help the patient, he should be brought to the hospital immediately."

"Yes, that would be best."

I did not have time to think about the irony. Taking the medicine from him, I thought how I held the life of my angel in my shaky hands.

I tucked the packets in my pocket and thanked him, then ran from the camp even faster than my inbound flight.

I burst through the back gate to the Fiske's yard and ran into the kitchen gasping for breath. Little Anna Marie and her brothers Ernst and Poli ate at the table and played, while Elsa tended something on the stove.

"I have medicine. Here it is," I shouted, patting the pocket that held it. "Two small packets. The doctor told me that it must be taken with a warm drink."

I collapsed on the floor.

Elsa grabbed a towel and wrapped it around my neck, and then, together with Ernst, pulled me to the living room and laid me down on the sofa. Big beads of perspiration rolled down my pale face, which she wiped and cooled with the wet towel.

Somewhat refreshed, I pulled the packets from my pocket and handed them to her.

"Take them to Frau Gottfried immediately."

She placed my head on a pillow and walked out the front door with the medicine and the small pot of soup she had just made.

I fell asleep, exhausted and at peace. The packets carried hope. I could once again have faith in her salvation.

I dreamed of her vanishing behind white curtains while I held tightly to her bare feet, but she slipped slowly out of my hands. With each burst of renewed energy, I grabbed her tighter, first under her knees, then pulling her to myself, bringing her back from behind the curtains, separating her from the thousands of hands that fluttered toward a far whiteness in an invisible aimlessness. With her in my hands, I exhaled the last breath from my fully spent lungs and fended off the deadly forces that pulled her away from me. I fought delirium and called her a name that I could not remember. Then I named her my butterfly and encouraged her to open her wings and fly toward me. Her eyes opened slowly, watching me through gloom and sorrow, while I called to her from a canyon of silence with the mute tongue of fate's prey.

When I opened my eyes, I saw Mile sitting next to me.

"Timo, brother, it's time for you to wake up. It's almost midnight. Here, eat some beans." He handed me a plate and a spoon.

I leaned on my elbows but everything swayed in my head. I watched him in my dazed state, while he took back the spoon and plate and started to feed me. I chewed slowly, mixing my tired thoughts with dreams.

I felt miserable and lay back on the raised pillow.

He continued to talk.

"You know, what you did was gigantic. To run such a marathon in such a short time! Elsa thinks you must have had wings."

He held a spoonful of beans to my mouth. "She went to Mrs. Gottfried's immediately and made tea for her to take the medicine you brought. A doctor from Walsrode will come day after tomorrow, and maybe he'll also have something to help her."

He fed me another spoonful. "Eat, brother, get your strength back. Your soul almost walked out on you."

I remained silent. Truly, I felt like my spirit had departed through my lungs and I was no longer breathing. Sometimes I would take a deep breath and my dreams would pull me back into a sweet drowsiness.

Mile jabbered on.

I stopped eating and fell into a deep sleep.

I swam down a rapid stream hanging onto an uprooted tree. I saw helpless animals swimming, when all at once everything was engulfed and pulled into a deep well right in front of my eyes. I tried to swim out, but the vortex proved too strong, and I saw myself endlessly sinking. I twirled on the invisible axle of eternity, where, at the center of all spaces, I searched for her image.

By some miracle, or by the crumbs of a miracle, My Butterfly's fever broke several days after the doctor's visit. Elsa went every day and took care of her until she recuperated completely.

Elsa attributed Mrs. Gottfried's life to the medicine I brought from camp, but probably the doctor had benefited her more. In any case, I believed that Elsa's care, soups, and other food, as well as the special plasters prepared by Mrs. Celler, contributed most of all to healing Mrs. Gottfried.

The children returned to school.

Life continued as before.

From some old newspapers, string and dry sticks of hemp that I had collected in my shop over time, I made twenty paper kites, and on Palm Sunday they flew high over the schoolyard. The children squealed with joy, enchanted by the magic paper birds.

Thrilled with their happiness, I leaned back with a deep sigh, while she, pale and translucent as a shadow, waved from the window to the kites and to me.

Invitation

The distant explosions of the Allies' more frequent bombardment tore apart the primeval peace of Lomnitz' forgotten valley. The locals turned their anxious eyes toward the horizon and tomorrow. On occasion, we heard the screeching of armored units with their Panzers lurching down the roads to the West. When that happened, attentions jolted into high gear, as everyone filled with fear and uneasiness. We continued to perform our usual duties, but the locals stopped their tavern discussions, birds fell silent, and only the children spread a few remaining sparks of joy through the abandoned streets of Lomnitz and Prezelle.

German Easter came and went, and almost no one noticed. Closed hearts celebrated the Resurrection in silence, while worries began to appear on the faces of children meeting the first true difficulties of their lives. Spring chased winter out through the doors of the village houses, and the trees in the forests and nearby hills once again turned green. Kitchens steamed from cooking meals and baking breads, while storerooms smelled of dried lavender and strawberries.

One Saturday afternoon, Elsa came to my shop smiling mysteriously.

My eyes questioned her.

"Frau Gottfried asked me to invite you to be her dinner guest. She wants to thank you for the medicine you brought for her."

I was stunned. I didn't know whether from happiness or fear. Paralysis gripped my heart. Finally, I found a few halting words.

"Why... me? I'm... nobody. I wouldn't even know how to dine with a lady."

Elsa laid her hand on my shoulder. "Don't worry. Tonight, you will be a gentleman."

She gently lifted my chin and looked into my eyes.

"As a young maiden, I served the nobles of Hanover, and I can teach you manners. We must first bathe you and dress you, though, and then I'll show you how to handle silverware."

She started to leave. "Come to the house. Mile's already prepared a tub of hot water for your bath, and I'll iron Berthold's suit and shirt."

She turned back to me and chuckled. "My long-legged Mile looks like a goose in his slacks."

As I entered the house, the rumble of children met me. Mile led me to the bathroom, handed me a big towel and soap, and pointed at the steaming tub. He walked out and closed the door behind him, and, still confused, I undressed and sat in a tub of hot water that worked like a medicinal spa for my tense nerves. I lathered every part of my body, so that a blanket of soapsuds fully covered me.

Elsa entered with a soft smile, apologizing, and brought a bottle of Berthold's after-shave. She showed me his shaving set and walked out.

In the bathroom corner, however, she left behind a mischievous little angel who, with her shining eyes, smiled innocently.

I called for Elsa.

She ran in and laughed, "Shame on you, Anna Marie. You're a curious turkey!" She shook her finger at the precious imp, then turned to me. "She does that to me too."

I smiled.

Little Anna Marie giggled excitedly, as she ran from the room. Her voice disappeared in the roar of children's rich and innocent play.

Shaved, with nicely combed hair, in a white shirt and blue jacket, with ironed slacks, I again looked different, strange. From Elsa's bedroom mirror, an unfamiliar face peered out at me as I smiled back. I recognized myself, but that new look hid Timo the carpenter from my view.

Elsa sent the children to bed, leaving the three of us alone in the kitchen. She set the plates and silverware and began to teach me:

"In front of you, the big, flat plate is used for the main meal, then a deep soup dish, a small flat plate for appetizers, and a coffee cup with a saucer. On the right hand side lie a soupspoon, and also a knife, used for cutting meat, potato, carrot or other vegetable. On the left, you'll find a little fork for appetizers and a big fork for the main meal.

"Frau Gottfried will serve the appetizer, and when she sits down at the table, then you take the small fork and knife and cut a small piece. When she begins, you also begin, chewing slowly without noise. You should sit straight, and you should act very dignified. When she gets up, you get up also. When she serves you soup, you wait until she tries it first, and then you can start, silently without slurping. Enjoy every bite. You should not take more than five spoons. That's gentlemanly. They don't eat much, but they enjoy every bite. That's why they are so slim," Elsa continued confidently.

"If she serves wine, drink only a swallow at a time and bow your head with an expression of gratitude. Never drink the whole glass at once, no matter how thirsty you may be."

She rolled her eyes. "The late Berthold used to do that. Simpleton. I could never teach him manners."

Absorbed in thought, she continued, "Cut small slices and chew slowly. Enjoy your meal and stay dignified, always aware that you're a guest in her home. You must never finish your meal before Frau Gottfried. When she puts her silverware in her plate, you should do the same, and then get up and toast in her name, and when you have drunk one more swallow, get up again and bow to her. Like this."

Showing me how to do it, she bent my right arm over my waistline, and pulled my left arm behind my back. And that's how I learned to bow like a gentleman.

Elsa persisted and repeated the whole ritual several more times before she let me go. Finally, she hugged me and wished me "*guten Appetit.*"

Dinner

Darkness fell on Lomnitz as I started for Mrs. Gottfried's. I walked slowly, thinking about the visit, and began to grasp the weight of what lay ahead. Frightened by the incident in Prezelle, I understood the seriousness of the situation and considered the possible consequences. Danger had planted the seeds of doubt, and I felt uncomfortable.

She is not a common peasant woman yearning for a man. She is a lady of the German elite, the example of honor, who proudly carries a title and a name. Why would she risk her reputation? Why would she bring a common war prisoner to her house at night? Does she mean to defy someone? Is it herself? the villagers? or maybe her husband, from whom she has heard nothing in years?

The Nazis enforced blackouts throughout the country even though the bombs fell far from here. All of Germany became dark once the Allies began their continuous bombardment. I approached her house with caution. Only a small, hardly visible light burned in her living room. Everything else remained dark.

I knocked on the front door and answered her call.

From a dark hallway she led me to the living room, where big blankets compliantly covered the windows. She showed me my place at the dinner table, already set just as Elsa had described. Colorful plates glowed their porcelain shine through blue flowers, and the forks, spoons, and knives glittered in the light of a small lamp. The starched white tablecloth had green stripes on the edges, and next to each plate rested a purple napkin, rolled and placed in a silver ring. Crystal glassware and a round silver dish in the middle of the table completed the welcome.

"Please, Timo, would you open this bottle of wine?" she asked, as she handed me the bottle and an opener.

I went numb as I took them, because I had never before opened a bottle with a cork. Our farmers plugged big jugs of homemade wine with hemp, wrapped in a piece of rag. Elsa had not shown me this.

I tried to discover the secret by looking at the spiral shape of the opener. Perplexed, I began to push the sharp point of the opener straight through the cork, but at the first turn it stopped. Then it dawned on me that it was nothing but a screw, and I began to turn the opener through the cork until it reached the end. I pulled back slowly and removed the plug without much effort.

Amazed and encouraged by my success, I brought the bottle to my nose and sniffed. I placed it in a little container that looked like a bucket and laid the opener with the plug next to it. This small triumph reassured me, and I began to relax.

We started dinner with some sort of cheese and pastry appetizer—we would call it pita because of the thin flaky dough. I think she called it "Kuchen." Then she served soup with noodles, which I ate exactly the way Elsa taught me. And then came a dish with baked potatoes, thin slices of pork, and cooked cauliflower topped with a sauce that I liked very much. I cut a small piece of meat and chewed it as Elsa had advised. The potato quickly disappeared from my plate while I imitated chewing with an empty mouth, praying to God that Mrs. Gottfried did not finish her meal too soon.

Fortunately for me, she too enjoyed everything, and the dinner lingered—to the joy of my stomach. With every bite, I said to myself, *be a gentleman*, and I made every effort to look as dignified as possible.

On the other hand, the wine we drank had slowly loosened the strings of my tense nerves, and after a third glass, I did not drink one swallow at a time but rather more, enjoying the pleasures that surrounded me.

The heat of the fireplace had spread through the dining room, and, under my wool jacket and slacks, it engulfed my body, drawing forth large drops of sweat to roll down my back and face.

Mrs. Gottfried noticed my discomfort and opened the door to let in some cold air that instantly refreshed me.

I wiped my forehead with a napkin and bowed gratefully. I finished eating and placed my silverware in the plate.

"Frau Gottfried, dinner was excellent. Truly, I have never had such a wonderful meal." I told her the truth, even though I knew it sounded like flattery.

"Thank you, Timo. I'm glad it pleased you. I've also prepared a cake from modest ingredients. Instead of chocolate, I topped it with honey. I hope you'll like it."

"I'll enjoy everything, as I have up to now," I blurted out, asking myself where I found the courage to flatter. *Is it the wine? Or my peasant impudence that dares?*

She returned with a rectangular plate carrying a beautifully decorated pecan torte, topped with honey that shone in nuanced yellows. She cut a slice and served me.

The first bite intoxicated me, and I smiled, my eyes wide and glowing.

On her face a lovely expression of joy appeared as she took her first bite.

Her image so bewitched me that I stopped eating. I watched her, enchanted by her beauty, her charm, and her noble perfection.

She looked at me, smiled and continued to enjoy the taste.

I turned toward the piano so that she would not take me for an idiot to stare at her for so long. My head rotated but my eyes still locked on her.

Finally I got hold of myself and instead let my thoughts wander toward the piano and Beethoven. Rista loved him so much that he often sang fragments from "Ode to Joy" when he needed to cheer himself. He had thus locked much of the melody in my memory, and I began unconsciously to hum something similar to that.

Even today, I can't imagine how and why Beethoven's notes came from my mouth, but I caught an astounded look on Mrs. Gottfried's face as she eyed me with disbelief. I stopped and bowed my head, ashamed.

She got up from her chair and sat at the piano. She looked at me, as if expecting to hear my voice, and then began to play slowly and softly the most exhilarating sonata.

I drowned in the sounds, and then lifted my head high, as though catching the highest notes that floated above the melody would bring air to my lungs.

I shivered. Then I began to whisper the familiar tones, while she played louder, encouraging me with her eyes.

My joy and her happiness entwined in a surge of all our unacknowledged feelings, splashing forceful waves against the barriers of temptation in a foaming rage to break the high walls between us.

Beethoven's sonata had turned my lunatic desires into a volcanic eruption of emotion. My enamored heart bolted lightning looks, sparks of longing, and tremors of the soul. *If only I could touch her with my fiery lips.*

Again I floated slowly on the scales of the angelic melody, closing my eyes, intoxicated, vanishing to the unknown realms of this magnificent musical orgy. I became all at once her audience, her admirer, and her spirit. The dance of her fingers bewitched me. The captivating sounds that I now truly understood in their rightful greatness had created an enchanted circle where only the two of us existed beyond the rude walls of reality.

Never before had I felt such sublime euphoria.

My thoughts wandered incoherently. My eyes became glued to her face. My heart pounded. I inhaled her scent.

She turned around suddenly and looked at me seductively. I felt the penetration of her enflaming eyes as I sank slowly in a sweet empty dream.

Then I disappeared from the scene of her concert and stepped into darkness.

Her soft voice woke me. "Timo. Timo."

She held a small flask under my nose.

I opened my eyes, confused. I was lying on a loveseat next to an open window.

"You were probably overcome by the heat."

She set the flask aside. "I removed your jacket and opened the window to get some fresh air."

She crossed the room to retrieve a pillow and placed it beneath my head. "This furnace always heats excessively."

She perched beside me on the edge of the sofa. "How do you feel?"

"Good. I don't understand. What happened?"

"You fainted. I laid you down on the sofa."

I made a move to sit up.

"Don't get up. I'll make you some tea."

She rose, closed the window, and went into the kitchen.

I stared at the ceiling.

Why had I fainted? Fear of the impossible? Timo the carpenter and Mrs. Gottfried? All invented, all a fantasy.

Crazy!

I got up slowly and leaned on a chair. I felt as though I would again sink in the darkness. I took my seat at the table.

"Timo, why did you get up?" she asked, bringing in a tray with a pot of tea and a cup that steamed profusely.

"Forgive me for interrupting you," I said softly. "It was really beautiful. Other than the piece you played for me before we cut the Christmas tree, it was my first concert."

She trembled as she placed the tray on the table.

"Timo, you are extraordinary. You remember melodies and fragments of arias you've heard only once."

With a shaking hand, she slowly lifted the teapot. "I've never met a person who, without a note of musical education, respects and enjoys classical music so much. So much love for Beethoven. So much regard for Wagner."

She finished pouring and set the teapot back down. "You also appear to have an unusual ability to get into the core of the composition and to enjoy it as well as the best authority. Unbelievable!"

She handed me the cup. "Please."

"Madame, your magical voice has inspired me to probe the secrets of classical music," I said, as I accepted the cup from her hand. "And perhaps I have indeed memorized some of the melodies I have heard you sing, but mostly I learned from my friend Rista."

I set the cup on the table in front of me. "In our free time, he introduced me to Wagner, Beethoven, Mozart, and

Strauss, and he taught me some of the themes from Beethoven's 'Ode to Joy.'"

I took a sip, then looked at her earnestly. "Rista studied music before the war and visited the Zagreb Opera House regularly."

"Rista?" The name meant nothing to her.

"The little fellow who works at Bauer's tavern."

"Oh, yes! I remember. The children call him 'Gopher,' because he always carries things in and out of the cellar."

"Yes, him."

"How wonderful!" She clapped her hands. "Two classical music lovers in my immediate vicinity. Really amazing!"

Old Weinlein shouting from the schoolyard surprised us.

"Frau Gottfried. Frau Gottfried. Please turn off the light, by order of the local command."

She complied.

The room lapsed into total darkness.

I felt her passing by me, her dress, like a light wind, touching my knee and causing a storm of excitement to rise within me. Blind to my own actions, my shaking arms shot out to catch her, to pull her to me. My lips burned with some maddening thirst.

The pale light of night cast a faint glow from behind the open draperies. Her silhouette emerged from them and startled me.

She was so far away. Yet only three steps separated us.

"Timo. Night is already far along. I've kept you too late. You must go back," she said quietly.

"You're right. I must go."

"It was a great pleasure having you join me for dinner."

I put on my jacket. "I'm truly grateful for your very gracious hospitality."

She passed by me again and brought my overcoat from the hallway. In the darkness I could barely see her by the exit door.

I put on my coat and started for the door when I felt her reach for me.

"This way," she said, taking me by the hand.

I felt us both shake. I could sense, through our contact, the trembling and fluttering of her entire body. Everything in me was on fire. Lava pushed toward explosion, and I began to feel everything around me collapsing. Vanishing.

She pulled me close.

I relaxed slowly under the gentle touch of her soft hand.

"Timo, you must not love me," she whispered.

Bewildered and stiff, I felt every grain of strength drain from me.

My mind screamed, *I do love you. I* must *love you!*

Her hand fathomed the drumming of my heart.

In a dream-like motion, she raised her head and kissed me passionately.

I hugged her gently, pulling her closer.

We held our embrace for a long time, without words, without thoughts, only the two of us, wild and unreal, surrounded by the blackness of war.

On my return to the shop, I floated.

When I arrived, I knocked on Elsa's window. I saw the sleepy head of my long-legged friend Mile and waved to him to come over. I entered the shop singing broken fragments of the *Appassionata*. I listened to my voice singing Her Sonata, which now, replete with joy, sounded believable and clear.

"What happened? Tell us," Mile pressed.

"Really, there's not much to tell."

I took off my overcoat.

"It was wonderful. Dinner was excellent," I said, hanging the coat on the hook near the door.

"And she gave me a real concert. She played a Beethoven sonata. I enjoyed it like never before." Then, turning to face them, "When I left—"

I stopped.

I thought about what to say, "we hugged."

They both looked confused for an instant, and then Elsa hugged me. She laughed.

"My Timo, the conqueror!" She patted me heartily, while Mile smiled in confusion.

I did not sleep that night. I daydreamed about Mrs. Gottfried and me. Ranging from one fantasy to another, I became elated with the indescribable happiness of perfect love. Inside myself I polished all the rough manners of our culture, trying to convert myself overnight into a charming prince, but my peasant reasoning took me back to my cradle to dress me in rags of shame. I did my best to hide the memory from my newly acquired face.

I had crossed the threshold into another world.

A New Request

Fear and courage make close cousins. Sometimes a man crosses from one to the other and back again suddenly and spontaneously. My blue angel did not call for me. Thus I felt an outpouring of alarm spike through my veins in violent rushes, raising its pressure to the highest level.

My mind opened the door of reality and rang the bells of panic at my inaction, only to have dark thoughts cloud the fields of bliss and extinguish the imagined brilliance of our ideal flame with heavy drops of black rain. With the blazing torch of a mighty love, I tried to disperse the clouds of death from the gates of hell, but my effort drowned in the emptiness of despair.

I wavered between bold overconfidence and total dejection.

For three weeks I opened my door early every morning, full of anticipation—only to close it again later with a deep, long-suffering sigh.

Finally, in the third week of June she invited me to visit her. She sent old Weinlein to ask for my help repairing a sofa.

My eyes lit up. My head began to float away from my body. My every motion became a dance.

I grabbed my tools and raced toward the prospect of seeing her happy eyes. Had I traveled alone, I would have leaped the distance in two ecstatic bounds, but I had to walk cautiously behind the old man.

His steps plodded so slowly, while my eagerness ballooned to infinity.

Around the curve of the village's main street, a black automobile appeared that looked like a giant bug rolling down the road. Dumbfounded, I watched this mechanical beast, covered with layers of dirt and dust, until it finally stopped in front of us.

The sunburnt face of Dr. Ingermann appeared.

"Good morning, Doctor," came from my companion, as I stood shifting my weight from one foot to the other to hurry the conversation.

Dr. Ingermann set the hand brake. "Good morning, Weiny. Who's that with you?"

"Timo, the carpenter from the work camp. I'm taking him to the school to repair something for Frau Gottfried."

"Ah, how is the famous lady? It's been a long time since I visited her. Please, give her my regards."

He raised his hand to shade his eyes from the sun and watch Weinlein's face. "Is there any news about Colonel Gottfried? . . . Nothing, I suppose."

He took a deep breath. "Well, I must go to Zutz."

He released the hand brake. My knees bent, preparing for a forward spring.

"Old Hans is ill. Otherwise I would stop by Bauer's for a small glass of brandy."

I sunk back into my heels.

Old Weinlein shook hands with the doctor and remarked playfully, "Ah, you city folk. Never enough time. Always in a hurry."

As Ingermann put the car in gear, Weinlein turned to go and, with a wave, shouted a farewell, a sparkle in his eye. "A glass of schnapps is healthier than all of your medications."

The automobile vanished in clouds of dust, and we—*at last!*—continued toward the schoolhouse through Borne's meadow.

When we arrived, Weinlein called Mrs. Gottfried from the gate. "Timo is here, Madame. I am going home. If you should need me, please call me."

Her figure appeared from behind a curtain, where she leaned from the second-story window. "Thank you, Herr Weinlein."

"Come in, Timo, the door is open."

The sound of her melodious voice streamed through the corridors of my tense nerves and flowed into a bay of tranquility. Happy tears surfaced and glittered on the golden rays of the afternoon sun, while a smile shone on my clean-shaven, pale face.

I entered the house and dropped the toolbox on the floor, then stepped into the hallway.

She appeared on the staircase, descending with dignity and grace. I watched her lithe figure dressed in a white gown with silvery ruffled lace at the waist and hem. Her hair made two even braids, joined somewhere behind her shoulders, and I felt a sudden urge to clap my hands for joy and delight.

I tried to compose myself, to find the proper words, but the allure of her appearance bewitched me. I stood stiff, mute, immobile.

When she reached the last stair step, our eyes met in full acknowledgment of our mutual joy.

In a moment of rapture I knelt down, took her extended hand and touched it gently with my burning lips.

"Timo, I'm so happy to see you again. I must admit that I missed you, but I couldn't call you before now," she whispered.

I listened to her words fade, and, as if in a mirror, I observed my own eyes, wide with disbelief and wonder.

Instantly I understood the differences between us. I saw myself in the worn-out uniform of a prisoner of war, in all my wretchedness. I watched the withered eyes in my exhausted face drip tears of happiness. And, across from me, I beheld an elegant lady standing on a far-away step, radiant and removed from the bitter reality of my captivity.

I swayed in a clumsy attempt to turn around.

I leaned on the wall.

I rushed toward the exit. My lips whispered words of apology while my heart pounded out the rhythm of insanity.

"Timo, stop!" She beckoned.

I came to a halt before the door and turned around timidly.

She approached me softly, swaying gracefully, a smile of encouragement lighting her face. Her shining eyes burned with inner torches of bliss.

She hugged me and held me tight. She leaned her head on my chest. I trembled as I caressed her hair, and then lay my warm hand on her back. She wrapped her arm around my waist and led me to the stairs.

One step at a time, we climbed together to the second floor.

We entered through a door to find a mirrored dresser standing next to a ceramic fireplace. A large bed filled the center of the room. It was covered in white cotton, with white silk pillows.

I felt her pull me closer and press her trembling lips to melt with mine in response to a primeval hunger that had already burned too long inside us both.

Not even the taste of ecstasy, the joy of pleasure, the smell of her divine body, nor all the sweetness in life could equal the fountain of love that poured out of our hearts to blend in our celestial rapture.

Wrapped in white starched sheets, we shared our love until dusk. After a short rest, bathed and refreshed, hungry for more passion and tenderness, we returned to lovemaking beyond anything I could ever imagine. In moments of great pleasure, she joyfully cried, shivered with currents of thrilling energy, and led me through unknown paths of sensuous satisfactions.

I burned, and then vanished with the last spark of my fire.

And again, after a short rest, I wanted her even more, if only just one last time.

That night I stayed in her arms, filled with new strength, new vision—and new qualms.

For fear had never left me. Life had probably nailed it to my footsteps, so it would walk with me always. A part of me gave in to it. With a quaking heart, I tried to protect myself by mustering an inner peace and a calm face, but nothing I did proved a satisfactory weapon against the challenges I faced.

Sometime before dawn I untangled myself from her embrace, covered her with a sheet, and dressed in my worn-out uniform.

I was happy—ecstatically happy.

She told me she loved me, that I was her Balkan Apollo. She said she had never experienced so much happiness in one day, that she was fortunate I loved her, that I was the most beautiful man she had ever met.

My hands shook as I turned these thoughts over in my mind.

I left without waking her.

I returned to my shop and went to bed, trying to sleep through the rest of the night. But the roosters woke me and interrupted my dreams.

Forest Fairy Tales

The next Sunday afternoon, we rode off in Bauer's buggy. Mrs. Gottfried had secured it from Bauer on the pretense of visiting a school in Soltau to learn about some new teaching methods they had successfully initiated there.

Late June had brought warmth and humidity to the valley. Mrs. Gottfried cooled her face with a paper fan. In her other hand, she held a small parasol that offered her pretty head little protection from the scorching sun, but provided a lovely addition to her attire.

While a chorus of insects and birds chattered loudly, I cracked my whip to drive the horse faster eastward out of town. Instead of turning north toward Soltau, however, we continued eastward along the country road that wound among cornfields, wheat fields, and blooming meadows. Occasionally the buggy jostled from potholes and road bumps, and Mrs. Gottfried squealed and snuggled closer to me.

With our heightened sensitivity, we delighted in the beauty of the scenery. We deeply inhaled the fresh mountain air. We passed the chapel and headed toward Dortich Forest. Once we passed the first rows of pines, the tall trees' shadows surrounded us with coolness.

The squeeze of her hand made me quiver.

We stopped at the clearing where we had cut the Christmas tree. We laid out a blanket and sat there, enchanted by both the panorama and our own enormous outpouring of love and desire.

A crystal mountain creek babbled near us. Its water, clear as the morning sky, fell over a precipice to dazzle the air and mix the occasional voices of forest birds with all the pleasures emanating from our unknown depths as they surfaced from the primordial veins of our passion.

We bathed in the cold stream, and then hid in a thick cover of low pine trees, wrapped only in towels and thoughts of eternity.

My eyes adored her with thirsty longing, while from her, an unimaginably enthralling fervor continually hummed.

She caressed me and whispered, "You are my wind from the south. You are my mountain lion. The moon that bathes me at night. My Tristan." She continued to lavish me with words, many that I could not understand, but I soaked them into the depths of my being.

Her outpouring of love puzzled me. I believed that God had gifted me with an exceptional body and handsome face, and that many young women had lustily turned their eyes my way in my bachelor days. But the war and captivity had dowsed this young man's natural bloom, erased the scent of a woman from my mind, and locked my playfulness in a dungeon.

What can she see in me? As Nature's serene lavishness swirled around me, I pondered the imponderable.

The warbles of the woodland grew quiet.

Rrrrrr . . . From the north, a loud hum of motors floated behind mountain peaks that damped the roar of engines. A concerted thunder erupted over forests and valleys, crescendoing into the unbearable metal blare that cut a path of *vroom, vroom, vroom, vroom*—so deafening, so powerful, so majestic.

Fluttering heralds of darkness defiantly danced on the eastern hillsides above the tall pines, slashing through strokes of sunlight with their dark wings. The rumble of flying fortresses spread forcefully over the region, pushing the air in throbs against us. Dark shadows changed into an endless wave of flying metal objects scraping our treetops. They extinguished the light of the natural world.

Mrs. Gottfried screamed as I embraced her tightly in this moment of doom. "Oh, my god, Timo. What'll we do?"

Her quivering body thumped against my thighs and chest.

"We've got to find shelter."

I frantically pulled her down under the pines. "Stay hidden until I can find a better place for us."

I could hear my voice break from my inability to breathe.

I groped around, almost smelling my way in the unnatural darkness. When my eyes adjusted, I spotted a cave a few yards in front of me.

Frenetic, my steps kept slipping out from under me on the wet grass, as I scrambled back to get her. *Not now, Timo. For God's sake, keep your balance! Fast and sure. Fast and sure.*

When I reached her again, she barely breathed from fright.

I helped her up and tried to calm her. "I've found a cave just a short way from here. We'll be safe there. I'm sure."

She trembled and held me fast. My muscles shuddered in reply.

The buzzing of engines engulfed us.

"Quickly, my love. We need to get to the cave, now. No time to lose."

I turned to go.

She held her arms in her hands and rocked back and forth, eyes glassy.

"Shall I carry you?"

"No, please, Timo." She choked back her tears. "No, I'll be fine."

She lurched forward.

I took her hand and led her, wavering and stumbling, into the dark hole that offered our deliverance.

Once inside, fear overtook us equally.

"If they bomb the mountain, will this cave really protect us?" she asked.

I could hear her hyperventilate.

"It should. But perhaps we'd have a better chance deeper in."

I tried to answer her calmly, all the while thinking, *what if the horse doesn't survive? Even if we're safe—how will we get back to Lomnitz? What if a bomb closes off the cave? No one could possibly know we're here, and we have only our hands to use for digging.*

Worst-case scenarios spiked my brain, impaling any possible composure with spears of reality.

I am not your enemy! I railed silently at the very Allies who came to free me.

We had heard of horrible Allied bombardments. But so far they had remained invisible to us. The Allies had not flown over our cocooned hideaway in Lomnitz. But now, these hellish aerial fortresses scoured forgotten villages, small towns, and forests, searching for hidden factories, underground installations, power plants, mines, and communication towers.

They bombed everywhere with no concern for innocent victims.

We inched our way deeper into the dark cave, crawling on our hands and knees to avoid slipping on the moss-covered rocks or knocking our heads against a low ceiling.

I dreaded the possibility that one of these monstrous birds would drop a bomb directly on us.

The deafening roar had subsided to a loud drone.

"We must be a good thirty meters in. I think this is far enough."

"Yes, Timo, I feel much safer now."

I hugged her tightly. She still shuddered violently despite her protestations of composure.

An eternity later the motors faded behind the southwest mountaintops.

A radiant spark appeared at the mouth of the cave when the sun again lit the clearing.

We emerged, squinting sharply in June's bright light.

Tranquility returned. Birds began to sing. The stream murmured again happily, and the wind passing through the thick evergreens resonated with hushed melodies.

We stood there bathed in the sun, nakedness—and quaking terror.

After gathering our things, we returned downhill, scrambled into our seats, and set off. We could hear bombs once again exploding in the distance. It seemed as though they came from the hills to the northeast.

I stopped the buggy and listened.

I tried my best to hide the panic in my voice. "Another squadron's coming."

Thunder billowed again over the hilltops and echoed even more strongly in Dortich Forest. I cracked the whip, and the horse stormed down the path in alarm. Filled with apprehension, I drove him faster than the poor horse could manage. Mrs. Gottfried held onto my arm, while I persisted in coaxing the frightened and bewildered animal with the whip.

We came rushing onto the main road.

I slowed the horse, and we continued at a trot toward Lomnitz, our "trip to Soltau" unexpectedly diverted.

I did not fear for myself. I had become numb to terror long ago. But I worried about her. She was so delicate, so tender, a German aristocrat. She embodied such complex emotions and sensibilities.

This sensual being quakes to meet my touch, then changes into a gentle butterfly whose life might vanish at the dawn of the next day.

My God.

Restoration

July brought very hot days. I busied myself restoring an old glass cabinet for the Schneider family. Young Erika Schneider told me she had wanted to restore the cabinet for a long time, but she could not find an artisan in the area skilled enough for such a delicate job. She had learned about my expertise from the people of Lomnitz and Prezelle, and she came to me with a sincere request to help her revivify this cherished piece. She offered to help, to find the materials and parts, and, if needed, to polish the whole cabinet under my supervision if I would accept the job. Her family had kept this stunning piece of furniture for several generations and had become quite attached to it.

Clearly over a hundred years old, the handmade cabinet's engraved mirror evidenced the destructiveness of time. Its loose frame barely held it. The drawers of the cabinet opened with difficulty, while the glass doors sagged on their hinges. The wood remained sound, but the veneer had worn, as years of neglect and abuse had dulled the surface.

I agreed to take on the task, and then dove into the new challenge, ready to prove my skills. We both hoped to bring back the finish's former depth and the cabinet's overall beauty.

I suspected that the old piece held many of classic cabinetry's secrets. I took it apart at almost all its joints and found numerous disguised screw heads, complicated mechanisms, and hidden drawers. I rebuilt the wooden grooves, glued joint guides, removed the thin veneer and decided to take off the surface.

Erika made sure I got good sandpaper.

Although unbearable heat plagued us throughout most of our labors, she came every day, brought paint and varnish, polished the hinges, restored their original shine, and oversaw every stage of my work.

Erika was a tall blonde with a narrow, pale face and a blush to her cheeks. She had pretty eyes and a long neck like that of a swan. Her upper body was quite shapely. She had, however, large feet, sizable hips, and a big seat, and—though she wore a full-length summer skirt—her habit of bending over revealed her large thighs. She was not attractive, but her enormous enthusiasm for the restoration of the old cabinet touched me.

She and Herbert Miller got engaged just before the war. The Reich then sent him to France, interrupting the many plans they had made. Ericka stayed in Lomnitz with her mother and younger brother, waiting impatiently for Herbert's return. She continued to make arrangements for the wedding, prepare her dowry, and take care of Herbert's house on the outskirts of town, where Herbert's old father Gerhard lived alone.

The cabinet became her obsession. As we restored each part, the artistic perfection of the marquetry and parquetry became recognizable and displayed the successful results of our combined effort. I was convinced that the cabinet constituted part of her dowry. She treated it with so much love, happiness, and hope for the life she expected to live with Herbert.

As the end of July approached, the heat grew unbearable. Humidity stifled the entire region. The winds died down, and the sun burned with flaming rays, transforming the valley into a giant pot, where clouds of evaporation percolated to infinity.

Sweat constantly soaked my shirt and shorts. It dripped from my head and entered my eyes. Then trickling over my muscles and buttocks, stomach and chest, it mixed with humidity and shop dust to become an oppressive mist that lingered everywhere.

Elsa and the children moved their mattresses to the yard in front of the house to sleep under the open sky in the cool of night. Erika stayed overnight with them sometimes. When everyone fell asleep, Mile and Elsa sneaked to the orchard behind the house and there shared pleasures until the roosters woke them and sent Mile back to the village camp.

I occasionally left in the evening under the pretext of returning there myself. Mrs. Gottfried and I protected the secrets of our relationship very cautiously. We did everything we could to hide our tracks.

News of the cabinet restoration spread quickly around the region. Erika engaged an entire network of suppliers, craftsmen, and regional museums to search for authentic parts with special manufacturers' markings to replace the missing hinges and locks. Little by little, restoration fever struck the area, and we gained many supporters. Cabinetmakers from all over stopped by daily to contribute their advice about how to return the old piece to its original state—as if anyone could possibly know the proper color and varnish after so many years. Even experts from the cities came to appraise the cabinet's origin and age, considering it an historically important piece of German artisanry.

One day a newspaper reporter from Hanover arrived at my shop with a photographer. While I polished a drawer front and held my breath that my "home brew" varnish would return it to the admirable artistry of its birth, Erika expounded on "the myth of the cabinet"—which I don't believe had existed the day before. But the rich imagination of the participants, along with the unproven yet detailed suppositions of museum experts, created a story of origin that only Germans, with their long history of antique collecting, could believe.

The photographer took several pictures, one of Erica in front of the shop, with various parts spread out over white tablecloths, one where she holds an old photo of herself standing in front of the cabinet, and finally, one of the two of us polishing a door.

The Sunday issue of *Hanover Zeitung* printed a full-page article—complete with photographs—the text of which follows:

> In the village of Lomnitz, the extraordinary restoration of a German piece of handcrafted art is taking place. The tradition of German artistic craftsmanship continues to dominate the world, in support of the ideology of Our Führer and of the Third Reich.
>
> Young Erika Schneider represents German Aryan superiority at its highest level. With this project, Erika expresses all the classic values of a true German woman: determination, faith in Our Glorious Nation, pride in German traditions, and enormous love for the antiquities that form part of her family's German heritage.
>
> According to the assessment of museum experts, the cabinet is the work of the famous eighteenth-century German cabinetmaker, Johann Heinrich Riesener. As such, the cabinet's restoration should not fall to one family alone. Rather all proud Germans should accept the duty of contributing to returning it to its original glory.

Only by working together can we maintain the strength and dignity of Our Great Nation.

In the restoration of this unique antique, Erika is helped by a masterful artisan from Serbia, who, with his unselfish effort and extraordinary skills, is restoring the original floral and figural marquetry and parquetry of Riesener's cabinet.

When we interviewed her, Erika promised that, as soon as they complete the restoration, she will call the reporters of this esteemed newspaper and conduct a ceremonial unveiling before the people of her own village and other honored guests from the rest of Germany.

With sincere wishes for success, the reporters and editors of *Hanover Zeitung* salute Erika Schneider.

Heil Hitler.

I gave thanks to Mary Magdalene that they did not include my picture along with the article.

New Work

Thus the news of my carpentry skills crossed the borders of our region and extended beyond the zone of the local media. It became a piece of Nazi propaganda and opened the floodgates to requests for my services.

The commandant at Staub called me in and assigned me my first job for Gen. Bruss in Nuremberg. He ordered me to take on this responsibility as soon as I finished the cabinet. He issued a special travel pass that enabled my conduct throughout the region, arranged for transport by chauffeur whenever possible, provided a permit for traveling by train, and also informed me that, in the interests of Germany, I must wear civilian clothes when not on duty. From a local tailor, the Commanding Officer of the Work Labor Department would promptly order me a light green specialty uniform that would identify me as a foreign worker. He would introduce me as an artisan from Serbia employed by the Third Reich. They promised to pay me according to the jobs that I would do, and while at work, I would eat in a restaurant and reside in a hotel or in the camps for foreign workers.

This sudden change in my status stunned me. I remained dumbstruck as I walked back to Lomnitz.

Then I began to think about the consequences of my new position. The thought of leaving Mrs. Gottfried disturbed me greatly. Other issues presented themselves, as well. *How will my comrades and other Serbian soldiers look on my change of status? Will they accept it, or will they call me a traitor?*

I wended my way back to the dormitory, and that night I told Rista and the others about my concerns.

"You know," Nedeljko's eyes widened under his thick lashes, "the Commies are spreading their propaganda all over the place here, and the ones back home are even talking against the King and the Yugoslav Royal Army."

He spread his hand out over his heart, as if to keep it from breaking. "They say our officers are a bunch of parasites and that we shouldn't follow them anymore. Can you believe that?"

He looked dumbfounded. "I think it's starting to have an effect on people. Can you imagine giving up your loyalty to the King?"

He shook his head. "You gotta watch out for those Commies, Timo. If they find out what you are doing, they'll shoot you to death if you go back."

"Yes, brother," Mile piped up, his large Adam's apple quivering. "The ones here consider it high treason to collaborate with the Germans."

He rolled his eyes. "Even though we're really just forced laborers or slaves, the Reds object to our labor camp as special treatment for a few POWs." He removed his hands from his knees and crossed both his arms and long legs with a jolt. "They think you have to be a traitor to accept such work."

Mile's statement upset and depressed me, although our distance from Staub provided us some protection from any direct attacks.

"Do you think we can manage to stay out of their sights and maintain our low visibility? Or are we in danger?" I asked, knowing they all shared the risk.

My compatriots thought for a while, then shrugged their shoulders.

"Our work is an everyday occurrence of no consequence. Why should they accuse us of any wrongdoing? We're forced to work here," said one of the men who worked in Prezelle, interjecting himself into our discussion.

"But you volunteered to work in this labor camp. Didn't you?" retorted another of the Prezelle workers. "When they asked for field hands, you stepped forward and joined us."

He raised his eyebrows and continued. "Now you wonder that the Commies accuse you?" He shook his head. "You'd better plan not to go back when the war's over."

"I don't know what to do," I sighed. "I can't refuse the German authorities' orders, nor can I protect myself from communist spies."

"Just do as you're told," the second Prezelle man added, his head hanging low. "We're doomed anyway, whether as

Yugoslav Army soldiers, as POWs, or as Serbs." He shrugged, turned, and walked back to his room.

"It seems to me," Rista offered, "what the Germans pay you is fair compensation to the Serbian people—and probably the only compensation we'll ever get from them in this war!"

He stood up and walked over to me. "So, by all means, do accept it, Timo, and with a perfectly clear conscience."

He patted me on the back. "You have nothing to be ashamed of."

The next evening when I talked to Mrs. Gottfried about it, she became ecstatic because she had accepted an offer to sing the role of Brangäne in Wagner's *Tristan und Isolde* at the Hanover Opera House, and it seemed to her that this latest event helped to bring her plans to fruition.

I did not understand. I went back to my workshop puzzled and confused.

The next day Erika remarked that I seemed far away and not at all myself. I shrugged it off and stumbled through the hours, halfheartedly varnishing and waxing.

That evening when I visited Mrs. Gottfried again, my beloved's exhilaration over my new status eased my worries and convinced me that it was the will of God. Content with her forecast, I felt less threatened about the consequences of my future employment. But a new gnawing concern about her departure for the Hanover Opera arose in its place. A quaking unease came over me.

I now threw myself into meticulously working on the cabinet to distract me from my worries. We finished toward the middle of August. Erika requested that the village mayor place it in the Town Hall, but the Council had already decided to exhibit it in the Town Hall of Celle, where reporters could take pictures of it in a more resplendent setting.

In the morning, before they loaded it on the truck, it stood for a while in the sun, where the play of light on the woods, the warm glow of the new hinges and mirrors, and the contrast between refined parquetry and trelliswork grounds shared their unfathomable past with every viewer's imagination. Intricate marquetry, perfect doors and drawers, ormolu mounts, shiny locks, curved legs, all so captivating.

I stared, admiring its extraordinary beauty. I searched for an answer to the question of how such masterpieces could have been made over two hundred years before my time.

I took pride in my craftsmanship, but I felt utterly insignificant in comparison to *this* cabinet's maker.

Chapter 5

First Assignments

Once I became renowned for the restoration of antiquities, time passed quickly. First they sent me to Celle, where I restored Gen. Bruss's dining table. For more than a week, I traveled from the guesthouse to the General's house in a chauffeur-driven automobile. The servant lady in the General's house prepared me very tasty meals for lunch and dinner and served them to me in a separate room next to the kitchen. With all these benefits, I felt like a guest, not a prisoner of war.

In my free time, I wandered around, looking in all the shops near the guesthouse. From my first pay, I bought some small gifts for my friends, as well as for Elsa and her children. One day, when I had nearly finished my assignment for Gen.Bruss, I happened on a pawn shop where I found a stunning old emerald necklace. I trembled at the thought of buying it, but I managed to find the courage to enter the shop and make my purchase.

When the time came for the next item on my restoration agenda, the chauffeur took me to the Officer's Club, where I spent the morning repairing a pair of leather chairs. In the afternoon he drove me back to Lomnitz.

Nearly ten days had passed since I had seen my friends and my love. I breathed a deep sigh of satisfaction at my return.

The long summer afternoon slowly inched toward evening like a snail mounting Everest. I listened to the conversation among Elsa and my friends, but I could not follow the discussion. I smiled dumbly, accepting their gratitude for my gifts, but my spirit wandered between the clock on the wall and the fading rays of dusk beyond the open window. Only Elsa's mysterious smile caught my attention, as it taunted me to part from them.

As I walked out into the darkness, the shaded windows of the houses in the village released tiny rays of light occasionally muted by silhouettes. Not even my deep desire to rejoin Mrs. Gottfried could erase the beauty of the night from my awareness. In the shadows of the trees, I tasted the sweetness of mulberry. Sometimes a horse neighed or a cow mooed. Night birds called and sleeping pigs grunted occasionally in the dark August heat. Even old Weinlein had turned off his lights and gone to sleep on the terrace under the open sky.

The bright light of the waxing half-moon bathed the path to her house, making my approach from the shade trees difficult and dangerous. Humidity from the mossy trees lingered to further heat the night. Wet branches touched my arms, making them sparkle and glow in unison with comets and stars passing in the black sky. It all danced gloriously in my mind, rushing and pushing me forward.

The light shone over my shadow, as my feet flew through the clearings. With one eye in the back of my head, my two frightened orbs searched for a path in the shade. Although I yearned for her unbearably, common sense took me on a longer trail under trees and through the schoolyard.

I knocked softly on her back door and, with quickened breath, listened for her footsteps.

The door opened, and her face glistened with joy in the blue and white moonlight. She flew into my embrace. Tender kisses softened our cries of happiness. Our bodies merged as we moved into the safety of the dark house, where whirling desires and insatiable love spun off into infinity. We made love in every corner, on all ottomans, sofas, loungers, and beds. Then we played hide and seek in the sweet darkness, drinking the distance between us like a potion to amplify our desire. We came together again, burning at each torrid embrace, scorching each other with unending kisses, and erupting with cries at the depth of our pleasure. We bathed each other, tenderly soaping and caressing our skin with excitingly soft touches. At last we submitted to an even stronger call of passion, plunging into a hurricane of whirlwinds exploding in harmony.

Sometime after midnight I retrieved and opened the small package I had with me. Hands shaking, I fumbled to fasten the emerald necklace from Celle around her neck. In the semidarkness, I could feel her excitement as she elegantly arose out of my arms like a water nymph and floated toward the mirror.

I sprang to the window and threw aside the draperies so that I could catch both her and her reflection in the last lunar rays. I crumpled to the floor totally stunned by this double dose of her beauty.

Her long blonde hair glimmered in the moonlight. Her face shone with happiness and contentment, watered with tears of joy that, like drops of dew, slid down her cheeks and over her divine breasts.

She smiled her thanks to me, and then turned back to the mirror to admire the necklace.

I sat down again on the bed to get a clearer view of her reflection. In the still of the night, above the buzz of insects, her stormy breathing trumpeted her exhilaration. She turned around and threw herself into my open arms, kissing me continually. I raised her above me, and her golden hair spilled over my cheeks. I kissed her hungrily, awakening a new thirst and new desires.

Oh, how deeply I love this woman.

"Did the Colonel love you as much as I do?"

I uttered it suddenly, involuntarily.

Surprised and perplexed, she lifted herself on her arms, shivered, and dropped to lie at my right side.

She was silent.

My heart stopped.

The silence choked me.

Her sad eyes met mine then looked away. "I was very young when I married the Colonel."

She propped herself up on one elbow. "We met at the Academy, where he taught art history. Almost twice my age, he couldn't have children, yet he constantly wished for them."

She sat up and scooted back to rest against the headboard. Then she looked at me kindly. "It pleased him that I accepted this temporary teaching assignment, and he came regularly to enjoy the children's laughter. He entertained himself with their games and foolishness until the last day before he left for the Eastern Front."

She looked down at her hands, then away. "He departed with tears in his eyes."

She took a deep breath. "I loved him very much. He was very attentive and gentle to me."

She turned back toward me. "He allowed me to continue at the Hanover Opera. He helped me in the early stages of my career. He taught me about acting. He did everything to arouse the opera star in me."

Becoming more animated, she repositioned herself to sit legs crossed and inclined forward, engrossed in memory. "With my first roles, he helped me overcome my stage fright. He invoked in me an unaccustomed courage that carried me through all the elements of the drama so that I would immerse myself in scenes spontaneously and subtly. He provided the pillar that I leaned on. And later, when I swept both the public and the critics off their feet, and when my career took me to the highest heights, when I traveled to Hamburg, Leipzig, Bayreuth, and Berlin, he always found time to join me."

She folded her arms, looked away, and took another deep breath. "He loved me, but in his own strange, rigorous way. Order reigned supreme for him. He lived within himself, inaccessible. He didn't know words of love. He never touched or extended any physical tenderness to anyone."

She looked down at her hands again. "It was hard."

Then she turned to me with anguished and puzzled eyes. "Half the time, I considered my own passion for him degrading, impure. The rest of the time, I wondered whether he really loved me, or whether I was simply an object he collected or a way to keep opera in the house."

She sighed deeply. "Before the war with Poland, when the cultural life of Germany had died out, we moved back to his birthplace. I disliked living at Hildesheim villa. The closed circle of the aristocracy stifled me."

She let out a cynical chuckle. "That's why I jumped at the offer to teach in this godforsaken village." She turned back to me in earnest. "As it happens, the Colonel had arranged it all when he realized how unhappy I was there."

Her voice softened as she peeked out at me through lowered lids. "I have him to thank now, because otherwise I would never have met you . . ." She paused, and gazed longingly at me, "and I would never have known the joy of true love."

The pain I had caused her with my untimely question pierced my soul. I whispered, "Please, forgive me."

"Oh, Timo, please. I love you more than you can imagine. Our love is a river without end, where we will travel eternally to our secret island."

"But what happens when the Colonel returns?"

She shook her head. "He won't return. They informed me some months ago that the Russians had captured the entire army of *Feldmarschall* Paulus. Otto was with them. Before his departure he said, 'The war with Russia is already lost.' His words proved true."

She looked at me, then cradled my face in her hands.

I froze. Learning from her of the defeat of the German army on the Eastern Front shocked me completely. She had known it. First hand. I could neither rejoice nor cry. I was confused.

She rescued me. "But I have good news. Friedrich Witting, the director of the Hanover Opera, is my good friend and admirer, a true scion of classic German culture, a nobleman and a gentleman, who has always had the highest respect for women."

A joyous smile spread over her face and she leaned toward me. "So I was not afraid to approach him about a job for you at the Opera House. He wrote me that he's heard of you and your exceptional skills, and he will happily employ you." At this, she gave a little bounce and her face lit up.

"He's wanted for some time to restore the main loge and the decorative façades. So he obtained a permit for your assignment. You start the week before opening night, 10 September, so you'll arrive in Hanover by the fourth."

She laid down on her back beside me, but the excitement in her voice kept increasing. "He's agreed to let you stay for the season. While you're in Hanover, you'll lodge with my aunt Rosa, who lives about ten minutes by foot from the Opera House. I wrote her that you're an artist friend from Serbia, working on the restoration of the Opera interior."

She turned on her side to face me and laid her hand on my arm. "She's replied that she'll be happy to have you as her guest. She lost her hearing, so you must shout in order for her to hear you, but she's a dear, my aunt Rosa, and she'll do everything to make you comfortable. You'll feel you're in your own home."

She looked down. "I too will stay there. But I'll arrive the day before opening. I must practice intensely till then, and Friedrich is sending a tutor so we can work on my *Sprechgesang*. The alto soprano Frau Wilke will arrive here on Monday. She'll stay with me until we leave for Hanover."

She hesitated. Then, touching my elbow, she continued, "We won't see each other for a while, *Liebling*.—Please, don't look at me like that. It's hard for me too, but it has to be this way."

She threw her arms around me once more, and, clasping her hands behind my back, she hugged me tightly there in the darkness. I thought about everything, about the opera, about her aunt.

And then, my thoughts returned to time, to the next long week I would spend without her. I looked at her with panic. She hugged me again, and caressed me, softly singing a comforting melody unfamiliar to me.

The first light of dawn slowly entered through the window. Looking somewhere to the east, we both stared blankly at the daylight, and automatically started leaving our love nest. I put on my pants and jacket and sat down again next to her.

I hugged her gently. The first rooster's distant call startled us. I kissed her and hurried out the back door. I ran through the backyard and disappeared in the shadow of the fruit trees.

The village was waking up. Roosters crowed loudly everywhere, while hungry dogs scratched at kitchen doors and barked for scraps. When I got closer to Elsa's house, I saw Mile vanishing in the shadows of the nearby forest on his way back to the village camp. My good old, long-legged friend had overslept again. But no one cared about it anymore.

Sometimes it appeared that all the villagers knew about him and Elsa, Radenko and Irma, and, maybe, also about Mrs. Gottfried and me.

Departure from Lomnitz

Tormenting days without her passed very slowly, though I kept busy helping Elsa and Mile in the fields and at home whenever the Germans didn't have some project for me.

They sent me all over the region to restore furniture, most of it worthless. I did wonders, however, at bringing the pieces back to their original state. Thrilled with the results, their owners praised my work and rewarded me with gifts.

On 1 September, the invitation from the Hanover Opera Director arrived with a work permit, approved by Regional Gestapo Headquarters, informing me that a truck from Uelzen would come to take me to Hanover on 4 September. I did not know what time the truck would arrive, so that day I got up early and waited impatiently on the bench in front of my shop.

I heard the thud of Horst's boots. "Good morning, Herr Timo."

I turned and saw a young man who, dressed in an army uniform, appeared older, different, and somehow foreign to my eyes. I had not seen Horst since he left for army camp with Hitler's Youth.

Is it possible that he has changed so much in just a few months?He has suddenly become a young man. No, older.

A soldier. A German soldier.

"Good morning, Horst. My God, you've grown so much I don't recognize you."

He laughed. "No, Herr Timo. It only appears that way. The uniform's large, and I look big in it."

"You won't join the army, will you? Who'll help me?"

An instant shadow appeared on his pretty young face. He kept his voice low so that no one in the house could hear him. "The entire unit of the First Mountain Battalion is moving to Bielefeld Gartenstadt, where they'll train us as field scouts for special assignments. We leave in three days, and I still didn't tell anyone."

"Not even Elsa?"

"No one."

"You must tell her immediately. You must prepare her. You can't wait until the last moment."

"I know." He looked down. "I attempted to yesterday, but you know my mom. Always chattering and never listening completely."

He took a deep breath. "I tried telling her with my brothers and sisters all around, and, . . . well, . . . But, I'll do it today." He nodded and squared his shoulders and became himself again, the same innocent boy who followed orders while facing his future stoically.

"I'm going to Hanover today and maybe we won't see each other for a long time."

Warm feelings toward him overwhelmed me, and I addressed him with a more caring voice, "Horst, listen to me carefully. Wherever you go, try not to be among the first. Wisely consider your position and choose the closest shelter. Germany's losing this war. The Allied armies may soon cross the borders. Defeat is on the horizon. Save yourself and run away from senseless orders. Only in this way will you survive. Do you understand me?"

I looked him in the eye.

"Yes, Herr Timo. I hear you," he answered quietly, eyes downcast. Then, looking up again, "Thanks."

I hugged him and slapped him on the back when Elsa appeared from around the corner. "What are you two talking about so early in the morning?"

"Herr Timo was teaching me about some stuff," Horst said. "Mom, please listen to me without interrupting this time."

His eyes pleaded with her. "On Wednesday, I'm leaving for Bielefeld. They transferred us to Gartenstadt, and I'll train there with the Scout Corps."

I watched her pupils widen, her chin shake, and her nervous fingers clean her apron of invisible stains. She did not, however, say a word. It seemed to me she started crying—but I could not interpret the expression on her face, whether spasms of pride, pain, or panic. She stepped forward and hugged him, then began to sway with him, like a little child. She cooed words to remind him of his childhood when she had rocked him to sleep.

At that moment, a truck engine roared around the corner. I said goodbye and departed for Hanover.

I never saw Horst again.

We arrived in Hanover at ten o'clock in the morning. We passed through the city checkpoint where they inspected all our papers. They stopped us several more times at major intersections. Then we finally pulled up in front of the opera building. The chauffeur dropped me off at the front entrance and went on his way.

An impressive creation, the concrete and marble Hanover Opera House had colossal round columns in front, resembling classic Roman or Greek architecture. Muses, the guardians of the opera, and one ancient emperor in a chariot decorated its roof. The Opera's main theater had a series of tall oval windows on all sides, and the façade also had a series of similar windows on both floors.

I walked through the massive doors of the main entrance, carrying my suitcase and toolbox. Overcome with awe, I stopped and stared at the tall glittering marble columns, stairways, and balconies. Turning around and around, not knowing what to look at next, I marveled at the exquisite sculptures, paintings, and other décor.

Totally dazed and enchanted by all this beauty, I failed to notice an older woman approaching me from the left.

"You are the carpenter from Lomnitz, Herr Tomić, correct?"

"Yes, Madame, I am." I removed my hat.

"Come with me, please."

She started up the stairs, went down a long hallway, and stopped in front of several offices with tall doors. She knocked on the third door and entered. "Herr Director, the carpenter from Lomnitz has arrived."

"Come in, Herr Timo, come in," a baritone echoed from the inner office. "I'm so happy you've joined us."

A tall man approached me with an extended hand and a cheerful face that expressed sincere welcome.

"I've heard so much about you," he continued, holding my right arm as we shook hands. "It will truly be my great pleasure to have you here as our guest." He moved to stand in front of one of the armchairs and gestured for me and the woman who had brought me to take the seats opposite him.

"Did you have a good trip?" he asked, as we all sat down.

"Yes, sir. The road was good, and Lomnitz isn't that far."

"You speak German very well. Did you learn it in school or university?" he questioned.

"No, sir. I learned your language after becoming a soldier. I had a good teacher, the garrison's doctor, Doctor Cvetić, from whom I learned basic conversational German. Later, I continued to study from a textbook, *German in 100 Lessons,* and lately a POW who speaks fluent German has helped me learn grammar and the rules of conversation."

"Unbelievable," he roared. "Truly amazing to hear such good pronunciation. Apparently you have a natural gift for languages."

He paused and turned to the woman. "I see you've already met Frau Hilda Kleist. She was one of our great divas. Perhaps you saw her portrait in the hallway as Mimi in *La Bohème*? She retired from a most successful career a number of years ago, and we have been honored to have her assist us here. We simply could not run this establishment without her. We've come to depend on her so."

He stood up again and Mrs. Kleist and I followed suit. He directed us toward the door.

"She'll take you to your workroom, and then she'll show you the theater hall where the objects for restoration are located."

He turned back to me and held out his hand again to shake mine. "I welcome you and wish you a happy undertaking. For everything that you need, please address Frau Kleist."

He accompanied us out of the office and disappeared behind the massive doors that—surprisingly—closed very quietly.

Grandes Dames

I followed Mrs. Kleist to a room on the lower floor that looked like a storage room. I left my suitcase and toolbox there and continued with her through a separate hallway that led to the entrance where she had first met me. She led me up the marble stairs to a wide marble platform in front of the main hall entrance.

I watched her graceful body sway in a cadence of rhythmic steps. *Why do men seem so blind to anything but a pretty face? Here walks an elegant form only God can sculpt out of human flesh.*

In striking contrast to her curves, a series of marble columns lined the corridors that led to the loge and lower orchestra seating. A little further along on each side, a semicircular staircase ascended, leading to the first, second and third balconies. On each corner of the platform stood various sculptures—also marble—and on the white walls, between the massive marble columns, oil portraits from the past dominated the area.

At the other end of the hallway, an older man appeared and called to Mrs. Kleist. She turned to me, excused herself, and walked back toward Dir. Witting's office to confer with the man.

While waiting, I decided to admire the beauty of the life-sized paintings of opera stars that hung on the walls behind the columns. Pictures of men and women dressed in period costumes, posing with such animation that one would expect them to step forward and perform, electrifying the space around them with the arias of their immortal roles.

After passing a few of these images, I recognized a face. *My Hanna!* The nameplate identified her as Mimi from *La Bohème*, and I remembered Director Witting saying that this was Mrs. Kleist. The many similarities of the two young faces puzzled me, but when I compared her with the other female opera stars, I realized they all looked quite similar: young, beautiful, and so attractive that the eyes of any young man could remain glued to any one of them for a very long time.

Mrs. Kleist returned and led me through the main theater entrance, where a magnificent view opened before me. In the middle of the hall, several rows of velvet chairs piped with gold cord descended gradually to the stage, spreading in a semicircle, and fitting perfectly with the theater boxes on both sides. The boxes continued the semicircular shape and interconnected from the first to the last, while the last on the first floor almost touched the stage. Again I found myself turning around and around to admire this magnificent auditorium.

Mrs. Kleist spoke up. "Herr Timo, Loges Numbers One and Two will require your attention, and also, mind you, the façade on the first balcony."

She stepped around to direct me. "Allow me to show you the entrances to the loges."

I hurried to where small stairs led from the corridor entrance. On the first loge, she showed me the worn out chairs, the broken arm support on the barrier wall, and a torn velvet tapestry on the back wall. On the second loge, two chairs had worked loose completely and the velvet tapestries on both the front and rear walls hung in pieces.

"That is not all, mind you. I shall show you the loges on the right side. They too need some repair, but these two loges *must* be completed for some very important guests."

Her brows drew closer and her face tightened. "You *will* be able to get them ready for the show, will you not?"

"Yes, Madame. But I don't know whether we can find the same velvet."

"Not to worry. When we did the last restoration twelve years ago, we purchased a great deal of material for repairs and maintenance. Old master Ulmann died a few years ago, and the young Ulmann joined the army, so things simply have not been kept up for a while."

She started back to the stairs. "Nevertheless I believe everything you need will be there. I'll show you the storeroom and the rest of the supplies."

She paused and looked directly at me. "If you should lack for anything, please inform me, and we shall do everything we can to find it."

As she approached the stairway, she continued, "And I should tell you about your work hours. You shall work from six o'clock in the morning until two in the afternoon, and then you are free to do as you please." She leaned toward me. "In the afternoon, opera and orchestra members practice here, and not even the slightest noise is tolerated. Mind you, remember, you need to finish your work in the hall by two o'clock, and by three you must leave the building. This will not be a problem, will it?"

"Surely, Madame, please don't worry. I'll have enough time."

"I do hope so, sir. Oh, and another thing. On the lower floor, in the dining room at the bottom of the stairs, lunch with coffee is served at ten o'clock every day."

She chuckled softly and leaned her head slightly to the left. "Our coffee, mind you, is not real coffee."

She reached the bottom of the stairs and turned to face me directly. "I shall come to collect you, and we can go down to the dining room together."

She started to go, then turned back. "When you arrive in the morning, ring the doorbell located on the left side of the main entrance. Someone will open for you. Today it will be best if you simply get yourself settled in and then get some rest. Is this suitable to you?"

"I have the address of Frau Gottfried's aunt. She's expecting me today, but I don't know how to get to her house." I pulled a piece of paper from my pocket and showed her the address.

Without looking at it, she said, "Ah, not far from here, maybe, a hundred meters. I shall show you how to get there," she replied, again not looking at the address.

We walked out of the theater hall and returned to my workroom. I took the suitcase and went to the entrance hall. She took me down the right hallway and showed me the material storage room, filled with tables piled high with rolls of velvet of various designs and colors, shelves with brushes, paints, varnishes, and glues, and under the tables, long pieces of mantles, oval façades, plaster pieces of décor for ceilings and walls, as well as various pieces of furniture.

I was both overwhelmed and satisfied. All my worries dissolved upon seeing such a wealth of supplies.

About a hundred meters from the opera building on the second side street, Schiller Strasse No. 15, Mrs. Gottfried's aunt's house made an easy walk from the Opera. It took me only five minutes.

I pulled the handle on the steel gate, and the clang of a large sheep bell replied. A moment later I heard the doors unlock, and a hefty woman in an apron and white bonnet appeared behind them, looking at me suspiciously.

"I'm Timo Tomić. You're expecting me, aren't you?" I asked.

"Yes, Madame's expecting you. Come in." She opened the gate widely for me to pass.

I presumed this was not Mrs. Gottfried's aunt, but her servant, so I simply followed her through the yard. Upon entering the house, we passed through a small hallway, then into a big salon with lounge chairs, ottomans and tables.

On one of the tables, a porcelain teapot steamed merrily. A very dignified woman, dressed in a beautiful brocade gown with white embroidered collar and cuffs, neatly arranged blond hair with streaks of gray, a tasteful brooch, a string of pearls, gold earrings, bracelets on both wrists, and rings with azure stones, sat quietly. She was quite elegant.

When she saw me enter, she stood up and approached me, extending her arm. I took her hand, kissed it, and bowed like a true gentleman.

"Ah, Herr Timo. You're a real charmer. Please, sit down and tell me about your travels."

"If you would allow me, I'd like to refresh myself and change my clothes," I said, but soon realized that she could not hear me.

"Frau Heinrich," the maid shouted, "the gentleman would like to refresh himself before he joins you in the salon."

Mrs. Heinrich turned to me and apologized, then hurried the maid to show me the bedroom and bathroom. When I walked away, she continued talking as though I hadn't left.

I felt a certain sadness for this genteel woman who did not hear the world around her. *But then, in this world of gunfire and explosions, perhaps not hearing might save her soul.*

At the back of the house behind a couple of other rooms and a bath, my room lay at the end of a hallway that led through a glass door into a garden. The bedroom was small but very nicely arranged. Along the wall stood a bed, covered with a silk quilt and two big white pillows, with a small nightstand and a dresser next to it. A mirror stood in the corner of the room next to the window overlooking the garden in the backyard.

I washed with cold water and combed my hair, changed into civilian clothes, and walked back to the salon.

Mrs. Heinrich sat like a sculpted figure holding a cup of tea in one hand and a plate in the other, taking tea with the elegance of a British *grande dame.* She seated me in a lounge chair and began talking, leading the conversation with stories. My words got lost in the hollow space between us, where sounds drowned in the oblivion of deafness. I nodded, listening to her disjointed monologue that began with her childhood, continued with various acquaintances from the past, flowed into the present on dreamy fragments of memory, then disappeared with charming words into a disordered celebration of a time when she could hear.

What an exceptional beauty, I thought, looking at her profile. *She and my Hanna are so alike.*

Exhaustion from the trip and the following excitement had tired me. I fell asleep in that comfortable lounge chair, dreaming about my love, my new job, and the day's impressions.

The Promise

I woke up early—in bed. The maid must have walked me there half-asleep, so I continued my wonderful dream on a soft mattress that smelled of wildflowers.

I dressed in the morning quiet. From the hallway, I smelled coffee. I followed it to find that, on the kitchen table, breakfast awaited me: a thin slice of dark bread, a pat of butter, and a small bowl of jam. I poured and quickly drank my coffee, smeared the bread with butter, and tiptoed out of the house.

Breathing in the calm, pre-dawn air and eating my tasty morsel, I walked joyfully down the main street to the Opera House. I rang the entrance bell. After several minutes, an older man in a robe appeared, looked at me with sleepy eyes, and let me pass into the empty hall.

I went to the workroom, picked up my tools, and surrendered to my job. First, I took apart the chairs from the loges, tightened the seat and back covers, glued the joints and grooves, then moved on to the walls. I removed the torn velvet, the baseboards and decorative mantles, cleaned the walls, and then went to the supply room for materials. When I finished measuring and cutting the necessary velvet, Mrs. Kleist arrived and informed me that I could go to lunch.

When we entered the dining room, I noticed two swinging doors that blocked the kitchen from view. Delicious smells emanated from there and spread throughout the area. Off to one side, a ten-meter long table with chairs on both sides nicely accommodated a large group when needed.

Director Witting and the company housekeeper had already taken seats at a somewhat smaller table. A young woman in a chef's jacket served them. Mrs. Kleist and I took a seat nearer the end of the same table.

When they brought in a large porcelain tureen of noodle soup, Mr. Witting—glowing with pleasure—complemented the young cook and filled everyone's plates. The rich soup was heavily peppered, with vegetables unknown to me, but very delicious. Small pieces of meat floated among the thin noodles, and the aroma of parsley summoned my dragons from hibernation.

During this transformative period in my life, I had, however, suppressed my peasant instincts and adjusted my etiquette to coincide with those around me. So I enjoyed every spoonful, swallowed slowly, sat upright and ate patiently with careful measure—an astounding accomplishment for a man with a dragon in his stomach!

After the soup, they served baked potatoes, along with ground liver dumplings, cooked cauliflower covered with molten yellow cheese, and warm dark bread with sunflower seeds sprinkled on a shiny crust.

Mr. Witting savored his meal, while Mrs. Kleist steadily chewed small cuts of food and occasionally cast a look my way. The old housekeeper chewed noisily, involuntarily emitting loud expressions of pleasure. The general satisfaction encouraged me to spontaneously applaud the feast.

Lunch lasted half an hour, and immediately after it, everyone returned to work.

I felt heavy from the sizable meal but adjusted quickly and began to glue the velvet to the walls. While I waited for the adhesive to harden, I glued the chair joints and grooves and secured them with clamps I had brought from Lomnitz. The velvet dried quickly. I cut and installed new baseboards and decorative mantles over it, transforming the walls into framed pictures.

My love, you should see how the color changes to deep red in the shadows under the windows. Like blood dripping from a tragically painful death in the classic operas that Rista often narrated to me. How magically those passionate scenes come alive when I am here in your realm.

As Mrs. Kleist had indicated, the orchestra always began its daily practices early in the afternoon. Members passing by the loges admired their new appearance, touching the velvet seat covers on their way to their chairs. The conductor took his place on the podium as would a gnome popping up unexpectedly from one of Grimm's fairy tales, and Mrs. Kleist came like clockwork every day to remind me of lunch and of quitting time.

On 7 September, I had just put the final touches on the balcony face, when I caught the whiff of a familiar smell and felt someone touch my back. A thousand doves rushed out of my heart. I lit up like the sun's reflection on the gilt ceiling of this splendid hall. Turning around, my pupils widened to discover Mrs. Gottfried's smiling face and shaking body. Our open arms became wings of delight, and we fell to our knees caressing each other.

I gasped for air and covered her with a thousand kisses.

She whispered, "*Liebling*, I rushed to come earlier, to see you, to touch you. I missed you so very much."

She looked down at her wringing hands. "Every day became an eternity. Every night a dungeon of suffering."

She fell silent for a moment, then, raising her tear-filled eyes, she spoke with a shivering, pleading voice, "Promise that you'll never leave me. Promise. Swear to me. Here, before my opera angels, before the only God of love and happiness!"

I took her hands in mine.

"My love, I shall always love you. You're my mind, my heart, my soul. I will love you forever. I pledge this to you before all your opera angels."

"And I you, forever and ever."

In that nightmarish space amid the uncertainties of war, in those torn and dangerous times, from both hope and suffering, our words of union poured spontaneously into a harmonious flow of oaths, the silent prayer of the heart and soul of two beings bonded as one.

We knew from that moment that we would live our lives together.

We did not wish for more.

Opening Night

Opening night arrived. A few hours before curtain, Mrs. Kleist told me the significance of Hanna Gottfried's role, gave me a history of *Tristan und Isolde*, a synopsis of all three acts, and a general profile of the audience.

"This performance," she said, "is mainly for Army and SS officers and their spouses. Some civilians will also have seats in the back rows of the main hall, mind you, and in the first and second balconies."

She pointed up toward the back. "Kirsten Fromm operates the stage lighting from the third balcony, where you and I can watch the performance in peace."

She guided me there and left.

Soon Kirsten arrived, waved at me superficially, and started working on her reflectors. A woman in her thirties, with breasts spilling out over her thin cotton blouse like a pair of cupolas, she smoked like a Turk, lighting one after another. A cigarette hung from her mouth as she busied herself testing her light board and other equipment—which she occasionally swore at. Between puffs, she guzzled a black liquid from an oversized cup.

From time to time, she intentionally lifted her breasts and looked shamelessly in my direction. When she noticed me ignoring her, she turned her rear toward me and continued to try to seduce me with vulgar movements.

I bent forward and looked directly at the stage and orchestra pit. I watched the musicians slowly fill their rows, listened as they tuned their instruments, and—for the thousandth time—alternately practiced segments and leafed through sheets of music. Behind the closed curtains, I could hear stage decorators running from one end to the other, preparing the set for the first act. The chorus also warmed up, and on occasion tenor and baritone vocaleses drifted from the back of the stage.

Only Mrs. Kleist stood at ease, waiting behind the curtains for the cue to have the doors opened. In that solemn moment, the tranquility of her spirit shone forth, as though she had formed a permanent part of the Opera House from the day of her birth.

Out of the shadows, people carrying dark window blinds soon appeared on all floors. Some climbed ladders to mount the blinds, rendering imperceptible even the slightest touch of dusk from outside. Reflectors brightened the stage, and gloomy lamps lit the walls of hallways, loges, and balconies to direct the audience to their seats. Except for those tiny traces of light, black engulfed the entire opera house. On the third balcony—which had no lamps at all—darkness prevailed, and my eyes couldn't adjust after looking at the illuminated stage.

I felt a hand pinch my bottom and I lurched to the side.

Kirsten giggled lustily and shouted, "Hey, boy, are you afraid of screwing?"

Bewildered, I glared at her. I wanted to scream, *You shameless bitch!* But I could not, for fear of attracting attention.

I moved to the left corner of the balcony about ten meters away from her, and set a chair in front of me as a protective barrier.

A half hour before the performance, the doors opened and spectators poured in. Police in black uniforms lined the orchestra walls like dark statues. With gleaming sparks, their quick eyes scanned for suspicious characters. Beneath ghostly white faces, a parade of uniforms—generals, colonels, and captains—as well as evening gowns of black, navy, or brown, seated themselves in the first orchestra rows. Officers of lower rank and their female companions sat next, and civilian couples dressed in formal attire took the last rows. All of them sat as one, then silence fell on the room, as if in a church—but without prayers or a God.

Once the balconies filled, everyone stood up, turned to the loge directly in my view, and shouted, "Heil Hitler! Heil Hitler!" Then a murmur started and the orchestra finished its warm-up with a loud flourish.

I shuddered and sat down again.

When the curtain began to rise, the violins started slowly as if to tune our ears. Then the rest of the instruments joined in alternating waves of turbulence and calm, until the entire orchestra became one harmonious flow of invisible propositions, rising and falling in a continuous overflow of excitement and intoxication. Following the command of the miniature conductor, the melodies climbed the heavenly stairs, conquering marble statues and pale faces with gusts of whirlwinds that broke open Wagnerian skies to reveal the magnificent décor behind the rising curtain.

In the first act, my angel, in the role of Brangäne, captured every moment with perfection—the expectation, the fear, the concern, the intensity. She filled me with immeasurable happiness and blissful exhilaration.

My first opera. I, Timo the carpenter, am experiencing this heavenly revelation in the shadow of hell, with my angel to guide me.

When the first act finished, after a long and thunderous applause, I noticed that Mrs. Kleist had taken a seat near me. She brought me a cup of coffee that I gratefully accepted. She did not ask why I had moved away from Kirsten. Instead she whispered, "That whore. Mind you, I shall stay right here until the end of the performance."

I was sincerely grateful.

She noticed and smiled discretely.

The second and third acts passed like a dream. I followed each scene as though bewitched, overwhelmed by the sad story of the lovers. I imagined Mrs. Gottfried and myself in the unfortunate roles and wished for a knight's ending.

The final curtain rang down to deafening applause from the enthusiastic crowd and innumerable bouquets for Isolde and Brangäne.

"You must wait here a short while until the reception for the official guests begins," Mrs. Kleist instructed. "I am sorry, but you shall need to stay here alone, because I must go down to help Herr Director."

She got up to leave, then stopped and looked back at me.

"Not to worry, mind you. I shall tell that vulgar woman she must not disturb you."

She gave Kirsten a stern warning as she passed her, then disappeared behind the balcony stairs.

I remained in my seat, a certain anxiety in my heart. This lascivious woman scared me. I sat subdued, my arms and legs crossed, impatiently waiting for what would happen next. Kirsten slowly packed the equipment and occasionally threw a look my way.

Although I tried to appear calm, I felt like a chicken trapped outside the coop at night.

When she finished her work, she came over, placed her right hand between her legs, brought her fingers languidly to her lips and said quietly:

"You don' know what you're missin', boy." She winked, puckered her lips, and slowly turned to go.

"Byyee." Her breathy farewell faded from my ears as she descended the balcony stairs.

Relieved, I took a deep breath. I shook my head and was trying to gather my composure, when I heard soft footsteps coming from the stairwell.

My angel appeared.

Thrilled to have that vixen replaced by the woman of my dreams, I rose and rushed to embrace her.

I did not let her out of my arms until Mrs. Kleist's voice discretely announced, "It is time to go."

"Good night, Frau Kleist. Thank You."

As we passed her on the way out of the building, I added. *"Sie sind ein Engel!"*[18]

"Sleep well, Herr Timo."

She closed the door behind us.

Everything was totally dark. The opera building seemed like a giant mausoleum in a large cemetery.

We arrived at the house. Hanna pulled out a key, unlocked the gate, then opened it to a slight creaking. When we entered the house, she asked whether I needed to eat.

"Yes, I'm a bit hungry, Madame. But, I could wait until tomorrow."

She looked at me tenderly. "Timo, I'm your Hanna. Please don't call me 'Madame' anymore."

---

[18] "You are an angel!"

I hesitated. I tried slowly: "Hanna, Hanna—that name sounds so breathtaking . . ."

"Ah, my beloved, from your lips, Hanna sounds like a nocturne."

My Hanna! My beautiful goddess! I could say it now out loud, and I basked in my private happiness.

I did not think of my hunger any longer. Embracing her, I kissed her with a passion already sparked at the opera. I picked her up and carried her tenderly in the silence of the night down the dark hallway to my room.

Overflowing with unquenchable love, we entered the room in a whirlwind of desire, searching for meadows of delight on white bed sheets. With every sip of her, I became more intoxicated, and eagerly drank deeply, crushing our bodies into a rich blend of passion, like vintage wine from the choicest grapes.

Flight from Hanover

Screaming sirens woke us. Distant thundering boomed. Shivering, Hanna hugged me in panic. I rushed her out of bed, dressed quickly, and ran out of the room.

I stopped in amazement at the dining room where Mrs. Heinrich sat in a big leather chair with a cup of hot coffee. Engrossed in some picture of the past, she looked perfectly peaceful as she undoubtedly imagined herself walking graciously through invisible gardens. Her deaf world left her oblivious to her danger.

"Auntie Rosa, we must leave."

Hanna's voice startled me.

"They're bombing us! You must hurry. I'll get your bag," she continued, as she ran to Mrs. Heinrich's room and retrieved her purse and jacket.

Mrs. Heinrich turned around slowly, put her cup on the table next to her, and, with a perfectly calm voice, replied:

"My dear child, I am not leaving my home. I am too old to run. I feel quite safe here in my house."

Hanna placed the jacket around Mrs. Heinrich's shoulders.

"Please, don't ask me to leave. And don't waste time because of me either. I will be happy right here, where God is watching over me."

She waved her hand for us to go.

I grabbed Hanna, picked up my toolbox, backpack, and her little suitcase, and we rushed out of the house.

Anti-aircraft guns fired into the sky all around us. Explosions from the first bombs blended with the thunder of detonating missiles and the roar of B-24 engines.

Widespread panic had broken out. Streams of frightened men, women, and children merged into an uncontrollable mob on the main routes leading southeast. Trucks and cars honked as they nudged their way through the wild flood of people. Screams and cries echoed off the walls of beautiful old Gothic buildings.

Bombs fell just behind our backs, booming and crashing.

As we reached the city's edge, I turned and saw a vast cloud of planes blot out the sky. The panic on Hanna's face urged me to run faster for cover in the woods.

The heat wave from blazing fires entered people's nostrils and came out as streams of blood. I grabbed a shirt from my bag, covered Hanna's face, and pulled her down to the ground into the thick grass to breathe the fresh morning dew.

A whirlwind from the blazing firestorm choked every breathing thing in its path. I tied the shirt around her mouth and nose and a scarf around mine.

We ran into the ravine leading to the creek behind the woods.

The air at the bottom of the ravine remained untainted. We inhaled rapidly and looked for the shortest route away from the attack.

We noticed a crowd of people who had also descended into the gorge in search of salvation from the fire. We all looked at each other helplessly.

Crash Boom Boom Boom Crash Boom. Bombs fell nonstop.

Huge bombers soared overhead, like condors in search of prey.

My God! That's my ally's B-24 about to bomb us!

As I looked up into the plane's belly, a huge shell bore directly down on us.

I jumped to cover Hanna with my body. In an instant, people cleared a large circle.

We heard a dull thud.

Silence.

Explosions continued—but somewhere far from us. We were still alive. The bomb had not exploded.

I lifted Hanna up, and we rushed down to the creek.

A stream of people followed us.

The air became cooler. We passed from one side of the creek to the other, distancing ourselves from the last houses of Hanover and from the path of the planes. We disappeared into the pine forest and stopped at a small clearing to rest.

About a hundred frightened old men, women, and children all looked at me, as if asking, *Where to now, Leader?*

I felt like shouting, *Where is your Hitler now? You want* me *to lead you? I am not German.*

Instead I looked at the hapless children, and my heart ached. I hugged my Hanna, then addressed the others:

"It's best to wait here a little while, then return to your homes. The bombardment will end soon, and you're maybe five kilometers from the city. The children must have roofs over their heads, even if the roofs have holes."

The children came closer to us. The women talked among themselves. The old men nodded approvingly, and through the atmosphere of fear dawned a ray of hope.

Hanna and I picked up our things to move on.

Someone asked, "Where will you go?"

Assuming that the bombing had ended the opera season, I explained that we lived in Lomnitz and that we had a long road home. A small girl asked her mother who would take them home. And then they all shouted with one voice, begging us to stay with them, to show them the road, to take them back to Hanover.

I looked at Hanna, thought of her aunt Rosa, took a deep breath, and agreed to lead them back.

We returned to Hanover that afternoon. Clouds of dust and fire still engulfed the city, as people worked doggedly to put the blazes out. Rubble from collapsed buildings blocked the main streets, and on the side streets, piles of trucks, cars, and horse buggies barred access to entrances, gates, and other streets.

We climbed several barriers to reach Mrs. Heinrich's house. As it finally came in sight, we sighed with relief to see both it and the entrance gate untouched.

Hanna ran through the door, loudly calling to her aunt. She disappeared into the living room—then screamed.

Mrs. Heinrich sat peacefully in her favorite chair, with her hands crossed over her lap. On the end table, a teapot and a half cup of tea stood coldly. A smile lingered on Aunt

Rosa's face, the last trace of the happy past she had returned to in her final dream.

Hanna started crying, and I left to find a mortuary to make arrangements for Mrs. Heinrich's cremation. They came for her body that evening, and, thankfully, my earnings allowed me to pay for the services, in addition to a good tip. I asked them to save the ashes for a later date.

We stayed there overnight and packed early the next morning for a long journey. I took another suitcase and filled it with warm clothes for Hanna, a pair of comfortable walking shoes, and the remaining food, sugar, and coffee, which I threw in my backpack. We left a message for Brunhilde, the maid, on our way out.

At eight o'clock, we took the first train for Celle. It was full. We searched for some time before finding a place to sit.

Autumn traveled north with us, as foliage turned from deep green to red and gold. Cornfields turned yellow, wheat golden, meadows cut, and thousands of haystacks appeared on both sides of the tracks. The train stopped almost every kilometer, so the trip lasted over eight hours.

Late in the afternoon we arrived in Celle and walked from the train station to the central bus station. The city buzzed with the arrival of refugees seeking friends, family members, and accommodations. Taverns and stores swarmed with new clients. Germans eagerly continued their daily routines, pushing the disaster out of their awareness.

Police, both in uniform and out, secured every corner, every passageway, every gate. Vicious German Shepherds on tight leashes growled, their iron jaws ready to grab any suspicious shadow, unwanted character, or innocent victim.

Tired travelers, nervous chauffeurs, bus drivers and conductors filled the restaurant. Crowds of people, piles of baggage, and street vendors surrounded the few buses left at the station. A line of expectant passengers meandered for half a block in front of the ticket window.

The departure schedule board reported a bus for Bergen: canceled; a bus for Nuremberg: on time; a bus for Soltau and Bergen: on time at eleven o'clock that night, but all seats sold out.

"Yes, I have only one seat for Madame. A long, slow ride, without lights," the haggard man behind the ticket window replied. "You yourself can travel to Bergen by way of Schwarmsted at 12:15 after midnight. Arrives at five in the morning. If you're lucky, you can catch a mail truck to Bergen."

He inspected me head to toe. "If not, twenty kilometers isn't so much of a walk for a young man like you."

He looked me in the eyes. "So Schwarmsted and Bergen, both?"

"Yes, please."

I paid and pulled free of the crowded ticket line. We walked away and sat near the end of the station, next to the bus for Bergen.

"Your papers, please," a voice above us thundered.

I shuddered. *Did we bring our papers?*

Panic . . . I searched through my bag and found my wallet. I handed my documents to the policeman and looked at Hanna, who combed her purse nervously. The officer, looking suspiciously at both of us, carefully read the permit and passes, then returned them to me.

Hanna finally handed him her ID and travel pass with a letter from the regional chancellor. The officer raised his eyebrows, looked with disbelief at this poor woman and her documents, then clicked his heels together and saluted.

He asked for a minute of time and walked to a nearby Gestapo officer.

A minute later both rushed back to her.

Raising their arms high, they bestowed her with "Heil Hitler."

"Frau Gottfried, the wife of honorable Colonel Gottfried should not be traveling incognito," scolded the officer.

"We escaped from Hanover, running for our lives. Half of the city is destroyed. If it weren't for Herr Tomić, who knows whether I would even be alive right now?" Hanna replied.

"I apologize, Madame. I did not wish to offend. We'll arrange for your comfortable return home."

He turned and beckoned two uniformed soldiers with machine guns, who ran over to him and stopped at attention.

"Send Emil here with a car," he ordered, then turned back to Hanna.

"Frau Gottfried, one of our vehicles will take you home. You still live in Lomnitz, no?"

"Yes," answered Hanna, surprised by this gesture.

"Please, get your luggage ready. You'll leave right away."

I stood up and handed over both suitcases. She looked at me, wondering, then addressed him:

"This gentleman will travel with me also?"

"No, Madame. He'll travel by bus."

His curt reply made my position quite clear.

"Please. Take my ticket." She hurriedly placed her ticket in my hand.

I bowed slightly to offer my thanks. *We dare not raise any suspicion.*

"I wish you happy travels, Herr Tomić. Please allow me to make your trip easier for you by taking your tools with my luggage," she said confidently.

I looked at the officer, who nodded approvingly, then I formally thanked her.

The automobile stopped in front of us, and she slumped in, eyes vacant with fatigue, while the chauffeur loaded the luggage. At the salute of the two Nazis, the automobile departed, followed by the curious looks of nearby travelers.

I put the ticket in my pocket and walked to the restaurant, relieved and pleased.

My Hanna is safe.

I ordered coffee and a sandwich, then sat at an empty table in the smoke-filled room. The smells of food, tobacco, and beer irritated my nostrils, as I foggily eyed travelers wending their ways through the crowds.

Eleven o'clock struck from the town hall as I boarded the bus for Bergen. We rolled slowly without headlights on a long, dark road. For a while I watched the markings along our way, following the curved shadows in front of the bus. I bounced constantly in my seat but finally fell into a deep sleep—deep nightmare—of the previous day's events.

We arrived in the small town of Bergen at one thirty in the morning. I stepped off the bus into an area that slept in complete darkness under cloudy skies. Behind the walls of perdition that surrounded the nearby concentration camp, silence stifled the last cries of the dying. A dog barked inside a fenced yard, but the yapping died quickly in the deathly stillness.

I shuddered and hurried down the main road to Lomnitz—undoubtedly the only well-fed traveler passing without an escort near this terrible death camp. Memories of dying skeletons and screaming cannibals in a crazy dance of demons besieged me. Frightened, I walked briskly on tiptoes, trying to muffle the thumping of my boots, praying to God to take me far from those evil ghosts. I did not look back, fearing that shadows followed me.

Soon I found myself at the edge of town, leaping with long steps toward Belsen. This tiny village also slept deeply, and I passed through undetected by their dogs.

Entering Lomnitz I finally felt at peace. My heart began to calm. I took a deep breath and thanked God for hearing my prayer.

I went to bed at dawn and fell fast asleep.

Pendulum

It was a bitter homecoming. The vicious winds of maniacal power returned to our valley with a stormy vengeance. Raging heedlessly, the logic of the Final Solution permeated all aspects of the Third Reich, as it fell in step with Nazi ideology. Changes came swiftly and brutally.

For us, it started at the top. An SS commander, Wilhelm Heller, replaced the old army commander at Staub. He immediately cut all tacit exemptions, brought back discipline and terror, and reduced food rations to a minimum. He gave orders to shoot to kill any prisoner caught trying to escape. He began punishing prisoners by making them stand in wooden sandals in the open yard, even when north winds froze their toes and legs up to their knees. Our workday started again at six o'clock in the morning and ended at six o'clock in the evening. He allowed only a few measly pieces of wood for heating the barracks, and that only on Sunday. We even suspected him of holding our mail, since no one seemed to receive any anymore.

Regulations rained down on our farm workforce like a hailstorm from a clear sky. The new rules forbade us from conversing with the locals. The SS caught our guard, poor

Stefan, sleeping at his lover's nest in Prezelle and sent him to the Eastern front the very same day. They replaced him with two harsh guards.

Heller took away my status and benefits and revoked my travel passes. I had to sleep in the dormitory and be escorted by a guard on every trip I took outside of Lomnitz.

They caught Radenko sleeping with Irma and hauled them both away, along with all three of the children. We had no idea what happened to any of them.

Autumn snaked by as we maneuvered to adapt to the new conditions. Uniforms ripped and boots wore out. Underwear shredded into rags. Prisoners carefully burned their Sunday log to the last spark and soaked up every grain of heat with the rags they wore, their exhausted bodies, and their blankets. The rules now forbade wearing civilian clothes, even peasant's vests and rubber boots, so we had no alternatives.

In these terrible times, however, the farmers of Lomnitz found a way around the new directives. They began to provide us food for dinner and breakfast—that we consumed to the last crumb—and over time they more and more frequently requested our services for work in the barns, silos, basements, and attics, bribing the guards with good food and strong brandy. The patience of these good people finally prevailed in our favor, and the guards loosened their vile grip after a few months.

As time went on, we, the Lomnitz laborers, came to have greater privileges than those of Prezelle, and we took maximum advantage of them. The guards did not oversee us much anymore, and they even let us return by ourselves, on time, while they continued to escort the other group of laborers to and from Prezelle.

Later, when the winter set in hard, they even let us go to work by ourselves, while they still accompanied the Prezelle workers both coming and going.

The seven of us had conquered the hearts of the Lomnitz people, while the twenty-one others ran into an iceberg that could not be melted.

Winter arrived and, in these new circumstances, the north wind's mighty gusts reminded us of our horrible first year as POWs. Memories of the last screams of the dying, of the primeval hunger, of the despair in the eyes of underground slaves, and of the eternal prayers for salvation, all haunted us with each tick of the clock.

I finally got the opportunity to see my Hanna. One day in December, after a long and painful separation, Elsa brought a message from her that she would wait for me at ten o'clock the next morning. My heart filled with joy.

At the appointed hour, I took my toolbox and went to her back door unnoticed. My face beamed when Hanna appeared at the door. Although I looked ragged and miserable, I stood proud and confident.

When the door closed, we fell into a long embrace, soaking in each other's passion. Tears rolled down her face, and adoration poured out after every sob. I followed her upstairs to enjoy with her the passion of our great love, and in our happiness we almost forgot that I needed to return at the end of the day.

When the shadow of dusk entered her room, she jumped from bed and reminded me that I would have to go back. She dressed me in the Colonel's warm undershirt and put his warm wool socks on my feet.

I left her, a bit astounded, but with so much happiness, sadness, and fear in my heart. I arrived at the village camp before the others and started a fire in the furnace with wood I had earlier brought from Elsa's.

I leaned on the wall and reveled in my thoughts. Then I crossed myself.

Alone and surrounded by a veil of fear, I whispered my prayer to the Divine. "Please, save my Hanna, Almighty God! Don't let evil and damnation overtake her."

Above the dark clouds of winter, Allied airplanes swarmed. They bombed Lower Saxony daily, spreading frustration and fear among the residents. Sirens howled panic, driving waves of residents to underground bunkers, basements, and nearby forest caves.

Nevertheless farmers covered their heads with big hats, their ears with wool muffs, and their faces with thick scarves, then went about their winter duties with the cattle, poultry, and pigs, never lifting their eyes to the skies.

I continued to meet Hanna at every suitable opportunity. Sometimes during school recess she went to Elsa's, where we would spend several sweet moments in Elsa's bedroom. Hanna ran to the house from school and threw herself in my arms at the door, absorbing my body heat, whispering words of love. I would hug her and kiss her, speaking my words of tenderness. Even a single minute together made us happy.

Our faithful Elsa kept a watchful eye, guarding us from any danger, and reminding us when to part.

Each time she left I would heave a deep sigh.

Day after day my countrymen in Staub died from the cold and from the hard conditions of captivity. When the news of these terrible truths reached us, we fell into despair and prayed for their unfortunate souls.

As they retreated from fierce Allied attacks, the recently crowned German conquerors turned into hordes of defeated, hysterical madmen who pillaged the occupied countries. Within Germany, traumatized soldiers joined SS butchers in a killing epidemic that rained disaster on innocents. East winds increasingly spread the white ash of human remains over the region, turning the last traces of erased existence into clouds of gloom. Reality became a vivid nightmare. To save a life became our only goal.

Deputy Sonnenfeld

One cold Wednesday morning in early January, Mayor Riedl sent for me to repair some furniture in the old Lomnitz Town Hall. At nine o'clock I entered the Mayor's office and found Mr. Riedl feeding dry wood into the upright ceramic furnace. At five foot ten, he dominated most of the townspeople by height alone, but his deep-set eyes and protruding lower lip belied a thinking man, a man who commanded respect by dint of his wisdom. He turned around, motioned for me to sit and, without looking back, closed the furnace door.

His face showed signs of distress.

It had saddened me to notice lately the same torment on the faces of many people in Lomnitz and the surrounding area. Their behavior and their conversations also reflected their pain.

He spoke to me absentmindedly.

"Timo, we have some work for you here."

He set his hand on top of his desk.

"My desk is falling apart and a couple benches in the main hall need repair."

He stopped, looked out the window, and then back at me, "The Regional Deputy from the military office in Celle is scheduled to meet with me and Mrs. Gottfried at 1p.m."

My curiosity exploded with the mention of Hanna. My ears sharpened and my eyes opened wider.

He didn't look at me. He stood deep in his own thoughts, his mouth slightly twisted with words that wanted to come but didn't.

After a minute or so, he turned to me. "Do you think you can do it all before he arrives?"

"I don't know. I'll have to see how much work there is."

"Well, if you can't finish everything by then, please do the desk first and then repair the benches. We'll have our meeting in my office, and if you still need to finish up here, I'd appreciate your continuing quietly."

"Yes, Sir, Your Honor. I'll certainly keep very quiet."

I moved toward the desk. "If you don't mind, I'd like to look at your desk and the benches to see what's needed. Then I'll bring my tools and the materials for the repair."

"Go ahead, please. I'll get out of your way."

The Mayor stepped over to the window, deep in thought.

I approached the giant antique piece, clearly long overdue for repairs. I pulled the side legs lightly and noticed loose joints. I opened the center and side drawers, where most of the front fascia had pulled away from the frame. But further examination of the piece revealed nothing more.

I looked up at the Mayor and said confidently, "This shouldn't take long. It just needs some regluing."

I stood back up and dusted off my hands. "It should set in a couple of hours, but I'll tack on some temporary braces to make sure it holds."

"Wonderful."

He pointed to the door leading into the main hall.

"We removed the benches from the front row and placed them to the side. They're rather long, and I wonder if you might need some help with them."

"I don't think so, Sir. But, if I do, I can bring one of my colleagues."

"Right. Go to it, then. You'll need to start the fire in the Hall's furnace. Although, it does get some heat from the air pipe of this furnace, you'll find it awfully cold in there."

"Thank you, Sir. Please, don't worry. I'll complete everything quickly and quietly."

I walked into the adjacent room and closed the door behind me. Some logs lay next to the stove. I lit the fire, then fed it a few pieces. The dry wood flamed up quickly, and the furnace started rumbling and crackling almost immediately.

I disassembled the two benches and laid the pieces on the floor.

I knocked on the Mayor's door and waited.

He came out, looked at the pieces, then at me.

"I'm going back to the shop for my tools and some glue. May I use the main entrance? Is it open?"

"Yes, it is."

"Please keep an eye on the furnace," I said, as I started for the exit.

"I will, and I'll also leave my office door open so you can get started on my desk."

The Town Hall clock announced 9:30a.m. when I returned. I fed the furnace more wood, then went into the Mayor's office through the open door. He had stepped out. The furnace in the office crackled joyfully. The heat rose to the ceiling and high windows, where cold droplets of moisture had formed.

I took off my jacket and started to work on the desk. I used a couple of chairs and some wood blocks to support the massive top when I removed the side legs. I quickly brushed homemade glue into the joints and legs, then pushed them back together and locked clamps to the sides and top to let it all dry. I pulled the drawers out and separated the front panels, brushed generous amounts of glue on it all, then put it back together. I clamped them tightly and set them near the furnace.

The Mayor returned and looked at the joints in amazement.

"Herr Timo!" he said admiringly. "You work very quickly."

"Thank you, Your Honor. Your desk is very heavy. It requires strong support, so I need to wait a couple hours before I can brace the legs with wood and screws. But I can still finish that before noon. Meanwhile, I'll work on the benches and hopefully complete everything before the gentleman arrives."

"Well, if you haven't, you'll be working in the other room anyway, so you shouldn't disturb us," the Mayor reassured me.

The robot-like work on the benches left my mind free to wonder why they had summoned Hanna. I shivered with fear that someone may have informed on us. I bit my thumb at the memory of the scene in Prezelle. My body twisted in pain, and I would have screamed if the hand in my mouth hadn't prevented it. Hallucinations and panic badgered my brain.

Can our life be any harder? The torment worsened. The suffering escalated. Time only hastened the executioner.

God! If we must die, let us die together in dignity. She is the princess and I am the pauper, but our love . . .

The Town Hall clock clanged noon, arousing me from my desperate daydreams and mechanical bench-mending. I rushed into the Mayor's office, secured the earlier-made braces to the desk and screwed them tightly together.

Since the Mayor had evidently gone home for lunch, I checked the desk by sitting on it. Then I pulled and pushed it to test the strength of the joints and braces, and, when fully satisfied, I stepped back into the main hall, leaving the office door slightly open.

At 12:30 I moved the repaired benches to their original position and rushed to secure the joints with wooden braces.

Time ticked loudly. My heart banged louder.

I packed the tools and materials, and then placed them in the hallway outside the main entrance.

Upon my return, I heard the screeching sound of an automobile stopping in front of the building. I heard a car door slam and boots pound the wooden platform around the Town Hall.

Oh, my God! I panicked. *They're coming through here!* My heart stopped.

Then the deep voice of Mayor Riedl—who had apparently also just returned—exchanged "Heil Hitler" with another man, and the pounding of the steps faded, as they walked around back to the Mayor's office.

I sat quietly near the furnace, barely breathing.

Mayor Riedl's loud voice came clearly through the door.

"Welcome, Herr Sonnenfeld. Please, sit down. Would you care for a glass of Schnapps, Sir? To wash down the road dust?"

The Mayor spoke cheerfully, obviously trying to lighten the mood.

The man didn't answer.

"Mrs. Gottfried will soon be here. Her classes end at 1p.m."

The school bell rang and the voices of children immediately erupted.

I listened intently.

At last the soft steps of her boots walked toward the back of the building and entered the Mayor's office. I heard chairs moving and the clicking of heels.

"Heil Hitler, Frau Gottfried!" A man's strangely shrill voice came through the wall.

"Heil Hitler, Deputy Sonnenfeld. How can we help you?" Her sure, steady voice echoed out to me.

Hearing her firm confidence dismantled my cage of fear.

That's my Hanna. Brave as a trooper.

The Deputy coughed lightly.

"Frau Gottfried. Our office has determined that students from your school district, especially from the town of Lomnitz, have not reported for military youth camp after finishing middle school. It is mandatory that all students of fourteen and over report to military training camp. *Die Hitlerjugend* is our future military force, and we must all take equal responsibility for their proper training, as well as for their instruction in Our Führer's illustrious ideology. We must all make an example to our children of what it means to be loyal citizens of Our Glorious Nation and to obey orders from Our Führer."

He cleared his throat.

"I understand that you have extended the schooling of seven students beyond their recruitment age, and that they continue to attend the same classes as in the previous grade year. Can you please explain that, Frau Gottfried?"

Silence.

I held my breath.

Mayor Riedl rumbled something I could not understand, and then I heard her crisp, vibrant voice.

"Herr Sonnenfeld, with all due respect, the seven boys you have on your list all have fathers who not long ago left their bones somewhere on Russian soil. They have no older brothers nor sisters to take care of their farms, to raise their crops, and put food on their tables. Their mothers have exhausted themselves raising their younger siblings and trying simply to survive."

She paused.

"You tell us to teach them loyalty and obedience, but you don't tell us how they will feed their families if they become soldiers. To you, these boys constitute nothing more than names on a list. To Lomnitz and their families, they have become sole providers, the only men in their households who can fill the roles of older brothers, fathers and grandfathers. How will you explain to their mothers that you'll leave no one to feed their younger sisters and brothers, their farm animals, their poultry? What will we tell our children tomorrow if we offer them no way to make sense of their future today? I'm sure the Colonel—"

The Mayor's warm voice gently interrupted her.

"Excuse me, please, Herr Sonnenfeld. Frau Gottfried simply wants to express that those farm boys have become the very essence of existence for these seven local families. Sadly, with the current level of rationing, the townships have no means to support them either, so without the boys, thirty-five good Germans would surely starve. I feel certain, Deputy Sonnenfeld, that your office has established exemptions for such cases."

Silence raged. The fire in both furnaces cracked loudly, like grenades exploding in my ears.

Deputy Sonnenfeld spoke calmly, but with a sharp edge to his voice.

"Of course our office provides exemptions for families without a man of the house, but Frau Gottfried must advise our office of such situations before the boys in question reach recruiting age. We must follow the rules, and neither Frau Gottfried nor you Mayor Riedl can change them. Those boys must report to the recruiting center by the end of this month, or I will send the police to arrest them, and we will prosecute them as deserters."

"Deputy Sonnenfeld!" Hanna raised her voice and spoke with fervor.

I quivered at the thought that she might offend this heartless deputy.

"If I have overlooked one of the Reich's formalities, Herr Sonnenfeld, I do apologize, but I was in Hanover preparing to sing for the Führer at the time these boys received word that their fathers had died in captivity after Stalingrad . . ."

Again, Mayor Riedl stepped in with his deep voice.

"Frau Gottfried, please, allow Herr Sonnenfeld to take all these facts into consideration. There may be some clause in the military books that would exempt them from service, particularly since they do still participate in our youth's exercises here, so they do receive some military training, in any case. Please let Deputy Sonnenfeld's office review their cases."

He paused. "You will make that possible, Herr Sonnenfeld?"

"Possible, but not likely. And at this point, Herr Riedl, Frau Gottfried must thank our merciful Führer that only her husband's suicide has saved her from prosecution herself."

I was stunned. *They would have taken her to prison over this if her husband had not complied with Hitler's insistence regarding suicide upon capture?*

I heard the Heil Hitlers and the clicking heels through a merciless fog.

Rista's Last Prayer

History would remember the last spring of WWII as having the greatest number of casualties per day ever recorded. Hitler's Final Solution raced at the speed of light to annihilate any remaining "unwanted people." Combat between Allied and Axis powers took the lives of young soldiers on all fronts. But the conflict over communist and capitalist ideals also blazed civil wars throughout the liberated countries. Hunger too took its toll all over the continent—especially among children—thus seriously endangering the future of smaller nations.

Although we fully expected continued Allied victories and looked forward to the end of the war, our shackles hadn't become any looser. With inhumane methods rivaling those of the Gestapo, the commander at Staub continued his brutal dominion over the living skeletons in his charge.

I consulted both Lubo and Rista to try to figure out a way that we might ease the burden for the families of the boys Hanna had tried to protect, but Heller blocked every effort.

Despite the return of spring, Hanna and I rarely met anymore because of the increasing danger. Guards, Hitler's Youths, and soldiers temporarily stationed in the barracks near Belsen now roamed the entire region like packs of wolves thirsty for blood and a kill.

I took it hard when I learned from Elsa that the regional SS unit would come the next day to pick up Rista. On the list of condemned Jews, he would die along with thousands of his faith. Now, when I think of it, I believe it undoubtedly pleased him to join his people, looking death in the eye with a defiant smile—but perhaps this too is a rationalization of the horror and the pain.

Rista breathed heavily and sighed, then walked out of the village house. Shaded with moist sadness, his eyes searched for familiar objects, but he could not see anything. Instead he merely sensed the weight of matter and space as he moved across the porch and down the steps.

I followed, not sure what he might do.

Then, walking through camp still unconsciously, he choked from the feverish nightmare. He turned and our eyes met, but I saw only darkness, turbulent clouds of fear in the face of an unavoidable reality.

Those black, sad, unwanted realities.

Oh, Lord, did I err in telling him? Does he hate me for it? Am I his hangman?

I struggled with the brutal fate awaiting him.

I thought of escape routes that might save him—now rendered impossible. The Germans had closed all means of passage and maintained heavy surveillance on all possible pathways. They no longer returned anyone to camp. Instead they shot escapees on the spot—everyone!—with no regard for the Geneva Convention or POW rights.

They will take him tomorrow.

Just thinking about it made me so distraught that I considered running away with him. *But where could we run? Maybe she would help us? How? We haven't prepared. Although we both speak German—he better than I—could we succeed?—We might run into Allied troops. . . .*

I walked over to him and spoke, "I want to escape with you. Tonight. We can sneak through the hole that our men have hid. At Elsa's we can change into civilian clothes."

He stepped closer to catch my face in the moonlight, and, seeing my tears, he hugged me.

Then, heads hung low, we walked together back into the house and went over to his bunk. He sat down on the edge of it, sighed, and looked up at me.

"Timo, my dear old friend, I have no more strength."

His eyelids drooped. He shook his head, and then raised his eyebrows.

"Nor will. Everything died in me in 1941 when the Ustaše[19] killed my beloved Rita and little Rebecca in Jasenovac.[20]"

He held his arms in his hands, rocked lightly back and forth, and then held his hands out in supplication. "Since then, I die a little more every day, praying to God to unite me with them." Looking down, he clasped his hands in front of his mouth.

He opened the chest that sat beside his bed and held his belongings. He pulled something from it, and showed it to me.

"Do you see this prayer apron?"

He held it momentarily to his heart. "I wear it to pray for the end of my suffering."

He touched it to his forehead. "And now, it has come."

He turned his eyes to me. "I have already known for some time, my dear Timo, about this final act of Hitler's demons. A few months ago I learned from my Jewish connections about the inauguration of the Final Solution—" He looked down and inhaled deeply. "—and if I had had any courage, I would've escaped already."

He shrugged. "But where to? My spirit is dead."

He let his arms drop lifelessly into his lap. "My life without the two of them has no meaning. My tears have dried up. My heart has hardened like a rock."

He displayed his arms to me, shaking his head. "Blood no longer flows through these veins. I am dead."

He sighed deeply. "This used body that sways on a worn out skeleton is only the symbol of a past they destroyed in me long ago."

---

[19] See footnote 9, page 77.

[20] A Ustaše concentration camp

He paused and looked down, fingering his prayer apron, then shook his head again.

"I cannot."

He looked up at me and nodded.

His face softened. "Thank you. Thanks for your sincere friendship. You Serbs are God's children."

I looked at him, ashamed. Pride and courage sat before me, and I was trying to cheer him with hollow hopes, to deny his stoic strength in the face of such brutal prospects.

Tears formed in my eyes.

He reached up and put his hand on my arm to console me, like *my* day of reckoning approached.

"Timo, when a man faces Death, his only salvation is in the Lord and in prayer. We all pray for something from Him, to save us from hell, to make us happy, to help us out of misfortune. Some pray for wealth, some for love and happiness, and some for health. We're always asking for something, but rarely do we give back. Yes, He's Divine. He grants everyone's prayers, but remember when you pray, pray for Him also. For He is in all of us, and we are He. And when you ask for salvation from Him, pray for His salvation too, salvation from us, from our damnation."

His devotion disarmed me. While he slowly pulled a small silk bundle out of his footlocker, I could think only of a shipwreck with no survivors. Shadows of ghosts swooped into the abyss waiting for us all.

I opened my mouth, and muted words came out on the putrid breath of anguish. My eyes drowned with dirty tears. My heart pounded with a weak rhythm, while its sound overflowed into an echo of despair.

The unbearable silence of the room where Rista now prepared his final ritual before us all choked me.

He spread a white tablecloth on top of his trunk, then placed a matchbox, a beeswax candle in a holder, and a small Jewish Bible on top of it. From his pocket he pulled out a little round cap and set it on his head. He tied his prayer apron around his waist, put on a clean shirt and, kneeling, lit the candle with a shaking hand.

He turned around, bathed me with his soft smile, and then drowned himself in his reading of *Torah*. His quiet prayer echoed through our souls with strange words of calling, singing, and begging that have stayed in my memory to this day.

"Shma Israel adonai eloheno adonai ehat."[21]

Rista continued to pray, reading from his little book. From time to time he would bring the smoke from the candle to his face and with the other hand lifted, he called on his Jewish God, asking for forgiveness of others' sins.

Tears bathed my face and the faces of my comrades, tears that we clumsily wiped with our sleeves, trying to hide our pain. His voice melted our hearts. We listened as his tender outpourings of sorrow became uncontrollable sobbing.

Then Rista turned to us, talking to his Lord in Heaven. "Almighty God, I am ready to enter thy Kingdom. The serenity of the soul I bring to you makes me happy. I hear heavenly music coming through the gates of grief and into my heart. I have fully repented. Forgive me, Lord, for leaving my brother Serbs to this hell on earth. I pray you, Oh, Lord, save them. Protect them and return them to their earthly paradise, to Serbia."

We all clung to each other in our sorrow.

The next day, early morning on the Sabbath, a truck arrived and took Rista away.

I tried to watch him through our foggy windows, but his shadow vanished, rushing quickly to the death chamber without a sound and without a trace.

---

[21] Hear, O Israel, the Lord, thy God, the Lord is One.

Our dormitory seemed demoralizingly empty after Rista's parting. But the sun still rose and set every day.

American Paratrooper

On my return from Prezelle one afternoon, I heard the thunder and rumbling of distant grenades.

Each day a little louder, a little closer. German regiments cross our area from both directions. The English and Americans should come from the West, but in this miasma of offensives and counteroffensives, who can tell which side is winning? The number of wounded and dead just continues to mount.

Frightened, all the locals slowly began to prepare for the unavoidable defeat that hung over Germany. They packed their underground storage with meat, wheat, and articles of all kinds to use in the looming catastrophe.

Lying only a few kilometers from Prezelle, Lomnitz differed from it immensely. Lomnitz' people carried on pragmatically, flexibly, adjusting easily to changes, while Prezelle residents held fast to stiff, hardcore Nazi ideology, extreme supporters of the Final Solution. They cooperated most closely with the local SS, and, as the end of the war neared, they became increasingly active in murdering Jews and other non-Aryans. I knew that they hated us Serbs as much as they hated Jews, but they treated us with a certain reservation because they needed the labor force.

On this particular day, as I cut through the meadows of Lomnitz not far from the last Prezelle houses, I saw a paratrooper dangling on ropes from a tree at the edge of a forest clearing. A brother Serb helped him get untangled, then pulled him down to the ground, and walked away to look after some cows.

I approached and identified him as an Allied paratrooper. Scratched and wounded, blood oozing from under his right sleeve, he lay there totally disabled, and when he saw me, he waved with his left hand to call me over.

I headed toward him.

Loud screaming off to my left made me turn to see several angry figures approaching, swinging sticks, hayforks, and shovels. I stopped frozen about twenty meters from the wounded man, and helplessly watched old Nazis throw themselves upon this poor victim and beat him with all their strength until he no longer moved. They continued to hit him and cruelly poke him with hayforks, while one fat man pointed a double-barrel shotgun, ready to shoot as soon as the horde around the soldier cleared away.

A few moments later, local policemen arrived with the Mayor of Lomnitz and stopped the hellish revelry.

The poor paratrooper had become a faceless hide, like those I had seen in the Russian prison camp.

Among that bunch of bloodthirsty old men, I recognized the fat man as the teacher for whom I had repaired furniture at Prezelle's middle school, the same man who had led the shaming of the Prezelle women. Although the paratrooper was almost dead, this brute still spat on him.

"*Schweinhund!*" he shouted, landing a final blow with the barrel of his gun, as the policemen surrounded the paratrooper to protect him from the mob.

I don't know where my courage came from, but I gathered the strength to address the attacker. "Herr Thielke, please don't spit on him. He's not a swine dog, and you must treat him as a war prisoner. The Allied forces have captured your soldiers, as well."

I did not continue because Thielke cut me off by pointing his gun at me and shouting, "Get the hell out of here or I'll kill you."

Shaking, I turned and started walking to Lomnitz. I had not gone five steps when his gun exploded. Several stones ricocheted off the ground beside me and struck my legs, causing momentary stings.

A huge rush of blood flowed to my head. My eyes sparked. My muscles shuddered. He had ignited my flame.

I turned back around like a panther and attacked the surprised old men. I pounded them with my legs, my fists, and with a hoe that I grabbed from one of them. Swearing in every language I knew, I waved it wildly over their heads until the policemen and the Mayor pulled me away.

My madness lasted only a few minutes. I did not even notice that some of my comrades from our camp had surrounded us and threatened to jump in at any moment.

Reason, however, prevailed, and we parted without any further consequence.

Two of my brothers helped to carry the paratrooper to the Mayor's house. Mrs. Riedl received the injured man, cleaned his wounds, and let him rest at their home until the local German Military Command took over.

I returned to Elsa's house, where she cleaned the cuts on my legs and smeared some pine tar over them.

"I'm surprised at you, Timo. You usually try to calm things down not exacerbate them."

I had never told her what I saw that day in Prezelle.

Night of Terror

I thrashed restlessly about, kicking my blanket onto the floor.

Howls in the distance. Waving hands calling me into a cave of horrors. Gunshots. Children crying. Me crying. *Why am I crying? Where am I going with my father?*

Alone. There is no one on the road. *Where have they all gone?*

Knocking. Someone calls, "Open up!" Someone is calling us. *Who is it? Who is knocking?*

Silence.

Knocking again.

I open my eyes.

Through the darkness of our room, I could see that everyone slept. But someone did indeed knock at the door.

Again I heard calling. I got up and walked over to see who.

No guards on duty.

Puzzled, I opened the door to the loud voice of Stefan Fiske echoing through the dormitory.

"Help us, please."

"What's happening?" I stepped outside.

"Herr Timo, Russian and Polish prisoners have attacked the villages. They're burning and murdering everyone. They burned Prezelle, and they're on their way to Lomnitz—if they're not already there. Frau Gottfried's in the school with the children and the older women. Old Weinlein, Herr Bauer, and Herr Hoffmann are guarding them."

Confused, I replied, "How? I don't understand. Did they escape from prison?"

"No, Herr Timo. The war's over. We surrendered."

Suddenly it became clear that our guards had run away. The noise and screaming I thought I dreamed was indeed real.

I urged Stefan to return to Lomnitz, then ran back inside.

"Germany has capitulated. The war's over. Get up! We must help our farmers. Russians and Poles from the prison camps are attacking, burning, and pillaging. They're killing old men, raping women and children. We must help them."

I dressed in a hurry.

The Lomnitz crew got up and was ready in a minute. The Prezelle crew stayed in their beds and stared distrustfully at me.

One of them rolled over and turned his back to me.

"Why should we defend them? They were pigs to us. Let the Russians and Poles take their revenge. They deserve it." He shouted his vitriol at the wall.

I looked at him and saw the shaming in Prezelle. For a moment I thought he was right. I would think the same in his place.

"But brothers," I tried again, addressing their conscience, "in the name of the Lord. In the name of our religion, please help us protect the children and women!"

Several grumbled, "Why?"

"All of them hated us," came from the corner.

"To hell with them."

Distraught, I entered the guards' room and grabbed both guns with their ammunition holsters. I handed one to Nedeljko, and we flew out. Mile, racing ahead with his long legs, had already vanished.

Children's screams in the distance ripped my ears. Wild barking, frantic squealing, shrieking poultry, and the prolonged mooing of cows mixed with blasts of gunshots.

We arrived at Elsa's house to an uncanny silence.

No one answered our call.

I followed the fence. Unspeakable horror confronted me. Mile lay there, eyes open, shot in the head. My Anna

Marie had crumpled beside him, her head smashed. Further along little Johann—at that very moment—took his last breath as I watched the life drain out of his tiny body.

I found myself hyperventilating. It took every particle of my strength just to remain standing.

A painful scream and a beastly roar echoed from the house, startling me out of my shock.

"Quiet everyone," I whispered, trying to ready myself mentally for what lay ahead.

On tiptoe, we swung open the gate. Through the open door, we could see three men raping Elsa, Wilhelmina, and old Berta, the widow who lived next door, who had helped when Hanna took ill.

I screamed in horror, then roared like a lion. With my gun butt, I threw myself on the first intruder and killed him with a single blow. But I continued hitting him until Spasoje pulled me off.

I saw that the second had a smashed face, while the third ran out through the back door.

I heard a shot from Nedeljko's rifle.

I saw the third man fall down prone, arms wide.

Elsa's daughter Wilhelmina had fainted. We lifted her and Elsa and washed their faces with wet towels.

The trauma had killed poor old Berta.

Spasoje picked up Wilhelmina and took her to the school. Nedeljko followed.

I grabbed Elsa around the waist and helped her walk with us. We passed through the back door, by the dead Russian, and hurried to join the others.

Elsa walked silently and with difficulty. Aleksa retrieved the third Russian's rifle, then leaned Elsa's other side against his shoulder, and, picking her up together with me, we managed to run.

Far off, fire raged through Prezelle. The white smoke on the horizon looked ghostly against this star-flickering May night.

Distant wailing echoed all around us.

A howling, horrendous choir of demons neared Lomnitz, as humans barked with the sounds of wild beasts, like a pack of wolves.

We made it to the front yard of the school, where old man Weinlein stood with a shotgun. Bauer had made a sort of barricade next to the school's west side that defended the approach from that end. I let Aleksa take Elsa inside, and then placed him with his rifle in the backyard, and Spasoje, with an ax, under the windows on the east.

"Fire when you're sure you can see them." I said to Bauer and Weinlein. "Don't waste ammunition."

In the classroom, frightened and sobbing children crouched in the front corner next to the door. Hanna was helping Frau Bauer and Erika Schneider with Wilhelmina and Elsa, so she did not notice when I entered.

Children screamed when they saw Nedeljko and me. Unshaven and unkempt, with torn POW uniforms and guns in our hands, we undoubtedly looked like beastly attackers to them.

In the back of the room, Erika's mother and old Gerhard sat along with several other older women. Frau Schwartz's children huddled around her in the back corner. Stefan and some of the older children peeked through the windows in the darkness, brandishing poles and sticks.

The flickering lamp lit the wall clock: four ten.

Erika and Hanna calmed the children and approached us.

Erika hugged me and cried, "Thank God you have come."

Hanna squeezed my hand, looked at me gratefully, and returned to tending Elsa.

"Turn off the lamp," I said to Erika. "They mustn't see us."

"You're right, Timo." She put out the flame under the glass shield.

The older girls calmed the younger ones, but their tiny voices belied panic and terror.

I moved Nedeljko to the window at the rear. The middle window already had a blanket over it, so when Erika and I pushed a large armoire to cover the front window darkness filled the classroom. Only an eerie reddish light from far away flames passed through the rear window and front door to dance on the white walls. It scared the children, who saw it as demons and witches.

Gunfire exploded from all corners of the schoolhouse. Weinlein's shotgun, Bauer's rifle, a burst of machine-gun fire, the whizzing and pounding of bullets on the bricks like large hailstones falling from the skies.

—A shriek.

I crawled to the main entrance where I saw old Weinlein buckled over the fence.

I called to Aleksa, who was lying not far from the entrance—but he did not move.

"Bauer," I cried, as he crawled to the door. He lifted his head, pointed the carbine at the gate, and collapsed. His head hit the brick pavement killing him instantly.

"Spasoje."

There was no reply.

I saw two intruders squeezing through the gate. I aimed and fired.

The first one stopped dead.

I aimed for the second, when a machine gun blast spread bullets around me. Concrete pieces flew throughout the hallway.

I pulled back behind the wall.

I got up and fired at the person holding the machine gun.

The firing stopped.

I heard a cry and swearing in Russian. And again, the howling of hyenas from several throats. Human imitations of Siberian wolves. A terrifying symphony of bloodthirsty wild dogs.

Shadows of murderers snuck around the fence, waiting for the right moment.

Nedeljko fired several times. Painful screams and swearing came from west of the fence.

Music from the record player spilled out of the classroom to engender a moment of calm. Beethoven's *Eroica* audaciously overpowered the human howling, gunfire, and explosions. It rose through the coming dawn above the valley and thundered with its mighty chords above the heads of the desperate.

Marshalling her music, her greatest strength and courage, Hanna defied them. She fought with the German weapon that conquered nations without force or bloodshed.

Silence spread.

The screaming stopped.

The howling deadened.

Everything became quiet, as we listened to this mesmerizing outpouring of courage and daring. The music stunned the beastly instincts of our attackers and extinguished the flame of hatred for a moment.

Adversaries' souls enjoyed briefly together the perfect harmony of passion, despair, and triumph.

Gunfire resumed, spreading again over the windows, spraying small pieces of glass throughout the room.

I killed two more by the gate.

The onslaught seemed endless. They jumped the fence, attacking constantly, through the windows, through the door.

I continued to shoot at the crowd that pushed in toward us like a herd of mad cattle.

Bodies covered the floor in the hallway.

Dawn arrived.

The light of day revealed a bloodbath in the front yard. Dead Russians and Poles lay piled from the gate to the entrance.

I heard a voice from behind the fence. "Brother Serb, why are you defending the Germans? We don't have anything against you Serbs. Go away. Leave the Germans to us."

I shouted, "Never. You're not people. You're beasts!"

"Damn you, traitor. I'll kill you with my own knife," came the reply.

"Come on. I'm waiting for you!" I yelled and fired.

The screaming, firing, and machine-gun rattling resumed.

Nedeljko bent over and fell.

Triumphant cries echoed through the yard.

Little Stefan jumped and grabbed the rifle from him. He pointed and fired at the first one who pushed his head through the window. The body folded over the sill, his arms swinging through the broken glass. Blood ran down his head and shoulders.

They breached the middle window.

I turned away from the entrance to fire at the first man coming through. But I suddenly felt a flame and began to lose consciousness.

In a swirling blur I saw Hanna. She screamed and ran to me. Little Stefan raised his carbine, but at that moment, a man with an ugly grin on his face smashed and cracked his head with his rifle butt, spattering blood and pieces of brain on benches and walls.

Unable to move, I saw with my last shred of awareness how they ripped the dress off my beloved, broke down tough Erika, raped her mother, jumped on bewildered Elsa, and violently shook Wilhelmina, who fainted once again.

The screaming of little girls who ran helplessly from these human beasts accompanied me, as I slowly drowned in a deep, dark waste.

I fell into an abyss, through a constellation of lost souls, to the last galaxy, to the last point of space, to nonexistence, to nondeath.

Chapter 6

Awakening Memories

Under uneven canopies, the long line of hospital field beds spread endlessly. Chatter in different languages blended with patients' screams, the rattle of metal dishes, and music from faraway speakers. The warm, humid air mixed with smells of strong tobacco, medical alcohol, iodine, anesthetics, urine, latrines, and gangrene. Masked medical personnel in bloody, white coats and dresses passed by beds administering medication, clean bandages, and bedpans. Occasionally one of them would stop by a bed, look at the patient's chart, feel his pulse, then continue to another, as if doing troop inspections on supine servicemen.

A doctor came to my bed, looked at the chart, and sat down next to me. He lifted the bed sheet, revealing a large bloodstain on the bandage across my chest. Calling to a nurse to hold me upright, he took the bandage off, and then said something to her that I could not understand.

I saw a reddish circle with a blue ring around a hole that dripped pus. They cleaned it, smeared the wound with iodine, rebandaged it, and laid me back down. I moaned and said weakly in German:

"Doctor, how long have I been here?"

He looked at me astonished, then turned to his nurse and asked her whether she spoke German. She replied negatively and ran out of the tent calling someone's name.

Soon a soldier appeared and said, "I speak German—not the best. I learned it from Oma and Opa when I was a boy. Can I aid you?"

"Ask the doctor, please, how long have I been here?"

After a short conversation with the doctor, he returned.

"The doctor says you are here during two weeks. A bullet hit over top of your heart."

He paused and looked at me with deep concern in his eyes. "Lucky they find you in time."

My throat throbbed with pain. "What happened to the others? Children? Women?"

The soldier questioned the doctor and the nurse. The negative movement of their heads cut my hopes short.

"The doctors and nurses know nothing. You came here in ambulance."

He clearly struggled with the German, carried forward by his sincere desire to help.

"They operate on you and keep you here with our soldiers. This is an American military hospital. They will keep you here."

He patted me gently on the shoulder. "When you can move, you go to German civilian hospital for rehabilitation. That hospital decides when you go back to your army. You are a Serb, no?" he asked, looking puzzled.

When I nodded, he continued, "Doctor Peters demands you stay quiet. Your wound very serious."

He winced. "He says you are in critical state. You must not move or try to get up. I will come to see you now and then, and if you need something, I aid."

I drowned again in a deep dream.

My thoughts seemed hidden behind the shadows of yesterday, haunting me with happiness, horror, and screams. *Horror? Screams? Whose screams are they?* The jaws of insatiable beasts hovered over me. On a faded screen, scenes from the past, unclear pictures of children. *What children?* Women. *What women?* I groped to remember.

I felt pain in my chest again. *Shots. Howling. Her beautiful face, and so distant. Where is Lomnitz? Who am I?*

The ID tag around my neck carried familiar numbers. *Tag numbers.*

Familiar faces popped up. Unknown names and strange talk persisted. That never-ending broadcast.

Nevertheless, I slept restfully and long.

Close to sunset, a nurse woke me.

I moaned from pain while she changed my bandages.

She fed me mush with a spoon, and I swallowed with dwindling interest. Nevertheless those few bites returned a portion of my strength, and I relaxed.

The next day she washed me with a wet cloth, changed the bandages, and made me sit up in my bed several times.

Awakened by the smell of strong American tobacco, I realized that the German Yankee had returned and had begun to tell me about himself. Né Ernst Dunst in Rochester, near Pittsburgh, everyone called him Ernie. He had enlisted several years ago.

He brought me a bar of chocolate and a can of Coca Cola, both of which I tried for the first time in my life.

Noticing the pleased expression on my face after my first taste, he exclaimed joyfully, "Good, you like Coke. In America everybody drinks Coke."

I nodded gratefully. "Thanks, Ernie. It's really an excellent drink."

"I will bring more second time." He leaned closer. "How are you feeling?"

"Much better than a week ago. Now I can walk. I think it's time for the doctor to release me."

"Not yet." His eyebrows knit. "You remain in critical state. The doctor will not let you go."

"But I *must* leave. I must return. I must find out what happened to the people of the village where they found me. The women and children," I continued with urgency, but given the physical strain and painful pressure in my chest and head, I felt ready to faint.

"Stop. Be careful," he said. "I will get more knowledge, and tell you very fast."

Released

Several days later, I could walk, and I felt much stronger. They processed my papers, gave me an old army uniform without markings, a shirt and slacks, and a cotton bag with bandages and medical ointment for my wound.

Ernie packed me some dry food, with a couple cans of Coca Cola, a chocolate bar, coffee, sugar, and a pack of Lucky Strikes.

I signed off on a hundred new marks and a release document from the American field hospital.

They drove me by Jeep to the local railroad station and gave me a travel pass for Lüneburg and a transfer pass to the German civilian hospital. The jeep took me to the station where the sign read Uelzen.

Uelzen? Memories. The chauffeur that drove me to the Hanover Opera House had said that Lomnitz lay only seventy kilometers from here.

Names started to come back to me—but confused.

"I need a ticket for Bergen, by way of Soltau. How much, please?"

The clerk glanced at me. "Two marks."

I counted the coins and paid. "At what time does the train leave?"

"In twenty minutes." The clerk handed me the ticket. "It leaves at ten thirty."

I thanked him and walked to the terminal. The train left on time. I sat by the window and stared at the area along the tracks.

Where am I going?

Clouded by the black smoke of the steam locomotive, my view of the surrounding area mixed with pictures of summer landscapes and unclear visions of Lomnitz that awakened minute sparks of memories.

I arrived in Bergen at two o'clock in the afternoon.

Crowds coming and going surged in and out of the station. A few ambulances arrived while others left. Wounded veterans roamed the terminals. Germans. War prisoners. Allied soldiers. Live skeletons in striped uniforms.

And the children!

Some appeared lively, full of joy and happiness, while others looked very sad and hungry, with hollow eyes, lost hopes, and faded dreams. A little girl of about five asked me whether I were her father. Not waiting for my answer, she walked immediately to the next man and asked again. My heart tightened in a fit of sorrow.

I found an old taxi parked in front of the station.

"Can you take me to Lomnitz?"

The driver, puzzled, looked at me, then said. "Lomnitz? There's no one there anymore. Everything's destroyed, burned down. There's no one alive."

"It doesn't matter. Can you take me there? How much?"

"I can." He shrugged. "Why not? Ten marks."

I got in. Clearly too weak to walk, I couldn't even think of challenging the fare.

We arrived in front of the Town Hall in about fifteen minutes. I stepped out and paid. He looked at me in disbelief and left.

The overwhelming silence seized me. Not a sound other than an occasional rustling of leaves in a puff of wind. I stood in the middle of the square and looked west.

The charred columns of the Town Hall stood like guardsmen around piles of burnt walls, ceilings, broken roof tiles, and glass. To the east, along the south side of the main street, I saw burnt houses, damaged storage bins, and the remains of the silos of the families Schulz, Fritz, Celler, Weber, Ulmann, and Joseph, and finally, the contours of Elsa's house.

My last pictures of Little Anna Marie, Johann, and Mile flickered in front of my eyes.

My knees gave out.

I turned to look at the north side of the street. The church still stood—but with its windows broken and its door ripped away. Bauer's tavern and house had burned to the ground. Beyond it, the minister's house had partially burned. The grocery was first ravaged, then destroyed.

Dreadful scenes arose in my mind. Ugly faces. Frightened children.

My Hanna. My beautiful Hanna. Oh, Lord, please help me find her. Hanna!

I bellowed her name through the desolate street, like a wolf alone.

I cried when I saw the school—broken windows, broken door, ravaged house, and torn fence.

Sitting on the edge of the stone fence that surrounded the now bullet-ridden monument to Berthold Hoffmann, the founder of Lomnitz, I sobbed, barely able to breathe.

Broken.

But the task at hand called.

I struggled to clear my clouded thoughts and move forward.

I wandered through Lomnitz hoping to find some lost souls.

Finally, exhausted, I arrived at our old dormitory building. Empty, its open windows invited all passing creatures to enter.

I answered its call. With every step, memories returned.

My fellow prisoners had scrawled their names on dirty walls, alongside words of despair and counts of the days, months, and years of captivity. Beds were left without blankets, but straw mattresses and pillows remained, strewn on the bunks and floor.

In the guards' room I found the bed still covered with its heavy bed sheet. I lay down, blanketed myself, and, looking through the window at a sky full of stars, went to sleep.

Peaceful and without pain, I slept to the chirping of crickets.

I dreamed that the faces of all my beloveds surrounded me.

Then—disturbing the silence and harmony of nature—I awoke, weeping happily. The Allied defeat of the German territories had extinguished forever the fanfare of the Third Reich.

Shackles at last fell away, and peace breathed calmly and painlessly for the first time in many long years.

Staub

The roosters of Lomnitz woke me with their familiar morning call. I jumped up ready to go to work, then stopped short at the entrance of the dormitory building, my time and place coming back to me in a bright flash.

I must go to the main camp. Someone from the group of Prezelle laborers may know something.

I walked slowly down the dusty road, chewing on a biscuit from my bag. Knowing the long trip ahead of me, I hoped I might get there by late afternoon.

I heard the distant roaring of an engine, and soon a truck approached from behind, bouncing and jostling on the bumpy road.

I raised my hand and waited for it to stop. When the truck pulled up, I saw a civilian behind the wheel in a sweaty blue shirt with a cap on his head.

He set the hand brake. Curious, he turned to look at me.

"Can you take me to the camp?" I asked in German.

He shook his head, then spoke in Serbian, "I don't understand you, Schwabo. I'm going to Staub, and if you want a ride, hop in."

Elated, I started laughing, and I shouted, "Brother Serb, there is no greater joy than mine!"

The puzzled face of my countryman made me laugh again. I repeated—this time in Serbian!—"This is my lucky day. To meet my countryman here!"

"Ha, who would've believed it?" He leaned out the window and tipped his cap. "And I thought you were some local German." He pulled back in and, looking somewhat dazed, put his hands on the wheel. "God Almighty, who would've known?"

I went around to the passenger side and climbed in, offering my hand. "I'm Timo, Timo Tomić from the village of Krusar, near Jagodina," I said as I settled into the seat, "a former prisoner of war, who worked almost three years in the village of Lomnitz. Where are you from, brother?"

"From Srpska Crnja [***Serp**-skah **Tser**-nyah*] of Banat."

"Ah, a Lala!" I exclaimed, happy to run into one of these easy-going but dedicated fellow countrymen.

"And proud of it!" returned the fellow with a broad smile. "I'm Milenko Prodanović [*Proh-**dah**-noh-vitch*]," he shook my hand, then turned back to the wheel, "also a war prisoner from Staub. I'm returning from Bergen."

I threw my hands in the air. "And I'm also going to Staub. That was my main camp before I got the job in the village. Are many of our people in the camp?"

"It's pretty much emptied out. Many returned home."

He released the brake and shifted into first gear. "I didn't want to go back to Tito.[22] I just can't, brother, go back to communism."

He shook his head, then looked at me with sad eyes, the light from unexpectedly seeing a brother now gone.

"I have nothing to return to."

He shrugged. "Before the war, I was poor and worked on a farm. All the communists here wanted to take me back. They told me that Tito had imprisoned the rich people. Nationalized all their properties."

He shifted into third. "Divided it among the poor. And now we're all equal. They said I would benefit from going back."

He shook his head. "'No,' I told them." He started nodding. "'Let the King go back and then I will return.'"

He dodged a pothole, then looked over at me as we rattled in our seats. His loyalty to the King reminded me of how these northern Serbs had successfully persevered for centuries against assimilation into the Austro-Hungarian Empire.

---

[22] Josip Broz, more commonly known as Tito, headed a Yugoslavian communist, anti-Nazi group of guerrillas during the war. He took control after Hitler's surrender and planned to rebuild Yugoslavia as an industrial state following Stalin's model for the USSR. Given that Hitler was the common enemy to both Britain and Russia, Tito initially won the support of the West after the war ended, despite his communist policies and known atrocities.

"So I stayed here with five or six hundred others who also remained behind."

His dulled eyes remained on the road and the corners of his mouth turned down.

"We farmers have no interest in communism."

He turned to me again, a little brighter. "I drove a truck before the war, and when we got this one from a nearby village, I became the driver."

We swayed to the left as he swung the truck around a sharp bend.

"We trade with the Germans. We give them cigarettes, chocolates, and such luxuries, and they give us food. The German Army Command left us without any food or supplies when they took off. And the Allies haven't come yet. So we manage with what we have and with what we can find in the surrounding villages."

He turned to address me with respect. "And you? Where are you coming from?"

While we bounced on the rough road to camp, I told him my story and questioned him about the Prezelle laborers. But unfortunately, he had not heard about them.

"I know the Russians and Poles led a horrible pogrom throughout the region, and that the Russians rained inexcusable revenge on the Germans, but the Americans prevented them from complete reprisal and chased them back East."

He looked away, out the window at his side. "Many innocents were mutilated or killed. Many women perished from beastly rapes, as the Russians abused them in the most horrible ways. When they fainted, the Russians shoved corncobs in their wombs, wooden sandals, boots, and sticks. Ghastly creatures!" He shook all over.

I shuddered with panic. I crossed myself and fell silent.

Is she alive?

I couldn't think about the worst.

The pain around my heart increased, and my mind became a blur on the sweaty seat of that truck.

I tried to exhale the frustration and helplessness, but it would not leave me.

We arrived at Staub just before noon, to a scene of forgotten slaves who wandered from one end to the other, looking for the exit from an open cage that would lead to the long-forgotten secrets of self-determination. For them, freedom was only a corridor to other dungeons, to other prison camps. Shackles had become part of their being, as eternal as the link between life and death.

They put me in a barracks with some soldiers from Kraljevo [***Krahl**-yeh-voh*] and surrounding areas, who fired thousands of questions at my tired ears. The soldiers finally let me rest for a while. Later in the evening, they gathered around me again with more questions.

I explained that I had been wounded and had therefore spent several weeks in a hospital, so I too had little knowledge of current events.

"Yesterday, I was supposed to go to a German hospital for rehabilitation, but I decided to search for some friends, and this is why I came to Staub."

I asked about the workers from Prezelle but got no answers.

I found a metal dish and a spoon in my barracks, and then lined up for dinner, but—thanks to the repellently familiar smell of the kettle—I walked away shortly after and went back to my bunk. In my bag, I found the last piece of biscuit and tamed my hunger. After my coma, sometimes even a small bite proved sufficient to satisfy me.

That old dragon inside me had died.

Milenko came to visit me after dinner and brought me a piece of bread. I ate a few tasty bites and put the rest in my bag.

I asked him again about the workers from Prezelle and about the people of Lomnitz.

He looked at me, deep in thought, and suddenly remembered something.

"There's a man who helped in Lomnitz during the harvest season. Maybe he knows something. I'll go find him," he said, as he rushed off.

I waited, burning with impatience. I wanted to run after him, but by the time I had my gear together, he had disappeared, and I did not know which way he went.

Everything was dark. People moved from one barracks to another like zombies. Doors and windows gaped open, as the fresh air cooled unfortunate souls until their next nightmare. Many wandered through the villages, meadows, and forests of the area, then returned to camp drawn by the magnetic force of habit.

Milenko came back with a small man named Ranko, who addressed me from the doorway.

"I knew Simo Matić [***See**-moh **Mah**-teetch*] and Pero Stojković [***Pey**-ro **Stoy**-koh-vitch*] from the farm labor camp."

He came in and took a seat on the bunk across from me, a look of sad urgency in his eyes.

"They worked in Prezelle, and a few days after Germany surrendered, the Americans brought them here to Staub. They told us they helped the Americans bury the dead from Prezelle and Lomnitz."

He bent forward, his eyes turned to the floor. "Someone counted about fifty murdered and almost as many wounded."

He looked up at me. "The Americans took many women and children to their hospitals. Simo told me that almost all the Serbian laborers from Lomnitz were killed on the school grounds. Our countrymen killed many Russians and Poles defending the school. But about five hundred furious prisoners from Bergen prison camp rampaged all night through the villages, with Prezelle and Lomnitz suffering the worst."

He leaned back with a smirk, his hands on the bed for support. "Simo and Pero left the camp with a group of others about ten days ago, and someone said they joined the convoy returning to Yugoslavia."

Then he leaned toward me again, fire in his eyes. "All sides solicited us to go back. Tito's communists came with the English to try to force us."

He waved his arms wildly. "In uniforms, Sir! With red star badges!"

He pointed to the ground. "Here, among us! Among the Serbian soldiers of the Yugoslav Royal Army!"

He slapped his knees and looked as though ready to spit. "We condemned those who wanted to go back. We harassed them. But Tito's henchmen succeeded in convincing almost half our comrades. The rest of us, here, they treat like traitors. These English pigs."

This time he did spit. He looked away in disgust.

"They sold out our king, and they also wanted to sell *us* out to Tito and his bloodthirsty butchers."

Hopeful nevertheless, I asked, "Where have they taken the women and children of Lomnitz?"

"I don't know, Sir." Ranko hung his head. "I'm sorry that I cannot help you."

Then, looking up, "But you can inquire in Bergen. There's a German office for displaced persons and the Allied Red Cross. They may know something."

Milenko caught my eye. "I'm going to Bergen tomorrow, and you can come along."

The Search Begins

At midmorning next day, Milenko dropped me off in front of an old building in Bergen and showed me the door to the office. I thanked him sincerely and said goodbye to this good man from Banat.

Refugees from the East jammed the German displaced persons office. People stood in two rows leading to a single desk, patiently waiting for their turn. Young secretaries pounded on old typewriters, asking dry questions, without concern for anyone's welfare, without mercy for their suffering.

"Name? Last name? Year?"

"When and where did the person disappear?"

"Who's inquiring? The address of the inquirer? Next, please."

One after another, somber individuals, depressed and humble, approached and left, routinely—as though waiting quietly in line to receive nothing had become a way of life.

"I'm looking for Frau Hanna Gottfried."

"Who?"

"Frau Hanna Gottfried," I raised my voice, "from the village of Lomnitz. The wife of Colonel Gottfried."

"Yes, yes, we heard you. When did she go missing?"

"The Ninth of May, after the Russian pogrom. Do you have any information about the people of Lomnitz?"

"How old is the Frau?"

"I am asking you, do you know anything about their whereabouts?"

"Your address?"

My voice became louder yet. "My address? I don't have an address. I don't even have time to wait for your answer."

I threw up my arms in exasperation and walked out of the office, enraged by bureaucracy.

I stood in front of the entrance and took a deep breath, then set out for the other side of Bergen, looking for an Allied barracks, or Allied guard posts, or an Allied flag.

After walking for about five minutes, I found myself in front of a building where the sign read, "Red Cross Office." I entered and got in line behind several other people.

A young blond man with glasses met me and asked politely how he could help. I repeated my story, throughout which he maintained eye contact with me. As I finished, he bit his lip and looked away.

"Sir, we're Red Cross representatives, and our duties are directed to the care of displaced persons, refugees, and families without a home, food, clothes, and shoes."

He took a small notebook and pencil from his pocket. "We can't help you now in your search, but I'll give you the name of an American Lieutenant Adams from the local Allied Command. He passed through those villages after the surrender, and he may have some information about the people you're looking for."

He offered me a sheet of paper with the name on it and looked at me again. "You wear an American army uniform without markings, and speak German with an accent. You're not either. Where're you from?"

"I'm a Serb. A soldier of the Yugoslav Royal Army. Former war prisoner. Hanna Gottfried is . . ."

My voice dropped to a whisper. ". . . my life."

I took the note, thanked the man, and walked out.

I quickly arrived at the military barracks of the Allied Command Quarters. The guard looked at the piece of paper, phoned an office, and directed me to a building in the center of a fenced area.

Lt. Adams received me heartily and began speaking to me in English—which I could not understand—so I apologized. He called for a middle-aged woman, Mrs. Wagner, and, with a deep sigh, started again, "Yes. I passed through several devastated villages."

He winced, then continued. "The dead and wounded were strewn all over the place, but the worst were the women and children the Russians and Poles had raped."

He paused for a moment, then looked up.

"Yes, yes. I remember the school. We chased a bunch of drunken fiends out of there and into the forest. They howled like savages. We shot some of them right on the spot, right over the bodies they slew."

He turned to the side, his eyes narrowed and blurred.

"My skin crawled, looking at all those bodies. Young women with smashed heads, torn limbs. Little girls with dead eyes and faces contorted, with mouths hanging open from screaming so hard."

He shifted his weight. "Boys with shattered skulls."

He faced me. "Anyone still living just moaned heart-wrenchingly."

He looked deep into my eyes. "But the expressions in the eyes of the women and girls . . . that—"

He looked away and swallowed hard. "That will haunt me forever."

I rose up on my toes. "Hanna! That was my Hanna. Tell me what happened to her."

I pressed him with questions.

Lt. Adams drew a deep breath. "I believe they took several women and children to Minden Sanatorium."

He shrugged. "Anyway, I know they separated them from the wounded and sent them by ambulance to Minden."

He crossed his arms. "We continued sweeping the area, then went on to Belsen. An infantry unit stayed behind to bury the dead and transport the wounded and injured to some nearby German hospital."

He shrugged again and shook his head. "That's all I know."

"I'm very grateful to you, Sir."

I turned to Mrs. Wagner. "Could you please tell me where Minden is located?"

"Between Hanover and Osnabrück," she replied. "It's a long distance from here. The train goes only once a day, in the morning. Today's train has already left."

Then she translated our conversation to the Lieutenant.

The Lieutenant spoke cordially. "Where will you stay tonight? You can stay with us in the barracks. There are many empty beds."

"I would be most grateful."

I extended my hand. "My name is Timo Tomić."

He smiled as we shook hands.

"I'm a Serb, a soldier of the Yugoslav Royal Army. I was a POW in this region throughout my imprisonment."

He raised his eyebrows. His eyes widened brightly. "If you survived that night in Lomnitz, you're some kind of a hero."

Hero? Dismayed, I thought for a second. *What hero?*

He put me in an almost empty barracks. My bed had a real mattress with white sheets and soft pillows. I wanted to rest my tired body immediately, but the Lieutenant had invited me to dinner.

We continued our conversation with the same interpreter, who stayed late with us that evening. We enjoyed a couple of American beers that got me lightly drunk, and I became again a calm observer and an eager pupil as we discussed our impressions of the war and its consequences.

When the evening ended, I savored the memory. *They treated me to an excellent meal, exceptional beer, the Lieutenant's company, and a very comfortable bed in the barracks.*

I slept like a hibernating bear.

The Lieutenant woke me. "Time to get up if you want to catch the train for Minden."

I opened my eyes, and then rushed to get ready.

Lt. Adams and Mrs. Wagner waited for me outside the barracks. He handed me a large backpack.

"Mrs. Wagner will take you to the train station. Here's some food, a few cans of beer, and some cigarettes. I hope your search is successful, and I hope we'll meet again."

He put a hand on my shoulder. "Remember, my name is Paul Adams, and if you're ever in Fremont, Ohio, look me up—please. It'd be great to see you again."

He shook my hand firmly and saluted with the American salute.

I saluted like a Yugoslav soldier[23] and walked away, sad to leave such a pleasant and helpful companion.

---

[23] The palm is perfectly straight with thumb tight against the forefinger. The arm from shoulder to the elbow is at 90 deg to the upper torso (on the same plane) and the other half is bent toward the forehead at an angle depending on the height of soldier's head, again perfectly straight, but the middle finger almost touches the right eyebrow with palm facing down.

Melancholia in Minden

The sharp sound of the train whistle woke me before we arrived in Minden. I stepped down and walked to the exit where two German policemen stopped me and asked for my travel pass. I faced them with an angry look and handed them my—English—documents. They looked confused and muttered something like "American" and let me pass.

Wonderful, I shouldn't have any problems.

Actually, those papers documented my transfer to the rehabilitation hospital, including the necessary travel pass for it. I did not have any other documents.

I thought nothing of it at the time. *Why should I need a travel pass? After all, we won, didn't we?*

I stopped at a street vendor's booth and asked a young lady for directions to Minden Hospital. She pointed in the opposite direction, so I started walking slowly along the west side of a street full of antique shops, markets, and restaurants.

Sudden hunger guided me to take a seat in a small restaurant. They brought me coffee and a plate of a chicken paprika dish, as well as two slices of freshly made bread that smelled of sweet yeast. I spread the bread with butter and enjoyed every bite. The coffee, made of rye and real coffee, tasted quite good.

A waitress informed me that the hospital was on the next street, right after the green market.

Blossoming hope and excitement at the thought of being so near to finding Hanna filled my mind and heart.

"You'll see it when you get close," she said.

At the entrance, a guard with an old cap on his head smirked and showed me the administration building. In the reception room, a woman's head bent over a desk. As I walked, she disappeared, for an instant, behind a row of books. She reappeared, tapping her pencil and singing quietly.

My cough interrupted her afternoon concert.

"I'm looking for Frau Hanna Gottfried. I received information that she was brought here from Lomnitz with several other women. Can you please help me find her?"

The young woman approached from behind her desk.

"I've come from the American Section. Here are my papers."

I handed her my documents.

"Yes, please. One moment, please." She walked into the next office.

An older gentleman in civilian clothes appeared behind her.

"I'm the Hospital Director, Doctor Bramstedt. Please step into my office."

I walked in.

My heart pounded with excitement, as well as anxiety over the possibility of being found out, but my determination kept me from crumbling. I introduced myself as an employee of the American military commission for investigating pogrom survivors and witnesses, and I requested to see all patients assigned to him from Lomnitz.

He took a seat at his desk, looked at my travel documents calmly, raised his head, and addressed me in English.

I shook my head to show I didn't understand, and he switched to German.

"These documents indicate that you're a patient at an American field hospital. Who are you? What's the reason for your visit?"

I blushed and shivered, losing my confidence as a sudden wave of fear passed through me. I lowered my head, covering my face with my hands and closing my eyes in prayer.

When I looked up, the Doctor motioned for me to sit.

His gentle voice, full of compassion, and understanding, reassured me, "Don't be afraid. I won't report you. But you must tell me the truth."

"Yes, Doctor. Please, forgive me. It's always better to tell the truth."

I cleared my throat and stared at him painfully. "My name is Timo Tomić, just as it says in my documents. I worked in the village of Lomnitz as a war prisoner for almost three years, and there I befriended many of the locals, who accepted me without prejudice."

I leaned forward. "That period was the happiest in my life. The Lomnitz villagers respected me, appreciated my work, accepted me as their own, and loved me. And I loved them equally. When the Russians and Poles attacked, I—and a group of my countrymen—defended them."

I looked away. "Four of them died there, and the attackers wounded me seriously."

I moved to the edge of my seat, as my eyes began to cloud over.

"Among the survivors, the Americans saved Frau Hanna Gottfried, Elsa Fiske, Elsa's daughter Wilhelmina, Erika Schneider, and several other little girls."

I retrieved a handkerchief from my pocket and wiped my nose. "I understand that the Americans brought them here to your hospital. Please, tell me how they are and whether I can see them?"

Tears rolled down my face.

He watched me in silence until I calmed down.

"I would like very much to help you and to ease your concern, but I'm afraid I must disappoint you. Frau Gottfried is no longer with us. The traumas of the attack and rape took a terrible toll on her psyche, and we were not in a position to help her. We have sent her with little Wilhelmina to a specialist at Berleburg sanatorium."

He sat up straight in his chair and took a deep breath as he laid his hands on the desk.

"But they do not allow visitors there. They specialize in severe cases and they have very strict rules. Only doctors and hospital personnel have access."

His words cut through my heart like a shredder, with small pieces bouncing off the floor of cold facts. I quaked from the pain in my chest, the immeasurable sadness in my heart, and from the pressure, pounding with a heavy beat, at the top of my head.

He came to my side and consoled me, patting me on the back. He called in the young receptionist, and she brought me a glass of water with a pill that calmed me completely within a few minutes.

I stared at the grayness of the world outside. *They have taken her to Berleburg—to a place where I cannot go to see her. What can I do until she's released? How will I know when I can see her again?*

I listened further and learned that Erika recovered very quickly and returned to the village with several little girls.

"Elsa's still with us. She's the last person from Lomnitz," Dr. Bramstedt continued, "but she's made little progress. She has adjusted to the hospital's work duties and has helped the sisters clean rooms, take food to patients, bath them, and wash bed sheets. She works constantly and always looks for more to do."

He shook his head. "But she's completely withdrawn. She talks to no one."

He frowned. "She simply works hard and keeps to herself. She sleeps very little. In fact, she's afraid of sleep.

At night the nurses often find her sitting in her bed staring at the ceiling."

He paused, looked down, and raised his eyebrows, still frowning. "And she doesn't eat much. She's lost a lot of weight."

He took me to her room—which was empty—and asked a nurse to find her.

When she appeared in the doorway, only a shadow entered the room. I could not recognize the sunken eyes on a bony face, sagging bosom, long skinny arms, and bony hands.

I whispered. "Elsa, it's Timo."

She did not look at me. She continued to stare at some empty spot while I tried calling her out of the deep dungeon of her lost mind.

I felt myself swaying as my vision went blank.

When we returned to Dr. Bramstedt's office, he waited patiently as I tried to compose myself.

"Would you allow me to take Elsa back to Lomnitz with me?"

"I'm sorry, but in my professional opinion, she's not ready to leave here yet. She'll need more time to recover."

"But Doctor," I pleaded, "she may come out of her shell sooner. She'll be with familiar faces and objects in Lomnitz. Wouldn't that rekindle her memories more quickly?"

"It may, but that may not be the best thing for her. Since her trauma occurred there, being back might trigger greater trauma and provoke further setback. She needs therapy and treatment here."

He watched the water spraying peacefully in the fountain outside his window. "Returning her to her former life would be risky and dangerous."

He looked back at me. "No, I cannot release her yet."

"Oh, my poor Elsa," I sighed. "How long will it take to bring her back?"

"Herr Tomić, we have treated many patients with similar conditions. Postwar trauma simply takes a long time. So much depends on the strength of her will. She fights her demons daily, but she's still far from recovered."

He turned away again.

"I can't tell you how long—months, years—or she may never heal."

Dr. Bramstedt stopped, then leaned toward me. "Why don't you stay a while and spend some time with Elsa. Perhaps your presence may plant some seeds of hope. We can arrange for your accommodation here as part of her treatment. Would that be possible?"

"Well, why not?" I said, not thinking.

"For how long might you stay?"

"A week or two would not matter much."

But then I thought of Hanna, and my mind rushed to resist.

I hung my head. "I'm sorry, Doctor, but I can't stay. My search has just started and I must continue to look for Frau Hanna Gottfried."

"I'm sorry, too. You could be of great help to Elsa."

He rose from his chair. "Forgive me for asking, but what's your connection to Frau Gottfried?"

I looked at him slightly confused, not sure what to say or how to say it. I feared the arrogant face of aristocracy would ridicule my petty role. But I quickly composed myself and answered confidently:

"Hanna and I love each other and nothing will stop me from finding her. I'll follow her to the end of the world if it takes the rest of my life. She is all I have."

He nodded warmly and shook my hand.

"Good luck, young friend. May your search be fruitful and may you find your Hanna very soon."

He opened the door for me. "Please write to us and we'll keep you informed about Elsa."

I departed with a heavy heart for leaving Elsa, but I understood the wisdom of his words and walked out satisfied that I had left her in good hands.

Return to Lomnitz

Leaving Elsa behind, I arrived in Lomnitz in the late afternoon to the familiar sound of silence. Once in my shop I set up a mattress that I found in a closet. I covered it with a dirty sheet and went to sleep.

Distant crowing alerted me to the approaching dawn. Upon opening my eyes, I saw that the door, hanging on only one hinge, had remained open through the night.

Poultry!

I sat up and listened more attentively.

The chickens chattered in the nearby garden, and soon the mighty voice of Elsa's rooster Koenig echoed throughout the village.

Koenig was the children's favorite rooster. Despite the pain of that memory, I almost jumped for joy. I ran out of the shop and found the entire flock pecking in the overgrown backyard.

Thank you, Lord!

Listening carefully, I ran through the village, and soon, in the woods near Hoffmann's barn, I spotted a sow with piglets running after her. I checked the storage bins and found one that still had corn at the bottom of the burned cage, but mice and rats had infested it. I grabbed a hayfork and chased the vermin, then found two large baskets and filled them with the seed. As I searched for a means to move it, I happened on old Hoffmann's ox-buggy. I dragged it back to the baskets, hitched myself to it, and pulled the buggy over to the last of Elsa's storage bins not damaged by fire. I repaired the fence around the pigpen, and, luring them with corn, got the sow and two piglets back inside.

To my great surprise, I found my toolbox behind the shop's broken door. It had somehow escaped the pillage. Thanks to my tools, I repaired everything easily and quickly, and what otherwise might have taken weeks now took only days.

I fixed the door and window on my shop. Then I repaired the house's broken entrance door and the doors to the children's rooms. I cleaned the debris in the kitchen, hallway, and bedrooms, and made all the beds.

Once I had Elsa's house in order, I went back to the village square. I walked from one house to another doing repairs, putting up doors, and covering broken windows, even though roofs had burned through and gaped open to the sky.

I wanted to restore the village, and, no matter how unrealistic this may have seemed, it made me very happy.

At noon one day, I found three sacks of wheat at Fluger's house. I sang *Ode to Joy* carrying them to Elsa's.

That afternoon I searched Bauer's barn and found a plow that I wanted to pull to Elsa's. Try as I might, it proved too heavy for my worn body.

I decided to leave it for the morrow.

A horse's neighs woke me the next day. I discovered the sun already shining brightly. I listened intently. The sounds of pigs squealing, chickens chattering, and birds singing occasionally broke the reigning silence.

Again, I clearly heard the distant neigh of a horse.

I jumped up and ran out—nude as a baby—to investigate. When I heard snorting, I ran up the street.

In front of the minister's house a black horse with a thick mane and blanket stood hitched to a wagon. A crash from the house startled me, and I ran to the broken fence and grabbed the biggest board I could find as a weapon.

I snuck up to the entrance and yelled, "Who's there? Come out!"

I held the board ready to attack, when, from the dark hallway, a young minister in a black suit appeared out of the shadows. His red hair shone brightly in the morning rays, as a few curls fell over his high forehead and almost touched his long eyebrows. His mouth twitched with fear, making it appear as though his tiny mustache reached out on each side to seek safety in his sideburns. He was tall and masculine, with a short neck that joined his large torso to a gentle face. His body sloped down over a rounded belly out of which poked two stumpy legs.

He looked dumbfounded—in total disbelief at my threatening pose. I had frightened him. With his hands up as if under arrest, he walked out praying. His two blue eyes fixed on my nude body.

I understood his panic. A meeting of religion and nature had occurred. I felt ashamed and threw the board aside.

"Please, forgive me, Reverend. I didn't expect anyone to be here."

We suddenly sensed the humor of the situation and started laughing heartily. I covered myself with my hands, and, after taking the blanket he offered me, ran to the entrance of my shop.

I dressed and returned to meet him at his cart.

He had news to report as he accepted the blanket back from me.

"Yes, Herr Timo. They murdered the old Reverend Gunther, God rest his soul. They stole the coffers and did a lot of damage to the church. In one night, their insanity destroyed more villages than the Allied bombs did in several days."

With eyes downcast and pursed lips, I nodded my understanding.

As we crossed the threshold, his tone turned positive. "The Bishopric sent me to restart life in Lomnitz. I heard about you and your heroic act. The villagers will be eternally grateful to you. God bless you."

Together we cleaned the minister's house. I repaired the door and windows, the old couple's bed, and a broken down dresser. The young minister, Norman Keller, brought in the bedding, pillows, towels, and dishes, and we put together the bedroom and kitchen for his future accommodations. Both of us felt fortunate to meet here, and our enthusiasm for the work did not flag until late that night.

Having cleaned the church, the young Rev. Mr. Keller lit candles. The flames flickered on the night breeze, turning the atmosphere mystical. The shaky sound of his voice in prayer echoed through the broken windows and over the abandoned valley, like the desperate call of a condemned soul eternally wandering.

The Rev. Mr. Keller's arrival with a horse and wagon contributed greatly to the speedy restoration of the standing homes, barns, and storage bins. We plowed the fields and planted corn and wheat. We also planted potatoes, onions, beans, cauliflower, cabbage, and other vegetables that the Minister obtained from the bishopric supply warehouse. We trimmed the orchards, sprayed them with insecticide and turned the soil around the young trees.

Once everything seemed under control, Rev. Keller took his leave.

A few days later, he returned with two older people sitting in the back of his wagon. When they stepped down at the Village Hall, they hugged the stone columns and, visibly shaken, started crying.

I recognized the Mayor, Walter Riedl, and his wife. Even at such a clearly longed-for moment of homecoming, Mayor Riedl exhibited remarkable poise and self-control. He gently reached an arm around his wife's waist. They turned their tired and blurry eyes to take in the vision of their beloved town, and they caught first sight of me.

They shook with joy when they recognized me. Now bent and fragile, these two former pillars of Lomnitz unsteadily approached and lavished me with words of gratitude. They squeezed my hands with expressions of warmth, happiness, and tenderness, and, in the Balkan way, tears shone in their eyes.

A few days after that, Ude Hoffinger and his wife, Mrs. Schüller with her son and daughter-in-law, the family Graim, and the Joseph Ulmann family arrived.

My new friend Milenko stopped by regularly to bring news from Bergen, informing me about the events at Staub and about the placement of POWs.

Thanks to a summer generous with both heat and rain, the crops grew quickly. The cows supplied enough milk. The pigs fattened and multiplied, and the chickens laid so many eggs that we had plenty to eat and to incubate. We divided all food equally among the villagers, and everybody worked hard so that we might make it through the winter without hardship.

I repaired almost all the roofs, and the young men helped in the restoration of the burned houses.

Lomnitz began to look like itself again.

But all that strenuous work could not assuage my longing for Hanna. She haunted me everywhere. Every board I carried, every nail I struck paid homage to her and to the life I prayed we might still live together.

Though rebuilding the town brought me much joy, my heart ached when we repaired the cemetery with the graves of my comrades. On the temporary crosses of rough-sawn boards, their ID tags hung without names. We easily identified Mile's grave by its length, but the graves of the others were all about the same size, and I did not know their tag numbers.

I prayed to God for forgiveness and put the names of Spasoje, Aleksa, and Nedeljko on the crosses.

The young Lutheran minister blessed the graves, singing, "It Is Well with My Soul," after which I sang "Our Father."

God is the same. Though they leave us behind, let the earth be full of light again, and let the Lord take them into his Heavenly Kingdom.

After the memorial, I sat down with Rev. Keller and talked about Elsa. I wanted him to help me find Wilhelmina and Ernst—her only surviving children—and to bring Elsa back home. From the Mayor, I had learned that Ernst was in an orphanage. The old couple wanted to return him to Lomnitz and adopt him.

Rev. Keller agreed to help. We wrote a letter to Dr. Bramstedt in Minden, asking him about Elsa's recovery and expressing all the villagers' desire to bring her back home. We sent the letter on 20 July 1946.

English soldiers came the very next day to take me to the relocation camp near Osnabrück.

Chapter 7

Black Army Service

Early in 1946 English Regional Headquarters had canvassed our POW camp for volunteers for the English Army Watchman Service. About eight thousand Serbs volunteered, including a few officers. I too offered my name, and thus they came for me on 21 July.

I loved my new status. I loved wearing an English Army uniform. Since they were black, we called it the "Black Army Service." I had the opportunity to learn English directly from Englishmen and to read many books from their library. In addition, I had free time to look for my Hanna in different hospitals and sanatoriums. Whenever I learned from someone that she might be somewhere, I would set forth anxiously, traveling thither and yon, scurrying from one gate to another—only to return disappointed and tired.

When on duty, we watched gun and ammunition warehouses round-the-clock—not at all difficult. Often some of us played cards all night while two other servicemen stood guard. Or, if we chose, one of us could read in the small guardhouse when two or three of us served at the same time.

Occasionally I would find someone who wanted to earn a little extra money to substitute for me. Thus my new friend Blagoje [***Blah**-goh-yeh*] stood watch day and night, while we gambled and while some of the others found solace with married women and prostitutes in the nearby town.

Blagoje worried so much about his wife and his little daughter that he tried to earn as much money as possible to send packages home frequently. We paid him for every shift he did as substitute, and he stoically stood from one to the next, sometimes for a whole week, as if he never wanted to sleep. The strength of faithful love carried him through sleepless nights and delirium for months. While many of us treated our money as "easy come, easy go," he carefully saved every penny to buy articles for his packages.

I also got to know a fellow by the name Vidoje Arsić [***Vee**-doh-yeh **Ahr**-sitch*]. He visited a local teacher and, while her husband cooled off in the kitchen with cheap brandy, he slept all night with the woman, then returned to the barracks. At times he would not leave her house for days.

He took me once to meet her, an attractive and smart woman. I could not understand what lured her to this brutal, rough character. A real simpleton, without any manners or morals, he had appeared sneaky and condescending as a prisoner but had turned into an aggressive brute now that he had his freedom. He made a shameful representative of the Serbian people.

We Serbs loved the children. We took them chocolates—sugar, flour, and canned food for their mothers. They all compensated us for it: joy and laughter from the children, pleasurable favors from the mothers. Almost every Serbian soldier had at least one German woman he went to during his free time. Whether single or married, young or old, the women constituted part of a former POWs' goods exchange.

German women proved accommodating for many reasons: Hunger, Hunger, and Hunger. Lack of food blinded their judgment. Abstinence overcame their deep-seated prejudices about partners outside their "pure race," and the desire for stability and peace made them ambassadors to all alike. They accepted this function—along with humiliation, mistreatment, and insults—with patience and determination.

They fed the nation, and the nation proclaimed them whores, kicking them out of their homes. Serbs accepted them, married them, and took them to the New World.

The first to make peace with Germany, we Serbs never received Germany's forgiveness.

Months passed and my search continued—fruitlessly—every chance I got. In July 1947, about a year after joining the Black Army, I received a letter from the Rev. Mr. Keller that made me very happy:

> Dear Timo,
>
> I write to you about a few happy events that have taken place in our village.
>
> Elsa has returned from Minden. She now helps around the church and the house, but she still doesn't speak. She always seems very far away, and she still suffers from nightmares.
>
> Radenko and Irma's return to Lomnitz pleased us all very much. They plan to marry. Radenko has promised to write you after the wedding.
>
> Erika's Herbert came back after his release from a POW camp, and they got married two months ago. The whole village celebrated this happy event.
>
> Also, members of the Fluger, Schultz, and Baumgarten families have returned, and some close relatives of the Rodenberg family have now settled in Lomnitz permanently. The village finally has a sufficient number of parochial families to form a choir, but we need children. I am planning to do my part. My childhood sweetheart, Marta, has agreed to marry me in September. She has

fallen in love with the people of Lomnitz and can't wait to move here to join me.

The school remains empty and a heavy melancholy hangs over it still.

We all hope that you will visit us soon. Many changes have taken place here, with so much new. Both great pain and great happiness have befallen us, all mixed in one big kettle of the Lord's blessings.

We talk about you often, we keep you in our prayers, and we ask the Lord to help you in your search.

Please come for a visit. Everyone wants to see you, and Marta is anxious to meet you.

May God light your path.

Pastor Norman Keller

No word of Hanna.

I had learned of her release from Bad Berleburg, but I could find no trace of her. For me, a tide of sadness flooded the space between the lines of this happy letter.

I fell under the spell of melancholy. The memories the letter evoked took me back through a symphony of voices, sounds, trumpets, and thundering drums mixed with uplifting violin, viola, and flute melodies, that whirled into a harmony of reminiscence where I became intoxicated with the potion of a yearning nostalgia. In the thousands of shadows that spilled over the heavenly arches, I searched for her beautiful face, now hidden behind the veil of a fast-receding past. Far away on the seas of the lost, I dreamed of her whispering image. The splendor of her smile—lips full of passion, gentle, wondering eyes under blonde locks—and her sensual calls of tender love that came from the depth of her being.

My Hanna, come back to me!

After more than twenty-six months, I continued my search, but I had nearly given up hope.

Eight months later I received the following telegram:

> On this day, 22 March 1948, in recognition of extraordinary services performed, his knowledge of the English language and his fluent knowledge of the German and Serbian languages, Jeftimije (Timo) Tomić is promoted to the rank of Sergeant in the regiment of the Civil Mixed Watchmen Services of the English Army.

A member of the Black Army for almost two years, the promotion nevertheless came suddenly, like thunder from a blue sky. They transferred me from the Civil Watchmen Services, where our unit was entirely Serb, to the Police Academy, outfitted by a combination of Serbian, Lithuanian, and Polish war prisoners.

Training lasted six weeks. My duties included translation and explanation of terms, regulations, and military laws.

By the second session, I became an instructor, and in the course of several months, hundreds of young policemen paraded in front of me for assignment throughout the English occupied zone. They served to protect the interests of both military and civilian institutions, as well as guarding the displaced persons camps, which were filled with the remaining Četnik [***Cheht**-neek*], Lotić [***Loh**-teetch*], Nedić [***Ney**-deetch*], and other surviving non-communist Serbian counter-revolutionary groups who could not return home to Yugoslavia.

My new position gave me much wider freedom of movement, including a free pass for bus and railroad. Thus I could continue my search more systematically and with greater efficiency.

Very well organized, Germans could, within a few years of the end of the war, find many of their citizens in the territories under occupation by Western Allies.[24] Nevertheless, I visited every mental hospital I heard about in the occupied zone, leaving my name and address with the hospital directors, doctors, and nurses, as well as with the administrators of various missing persons bureaus.

When Radenko's promised letter arrived, I read it eagerly. I examined every word, trying to find even a small trace of hope about Hanna's whereabouts. I read the letter again aloud, listening to the tale of Elsa's complete recovery, and the return of Wilhelmina and Ernst—*Oh, how I wish I could have been there*—then about Erika and her marriage to Herbert, about the rebuilding of the village, and about the villagers who often mentioned me and prayed for my health. The young Lutheran minister had married, and the couple expected a baby in June, the first newborn in Lomnitz since the war. Everybody anxiously awaited this event. Radenko wrote that they had placed monuments to our fallen comrades in a prominent location of the cemetery, and that he was very proud of his new countrymen.

---

[24] Any information about prisoners of war, civilians, and children from the Soviet occupation zone, however, proved inaccessible.

New countrymen! Besides getting married, Radenko, it appears, has decided to remain in Lomnitz. How wonderful for them!

He ended by inviting me to visit.

The bottom of the page included the scribbled signatures of the old mayor, Ernst, Erika, Irma, Wilhelmina, plus a note from Elsa:

"My sweet Timo, my strength and courage, please come soon!"

The joyful tears in my eyes at all this good news became a dark veil of despair over the one signature that the letter lacked.

A New Lead

Spirits beckoned insistently.

I decided to revive, from the depths of oblivion to which I had sunk them, the beautiful pictures of our brief time in Hanover.

In late April, I arrived at the front gate of Mrs. Heinrich's stately home and pressed the latch. It was locked. At our departure, Hanna had hidden a key under a loose brick. I squeezed my hand through the gate behind the stone column and found it still there.

The gate groaned deeply from the heavy rust, then stuck half open. I passed through into the front yard. The grass now covered the brick patio with nearly four years of uncontrolled growth. I went into the house, and the heavy odor of the closed rooms struck me.

I felt queasy.

Death still lingered in the air. No one had entered since we left. Everything remained untouched, covered with cobwebs, a gray layer of dust, and stale odors.

My Hanna is not here.

Dejected, I walked out of the house and took a deep breath. I exhaled the smell of death and turned my eyes to the Opera House. That devastated old beauty stood defiantly among other ruins, calling its guests to a performance that could take place only in their memories.

I returned to my duties, but at my next opportunity in early July, I journeyed deep into southeast Germany, a hundred kilometers from the Czech border, near the Bayerishcher Wald mountain range, to the beautiful town of Regensburg. There, remarkable old Roman, Romanesque, and Gothic architecture stands along wide avenues—monuments to different eras, religions, and rulers. The tall crowns of centuries-old oak, birch, beech, and pine line the main street, offering permanent shade for the sidewalks, colorful shops, offices, and restaurants, transforming the entire neighborhood into a magnificent atrium, the Bismarckplatz.

Somewhere as I wandered through, I passed the famous Theater Regensburg, with its flying banners announcing their presentation of *La Bohème.* Scenes of my angel's opera stormed and whirled suddenly through the skies above the Bavarian Mountains.

Hanna is so close. I feel her breath. Her touch.

I reported to the administrator of the Regional American Hospital and received permission to visit the mental hospital and talk to the doctors and nurses on duty. The Director's words tumbled out in a cyclone not waiting for an answer to its questions.

"You have traveled so far. I don't understand. Who sent you here? You say that the British military office advised you she was here? I'm sorry to disappoint you, but Frau Gottfried left us some time ago."

Two days of travel, a change of time zones, holdups, crowds, and now back again empty-handed.

Seeing my complete chagrin, the man addressed me with patience. "But, please, wait a moment. We'll check her file. Frau Breuer, please bring Frau Hanna Gottfried's file from the archives."

He turned to me. "Would you like a cup of coffee, Herr Tomić? We now have good, imported coffee from Brazil."

For a moment I had felt her warm breath, but now her touch turned to a will o' the wisp. Her image floated and disappeared behind tall pines skirting a faraway clearing. Everything flowed into blankness, whiteness, and desolation.

She is my love. For her I learned a new language, music, and history.

Frau Breuer returned and handed the Director the requested file.

"Thank you. Aha. Aha. Hm," he mumbled, as his eyes ran over the pages.

He looked up. "I'm not finding any further directives. It's really unusual. She was released on 12 May. Doctor Geller signed her off to the custody of Frau Hilda Kleist."

"Kleist? Frau Kleist!" I shouted. With joyful relief in my heart, I jumped up and, on my way out, hugged Mrs. Breuer, who was standing at the door.

Waves of happiness overwhelmed my soul as I floated back to Hanover. I went back to Hanna's aunt's house. It was still empty. I left a message with my address, dated 14 July 1948.

The Opera House was now in the process of restoration. I read that Dir. Witting had perished in the bombing.

Madame Kleist? Perhaps someone from the musician's guild and art association could tell me something about her. . . .

"Yes. Yes. I remember Frau Kleist. How can I not?"

But the old musician looked doubtful. "I heard that she was killed in the last hours of the bombardment."

"She was killed? Impossible! No, no, she's still alive. Do you know where she lived?"

"I'm really sorry, sir."

Traitor

The pain in my heart at the thought of never seeing Hanna again spread day by day through my tired mind and body, exhausting me, making me slow and sleepy. I walked the streets drowning my sorrow in senseless streetcar rides and occasional bouts with a bottle of brandy in some smoke-filled parlor or colorless bordello, full of drunkards, scum, and wasted whores on their last gasp of life. At times, after quenching my pain with alcohol, I even fell into oblivion in some stinking gutter.

Whenever I passed an opera, theater, or school, though, I heard her angelic voice sing, enchanting my heart and reawakening fond memories. A veil of warmth fluttered around me, exciting my senses, reopening the windows of longing, and jumping me forward to the freshness of a spring that would not arrive until months later.

Two letters awaited me at my barracks one cold afternoon in late February 1949. The wind of tattered memories blew the old shaky handwriting of my father to me. Astounded, I feverishly opened it.

20 January 1946
Dear Son,

Since the day of liberation, we have not received a word from you. Are you alive? Have the winds of war swamped you? When Milutin returned and told us that you were alive, your mother and I thanked the Lord and cried a bit with our few remaining tears.

We wrote several letters, but they must not have reached you. When Milutin returned, and you did not, it was hard on us, and your mother took it with much sorrow. She cries by the stove and sighs, and she is waning like an old apple, thinking of you only.

I have gotten over the pain, and I am glad that you did not return. For you, there is no life in this country. First, they took away the best plow fields we had, and then they took half of our sheep and pigs, all for the people, as we are all equal now.

We don't know these people running our new government. They don't believe in God. The church is closed and our beloved priest Arsa was led through the village barefoot and almost nude with a banner hanging from his neck so that everyone could read: Traitor. Collaborator. Četnik's accomplice.

They named you also. They listed you as a traitor for working for the Germans, and if you return, they have issued an arrest warrant. Please, son, don't come back. Stay there, because a thick cloud of darkness has fallen over Serbia. Milutin has decided to escape from here and go back, and, God willing, this letter may reach you, but if not, I will not sign it or mention any names. And so, let our Lord take care of you. Write to us when you can.

Your father and mother
On St. Jovan's day

Traitor? Traitor? echoed through my head. *With lost youth? With a skeleton body from starvation? With the tormented soul of a slave? With a broken arm and a gunshot wound close to the heart?*

My poor old parents! Damnation is the shadow of my life. If I have sinned so much, and—Almighty God—often doubted you, my elders have always been obedient, devout, and without sin. The Holy Spirit always shone from their faces. The Mother of God has blessed them. I remain beholden to you, but this debt I will not return. I will no longer believe in the Holy Secrets nor walk Your path again.

I parted from God and locked the door to my heart.

The following day, after terrible nightmares, I decided to report to the American Immigration Commission and request a visa for the United States of America. From the representative of the Serbian Brothers Help Organization in Chicago, I obtained the guarantee, and with my paper forms and military documents, I started the long walk to America, entering mechanically into lines, columns, and divisions of war prisoners, only one among the hundreds of thousands of human tragedies, all on the road to uncertainty, to a new oblivion in a New World.

We did not know whether we traveled to a new incarceration of soul or to a reprieve from this miserable stagnation of life. With tired, yellowish faces and hunchbacked bodies, we carried sadness and weariness on a path of promised hope and left behind our youth, courage, and confidence.

Listless, I remembered the second letter. I found it squashed in my back pocket and tried to unravel the name of the sender. I opened it slowly and read over the first few lines.

Honorable Herr Timo,

I have tried vainly to find you before now, and it appears our paths have crossed several times; however, I learned about your continuous search only recently.

Who? Who is this? My eyesight hazy, I pushed myself to read further.

You could not possibly imagine how much I have wanted to find you. Ah, please forgive me for torturing you. You do remember me? My name is Hilda Kleist, secretary to the Opera Director in Hanover.

Oh, my Lord, is it possible?

I took a deep breath and concentrated, staring at the words that jumped in a promising dance. I stepped out of my place in line and sat on a low concrete wall.

No one noticed me—just as in the march of death, the corpses walk, while the living lie dead along the road.

I do not know where to start, but before all I am sending you news that Hanna Gottfried is alive.

OK, yes, I know she's alive. They released her to you last May, but where are you? Where ***is she****?*

The letter continued:

Unfortunately, she is still totally withdrawn. The horrors of the past still surround her, and she continues to wander alone in the darkness of her mind. She has undergone many therapies, been

> admitted to many hospitals, clinics, and sanatoriums, and everyone just tells us that she needs more time to recover, more peace and quiet.
>
> It seemed to me that she had spent too much time sitting in dungeons. I took her out of the Regensburg hospital in May of last year. We lived for a while with my brother near Dortmund and stayed there until the end of January, when I decided to return to Hanover, to the house of her aunt Rosa. I found your letter, but when I showed it to her, she hardly gave it a glance and seemed not to comprehend at all.
>
> We moved in after a quick rearrangement and house cleaning. I can tell you that Hanna has felt more at peace surrounded by her dear memories from the past.

Upon reading this news, I exhaled a mountain of burden.

"I must go back."

I imagined the masses of Serbs standing in line calling out to me. *Hey, wait. Where are you going? You can't leave us.*

"But, I must. I can't live without her!"

No, you are a part of us. You swore to the King and to the Fatherland, and it is your holy duty to remain with us.

"Crazy corpses. You died a long time ago. I want to live. Only Hanna's love can nourish and sustain me!"

You fool. You're crazy. Don't go back. Stay with us. We will all be together in the New World. We will start a better life. Don't leave. It's just another false lead among the thousands you have already uselessly followed.

My murmuring columns whispered to me with force and determination.

I walked to camp trying to read more. Sentences floated in an unclear whirl of words. The thought that I could find Hanna in Hanover carried me forward. When I reached my bunk, I quickly packed some clothes and started for the railroad station.

On the way out, Milan, the postal carrier gave me a special delivery registered letter for which I had to sign. I glanced at the envelope and recognized it as an official letter from the government of Lower Saxony.

I placed it in my pocket and rushed to catch the next train.

Few people bound for or through Hanover had boarded, so I easily found a seat in a quiet corner. As we pulled out of the station, I continued reading the letter from Mrs. Kleist.

> I hope that this letter will find you before you return home to Serbia. I search for words that will offer you a certain solace before you decide to fly to us in exhilaration. Unfortunately, with great pain I write to tell you that Hanna left the house a few days ago and has not returned. I have gone mad waiting and hoping that she will come back, but with every day that passes a greater wave of panic sweeps over me, choking me with thoughts of some terrible outcome.
>
> When I learned a short time ago from my opera colleagues that you had searched for her, I was overjoyed, and in despair over Hanna's whereabouts, I started writing you. I had hoped you might know what paths Hanna took when she left here, but then I realized that she is not really conscious of what she is doing, and I

believe she is not even aware of the world around her. Please, do not hold it against me for painting a dark picture, but the situation pains me deeply, and each day brings less encouragement. She always maintained some ray of hope, and I remain optimistic that she will return.

I will wait here for her patiently and devotedly. And if fate should separate us and we become but memories from the past, let the Almighty God protect you and follow you in your future endeavors.

With sincere greetings,

Hilda Kleist

Vanished? Left the house? Where?

Crazed thoughts bombarded my tired brain.

That wonderful lady. That beloved angel. She took care of my Hanna.

Oh, Damnation, why do you rob me of my only path to happiness?

I will find her, and she will be happy again. We will both be happy again.

I tried to cheer myself by thinking about the prospect of visiting Hanover once more, but only an emptiness of soul and vast, new longings flooded over me. Doubt crawled beneath my skin and a fog of fear wrapped my heart in its clammy fingers.

I stared out the window seeing nothing.

Hero

After an hour or so my stupor began to lift. I carefully opened the official letter from the Secretary of the Office of the Chancellor, State of Lower Saxony, and read the contents in disbelief:

Honorable Herr Timo Tomić, the Carpenter:

It is our great pleasure to inform you that the Office of the Chancellor for the State of Lower Saxony, in the name of the German people, has made the decision to present to you and to your fallen Serbian comrades, the former prisoners of war who have sacrificed their lives in the battle against the terror carried out by Russian and Polish war prisoners, *The Knight's Medal of the First Order*, in recognition of your heroic defense of the innocent residents of the village of Lomnitz and its surroundings.

Herr Sebastian Gerhard, the Chancellor of the Regional Government of Lower Saxony, requests your presence on 18 March 1949 to present to you this highly respected decoration from the German people, as a sign of appreciation for your heroic act. The Christian Democratic Union, as a leading political body for occupied Germany and her people, also expresses deep gratitude for your Knightly Serbian courage in the defense of the villagers of Lomnitz and the surrounding area.

The people of Lomnitz, as well as our office, await with great anticipation your confirmation and acceptance of the invitation from Herr Gerhard, as we all sincerely hope that you will attend this historic celebration.

We kindly ask you to confirm your arrival with the attached letter and envelope, enclosed for your convenience.

Sincerely,
Stefan Brahm
The Secretary of the Office of the Chancellor
State of Lower Saxony

I closed the letter and gazed at the blur of passing landscape. With a sharp contraction of my diaphragm, I grasped the irony of my circumstance.

The nation that ordered me to put on a uniform and defend the borders of a disintegrating country has proclaimed me an enemy of the State, and the reward for return to my Fatherland will be the chains of a war prisoner and a trial for treason.

—For unselfish sacrifice in defense of innocent village people, the government of my former enemy will give me the Knight's Medal of the First Order for my heroism!

What a world!

I arrived in Hanover late that evening. The streets were lit, yet the city appeared empty in the somber winter night. My shadow wandered through the wide boulevard, dancing occasionally under the big shining windows. It disappeared behind me as I passed street lamps, only to return faithfully to my quick steps.

Rising proudly in the evocative veil of artistry, the Opera, now renovated, stood bathed in the light of numerous powerful reflectors. Tall lampposts lit the entire street around her. She had been painted in winter white, with shades of blue on her façade and golden sculptures on her roof.

Spellbound at this magnificent site, I passed her and secretly expected to hear the symphony through the open windows of the upper balcony.

Only a short walk remained. My heart beat with a mighty rhythm while my sweaty palms grabbed the gate and pressed the electric bell that rang in the quiet yard of Mrs. Heinrich's house.

I heard steps and stopped ringing.

The familiar voice of Mrs. Kleist asked who rang.

I trembled. I felt an unknown fear and cleared my throat by speaking my name.

The gate opened wide and Mrs. Kleist hurried to hug me, extremely happy to see me. We entered the front yard, she locked the gate behind us, then stopped before the front door and hugged me again and sobbed. I felt her aging body shake for a moment, then return to the original posture of her inborn dignity as she composed herself after the avalanche of emotion.

We entered the living room in an atmosphere of lightness that suddenly drained my strength. Exhausted and beaten, I took a seat in a lounge chair. Mrs. Kleist rushed to place a small pillow under my head, and then walked away to the kitchen while I gazed about the room in search of my beloved.

The burden of loss weighed so heavily on me here in this room that it felt as though I sensed every detail of every memory written on every molecule of my being. I hungrily inhaled every touch of her body and gulped even the smallest traces left of her delightful charm. Soon my eyes fogged with sadness, and I felt tears spill down my face—my mind utterly exhausted from years of searching.

"I have prepared some tea for you, Herr Timo."

The soft voice of Mrs. Kleist woke me from my reveries. "Herr Timo, would you care to refresh yourself?"

"Yes, Madame. Thank you."

I went to the bathroom and washed my hands and face with soap that smelled of wild flowers. It suddenly breathed more life into me than I had felt in a long time.

The hot tea tasted warm and sweet. As I drank it, I watched Mrs. Kleist sitting in the lounge chair in almost exactly the same position as the late Mrs. Heinrich had. She lifted her cup of tea on the saucer at almost exactly the same height and showed almost exactly the same extraordinary features of aristocracy.

Surprised by the strange likeness of these two ladies, I wondered about the link between my hostess and my Hanna.

Mrs. Kleist began the conversation with a tender voice.

"Herr Timo. I am not sure that Hanna will come back here. I am afraid she may not consider this house hers, although she grew up here from a very early age."

She set her empty teacup on the table in front of her.

Her voice became more urgent. "I am concerned that, without our help, she will drown in this nightmare of lost souls we currently find ourselves in and will end up helpless at the bottom of some human pit."

She inhaled deeply. "Mind you, I have searched through all corners of Hanover. I have reported her to the police, to the English and French occupation authorities, to the Red Cross, to the office for displaced persons, to the missing persons office, and to nearby sanatoriums."

She raised her shoulders and her eyebrows. "And everywhere I go they promise to help, but, mind you, no one knows anything about her."

She shrugged and poured me another tea, then one for herself. She left hers on the table and sat with her hands folded in her lap.

She winced. "I have aged, Herr Timo, and I am helpless. Her disappearance is destroying me."

Her voice trembled. She took a sip of tea. Then, with a still quivering voice, she continued, "You see, dear Timo, Hanna is my daughter."

Flabbergasted at this revelation, I fell back in my chair as though receiving a punch.

"Hanna's mother?" I gasped, stunned.

Her breathing became shaky. "Yes, Herr Timo. Because of my career, she spent most of her childhood with my sister Rosa. Although the separation pained us both, she grew into a fine lady and followed my footsteps into the world of opera. I wish . . ." She closed her eyes and sobbed softly, covering her face with her hands.

I felt helpless.

I wanted to pour the compassion that overflowed my heart into her ears, but I could only choke and cough.

The silence between us grew so thick we couldn't hear each other.

Finally, my desire to find Hanna overwhelmed my stupor, and my words broke free. "Madame, is there anything in her youth, in her childhood, that would lure her to some happy surroundings?"

She moved forward in her chair and looked at me with surprise. "I really cannot imagine that she loved any other place better than Hanover and the Opera House."

She set her teacup and saucer back on the table. "Rosa raised her here and had her educated in culture, philosophy, and social sciences. When I was not on tour, she went with me to every single performance, even at a very early age. She received music and voice lessons from our best teachers. She sang in a choir here starting at age seven. And when she turned fifteen and had such a gossamer voice, I gave up my career to devote myself to furthering hers. She has simply spent all her life devoted to music."

Somewhat pensively, she picked up her tea again and returned to her former position, back straight, teacup raised. "She is not a child of nature, though she did become excited with the beauty of forests, meadows, and country life. But I believe all that related to her decision to teach in that village during the war, a concession to the life and times of the era."

She paused and her face became slightly stern. "Her sudden marriage to Colonel Gottfried seemed somewhat incomprehensible to me—though she was raised without a father—and, mind you, I know she was uncomfortable with the Colonel's family at Hildesheim."

She turned and looked directly at me. "I quite frankly do not know what other place could pull her more strongly than this."

We continued our conversation, examining every possible path for her wandering. I mentioned my plan to return to Lomnitz in a few weeks, but I did not tell her the main reason for going, as I secretly prayed that Hanna would turn up there prior to my arrival.

But my heart told me differently. It would be the last place she would return to.

Mrs. Kleist told me not to lose hope, but that she secretly believed Hanna would never wake from her dark sleep. This possibility affected me deeply, and I shook, thinking of the horror of such a life.

Mrs. Kleist then calmly reasoned with me about my future and compassionately encouraged me to emigrate to the New World with the rest of my countrymen. "Here," she said, "there are only ghosts and shadows."

She lowered her eyes and shook her head. "You are still so young. To wither away trying to find a lost soul would be a tragedy for you."

She promised to write if she learned anything about Hanna.

I listened, her words echoing loudly through my dark mind, hitting my most tender spots with deeply penetrating needles. She understood the human condition, but I knew that at some level Hanna and I could never live apart.

I slept in the same room where I had slept before, and the next morning, after a hot tea with biscuits, I said goodbye to Mrs. Kleist and went back to my Black Army barracks, empty once more.

The Sermon

I arrived in Lomnitz two days before the Chancellor of Lower Saxony's visit. Unannounced and unexpected, I took a taxi from Bergen and stepped out in front of the new Town Hall. A Wednesday, villagers kept busy and paid no attention to passersby.

The clouded sky let through a few broken sunrays that spread, without harmony or reflection, over roofs, backfields, country roads, and far away forests. The squeaking of rusty door hinges, the cackling of chickens, and an occasional barking dog broke the silence.

I recognized everything, except for shadows that now fell at a different angle, changing the familiar past into an unfamiliar present. My eyes wandered over the new village, trying to connect with places I once knew so well.

A familiar voice broke my daydream. "Are you looking for someone, sir?"

I turned around and recognized the Rev. Keller.

Dressed in tailored civilian clothes with an overcoat made of black English wool and a new wide-brimmed hat and mustache, I must have looked quite different from the board-carrying figure I was the first time we met. My heart leaping, I removed my hat and stretched my arms out wide to greet him, "Reverend Norman, it's I, Timo."

He ran over and hugged me.

"It's been almost three years. Welcome."

Then he turned to his house and hollered loudly. "Marta, come here, quick. Timo's arrived."

Marta ran out shouting with such enthusiasm that everyone in the vicinity heard her.

Soon Lomnitz Square turned into a real celebration at the news that I had returned. Everyone hugged me and waved their arms with joy. Some had tears in their eyes, and some stared with unusual expressions of admiration, trying to get to know as much as possible about me.

All at once, the crowd parted to allow the passage of two older persons, the old Mayor and his wife. I stepped forward to meet them. We fell into each other's embrace and sobbed together.

The whole village stood silent, choked and dazed by their depth of tenderness, tears running down their faces. Old Mrs. Riedl caressed my head and spoke some soft words of consolation, while Mayor Riedl tried to wipe away the flood of tears that ran down his wrinkled face.

I heard a familiar, loving voice behind me, sounding hardy and excited. "Timo, my apple, my sweet Timo!"

Elsa ran with open arms and threw herself at me, kissing my face.

I am home.

Soon Radenko and Irma arrived, and our reunion became a homecoming laced with immeasurable joy. The surprise gathering and celebration of my arrival continued late into the afternoon and might have gone on through the evening, if not interrupted by the church bell, calling its parishioners to evening service.

We all filed quietly into the nave, shaking hands and hugging as we congregated briefly here and there along the way. The Rev. Mr. Keller gave the following sermon that will remain in my memory forever:

> Our Fatherland lost the war. The English, Americans, and Russians won. Maybe they had better materials, more soldiers, wiser leaders. But that was, in essence, a material victory. The *material* victory was theirs.
>
> Here, among us, lives another kind of person, and this kind of person has achieved a much greater victory—a victory of spirit, heart, and honor, a victory of peace and Christian love. These victors are the Serbs who fought shoulder to shoulder with those that the world considered their enemies. These victors are the Serbs who fought beside our villagers to protect our families. They laid aside all care for personal safety. They laid aside every nationalistic concern, and they laid down their lives to save the lives of our women and our children.
>
> Formerly we knew very little about them. But we *have* known what *we* did in Serbia. We knew that for every one of our occupying soldiers killed, we killed a hundred Serbs defending their homeland. We knew that we not only committed this outrage, but we also directed others to commit similar outrages, so that Serbia was besieged from all sides: from Italy, from Hungary, from Albania, from Bulgaria, and even—and perhaps most horribly—from its own Yugoslav sister, Croatia. We knew that here, among us, several

thousand Serbian soldiers—who not long before represented their homeland's finest—endured their imprisonment as skeletons, exhausted and devastated from hunger, barely able to put one foot in front of the other. Yet we had them build their own housing and our concentration camps. We had them dig our ditches and our trenches. We had them work in our iron foundries, and we even had them carry the very munitions that would destroy their homeland and those of their allies.

All of us have heard the Serbian saying, "One who does not take revenge will not be honored in heaven."

Who among us did not fear the revenge of those suffering souls? We feared that if we lost, they would do the same to us as we did to them. We imagined our children floating in sewers or roasting on spits. We imagined the murder of our people, the raping of our women, and the destruction of our homes by Serbian prisoners of war.

But instead, the opposite happened.

When the POW camp fences burst and hundreds of raging Russians and Poles went on a rampage to pillage, burn, rape, and kill, our Serbian knights confronted the attackers and put their lives on the line to protect our villagers from that beastly reprisal.

Only one of these knights is, by God's will, still alive, and he is with us tonight, here in our village, here in our church. *Serbs* sacrificed their lives for *our* children, for the children of our mourning Fatherland.

> Only now can we understand why our great poet Goethe learned the Serbian language.
>
> Only now can we comprehend that Bismarck's last word on his deathbed was "Serbia."
>
> This victory of the Serbs was far, far greater, far, far richer than *any* material victory. Raised in their St. Sava[25] tradition, with a spirit nurtured by the heroic tales that Goethe loved so much, they won our hearts and our love.
>
> The souls of our surviving villagers have recorded this victory in their hearts. They will carry it forward for generations, both here in Lomnitz and in the surrounding areas, as an immortal story of brave Serbian men who won the greatest battle of the war, indeed, the greatest and most glorious battle in life, the battle that we all face each and every day, the battle to set aside hatred and to take up the cause of Christ, the cause of Love.
>
> I wish to dedicate this commemorative service tonight to our Savior and our saviors.

His speech echoed strongly from one end of the church to the other. His powerful words entered the hearts of the

[25] Saint Sava (also Saint Sabbas; born: 1174; died: 14 January 1236) was a Serbian prince and Orthodox monk, the first Archbishop of the Serbian Church, the founder of Serbian law and literature, and a diplomat. He is widely considered one of the most important figures of Serbian history and is canonized and venerated by the Serbian Orthodox Church as its founder. He is the patron saint of Serbian schools and schoolchildren.

parishioners and spread through the open doors and windows over the village houses, farmlands, and forests.

No birds sang. Nor dogs barked. No breeze sighed. Everything rested in heavenly peace.

Radenko and Irma

The sun had set by the end of the service, so the villagers left for their homes. Many of them invited me to be their guest. Holding Elsa's hand on one side and Wilhelmina's on the other, however, made my determination to be with them obvious, so the Rev. Keller and Mayor Riedl said goodnight.

We started back with Radenko and Irma and soon found ourselves in front of the school.

I stopped involuntarily and stared at the renovated school building, at the pretty, white fence, and at the tall trees in the yard, but I shied away from looking at her house. I knew that she was not there, although I wished desperately to see her at the door or window.

I stepped back and, when I finally turned to look in that direction, shivered, at the sight of a foggy white form waving to me.

Finally, my vision cleared and I could distinguish a white window curtain fluttering on some unknown air.

Elsa pulled me close and whispered, "You didn't find her, did you?"

Our heads hanging, we slowly walked away, in silence.

At last we came to the end of the street where Elsa's house stood washed in lamplight. The workshop had been torn down, and in its place Elsa had added more rooms, rebuilt the entrance steps, newly tiled the roof, plastered the exterior walls, replaced the old windows and doors, and painted the house with clear white.

This enchanting renovation made me very happy. Beaming, I hugged both Elsa and Wilma tightly. "Mile would be very proud."

"Yes. My long-legged man would be really happy," she said and ran into the house sobbing.

"I am truly an ass," I said to Radenko, as soon as Wilhelmina had joined her.

Radenko answered in Serbian. "Don't worry, brother, Elsa's a very strong woman, much stronger than we could imagine, when you think of what she's been through."

He watched his foot as it shuffled some stones out of the way. "Reverend Keller and Marta have given her so much love and care. She was so lucky to have their help."

He looked up at me. "After Wilhelmina and Ernst came back, she finally recovered, and she's almost the same as before, but with a sadness in her eyes that's always there."

"And the children? How are they?"

Radenko nodded. "The children are fine. Wilma totally wiped that event out of her mind, and she never thinks about it. As you can see, she's become a beauty that many of the young boys follow about. Ernst is learning a trade in Celle. He wants to be an auto mechanic."

I put a hand on his arm. "Tell me about Irma and you after they took you away. What happened?"

"Oh, it was awful," he said looking down. "The Gestapo came that morning, stormed through the house, handcuffed both of us, and forced the children to come too."

He took a deep breath and looked away. "They loaded us in a truck and took us to Gestapo headquarters in Celle. The children screamed and cried when they took Irma off the truck and led her away."

He faced me again, his arms reaching out into nothingness. "I tried to hold on to her, but a guard in the truck knocked me unconscious."

He took out a cigarette and offered me one. I declined.

"I woke up in jail, and the children were gone. I had a terrible headache and a big lump on the back of my head. Finally, a medic came and took my pulse, then put a cold pack on the lump."

He patted his cigarette on the front of the pack, then put the pack in his pocket and lit up.

"When they lifted me, I almost fainted. They walked me out slowly and took me to a motorcycle with a sidecar."

He shook his head in disbelief. "Somehow, they got me in, although I was probably out cold, because I don't remember a thing about how it happened."

He took a puff. "The road was bumpy, full of bomb craters. I don't know how that medic managed to drive through, but we got to the hospital just before the Allies started carpet bombing us. The bombing was so heavy the ground shook, the hospital walls cracked, and glass shattered all over the place."

He took a long drag and started to choke. When the coughing stopped, he continued.

"So we took cover in a horse stall, but the horses went crazy. They neighed and reared up on their hind legs. Then they kicked their stalls open and ran right out into hell. I saw horse legs, heads, and barrels flying in the air like feathers in a hurricane."

He took a deep breath. "All the folks in the hospital kept screaming until the last bomb exploded in the distance and we finally had some quiet again. The only thing that saved us was that hospital sign on the roof."

He stopped. His eyes glazed over as he went into deep thought.

"Then what happened?" I insisted.

He lifted his eyebrows, looked up at the sky, took another deep breath, and wistfully said, "It's going to snow again today. I really should cut some firewood and keep the furnace running. Irma shivers all the time. Nothing warms her anymore."

I cradled his face in my hands and made him look at me. "Brother, speak to me. Let it out. I can share your pain."

I hugged his trembling body and tried to calm him down. He inhaled and exhaled slowly, his breath visible in the cold.

After more quaking and crying , he said, "I was lucky. They dressed my wound and took me back to Staub."

Then he sneered. "Like nothing happened!"

He looked puzzled, but less shaken. "I wondered what was going on, then I realized they didn't have time for me. The war was over. The guards abandoned us. That slimy soup ran out, and we had nothing to eat. We were sure we wouldn't last, and dozens did die every day."

His cigarette had almost burned down by then. He took a final puff and threw the rest in the grass, then smashed it with his foot.

"The Allies came a few days later. They took one look at us and they couldn't even breathe. Some of them screamed, some wept, and some just turned away, angry as hell. I couldn't tell how many, but they took truckloads of us to mass graves somewhere."

Radenko blew on his hands to warm them.

"They fed me pretty well and I started getting back my strength. About a week later, I asked them to release me so I could find Irma and the children. The Brits gave me a pass and told me to go to the local missing persons office. There they sent me to a women's prison camp near Bremen."

He put his hands under his arms and began to sway slightly.

"It took me a week to find Irma. She was in one of the field hospitals. She had pneumonia and the nurses had very little hope for her."

He winced. "She was just skin and bones. Even with her eyes open, she looked dead. You could hardly see her breathe. They gave her an IV. I tried talking to her, but my throat just closed up, and I cried."

He rubbed his eyes with his fingertips. Then he hunched his shoulders as he pulled his fingers down over his face in a look of sheer agony.

"A woman in the cot next to hers saw me and waved me over. She was like a skeleton mumbling something I couldn't understand. So I put my ear next to her mouth, and she whispered: 'Irma. Is she dead?' 'No,' I told her. Then she said to me, 'She has a strong will. She told me she has to live for her children.'"

Anguish in his eyes, he shook his head. "It was so hard for this woman to talk. She asked me if I were Raden, and I nodded. Then I put my finger on her mouth and told her to rest, that I would talk to the doctor to find out more."

He pulled a handkerchief from his pocket, wiped his nose, and put it back.

"I found an old German doctor and talked to him about Irma's condition and her chances for recovery. He said she had a burning desire that kept her going, but that she was in really bad shape and would need a long time to recover, even if she managed to survive the pneumonia. He said they had started her on a new American medicine, and he thought it would help, but he wanted to make sure I understood that she was terribly weak and that nursing her back to health would take months."

He warmed his hands again with his breath, and his mood lightened slightly.

"The medication did work and she started showing signs of life. She slowly began to eat again and to move her head and arms. She knew someone was there but she couldn't recognize me. I slept on a cot next to her and held her hand the whole time. After a few days she got a little stronger. The nurses helped her get up and walk, but she kept holding my hand and wouldn't take a step without me."

He looked at me. His pain pierced my soul.

A slender smile appeared on his lips and flickered in his eyes. "Finally it was clear she knew me. I was so happy I cried."

He dug his hands into his pockets and pulled his shoulders together. "Helga, the woman in the bed next to her, recovered a little more quickly, and she was able to talk. She told me horror stories about their imprisonment. I can't even think about it."

His eyes darkened once more. "Listening to her made me cry."

He warmed his hands again. My eyes urged him to go on. "Helga told me the Nazis took them to Uckermark on the fifth of December. The camp was for young German women—about sixteen to twenty-one—that the Nazis had accused of racial defilement.[26] She said the barracks were

---

[26] Nazi lawyers designed the law called "racial defilement," ordered by Heinrich Himmler, the head of the SS in 1940 stating: "Fellow Germans who engage in sexual relations with male or female civil workers of foreign nationality shall be arrested immediately." At

packed tight with girls, but it was so cold, they were happy to have some new warm bodies join them on the big wooden platform they slept on."

He raised his shoulders and pulled his coat collar up over his ears.

"She said they gave them numbers right away and never used their names again. She was 395 and Irma was 430. They had female guards who carried switches and beat them all the time, right from the start. They would even whack them on their way from the barracks to the showers and back."

He put his hands in his armpits and hugged his chest, as though trying to keep it from bursting. "The very first day Irma got really beat up, because she stumbled and fell right in front of the head woman. Helga said that the woman's beating was an act of pure brutality. That guard was so mad that when she talked, she spattered all over Irma, to the point that it scared everybody to death. When she was finished with the beating, she ordered a couple prisoners to pick Irma up and carry her to the barracks. Someone brought out a can of pine tar and smeared it all over her."

He shook his head and wrung his hands. "She said Irma just trembled and moaned, so she took Irma in her arms and wrapped Irma's overcoat around both of them to keep her warm."

Then his hands moved back under his arms. "The next morning all they got was cabbage soup and a piece of bread, and then they had to march to the center of the camp where they had to strip again and stand naked for almost an hour. She said snowflakes fell on them and didn't even melt, they were so cold. When they finally

---

first, this applied only to relationships between Jews and non-Jews, but the racist law was later expanded to include Slavs.

ordered the women to dress, some of the women went unconscious because they just couldn't tolerate the frozen clothing on their naked shivering bodies. . . ."

Elsa's call interrupted our conversation.

I no longer wondered why Irma had still not spoken.

As we entered the house, we could see that Elsa had full glasses of brandy waiting for us.

"Welcome home, my dear Timo," she said, lifting her glass.

Radenko and Wilma grinned at me and toasted with joyful welcomes. Irma smiled and I smiled back, toasting to everybody.

I shook from Radenko's story, but I made it look like the strong brandy had done it. I rumbled, "Brrrrrrrrr!"

We burst into laughter, and suddenly the atmosphere of tension changed into a relaxed and happy meeting of old friends.

Radenko and I started singing spontaneously "By the River Morava," filling our hearts with the joy of familiar words and melody, and a little later, Wilma and Elsa joined in.

Different folk melodies echoed late through the night, summoning further the spirit of celebration after years of dejection, suffocation, and exhaustion in a decade of hardship.

I was home.

Knight's Honor

At daybreak, through the window in the new bedroom of Elsa's expanded house, I watched unspoiled snowflakes fall and pile up on the windowsill, reminding me of the cotton stuffed around Christmas ornaments in the shops for the wealthy people of Münster. My gaze then fondled the snow-covered rooftops, barns, and storage bins, bringing back memories of the many changing scenes of my dark history.

I felt a heavy longing for Hanna. I thought of the cold tunnel where she now wandered, and I took a deep breath of the sharp morning air, calling to her spirit with bursting lungs and the uplifting hope bestowed upon me by my circle of reunited friends.

Radenko came early to fetch me, and after partaking of the abundant breakfast Elsa had made, we took a walk to the cemetery. Radenko's letter had told me that the people of Lomnitz had raised monuments to our fallen countrymen, but I did not expect to find the magnificent sight that stood in front of us.

Behind the cemetery's main entrance wall, very close to the gate, in the first row lay four beautifully sculpted monuments of white marble with Orthodox crosses on each one and the names of Spasoje Užičanin, Miodrag Stojković, Nedeljko Polovina, and Aleksa Pitić. In the second row behind them stood monuments to old Weinlein, young Stefan Fiske, Bauer, and the rest of the innocent victims of that horrible night of pogrom on the first day of Germany's surrender.

MIODRAG STOJKOVIĆ
Brave soldier of the Yugoslav Kingdom
Killed in the defense of Lomnitz residents
9 May 1945

Mile's monument was beautifully edged with white bricks around the perimeter. A spray of flowers lay on top of the grave.

My heart ached when I passed the grave of little Anna Marie. Tears filled my eyes as I put my lips to the icy surface of that dear angel's picture.

Radenko, noticing my sudden dizziness, caught me and brought a lit cigarette to my lips. Having picked up the habit in the Black Army, I took a long drag and tried to choke back the mighty pain in me and to calm myself down, but the sudden strength of the tobacco smoke only blinded me.

We sat next to the chapel for a while and smoked, staring blankly at these mute remains of the past.

Why?

We walked to the village square, and in front of the Town Hall, we met Mayor Riedl and the Reverend. We exchanged warm greetings and talked about the next day's events.

Always a man of precision and efficiency, Mayor Riedl shared his information with us. "We have prepared the program for tomorrow with the following schedule. At ten o'clock in the morning, before the arrival of the Chancellor, we will meet briefly in the Town Hall, then recess to the cemetery. There, we will begin the ceremony by paying our respects to the fallen victims."

Mayor Riedl continued with a nod toward the town's pastor.

"The Reverend Herr Keller will give a memorial sermon, and then the church choir from Celle will sing an appropriate hymn."

He cleared his throat and went on to describe the rest of the program.

"Chancellor Gerhard will arrive at eleven o'clock. He will place wreaths on the graves of the fallen heroes, and then he will make a speech in the Town Hall and present you with a medal, which he will pin on your chest."

He smiled at me. "If you wish to make a speech, Herr Timo, that would please us all very much. The residents of Lomnitz have all expressed their desire to hear you. But if you do not wish to speak, I'll close the ceremony expressing our gratitude to Chancellor Gerhard and to you."

Mayor Riedl's words eased my mind. I could not even think about speaking of anything related to that damned night while my poor love still walked the streets or lay dying in some remote corner of some godforsaken hovel.

Breakfast

When I got up the next morning, Elsa noticed that I was upset and she tried to cheer me. She asked if I slept well. I answered indifferently, and then, feeling ashamed of my insensitivity, I gave her a hug.

When I squeezed her in my arms, I felt her trembling, boiling with the excitement of body contact, and I felt her hold me tighter, with her murmuring tender lips nearing mine. I kissed her softly next to her lips, and then separated from her quivering body, embarrassed by my unrestrained emotions and besieged by images of Hanna and Mile.

I walked out into the front yard. More snow had fallen, and everything was white. I shivered, more from the memories of a snow covered past than from the present cold.

Nothing had changed. Everything was like before. Cold. Distant. Unreal.

I waved my hand, attempting to chase away the ghosts of the past, then turned to the window, where I saw Elsa's crying face. I walked out through the gate, subdued and miserable on the very day when they would celebrate my name.

I arrived at the school and stumbled, unable to take a step that didn't raise ghosts. My feet walked a red carpet of blood. Silent screams blared. My hands pulled a body without a head to the bottomless pit in the yard. From the dark depths of the walls, wolves in human form jumped out at me. Black clouds of thick smoke choked out any flicker of daylight.

I dared not venture inside. Trembling in my turbulence, I jumped back, walked away, and slowly meandered toward the cemetery.

I stopped in front of my comrades' monuments and raised my head to the heavens. I thought of them looking at me from their new home in Paradise and, shaking, crossed myself and prayed. I reminisced about our happy moments together and smiled thinking of Nedeljko's comic expressions, Mile's clumsy, long-legged walk, Spasoje's quick eyes, and Aleksa's child-like excitement at every package from home.

I sobbed for my lost friends, and suddenly I felt very lonely, very much in a foreign land, without anyone of my own.

At nine o'clock, I reached the front of the Town Hall. Many people had already arrived. Inside, villagers crowded the auditorium, some sitting on benches, others standing by the wall, and some simply milling around. On the stage, which the people of Lomnitz had built for this occasion, the Celle Choir practiced their songs, although loud conversations and children's giggles drowned out their voices.

Reverend Keller interrupted my thoughts. "Are you ready for the ceremony?"

"I think I am, Reverend Norman."

"Did you sleep well? You look tired." He rested a hand on my shoulder. "Did you have coffee?"

I shook my head.

"It would do you good. Come home with me. Marta will have coffee and serve us some of her delicious cake."

Reverend Keller escorted me to his house.

From the front door, he called loudly, "Marta, I'm bringing Timo for coffee. Is that all right, dear?"

"Of course, silly. Come in, come in, Timo. Everything's ready."

The captivating smells of coffee, freshly baked cake, and wild strawberry jam reminded me, as I walked into the warm kitchen, that I had missed breakfast.

"Is the Little Destroyer up or sleeping? I don't hear him."

"Oh, Norman, our Klaus is not a destroyer. Don't say that. He's just a baby," Marta scolded. "Strong for his age, maybe, but otherwise just a curious little ten-month old."

"'Strong, maybe'! Ha! He almost pulled the tail off our Felix."

The Reverend removed his coat and hung it on a hook by the door. "That poor cat hides every time Klaus rolls down from his room."

Although Reverend Keller looked away as he described his son, I could hear the pride in his voice.

"You know, Herr Timo, he just started walking and he mows down everything in his wake. We've moved all our breakables to upper shelves and barricaded the stove." He shook his head and chuckled, as he took my coat and hung it beside his.

"Ula, his *Kindermädchen*, can barely keep up with him. She's young and full of energy, but by the end of the day, she's exhausted, God bless her. She has so much patience, and she's so good with him. We . . ."

A crash above us interrupted him.

Marta ran upstairs and calmed the little one's cries with her soothing voice. Once the sobbing stopped, she brought the baby down, straining slightly at his unusual weight and talking to him in a sweet, motherly way, as he rubbed his eyes.

She set him down on his feet. He wobbled for a second or two, then flashed a smile of joy at his father and hobbled over toward me with arms extended.

Just then the young nanny joined us in the kitchen. Klaus turned to smile at her, then plopped down on his butt and laughed.

Reverend Norman joined the baby's laughter, while Marta looked puzzled, and Ula sat down next to the child. She pulled him over to her. He twirled and twisted to get free, but her manner calmed him down, and he finally sat quietly in her lap, staring at me as though trying to remember my face.

"What did he break now, Ula?" Reverend Norman chortled.

"I was picking up his toys, when he gave a good yank on the curtains and pulled the rod right off the wall. We're going to have to tie those up out of reach, I believe."

The blond Destroyer had a devilish look on his face, as though he understood exactly what Ula said.

Reverend Norman took the baby from Ula and threw him up into the air, joining him in squeals of delight.

Marta held her breath at each toss, then relaxed and shrugged when the baby returned safely to her husband's hands. She gestured for us all to sit down at the table, while Ula took the baby from Reverend Norman and set him in his highchair.

Marta served our coffee, while her husband cut large pieces of cake—still a superb delicacy—for each of us.

The taste of Marta's cake with a sip of real coffee revived me. I ate and watched Reverend Norman enjoy every forkful, licking his lips continuously to make sure he was not dropping a single crumb. Little Klaus followed his father's lead, lapping up every morsel, licking his fingers, and bouncing in his seat, arms wide, then clapping, asking for more.

"That's enough for you, Klaus," Marta advised, as she took his plate away before it became a missile. "And Norman, you leave a little too for Herr Timo. Don't eat everything," she said teasing him.

She turned to me, "You know, Herr Timo, my Norman loves sweets very much."

"I'm not half so bad as your son," the young minister replied with mock indignation that turned to mock arrogance. "And furthermore, I'm not worried about it, my dear, because I know you've made two cakes."

"Ah, you naughty boy! You're always snooping through the cabinets. Just like Felix."

Wonderful couple, I thought as I laughed with them. *What strange contrasts in the character of the German people, both soft and hard souls, in a jumble of social relations—no different really from any other nationality.*

Ceremony

Promptly at ten o'clock, Mayor Riedl opened the ceremony. He read the program, reminded the locals about behavior appropriate to this historic occasion, and asked that they not crowd the honored guest, Chancellor Gerhard, but rather provide a wide corridor for him and his entourage.

"Lomnitz will this day be recorded in German history. Let us all do our part to demonstrate that we truly deserve this great honor."

After his introductory speech, everyone left the hall and walked in an orderly manner to the cemetery. People lined up along the low fence on both sides of the entrance gate and allowed only a few of us to pass through, among them Mayor Riedl, the Rev. Mr. Keller, and myself.

The Rev. Keller gave a short commemorative sermon. The surviving villagers laid flowers on the graves, and the choir, with their angelic voices, sang suitable hymns.

Large, fluffy snowflakes drifted down on us. In that absolute stillness, only our voices rippled the silence of the valley.

Then the church bell clanged, rupturing both harmony and peacefulness.

The announcement came that the delegation had arrived and the bustle began. The local brass band played the welcome march. Everyone gave way to the Chancellor as he approached the graves to lay on them huge wreaths of red roses, studded with both the German and Serbian flags. The Rev. Mr. Keller then gave the benediction.

As the Chancellor shook hands with the Mayor and the Reverend, the crowd dispersed.

We all returned to the Town Hall and took our places. At the word from one of the Mayor's assistants, everyone rose proudly, watching for the Chancellor's entrance. Soon a tall functionary from the Chancellor's entourage appeared at the door, scanned the hall quickly, and nodded his head. A pair of escorts passed through the door and lined up against the wall. Then the Chancellor of the Regional Government of Lower Saxony, Mr. Gerhard, walked in, and the public started applauding, giving a sincere welcome to the Head of the Region.

Sebastian Gerhard, a tall man in his seventies—with grayish blonde hair combed straight back—and very attentive eyes, carefully observed all the faces that silently hailed him. Mayor Riedl greeted him and seated him at the center of the main table, along with his secretary and his immediate escort.

When our eyes met, I nodded. Piercingly, he read my every detail. His face fascinated and encouraged me. In it, strong, deeply engraved gorges of suffering, pride, and defiance glowed. I knew this look so well from our old peasants, who had passed through many devastations of their homeland—the Turkish wars, the Balkan wars, the First World War—and who, without fear, proudly wore the history of their people on their old faces. Perhaps fate had similarly played with this man as well.

He took his place at the podium, and, after looking briefly at his notes, he began.

"On the eighth of May 1945, our Fatherland surrendered unconditionally to the Allies. The doors of our prisoner of war camps flew open and released a reign of terror that superimposed utter panic on the aching despair already in the hearts of Germans across the Country. The violence of that night left no one untouched. The war exacted a terrible price, and our surrender an equally terrible one.

"But here in this small village of Lomnitz, a chivalrous act shone so brightly that it has cut through the gloom that envelopes our nation. When Timo Tomić, a Serbian prisoner of war at Staub, got word that the women and children of the town were under attack, in the dead of night, he gathered four of his fellow countrymen and raced to their aid. Together with Lomnitz' old men and boys, they held off the bloodthirsty hordes of raging Russian and Polish former POWs who, otherwise, would most certainly not have ceased until every last villager lay dead."

He paused to look at each and every person in the crowd. "Those of you here who survived that night have this man, Timo Tomić, to thank."

He grabbed the podium firmly with both hands and leaned forward. "The measure of the horror this man confronted is symbolized in the wreaths we have just laid on his fellow countrymen's graves. His valor in the face of utterly overwhelming odds teaches us the meaning of honor and sacrifice. Only the brave can become Knights of the First Order, and today we have the privilege of honoring a man who we can truly say, without a moment's hesitation, is among the bravest."

He nodded to me, then turned back to the crowd.

"Many innocent people lost their lives that night, but this village will be eternally grateful to the knightly Serbians who sacrificed themselves to protect Lomnitz' locals. Please feel free now to express your gratitude to the sole surviving Hero of Lomnitz, the Knight of the Serbian nation, Herr Timo Tomić."

Thunderous applause answered Mr. Gerhard, who applauded too as he stepped back from the podium to face me and smile.

I was touched. My throat became tight as I tried not to sob.

Heroes do not cry.

The Chancellor returned to the podium, picked up the medal, and displayed it to the crowd. "The people of Germany, on behalf of the residents of Lomnitz and the surrounding areas, have today the great honor of placing upon you the Knightly Medal of the First Order. In the name of the future Federal Republic of Germany, we thank you for your sacrifice."

Having finished his speech, Chancellor Gerhard turned to me and pinned the medal on my chest. He congratulated me heartily, and then joined the others in applause that lasted several minutes.

As I waited for the room to quiet, I pondered scenes from the past. I was enchanted, confused, and exhilarated.

But a perpetual veil of discontent clouded my heart in this moment of happiness.

The crowd startled me out of my thoughts with loud chanting: "Speech! Speech! Speech! Speech!"

I looked around and again the piercing eyes of the remarkable Sebastian Gerhard met mine. His smile encouraged me, so I turned to the villagers.

The hall became silent, and suddenly stage fright overwhelmed me. Yet something pushed me to speak.

What shall I say?

I started with words I remember to this day.

"I came in chains to your country, suffering through most of the war, just as thousands of my countrymen suffered, just as we *all* suffered. By a strange turn of events, I learned your language, your music, your culture. I learned to respect your people, and in the end, I fell in love with the most beautiful woman of my life, your schoolteacher, Frau Hanna Gottfried."

I heard sobs from several women and children at the mention of her name.

In pain, I continued.

"The people of Lomnitz are exceptionally good people. Kindhearted and unassuming by nature, you opened your doors to those of us POWs who worked on your farms. For the seven of us, you made a small haven in the midst of hell and protected us from evil during most of our captivity."

I paused and looked deeply into the eyes of my Lomnitz friends in the audience.

"We never forgot this. We were grateful, so we worked hard and honorably. You accepted us, shared your food with us, your clothes and your beds, and gave us more than any war prisoner could hope to receive. We felt at home, and slowly we began to understand and forgive you."

I turned to the Chancellor.

"I thank you in the name of my comrades for this Knightly Medal of the First Order that I will display with pride for the rest of my life."

Then, smiling at the people of Lomnitz, "I hope that my path may take me to another happy village just like this, in faraway America, my future homeland."

I hung my head and looked at my hands, as I clasped them in front of me. "Although many of you have asked me to stay and become a part of your wonderful new community, unfortunately, I have too many sad memories that place a heavy load on my heart here. I do not have the strength to continue to confront the past when my soul and heart now feel so empty."

I looked up and held my hands out to the crowd. "Yet there are two things that would give me joy and happiness. I'm hoping and praying to God you may help."

Everyone seemed receptive and anxious to hear my request. "As you all know, we had a wonderful man, a great Serb, and an honest worker for the Bauer family, who became a victim of Nazi tyranny in the last days of the war, Rista Kohn."

With heavy hearts, the villagers all nodded.

"A good-natured and highly educated man, he was a mild-mannered Jew who would have never hurt anyone. While devoted to his religion and traditions, yet he instructed us simple Serbian peasants on matters of culture and history. He taught me—especially—about German art and music."

I took a deep breath and crossed my fingers behind my back.

"I would like to see his name engraved on the memorial stone along with those of my fallen comrades, as part of your sincere gratitude for our deed."

Mayor Riedl cleared his throat. "It will be done. We give you our solemn promise."

Everyone got up and began to applaud along with the honored guest, Mr. Sebastian Gerhard.

I waited until the hall quieted again, then smiled on the crowd in satisfaction.

"My heart is already half full of joy with your promise. And my late brothers are grateful, I am sure."

I nodded my appreciation to all those sitting at the table, then to the crowd, as well—then sighed a deep, deep sigh.

"But it will take a long time for the other half of my heart to ever feel full again."

I looked away and brought all my strength to bear on composing myself.

"As you know, Hanna Gottfried, with several other women, survived the tragic and hellish trauma of that terrible night. She never recovered from it. For four years, I have searched for her, and my love has only grown deeper and stronger, but my efforts have remained fruitless and empty."

In the first row of villagers, I could see tears trickle down Elsa's face, as she sobbed silently, her breast heaving with unbearable pain.

"A few days ago, a letter I received from Hanna's mother rekindled my hopes. She and Hanna had returned to Hanover, but when I got there, fate had again deceived me and disappointed me terribly."

I rubbed the back of my neck and took another deep breath.

"A few days before my arrival in Hanover, my beloved Hanna had left the house and disappeared. She's helpless now and unable to protect herself in her dark mental state. I fear that something horrible may happen to her as she wanders through streets and squares unknown to her."

I stared at a spot on the ceiling above the group, then gathered my strength again.

"I accept that I cannot bring her back from the depth of her illness, but I pray God that, before I leave this country, Hanna Gottfried is safe and in good hands. That would heal the wounds in my heart and allow me to leave with peace in my soul."

I turned back to the crowd with pleading arms. "If by any chance any of you learns anything about her, I beg you to inform the Reverend Keller and her mother, Frau Kleist, in Hanover."

I made a deep bow. "May God bless you and protect you from other misfortunes. I, again, thank you in the name of my comrades, my Serbian brothers, for everything that you have done for us."

Again applause thundered through the hall. Women cried, children sobbed, and tears rolled down the faces of wrinkled, tired men, in a show of respect for their Serbian heroes.

The Chancellor approached me, shook my hand heartily once more, and said goodbye as he turned to leave through the corridor of people.

In the back of the room, behind the last group of attendees, I noticed reporters and a photographer documenting this unusual event that took place in one small village, at a single moment in history, for a few forgotten warriors.

I prayed that my parents would not pay the price for my medal.

Leaving for America

After completing the American Immigration Commission's investigations and examinations, I spent the last days in our camp wandering through the surrounding area, absorbing pictures of snow-covered parts of the city, and slowly preparing my spirit for another giant step in my life.

After four years of fruitless searching and with Hanna's mother's blessing, I could finally let go.

Hadn't all the uncertainties of being a prisoner of war led to the glory of loving Hanna? Who knows where my next step will lead?

At least that's what I kept telling myself.

I did not know the geography of the United States, but from an old torn map on the wall in the Commission office, I located Chicago and decided to make it my future residence—assuming it the center of America. I envisioned a city occupied by millions of people exactly like the kind American soldier from Fremont, Ohio, who had helped me in my search.

Nevertheless, Chicago seemed distant and strange. But the challenge of the unknown appealed to me, and my imagination somehow managed to create a new and happy future for me there.

In America, it doesn't matter who you are or where you come from. Everyone there is an immigrant. Croat or Serb, who cares? Prejudice doesn't exist. Everyone has the same opportunities. Surely they will need carpenters and cabinet makers.

At dawn a group of us refugees took the train to Bremerhaven, and after several boring hours of travel, we arrived at the huge seaport. The train unloaded its full complement of passengers, who represented many different nationalities and, like me, journeyed into the unknown.

A dozen ships lay anchored in a line along the docks, with huge bridge-like stairways going to each ship. They loaded passengers through various entrances, lower stairs for lower decks, higher stairs for upper decks, alternating and continuing from one ship to another.

The columns of people loaded very slowly, so lines stretched for several hundred meters in front of each vessel. Watching this mass of people along the tall gangways subdued me with the minuteness of the human form. Loneliness overcame me, and not even the hundreds of people before and behind me could assuage my empty heart as I wrapped my fingers around the handrail to ascend the long stairway.

Once aboard, I searched for the most remote corner of one of the lower decks—far from people, far from the past.

I stared at the gray sky and inhaled air full of diesel smoke.

I thought of nothing and slowly fell asleep to the hum of engines somewhere below me as they flexed their muscles in preparation for the rigor of the long journey ahead.

"Hey there, are you by any chance Timo Tomić?" The strong voice woke me.

"I am."

"There is a letter for you." He handed me a folded paper. "Here."

He walked away.

I opened the letter and jumped as though scalded when I recognized the handwriting.

> My dearest,
>
> You're alive! I cannot describe how happy learning that makes me. I have opened my eyes again and can now see the blue skies.

"My Hanna's alive. She wrote me!" I shouted and waved the letter around insanely.

I brought it back to my eyes, now filled with tears. I could not recognize the words. I shouted with all my strength: "My God, My Hanna!"

> Perhaps the picture staring at me from the newspaper revived me—but suddenly, all at once, everything became clear.
>
> I had somehow ended up in a hospital in Spandau, where my awakening astounded the medical staff. When they informed my mother by telegram, she almost died of happiness.
>
> Tears of both joy and grief bathed our reunion and my return home.
>
> She told me about how she found you and met with you, and about your persistent search for me. Oh, my darling, if only I had known that you were alive, I believe I would have healed immediately, but it appears I never realized it

when Mother showed me your note, and her words simply failed to penetrate my darkness.

Now that you have returned to my life, my fear that fate will separate us again causes me constant panic—especially when I read of your decision to go to America.

I rushed to catch you in Münster, but unfortunately, you had left just the day before. I inquired at all the immigration commissions without success and finally decided to travel to Bremerhaven, in the hope of catching you here.

In this sea of humanity at the port, I tried to find you, to stop you from climbing those enormous gangways that swallow thousands. I repeatedly called out to you from the shore, expecting that you would hear me and recognize my voice.

But, my beloved, I have searched for you frantically for two days on these docks, and I fear I will never see you again. This is the last in a series of letters I write at night, on the dock. I give them to every Serbian passenger I can find, and I plead with everyone to deliver them to you before you depart.

Tomorrow, the last ships will leave and I will fall into despair again if I don't see you.

If our God exists, He will hear our prayers and the thousands of prayers I have made to His Son, and I will be with you again.

If you are already aboard, look along the shoreline, my only love. Send me a sign from your deck and wave to me so that I can die happy though alone, if I cannot—as is my fondest hope—die with you.

Your dove, your Hanna, forever!

"I must get to the deck! Let me pass!" I screamed wildly.

"Who gave you this letter?" I asked the man who had delivered it just minutes earlier.

"I don't know. Some woman in white on the dock."

I raced off.

He shouted after me, "Hey, are you crazy? Where're you going? The ship's moving."

"I have to go back! I must find her," I replied, turning momentarily.

Then, to those in my way, "Let me pass!" I yelled at the people standing along the rail of the lower deck.

Finally I got through and thought I saw my white angel standing all alone, on the now-abandoned dock from which our ship slowly departed.

I screamed as loudly as I could, but my voice dissolved in the sirens of ships that sounded their deafening signals across the port.

I felt a howling scream echo from my torn heart, as the final scenes of *Tristan* flashed through my mind.

I see her, my Hanna. It is *her! I am not dreaming.*

"Stop the ship!"

But no one could hear me.

We moved further and further from the dock with every minute. A cold sweat rolled down my back.

I ran to the spot where a tall gangway had moments before linked ship to land. The gate was now closed, and the ship had moved about twenty meters from the dock. The cold deep sea yawned between our vessel and the seaport.

I spotted an American sailor and—with a strong burst of hope—ran to him. Breathing heavily, I explained my need to go back. I asked him to call his captain and stop the ship, but he shook his head and said it was too late.

Too late?

The people on deck turned to look at me as though I were crazy. The ship had already travelled about fifty meters from shore.

"Stop the ship!" I hollered angrily.

They did not listen.

I went back to the gate and caught site of her again at the dock.

She stood, waving.

In all this sea of voyagers, she found me.

I did not wait any longer. I took a few steps back and hurled myself over the barrier into the sea. In the split second before I hit the water, I saw her face fill with panic.

I did not feel the cold.

I surfaced about five meters from the ship.

I started swimming to shore, when I heard from above—"Man overboard"—and near me, the splash of a life preserver.

I grabbed the lifebelt and continued to swim toward shore, my strokes now stronger. Voices from the upper and lower decks cheered and encouraged me on.

I raised my eyes to look for her and found her about twenty meters from me. Her joyous face glittered with radiant light that made her look even more divine.

I am so close. Only a few more meters.

Again happy cheering and shouts of joy from the moving vessel. Even the sailors now waved.

I seized the concrete dock and climbed out of the water.

She ran to my embrace, and we both fell back into the sea. Like two swans so deeply warmed by each other's presence that Arctic waters cannot chill them, we fluttered there in capes of foamy tide, kissing each other and spontaneously murmuring words of love. In a melodious array of sounds, we created our own ode to joy.

Moments before the last grains of energy drained from us, we climbed back onshore. Dripping wet in the icy sun of Bremerhaven, we stood there together, surrounded by a crippled and grieving world, yet, in each other's arms, whole again.

***

No words can express, my dear Andrew, how, in a world of turbulence, loving your mother and everything she represented brought peace to this artisan's heart. I can only hope that your decision to enter a similarly unforgiving world may somehow bring you a similarly exquisite joy.

Your loving father

Serbo-Croatian Pronunciation Guide

Adapted from Dick Oakes

Serbo-Croatian has 31 Latin (or Roman) letters, referred to as "Latinica." This alphabet is in general use in former Western Yugoslavia, while in parts of former Eastern Yugoslavia, "Ćirilica" (Cyrillic alphabet) continues to be used. For our purposes, Ćirilica has been transliterated as Latinica, the official Slavic phonetic Latin alphabet proclaimed at the La Haye Slavistic Conference in 1955. Although these days the language has been separated into Bosnian, Croatian, and Serbian, the language of any one area is still between 95 and 100 percent Serbo-Croatian. It is a Slavic language (Indo-European), of the South Slavic subgroup.

When vowels are combined, they are pronounced separately. Thus, "hodio" is pronounced hoh-dee-oh and "čuvao" is pronounced choo-vah-oh. **In this novel, I have provided pronunciation guides for Serbian names, written following the examples in red in this paragraph, using letter combinations as found below in "Designated as."**

The letters k and p are not aspirated and the letters d, n, and t are dental.

Letters not listed below are pronounced approximately as in English.

Pronunciation Guide

	Pronunciation	Designated as
A, a	- a as in father	ah
E, e	- e as in let;	eh
	also e as in grey	ey
I, i	- i as in pin;	i
	also i as in machine	ee
O, o	- o as in note;	oh
	also o as in gone	aw
U, u	- u as in duke	u
Ŭ, ŭ	- u as in sun	uh
C, c	- c as in dance	ts
Č, č	- c as in cello	ch
Ć, ć	- tch as in latch	tch
Đ, đ	- g as in germ	dge
Dj, dj	- dy as in bad year	dy
Dž, dž	- dg as in edge	dg
G, g	- g as in go	g
H, h	- ch (guttural kh) as in loch	kh
J, j	- y as in yes	y
Lj, lj	- ly as in halyard	ly
Nj, nj	- ny as in canyon	ny
R, r	- slightly rolled;	r
	when used as a vowel as er in pert	
Š, š	- s as in sugar	sh

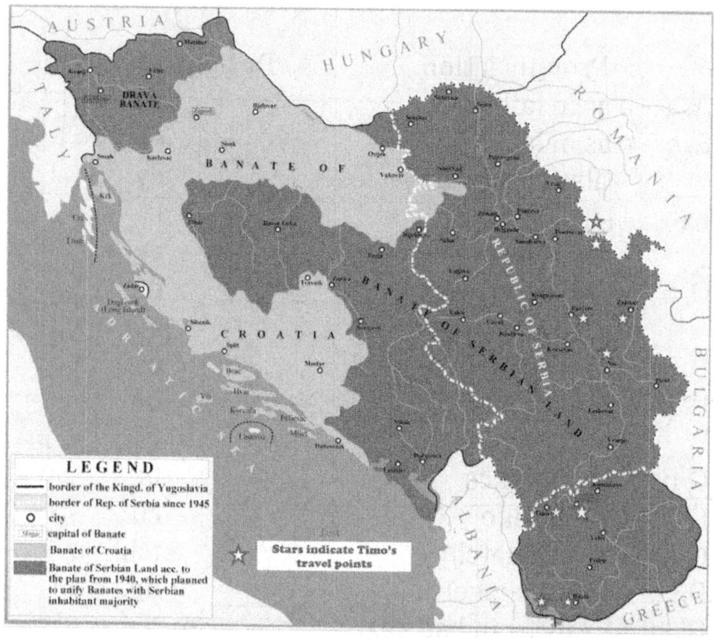

Figure 1: Yugoslavia before WWII

GENE LUKE VLAHOVIC

Gene Luke Vlahovic is of Serbian origin. Born and raised in the former Yugoslavia, he acquired his love of literature from reading European Classics at an early age. At fourteen, his first work was published by his hometown magazine, and at nineteen, several of his poems were published by the University Press and the Literary Magazine for Young Poets. *The Subtle Times,* a book of stories, and *The Chronicles of the First Serbian Soccer Club in America* were published by JR in 2000/2001, and his first novel *Tima Tisler* was published by Prosveta in 2004, all in Serbo-Croatian. The award-winning novel, *The Artisan* is the author's first novel in English. Gene Luke lives in Florida and continues to write stories in his second language.